CAFÉ BABANUSSA

CAFÉ BABANUSSA

A Novel

KAREN HILL

With a Foreword by Lawrence Hill

HARPERCOLLINS PUBLISHERS LTD

Café Babanussa
Copyright © 2016 by Karen Hill.
Foreword copyright © 2016 by Lawrence Hill Creative Services, Inc.
All rights reserved.

Published by HarperCollins Publishers Ltd

First edition

HarperCollins books may be purchased for educational, business or
sales promotional use through our Special Markets Department.

HarperCollins Publishers Ltd
2 Bloor Street East, 20th Floor
Toronto, Ontario, Canada
M4W 1A8

www.harpercollins.ca

Library and Archives Canada Cataloguing in Publication
information is available upon request.

ISBN 978-1-44343-892-6

Printed and bound in the United States

RRD 9 8 7 6 5 4 3 2 1

Café Babanussa: The Work of Her Life

(KAREN HILL: JANUARY 27, 1958–MARCH 27, 2014)

BY LAWRENCE HILL

IN THE FALL OF 1984, DAYS AFTER I HAD FINISHED reporting on the federal election campaign that ushered Brian Mulroney into his first majority government as prime minister of Canada, a phone call awakened me in the middle of the night. It was about the health of my sister, Karen Hill, who was living in Germany. The call came from my sister's husband. They lived in a rundown coal-heated walk-up flat in West Berlin. They had married in a civil ceremony—without fanfare or family—a few years earlier, so that Karen could work in Germany. Her husband and I had never met, or spoken, so I knew something was wrong.

Karen, who was twenty-six at the time, had moved to Europe five years earlier, after graduating from the University of Ottawa. My sister had a lifelong travel bug, and an equal passion for learning languages. English was her mother tongue, but she also spoke French and Spanish and more recently had learned German. In Berlin, she worked as a secretary at the Max Planck Institute (which carried out research in the fields of science and social science), had a crowd of expatriate friends and—from what she told me in her letters—had zero intention of returning to Canada.

West Berlin was a long way from Don Mills, the sleepy and almost entirely white Toronto suburb where we had grown up, and that was precisely why Karen had taken off. She wanted to escape our controlling and overbearing father. And she wanted to step out of the long shadows cast by our father and older brother, both named Dan, and both successful in their fields—our father as a human rights activist and our brother as a singer-songwriter. As well, she wanted adventure. She wanted to come of age racially, sexually, linguistically and politically, and Berlin seemed to her the perfect place to shape and define her life. It was cosmopolitan, multilingual and multiracial. Most important, it was an ocean away from Don Mills. Karen had met her husband in Portugal and followed him back to Berlin, where they moved in together. She drank, smoked, danced, devoured newspapers and politics, visited museums and art galleries, made a decent living with her job, studied German, learned about European politics and began forming connections within the Afro-German community.

When the phone call came to me that night, I had imagined it would be Karen herself, to commiserate about the fate of Canada in the hands of a Conservative government. But it was Karen's husband on the phone, and he was distressed.

Karen was sick, I was told. She was not making sense in her head. She was pacing the apartment, acting irrationally and speaking in gibberish. He did not think she could be left alone.

I was fully awake now.

During her periods of good health, our mother was lively, intelligent, inquisitive and playful. Our mother, Donna Hill, had struggled with bipolar disorder since she was a young woman. So had her twin sister, as well as a paternal aunt. But Karen had never shown any signs of mental imbalance.

As children, adolescents and young adults, Karen, Dan and I had coped with our mother's hospitalizations and long absences from the house. We had learned to recognize when our mother's health was starting to deteriorate: she would not sleep and would pace frenetically at night. I developed a term—*hospital ready*—for the right time to take Mom to emergency: hospitals were too crowded and too busy to admit a person who was simply pacing the house. *Hospital ready* meant that Mom had become a danger to herself, and that we could now convince doctors to admit her for psychiatric treatment. We witnessed our mother locked in a fetal position on her hospital bed, and counted the days before she would get up and start moving again. Her mind would begin to return, and eventually we would bring her home.

Dan, Karen and I had all asked each other, "Which one of us is next?" When that phone call came, I finally had the sad answer.

Within twenty-four hours I was on a flight to West Berlin, with instructions from my father to bring Karen back to Canada. I landed on a cold fall day, the air acrid from the smoke of thousands of coal furnaces. Karen's husband greeted me warmly, and with relief. He was sleep deprived and beside himself with worry.

Karen barely recognized me. She was dishevelled, agitated and pacing the flat. She would scribble feverishly in a notebook one moment, put on a record of Aretha Franklin the next, and then plug in a kettle, turn on the shower and return to her notebook. I peeked at the pages: they were full of incoherent ramblings that nobody but she could interpret.

Karen's family doctor in Berlin had been trying to help her ride out her episode at home. However, as I learned that first time and would learn again in the coming decades, when Karen was becoming ill, almost nothing could prevent her from sliding into the pit of madness. She would have to hit bottom before she was able to begin climbing the long and difficult path back to sanity.

Eventually, even Karen's sympathetic doctor gave up hope that she could recover without active medical intervention. Her husband and I had no choice but to have Karen committed to a psychiatric hospital. Karen was diagnosed as having bipolar disorder—the same illness that had affected our mother and her twin sister at about the same age.

It broke my heart to leave Karen in that state. She was so far gone, so deeply locked in her own psychosis, that she seemed to have no idea what was going on around her. Unable to carry out my father's wishes, I returned to Canada feeling sad, worried and defeated.

It took months, but Karen—bolstered by medications including an antipsychotic called Haldol, which she detested because it stifled her creativity and made her feel mentally sluggish—eventually recovered. She started functioning again, more or less normally. She left her secretarial job and eventually took courses to complete a certificate in Teaching English as a Foreign Language.

A year after Karen's illness, I quit my job as parliamentary bureau chief of the *Winnipeg Free Press* and moved to the tiny village of Sanlúcar de Barrameda on the southwest coast of Spain, where I began writing fiction every day. Karen came to visit, and she was full of spirit, adventure and laughter. She flew from Berlin to Malaga, where we met up and took a two-day bus ride back to my village. We passed through the interior of Andalusia and stopped the first night in a gorgeous hilly village called Arcos de la Frontera, where we stayed in a cheap *pension* room with two single beds. We were supposed to catch an early-morning bus the next day, but when I awoke around five, Karen was not to be found. I got out of bed and stepped outside. Just down the street, my sister was knocking back brandy at a bar, collecting free drinks from men who were happy to take her German cigarettes. I reminded her that we had a bus to catch. She replied, with a grin, "Just brushing up on my Spanish, brother."

I loved every minute that I spent travelling with Karen in Europe. There wasn't a museum or art gallery that she didn't frequent, a café she wouldn't stop at, a street she wouldn't walk or a foreign newspaper she wouldn't peruse. In Berlin, to which I returned twice to see her when she was healthy, Karen introduced me to her working-class quarter called Wedding, and to the vagaries of heating a frigid apartment with a coal-fired furnace. "Careful," she said one day as she headed out the door to work. "If you do it wrong, you'll blow yourself up."

I found, in travelling together in Europe and later in Canada, that we could talk about anything. How my fiction was going, and how she was enjoying writing poetry. How our first marriages—each of which would end in divorce—were faring. How our children were growing. And what had happened to ignite Karen's mental illness. She said that she had been drawn into management-labour conflicts at the Max Planck Institute, and she had found them overwhelming. Her marriage had also been troubling her. She had developed insomnia. Pacing at night, she had become increasingly anxious and finally entered into a period of psychosis, to be followed later by a pronounced depression.

Karen fared well for a year or two after her initial breakdown. She commenced a cycle of treatment and wellness, but it did not last. The illness returned, and she struggled with it for the next thirty years.

The side effects of her numerous and ever-changing medications involved trembling, weight gain and, perhaps most frustrating of all, a numbing of Karen's artistic and intellectual vigour. Karen detested the medications, and often changed or reduced them—sometimes closely following her doctors' instructions, at other times acting on her own. Usually, she enjoyed good mental health and was able to function normally. But then she would become acutely ill, which invariably ended in hospitalization.

I have lost count of the number of times I took Karen to emergency wards and waited long hours for her to be admitted. She despised being hospitalized as much as she hated the drugs, and twice she escaped from the hospitals where she was supposed to be locked up. The first time, she slipped into street clothes and blended into a group of people who were visiting her psychiatric unit at the Toronto General Hospital, got out unnoticed and walked home to her apartment, where we found her hours later. The second time, a few months before she died, she ripped an IV from her arm and slipped out of Sunnybrook Hospital, walking for hours in scant clothing in freezing winter temperatures, again on a path towards her apartment. I found her at home that time too, with blood—from her IV wound—all over the bannister and the walls. The police arrived a few minutes after I did. They didn't know me, and it took some time to explain the situation. They escorted Karen back to Sunnybrook. My sister, the linguist, traveller, poet, gardener, writer—and escape artist!

After Karen's first marriage ended, she stayed in Berlin and became involved with a Sudanese political caricaturist. They married, and although the relationship eventually ended, it led to the great joy of Karen's life—her daughter, Malaika Hill. About a year before the Berlin Wall came down and the Soviet Bloc crumbled, Karen moved back to Toronto. Malaika was born there in May 1989.

Karen moved into the Bain Co-operative Apartments,

near Withrow Park in Toronto, when Malaika was an infant, and they lived there together for more than twenty years.

From her first days back in Canada until her death in 2014, Karen lived a complex and rich life. Right away she began writing about her experiences in Berlin: her romantic adventures, her marriages, her experiences coping with mental illness in the hospital in Berlin, her travels throughout Europe, her experiences with racism in Germany, her connections to the Afro-German community, and what it had been like as a young Black Canadian woman to live in Germany through the 1980s.

But hers was also a difficult life. She worked at many jobs, including a few years managing an adult-education program in English as a second language at the Toronto School Board and a stint with the Canadian Race Relations Foundation. However, each time Karen had a job, the stress of work—not the intellectual challenges, but social challenges such as dressing and getting to work on time, and dealing with colleagues or bosses—seemed to catalyze another period of acute mental illness. After several cycles of taking a job only to suffer another devastating breakdown, Karen grudgingly accepted that she would be unable to keep working. She went on a form of long-term welfare and entered into a life of poverty alleviated only by the generosity of friends and family and by a fortunate housing subsidy at her beloved Bain Co-op.

Although she was unable to work for a living, Karen still pursued countless interests. She was a phenomenal cook and baker, and at holiday gatherings everyone devoured her linzertortes, cheesecakes and pumpkin pies. She adored her daughter, Malaika, who became the love of her life. She gardened outside her own modest apartment and in the backyards of friends and relatives. She drew, painted and created multimedia art at the Creative Works Studio, a Toronto arts program for people living with mental illness or addictions. She was a loving sister to Dan and to me, and a regular confidante and companion to our parents. She travelled to Cuba, Germany and Eastern Europe whenever she could come up with the money. She loved her cats, maintained many friendships and had a steady stream of visitors, both at home and during her hospital stays.

For the quarter century that she lived in Toronto, Karen created. She wrote dozens of poems, two of which were published. "What Is My Culture?" appeared in the anthology *Other Tongues: Mixed-Race Women Speak Out* and "A Breath of You" in *The Freedom Seeker: The Life and Times of Daniel G. Hill*, a curated exhibit in the Ontario Archives about the life of our late father. And from 1989 to 2012, she worked on *Café Babanussa*.

I have known writers who have faced all sorts of problems—unemployment, poverty, poor sales, hostile reviewers—but I have never personally met a writer who, in order to write, had to confront mental illness for a quarter of a century. Karen wrote whenever mental illness did not completely disable her. I imagine that for my sister, writing must have felt like hauling a brick-laden wagon uphill. She had to calm her mind and focus on her work, but the writing process stoked her anxieties. Still, Karen never complained about creating under the stress of illness.

Karen began *Café Babanussa* as a collection of short stories. Then she toyed with converting it into a memoir. Finally, she settled on a novel. She named her protagonist, Ruby Edwards, after our two American grandmothers: Ruby Bender was our white maternal grandmother and May Edwards, our Black paternal grandmother. The novel explores the life of a young Canadian woman of mixed Black-and-white identity, coming of age in a community of African expatriates and refugees in Berlin, and also experiencing a sudden, debilitating form of mental illness. The Café Babanussa draws its name from a real place: it was the café-bar where Karen began to step into Berlin's Black community. It was where she met her future husband and father of Malaika. For Karen, Café Babanussa was a home away from home.

Karen showed the manuscript to me many times over the years. We talked about matters of craft, how to improve it and how she might get it published. She also showed it to our brother, Dan, who had also written a novel and a memoir. Over the course of a decade, she took courses or mentorships with the writers James FitzGerald, Susan Glickman, Cynthia Holz and Ann Ireland. She was also mentored by the writer Sarah Sheard through the Humber School for Writers. I asked Sarah by email if she could share a remembrance of her time with Karen, and she replied within hours: "I remember enjoying Karen's kindly spirit and her determination to press onward with her manuscript despite the difficulties in her life. She was always open to feedback because she really did want to write the best pages she could. She never appeared to mind tackling revisions, never grumbled and never went defensive. She persisted. She per-f*****g-sisted. I admire that quality a great deal in a person. She did what it took to complete her project. It doesn't get any better than that."

Karen attended the Humber School for Writers on scholarship, and a memorial scholarship now exists in her name to help other student writers in financial need to hone their craft.

By late 2012, Karen had finished the last of her many rewrites and was ready to send her novel into the world. With the assistance of Margaret Hart at the Humber School for Writers Literary Agency, Karen began showing the manuscript to Canadian publishers. Her efforts to find a publisher lasted more than a year but were not successful. In the meantime, she wrote the essay "On Being Crazy," which is appended at the back of this book. It is an intimate, detailed and fascinating account of living with mental illness in Germany and Canada. Karen was not able to publish this piece either.

In early 2014, Karen became acutely ill again and was admitted to Sunnybrook Hospital. After many weeks of being hospitalized, she was released on a weekend pass. The plan was that if she fared well, she would return on the Sunday and be released the following day. That weekend, while out for a celebratory restaurant meal with her daughter, Karen choked and lost consciousness. She was rushed to St. Michael's Hospital, but she had entered a coma and she died a few days later, in the same intensive care unit where our father had died eleven years earlier.

I miss Karen more than I can explain. Some days I still find it hard to believe that she is not sitting at home in her living room, putting Aretha Franklin or Joe Williams, Billie Holiday or Ella Fitzgerald on the record player, happy to dance with any free spirit who would join her. I couldn't have loved her more than I did, and I am lucky and happy to have had her in my life for fifty-six years. My sister's courage is an inspiration to me to keep loving and to keep writing, day by day and page by page.

Posthumous publication is a sad thing. It is depressing to think of a writer putting years into her work and then not being around to see it ushered into print. But I find it beautiful to think that Karen's words may reach other readers. Her story will resonate particularly with those who care about issues of racial identity, with those who have travelled far from home to find themselves, with people who are curious about intersection between Canada and Germany, with people who live and work while struggling with mental illness, and with many more still whose loved ones have mental illness. But a writer can only be around for so long. If the written story is especially powerful, it is bound to outlive the teller. In Karen's case, the outliving began one or two acts too soon.

Café Babanussa appears here virtually as Karen wrote it. Jennifer Lambert at HarperCollins Canada edited the novel respectfully and conservatively, and I also suggested some minor edits. We have deleted redundant bits, but apart from a few bridging words, we have left the novel intact so that the reader can discover it as Karen wrote it.

Karen Hill has left us, but her poems, her essay "On Being Crazy" and her novel, *Café Babanussa*, are welcome to hang around and befriend us for years to come.

CAFÉ BABANUSSA

CHAPTER ONE

Home

THE TABLE WAS SET FOR FOUR. RUBY HAD CHOSEN
plates from her university days, a motley but bright assortment
of red, yellow and blue. She cut fresh lilacs from her mother's
garden and placed them in a tapered glass vase in the centre of
the large oak table. The house smelled of rosemary and thyme,
which had been sprinkled liberally over the pissaladière.

"What's that in the oven? Pizza à la derrière?" her father
joked as he joined her in the kitchen. James Edwards was a
no-nonsense type much of the time, but indulged in much
rib-poking with his two daughters. He had a deep, honey-
sweetened voice and frequently burst into song, riffing and
scatting away à la Ella: "Doo bop re bop wop doo bop, oh
yeah." Ruby would often sing back an answer, as she did now.
"Scooby dooby bop bop, till you drop, drop, whoo hoo, yeah."

"Atta girl, that's my Ruby," her father said and patted her
on the back with his big brown hand.

Ruby peered into the oven and poked at the crust with her
finger. The scent of olives and roasted tomatoes intermingled

with the herbs. Standing, she brushed slender hands down the front of her apron, which was tied around her waist. On the stove a pot was bubbling. Ruby lifted the lid.

"You've outdone yourself, my dear," her mother's voice chimed in as she too came into the room. "Mushroom soup— and I can smell the sherry, too. Another wonderful round of food. What's for dessert?"

Ruby opened the door of the fridge and gestured inside. "Grape tarte with crème anglaise," she said. She had worked hard to create concentric circles of green, purple and red grapes. It was a Sunday afternoon in the spring of 1980 and she had spent the morning preparing lunch.

Ruby's mom had spent the morning tidying the main floor of their large suburban house. As a finishing touch she had put the last of the white tulips into a pewter vase on the table by the front door.

Ruby's older sister, Jessie, flounced in from outside, her long curls swirling about her head. Jessie's hair was light brown and her skin was a shade paler than Ruby's, but Ruby, along with her jet black hair and darker skin, had her mother's aquiline nose and thinner lips.

"Ruby, it smells fantastic in here. What did you cook for us?" she said, her hands waving in the air as her sister came to greet her. Jessie surveyed the living room, as if deciding whether to seat herself on the plush coffee-coloured sofa or on the Scandinavian-style chairs. She was taller than Ruby and not so curvy—she had her mother's angular features.

"I'm not telling. You'll have to wait and see."

"Just like you," muttered Jessie as she sank into the sofa. She stared at a black-and-caramel-coloured African mud cloth that hung on the wall and at the top two rows of the bookshelf that were decorated with African and Inuit masks and sculptures. "Mom and Dad really do have an interesting collection of things," she said. "I kind of miss it where I am now." Turning to Ruby, she narrowed her gaze. "So, how's it going, Sis?"

Ruby sat down in an armchair and sighed. "Okay, I guess. I'm playing at being the official cook in the house. Just reorienting myself and enjoying spring. Do you remember Jackie from high school? She's pregnant."

"She's starting off young," said Jessie.

"I'm glad *she's* doing it, 'cause I'm sure I couldn't. I'm just not ready to do the settling-down-and-having-kids thing. Don't know if I *ever* will be."

"Why not?" asked Jessie.

"I want to hit the road. I want to travel and see the world first. Anyway, I don't really believe in marriage."

Their father stepped into the living room. "Ah, Jessie, here you are." He gave his daughter a big kiss on the cheek. "Glad to see you. How's the studying going?"

"Just fine, keeping me busy."

Ruby jumped up and strode to the dining room. "I'm serving lunch! Come and get it!"

Jessie brought the full soup tureen to the table. She lifted the lid and soaked up the scent of mushrooms, sherry and thyme. "Mmm. This looks great. What else is there?"

"Pissaladière," said Ruby.

"Wow, we're getting the special treatment. What's up?"

Jessie served the soup and everybody sat down to eat. Ruby's family was not one to mince words and immediately started asking each other, and then Ruby, what the special occasion was. Ruby squirmed in her chair.

"Soup's delicious, my daughter, but you can't keep a secret from me. Why all the fuss?"

Finally, she cleared her throat. "Remember Great-uncle William who lived in Berlin in the twenties and thirties? Well, I've decided to follow in his footsteps and spend some time there. I want to see different places in the world and I thought Berlin would be a good place to start. I'd like to see where he lived, and find out what kind of life he led." A note of sarcasm crept into her voice. "I mean, who wants malls and suburbia, anyway? I didn't save all my money from my work at the bank and at the university library to spend it on nothing right here. I want to get away from home and see new places. Plus, I'd like to travel in other countries and work on my French and Spanish."

Ruby's mother was from Montreal, and Ruby had grown up listening to her sing songs and tell little stories in French. Louise Edwards spoke French to her daughters often enough to pique their interest and give them an edge.

Jessie laughed. "Oh, the story of old Uncle William. You're really taken with that. He went off to be a singer and study music at the Academy in Berlin, and his gay ass was thrilled with the wild and open life he could live there." Jessie paused. "That didn't last for long, eh?"

Louise's singsong voice followed Jessie's. "It's wonderful that you have a dream like William did. I really think you should step out into the world any way you want. But . . . I hope it's not for too long."

Ruby's father moved his empty bowl aside and snorted. "That's a foolish, crazy-minded idea if I ever heard one," he said. "You need to stay right here and find a permanent job. Look at how hard your sister is working to finish her degree. But she'll be set once she's done. Set for life as an architect. I don't like this idea one bit."

"Dad, don't drag me into this," said Jessie.

Ruby felt her eyes start to tear up. But she had known this would happen and was angry with herself for going soft. She had wanted a family meeting to make her announcement. At least her sister would stand up for her. And her mom, too. Ruby pushed her chair back from the table and began to collect the soup bowls. On her way to the kitchen, she stopped in her tracks and then faced her father.

"Dad, you know I love you, but you are wrong. Sometimes people need a change of scenery and a little freedom."

"I concur," said her mother. Ruby's mom had moved to Toronto in the fifties to teach French and had met her dad at the old Park Plaza Hotel, which was one of the few establishments in the city to serve both Blacks and whites in those days. They met while whooping it up on the dance floor in the hotel's ballroom. A month later Ruby's dad proposed, and they'd been together ever since. They had a really hard time at first, with all the prejudice. Her mom even had to go with

7

a white friend to look for an apartment, because landlords wouldn't rent to mixed couples.

Ruby brought the main course to the table. "Here we go, pizza à la derrière," she said, and chuckled to lighten the mood.

Jessie patted her sister's hand when she stopped to serve her portion.

"When Ruby's got a plan, there's no stopping her," said Jessie. "Maybe she wouldn't be so driven to get away if Dad hadn't kept shoving so many ads for government jobs her way. Or maybe if she didn't feel like she had to measure up to me . . . But when I'm done, ha ha, I'll join Ruby overseas, if she's still there."

"I have goals and ambitions, too," Ruby said. "Just because they don't have to do with a set career doesn't mean they're not as valid." She spoke a little more about her great-uncle, how she felt he would help guide her way in Berlin.

Her father continued shaking his head in disbelief. The family ate in silence, the girls not daring to provoke their father. Ruby knew she risked her father's wrath, knew he would not understand. She realized that it was just like she had expected, and that he might never change his mind before she left.

Ruby served dessert while Jessie prepared a pot of tea. Everyone oohed and aahed about the grape tart and then fell into silence again.

Ruby and Jessie were left to tidy up the kitchen. Their parents had always made them do this kind of work together, so they fell easily into step.

"Ruby, you know I'm with you, whatever you decide to do. But maybe you ought to earn some more money before you head off."

"Well, I'm still working a few days a week at the bank. But even if I got a good job, it would be ages before I could afford to move out, and I don't want to live with Mom and Dad anymore. I have to get away, Jessie—I've started having nightmares again, where someone's holding me down and I can't breathe. And they've gotten worse. There's a man actually lying on me, trying to smother me. I end up blacking out in the dream, before waking up. They stopped for a while at university, but as soon as I came back to this house, they returned."

"That's awful."

"I can't live up to Dad's expectations the way you do. I have to make a life for myself somewhere else."

"You're probably right about it being about Dad, but be careful about running away. I want you to go as much as anyone else, but I think you'll just carry your fears with you. I know you'll think I'm crazy, but maybe you should try a little meditation. Maybe that will help keep the dreams away, if you can relax your mind."

"You're not crazy, Jessie. But I have a jumpy mind, one that doesn't calm easily. I don't think I can make it be still."

"Well, I mean it about coming over to visit you, wherever you land. You better find a place with enough space for visitors!"

"Oh, I will. And I promise not to bring a German lover back to Canada like Uncle William."

9

Jessie's face lit up "What? I don't believe you. Nobody told me that!"

"I wrote Aunt Lettie last fall. She's the family historian so I thought she might know something about him. She was hesitant at first, but she finally sent me copies of some letters to her and to his sister Ella. He told them about the lover he was bringing home." Ruby's eyes sparkled as she exposed this little secret to her sister.

"You're kidding me!" said Jessie, her face even more incredulous. "That's incredible. Do you have those letters here? I'd love to see them."

"Yeah, I do. We can look at them later, downstairs."

Ruby's mom came into the kitchen, a big smile on her face. "Nice work, girls. Good to see the two of you keeping each other company."

Ruby's dad joined them in the kitchen. "Ruby, is there any of that grape tart left? Would you cut me another piece?" Like Ruby, he had a sweet tooth.

Jessie said, "If there's enough left over, cut another piece for Mom and me, too. And is there any more tea?"

Away from the formality of the dining room table, the family hovered around the kitchen table nattering and joking with each other. Their father finally motioned to Jessie to follow him upstairs, and Ruby wondered what on earth he was up to. After they had been gone for a few minutes, she crept lightly up the stairs and stopped just before her parents' bedroom. The door was only partially closed. She overheard her father start in on Jessie. "You have to do something about

Ruby and this talk about travelling. I want you to convince her to get this cockamamie idea out of her head."

It was all Ruby could do to stop from barging in on them. There was a long silence before Jessie replied.

"Dad, I can't believe you're asking me to do this. Ruby is a grown-up now and she will do whatever she decides to do. Remember that poster I had in my room with that quote from Kahlil Gibran?

Your children are not your children.
They are the sons and daughters of Life's longing for itself.
They come through you but not from you,
And though they are with you yet they belong not to you.

Jessie had long ago memorized the whole quotation. "Remember now? Well, it's time for you to let go of Ruby. She'll be fine. You and Mom taught her well."

"But I had great hopes for Ruby," her father said. "I don't want her to fritter away her time."

"Just because she's going to travel for a while doesn't mean she won't come back ready to plant her feet on the ground. Anyway, you talk to her. I won't do your dirty work."

Ruby ducked into her mother's sewing room before she could be seen, then snuck down into the kitchen. Her face felt flushed; perhaps realizing that something was wrong, her mother gave her a hug and a peck on the cheek. Ruby stared out the kitchen window at a trail of cream-coloured gauze crossing the skies, brightened up by threads of pink and orange. The day was ending. But spring was in the air, and Ruby could hear the birds twittering in the tree just outside the door. Despite her father's negative machinations, the breeze carried with it a sense of promise.

Jessie burst into the room. "You won't believe what Dad—"

"Shhhh," said Ruby, placing a finger on her lips. "Mom, come quickly, there's a cardinal on the cherry tree."

The three women stood shoulder to shoulder at the window. The garden was bursting with white tulips and narcissi of different sizes and shapes, doubles and singles, beginning to fade as the lilacs reached their peak. With the pink blossoms bursting on the cherry tree, the garden seemed like it was right out of a fairy tale. The cardinal was hopping from branch to branch.

"Spring's coming, Ma. The little ones will soon be leaving the nest."

"That's what you should do, Ruby. Go see the world. I know your father disagrees, but there's nothing special waiting for you here."

The windows of the kitchen were wide open and they could hear a bird begin its song: sharp, high notes sung in measured sequence. Ruby's mom laughed and then quietly slipped out the back door, where she stood on the porch with her hands on her hips. She whistled at the bird, repeating the same staccato tones. A call and answer went on between her and the bird, the notes increasing in number with each round. Ruby's mom would tilt her head and laugh before listening once more. Her laughter became a coda to their song.

Appearing behind them, Ruby's father said: "Two twittering fools." Ruby's father could not stand birds. As a teenager he had worked at a resort where he had to serve rich white folks outside on the patio. One day a number of birds swooped down at his head, and frightened, he dropped the tray on which rested several meals. He was fired, and from that day his fear expanded into outright hatred. Her father gave his wife a hug. "Louise, I'm going downstairs to put some laundry in."

Louise moved back indoors, cheeks flushed. "My little songbird," she said to Ruby and Jessie. "We sing to each other every day."

Ruby reached out and touched her mother's arm. "That was nice, Mom." She and Jessie stared at each other for a moment and then they shrugged. "Too bad Dad can't appreciate the beauty of the bird and its song," Ruby said. Her sister nodded in agreement. "Okay, guys, I'm going to write out a list of what I need to pack."

Ruby skipped down the stairs and stepped into the bedroom where she had been staying for the past weeks. Her father was in the far corner of the room, standing over the night table with a book in his hands. He was humming "Stardust" as he read. His daughter moved towards him in a flash.

"Dad, what are you doing in here? What are you looking at?" Ruby peered over her father's shoulders. "My journal! What are you doing reading that?"

"I was coming in to close the windows. It's supposed to rain tonight. But I found this lying on the table."

Ruby reached to grab the journal from his hands, but he raised his arm. Ruby levelled her gaze at him. "This is my personal business. There's nothing in there that you need to know about."

"Well, how about I read a snippet. 'May 1st, 1980. Only a little more time till I fly the coop. I'll be so happy to be gone from here. Dad is driving me crazy, trying to suffocate me and extinguish all life.' Ruby, I'm not trying to suffocate you. Look at your mother and all the difficulties she's had with her health. Think about my worries. I'm just trying to protect you from pain that you don't need to experience. I'm sorry if I hurt you. Maybe you shouldn't have left your journal out."

"I thought I could trust you!" Ruby shouted. "How could you do such a thing? You're always using Mom as an excuse to be overbearing. I'm not going to live my life waiting to see if something *might* happen to me. Why are you picking on me? Because I'm the youngest? Because I'm not as smart and stable as Jessie?"

"You're just as bright as your sister. But you're more sensitive. I've always used kid gloves with you. You're more like your mother than you know. Why don't you work for a couple of years, and once you've established yourself, then you can take off?"

"Kid gloves? Are you kidding me? More like a straitjacket. I want to travel before I settle down. Can't you understand that? Now leave me alone. Go!"

Her father turned away in silence and left the room. Ruby threw the journal against the wall. Her father was a loving man, but always imposed his will, and Ruby was tired of being his good little girl, of feeling she had to perform to please him.

Ruby's sister knocked at the door. "Can I come in?"

"Sure, but I'm in no mood for joking around."

"Yeah, me neither. I heard the yelling. I'm sorry about Dad."

"He's worse than ever lately. I have to get out of here."

"You're right to leave, Ruby. But you should cut him some slack. Think about what he's gone through with Mom."

"Oh for chrissake, he protects her way too much! She's not some precious doll. Her illness doesn't prevent her from having inner strength."

"But think of all the times she's been sick. It's been so disruptive, yet he's always there for her. He works so hard to maintain a stable life for her."

"It's too much. She needs room to breathe, too. He told her not to go back to work, that she didn't have to teach anymore. But I know he loves and supports her. Jessie, you know I love him. He's a good man. But I can't stand the fighting any longer."

"Sis, it's automatic with him. Remember, he grew up as the oldest child in a strict, religious household and he had to look after three younger sisters. He's just doing what he knows best. Besides, he might be worried about you—and me, too? Worried that maybe we'll become manic like Mom?"

"I know," Ruby whispered. "I have thought about that and I struggle a little with that myself. But I don't want to *not* do things because maybe someday I might get sick. I can't live my life that way."

"Oh, Ruby, you're so brave. And stubborn, too!" Jessie hugged her. "Now let's see those letters from Uncle William. I'm dying to read them."

Ruby opened the second drawer of the oak dresser and pulled out a flurry of papers. "Aunt Lettie sent me these. I had to really beg her. Plus, look, look—I have a photo." The two young women sat down on the bed and peered at the slightly crinkled photograph that Ruby held. There was a dapper young man in what looked like a camel-coloured suit with a snappy light brown hat on his head. His face was cracked open into a wide grin, with dimples marking his lower cheeks.

"Wow, he looks really snazzy," said Jessie. "You can see how he'd attract someone's fancy."

Ruby unfolded a letter, date-marked June 1930. "I'll read it to you," she said.

Dearest Ella,

I have been here in Berlin for several months now and I am sorry that I have taken so long to write. Europe and Berlin in particular have been an eye-opener for me. Paris is ablaze with history, and one of my favourite spots to stop and think was Notre-Dame Cathedral. I spent a long time looking at the gargoyles and thinking of the fate of poor Quasimodo. I know that this is no longer news, but Black men are treated with great deference here and much is made of jazz music. There seems to be a club full of American and French folk on almost every corner. Everyone is talking about Josephine Baker. I saw her perform at the Folies-Bergère and you can say that dance breathes fire into her limbs. It is a wonderful place, this City of Light.

Berlin is an odd mixture of carefree and cautious. It is stately and chock full of gardens and parks. My favourite pastime is to take the train to Wannsee and read on the beach by the water.

The National Socialists are waiting everywhere in the shadows; their presence seems to become stronger every day. They are so full of hatred for Jews and Blacks that I am worried that I will not be able to stay if they get into power. This makes my stay bittersweet and I vow to make the most of my days. In any case, my musical studies take up most of my time. My singing voice is getting stronger every day. The hours of leisure that do come my way are spent in museums, clubs and the theatre.

I have a young German friend, Heinrich, who accompanies me most places I go and acts as a guide. There is one place we frequent, known as the Eldorado. My guess is that its mood would be too boisterous for your wise ways.

Hope all is well with you and the family.
Your loving brother, William

Jessie clapped her hands. "Isn't it amazing that he saw Josephine? I'm so jealous!"

"There's at least two places for me to look up on my travels," Ruby said. She lay back on the bed and thought about her uncle. Her eyes strayed to a family picture on the wall. The girls wore matching snowsuits and stood with their dad. Ruby longed to see Berlin and Paris. She longed for the days when their world was simpler, if not perfect.

Ruby's feet went *crunch, crunch, crunch* through the snow. She held on to her father's hand tightly, her fingers and palms covered by hand-woven red wool mittens. In her father's other fist was the rope for the toboggan that bounced along behind them. The houses had big snow-covered lawns, with little Japanese cherry trees popping up along the boulevard. Ruby loved that the snow was like a blanket, protecting the grounds from the wintry winds. She skipped along the sidewalk, still grasping her father's hand. "What kind of tree will we get, Daddy? Can we get a big one?"

Her father answered, "We will see, my dear, we will see."

As they reached the bottom of the street they rounded the corner and then stood in front of a small plaza with a restaurant, a grocery store and a drug store. In the parking lot was a large fenced-in area full of Christmas trees. Ruby marvelled at all the different sizes and types. She pulled off her mittens so she could feel the needles in her hands. "Daddy, how 'bout this one?" she yelped every few minutes. Her father kept looking around. Finally he made a decision, choosing a medium-size balsam fir that was full around the middle and tapered to a perfect tip. He went to get some help, Ruby following behind him.

The man dressed like Santa would not look her father in the eye. Instead, he turned to help someone else who had come after them. Her father waited patiently and then asked for assistance again. And once again, the man turned away to help another customer. Ruby tugged at his hand. "Daddy, ask him to get our tree for us!"

Ruby's father mumbled something about how not everyone was free in this world and what had happened to the spirit of Christmas?

The man snapped to attention and gave him a dirty look. "Okay, buddy, whaddaya want?"

"I'd like to purchase this tree and I'd like to be treated politely like anyone else while I do so."

"I wouldn't have expected you people to be out in this kind of weather. Better get on home."

Ruby's father refused to reply. Ruby tugged at his coat. "What does that mean, Daddy? Why do we have to get on home?" She turned to the man. "Mister, you're not Santa, you're mean. Santa's not like that."

Ruby watched with a kind of horror as the man's face turned a purply pink. "Get out of here *now*," he sputtered.

Ruby's father said quietly, "Sir, where is your Christmas spirit?" Then put a couple of dollars down on the wooden table, plunked their tree on the toboggan and led Ruby away from the parking lot.

"Ruby, you were right—that was a very mean man. Unfortunately, some people are cruel and don't like Black people. But don't you worry. We won't let him ruin our day." Then he chased her all the way back up the hill, the toboggan swinging to and fro behind him. Ruby laughed as she watched

her father's glistening brown face bobbing up and down in the
sea of white that surrounded them.

Ruby had been lying on top of the bed and now she went
to snuggle under the thick, brightly embroidered duvet from
Tibet that her mother had bought on one of her shopping
sprees. Over the years, Louise Edwards had been prone to
bouts of mania and depression, diagnosed as bipolar disorder,
but these episodes seemed to be receding as she approached
middle age.

One time, Ruby's mom had lost her wits when her father
had been away on a business trip. Jessie had been the one to
phone him and whisper that Mama wasn't well—one moment
she would be short-tempered and the next cuddling her girls,
laughing and smiling and full of love. You just didn't know
who she was going to be from one minute to the next. She
was also spending a lot of money on new decorations for the
house. She had bought a huge painting of a nude woman,
which she hung in the living room. As soon as Dad arrived
home, he took it down and marched it right back to the store
where it had been bought. Her mom ended up in the hospital
that time. Ruby was ten.

When she went to visit her at the hospital, her mother
started wailing that she loved her so much, and then a split
second later she ran down the hall screaming and banging on
walls. Ruby didn't know who this woman was; she didn't recognize her and was afraid of her, of whatever she had become.

Ruby sat there nervously waiting for her real mother to return, not knowing what to do. The nurse brought her mom back, but Ruby didn't want to stay anymore, and the nurse told her that it would be better if she left since her mother needed some rest.

Ruby was relieved to be able to go. This woman wasn't her mother.

Her father never talked to his daughters about what was wrong. Ruby guessed that he was too proud to admit that she wasn't perfect. Maybe he was scared, too; he didn't know how to explain any of it to his daughters and so just kept things hush-hush. Ruby realized that it was probably this same fear that was driving him to keep her so close to home.

When Ruby went back to the kitchen later that afternoon, her mother was busy fixing a salad for dinner. "I thought we could have the rest of the soup with this for dinner," she said.

Ruby pulled the soup out of the fridge and found a piece of baguette that was left over from lunch. "I'll make garlic bread," she said, grabbing a nearby mortar and pestle. As she pounded the garlic, she said: "Are you happy, Mom?"

Ruby's mother looked at her daughter and sighed. "Is this a roundabout way about asking about me and your father? Right out of left field, eh? Ruby, there are *always* kinks to work out in a marriage. You can never find that perfect person. Your father may have his faults, but I know he loves me and cares for me. That's as much as I can ask for."

"No, Mom, he should treat you more equitably, and he should stop trying to keep me under his wing."

"Your father has stood by me all these years, even when I

wasn't well. But what you're really angry about is you, isn't it? We'll have to try to talk some sense into him."

"I don't know how, but in any case, he won't stop me from going." Ruby had begun smearing garlic and butter onto the bread when Jessie walked in.

"I'm starving. Is it almost ready?"

"You still here? Just hang on for ten minutes, and there'll be food." Ruby pulled knives, forks and spoons from the drawer.

Her father came in and sat down at his usual place at the end of the table. "Smells yummy—I know there's good food coming my way."

The mood in the kitchen was tense, and they sat down to eat in silence. Jessie asked her father if he wanted to say grace.

"Rub a dub dub, thanks for the grub," he replied. The only time they blessed the table was when they had visitors who were religious. When that happened, the girls would check to make sure everyone's eyes were closed and smirk at each other across the table. The sisters shared a smile now.

"You may have done all the cooking today," Jessie teased, "but I sewed up a new dress for Mom at home this morning."

"I guess we're even, then."

Ruby's father looked up at her. "You'd be even more even with your sister if you worked on getting a good job."

"James Edwards, don't you dare ruin this meal."

"Ruin this meal? How about ruin her life? That's what *she's* trying to do."

"Dad," Jessie said, "for crying out loud. She's only going on a trip."

"She can go on a trip any old day. I want her to get established first. Besides, I don't want her to be so far away."

"That's it! I'm outta here." Ruby shoved herself away from the table and went outside to get some air. The flowers in the backyard were fanning themselves in the cool breeze, heads slightly bent. Ruby went over and picked some lilacs from the bush and then snapped two white peonies off their stems. She wondered if the plants felt pain.

Her mother came outside and rubbed her daughter's shoulder. "I'm sorry, honey. He's just having such a hard time with this. He doesn't want to lose you."

"He's not losing me, for chrissake, Mom. I'm not disappearing off the face of the earth."

"Come back inside and eat with us. You'll be hungry if you don't finish your food."

"No, Ma, I'll eat later. I'm going to my room." Ruby went down to the basement and found a glass for the flowers. She lay back on her bed and stared at the ceiling, her mind going over the conversation at the table. The more she thought about it, the more she wanted to go immediately to West Berlin. Her uncle had studied at the Academy of Arts there until Hitler's fascists had chased him out. When he returned to Canada, he and his partner did indeed move in with his sister, Ella. His sister refused to meet his boyfriend but let them set up house together in the basement, which had had its own entrance. Some members of the family said he was a bit of a scoundrel, mooching off them all the time.

Her uncle Walter's story piqued her imagination. What

on earth was a gay African Canadian doing in Nazi Germany in the 1930s? It tickled her that she was the only one in the family destined—chosen?—to follow in his footsteps. She felt compelled by some crazy idea of cosmic karma to see if she could find his old haunts in Berlin.

An hour later there was a knock at her door.

"Who's there?"

"It's your broken-down old father. May I come in?"

Ruby sat up in her bed but then slumped back down. He knocked again, and finally she said, "Come on in."

Her dad sat down at the foot of the bed. Ruby rolled over to face him.

Her father fiddled with his hands for a moment, head down. "Listen, Ruby, this is hard for me to say. I won't try to stop you from going. I can't anyway—you have a mind of your own and you're going to do whatever you want to do. It's just—I've spent so many years looking after you and looking out for you. It's hard to let go, hard to realize that you have to head off into the world on your own. I still hope you won't be gone for long and that you'll focus on a career when you get back. Your family is here, and you are an integral part of it. What are you going to do there in Berlin, after you've seen all the sights? But in the meantime, I don't know what else to say but be well, my dear, and travel safely. Let us know when you're leaving."

"Did Mom tell you to say that?"

Her father struggled. "Yes, Ruby, your mother and I had a chat. But this is me. Solo. Here to talk."

"It's just so strange . . . don't you remember when you were young?" Ruby asked.

"I guess different people have different impulses. Mine was to get an education, settle down and raise a family. That's what my parents taught me. Study hard, work hard, improve your life."

Ruby looked at her father and realized he had followed the dream of many Black Canadians. She stammered, "Maybe you didn't go far away, but you still set out on your own. That's all I'm trying to do." She quieted her anger and reached out to her father. "Thanks for coming to talk to me, Dad. It means a lot to me."

Her father opened up his arms and Ruby slid into them for one last bear hug. He hummed a familiar tune that made Ruby smile. Together they sang as they held fast to each other.

CHAPTER TWO

Landing

SHOTS RANG OUT FROM A TOWER UP ABOVE. IT WAS
nighttime and everything seemed grey and bleak. A man's
hands, pierced and bloody, gripped a barbed wire fence at the
top of a tall slab of grey concrete. He was gasping; his face was
etched with desperation and terror.

As a child, Ruby had sat with her father as he watched
a film in the family room, and had ended up burrowed into
his lap, too scared to watch the rest of the movie. Her father
had told her it was about spies in Berlin, but she hadn't really
known what that meant. He had shooed her away, and she
went off thinking that Berlin seemed like a horrible place.
This early image of Berlin haunted her now, along with the
romantic associations she had of her uncle, so she delayed her
descent into the complete unknown by stopping over in Paris
for a week to soak up the sights and sounds of the French
capital.

Ruby touched down in Paris mid-morning, mid-week.
Her parents had taken her to the airport the night before and

there had been repeated teary goodbyes. Her first transatlantic flight had felt long and cramped, and it was a relief to disembark into the busy airport. Ruby had chosen a simple *pension* on Rue de Nesle on the Left Bank, and she admired the quirky decorations and artwork when she arrived to drop off her bags. There was no restaurant or café at the hotel, so she walked down the cobblestone road, which burst out onto a large square. She happily noted there were at least four cafés with patios stretching into its hub. She sat down at La Pleine Lune and soon she was munching on a chocolate croissant and sipping a grand crème as she took in her surroundings. She tried to imitate the French and their very essence of nonchalance by just glancing at the people all around her, but there was so much to see. She noticed a slight young man with wavy blond hair staring at her on and off from the other side of the patio. He waved at her. She waved back. As she got up to go, she wondered if he was from around here and whether she'd ever see him again.

Ruby hopped onto the Métro at Odéon and found her way to the Jardin du Luxembourg. The air was fresh in the park and the sun now high in the sky, casting thick rays of gold over the beds of flowers. She feasted on the bright array of colours as she strolled around. She bent to touch flowers as if she were talking to them. As she took in their scent she felt she was inhaling the promise of the city. It helped to lift the fatigue settling down on her, so she decided to remain in the open air and go on to Père Lachaise Cemetery. She had heard that it was beautiful, full of the graves of the famous amidst bounteous nature. In particular, she wanted to visit the graves of Colette, Guillaume Apollinaire and then Jim Morrison.

During the week that followed, Ruby always had breakfast at La Pleine Lune before heading out to explore the city. She loved Paris, but she began to feel lonely and wished she had someone to share her experiences with. How would she cope in Berlin? Her confidence began to ebb. Maybe she wasn't quite as independent as she had thought. But she was determined not to go crawling back to her father so soon; it was important to prove she was capable of surviving on her own.

On the night before her departure, Ruby picked up some cheese, a baguette, some fruit and a bar of chocolate and went to the river. As she sat down with her picnic by the Seine, the same blond man she had seen on the patio her first day in Paris approached and joined her on the bench.

"At last," he said in French. "No more waving. I can look you in the eyes and tell you how pretty you are."

Ruby felt her cheeks warm as she smiled awkwardly at her new companion. His rather large nose reminded her of Gérard Depardieu, but his slate-blue eyes were welcoming, with a hint of laughter at their edges. His hair was so thick and wavy that she wanted to run her fingers through it.

"Yes, well . . . Um, what is your name?" asked Ruby. His accent seemed Eastern European, but she wasn't sure.

"I'm Werner. You are not from here, I gather, though you speak beautifully. What is your name, my little American?"

"Ruby," she said. "And I'm Canadian."

He took her hand in his and kissed it and said, "Hello, Ruby, *la Canadienne*. Pleased to meet you."

His eyes seemed to devour her. Ruby squirmed a little. "You're not French, are you?"

"No, I'm German, from Stuttgart."

"Oh! I'm going to Berlin tomorrow."

"Berlin, eh? That's where I live. Why are you going there?"

Ruby chatted easily about her life back in Don Mills and how her great-uncle's time in Berlin had inspired her to travel, though she could see Werner struggling to follow.

Werner switched to English. "Do you speak German?"

"*Nein*. Not one bit."

"Let's go for a walk and I can give you a crash course in swear words, teach you how to count, that sort of thing. We can do at least that much in one night. Are you staying there for a while?

"Well, I don't really know how long," Ruby said, rising from the bench. "Maybe a year."

"Then you *must* learn some German," he said firmly, and took her hand.

Ruby laughed out loud. Somehow she felt comfortable around this man. He spoke simply and was straightforward and seemed genuinely interested in her. And he was nice to look at. *Ah, what the hell, what harm can a little hand-holding do*, she thought, wrapping her fingers around his as they headed off towards Notre-Dame.

"Why is your English so impeccable?" she asked.

"Impeccable?"

Ruby smiled and said, "It's excellent."

"I always had a thing for English and English literature, more so than French. We start early in school, and also I travelled to London a few times. What about you? How do you speak French so well?"

"My mother is from Montreal. I love the romance languages. French, Spanish, Italian—love them all."

"What about your father, where is he from?"

"He's from Canada. He's Black."

Werner nodded as if he had thought something like this all along. "*Mischling* . . . ," he said.

"I don't know what that means, but it doesn't sound good."

"You're mulatto."

Ruby stopped and dropped his hand. "That word is offensive. It should never be used anymore. Call me Black, call me mixed, but not that!"

Werner apologized. An awkward silence fell over them.

"It's okay. You couldn't be expected to know how awful that word is." Ruby took his hand again and they stood looking out over the Seine. The incandescence of the city stretched out before them, and she felt like each and every twinkle that lit the sky was something to be discovered. Werner began chatting about Berlin, and he too seemed full of light, matching the Parisian night.

They sat outside Notre-Dame de Paris for a while, taking in its grandeur and murmuring about hunchbacks, and then they walked back through the streets to La Pleine Lune. After eating, they ordered drinks and sat chatting some more, the cool night air blowing gently around them. Ruby felt intoxicated in more than one way. Werner's intelligence and sunny humour had cast a spell on her. After an hour or two of earnest talking, staring and hand-holding, Ruby felt she was ready to begin her journey into independence and liberation. She asked Werner, "Okay, your place or mine?"

"Oh, I like your style. Straight to the point."

"Well, why bother waiting?" Ruby said. "Tomorrow I'll be gone and we'll have never known."

"Never known what?"

"Why, how we taste . . . the best dessert of all."

"Hmmm . . . I think I'm going home on the train with you tomorrow," said Werner.

The two of them wandered down the road and quietly climbed the stairs to Ruby's room. Amidst awkward fumbling and giggling, they doffed their clothes and drank in the essence of their dissimilar bodies. His was long and gangly, skin rough and mottled next to her rounded café au lait limbs. Werner struggled with her bra straps, yanking at them impatiently until they snapped against her skin. "Do you need help?" Ruby teased.

"German women don't wear bras," Werner said. "You'll be rid of this contraption in no time." They laughed as their bodies melded.

"Please, make me one promise," Werner whispered as he licked her earlobe later on.

"What's that?" Ruby asked.

"Don't say 'I love you' to me tonight."

Ruby giggled. "You must take me for a fool," she said.

"But why is it that so many Americans always say they love people they are just screwing?"

"I don't know about 'so many Americans,'" Ruby replied, "but Canadians are different from Americans. Don't lump us in with the Hollywood lot. Personally, I don't know how you could tell if you really loved someone without having sex with them first."

Werner began to massage Ruby's feet. Then he took her big toe in his mouth and said, "Mmm, juicy, smoky and a little salty. Just like a piece of ham."

"Are you calling me a pig?" asked Ruby as she wriggled around.

"I will worship them one by one, how do you say, until the cows come home?"

"First a pig, now a cow—Werner, you're not very flattering."

"This little piggy goes to market, this little piggy comes running *all* the way home. That's right, come to Werner, baby."

"Oh my god, get off my toes." On and on they went through the night, with Werner joking all the way.

Ruby postponed her departure to Berlin. She and Werner spent the next two weeks wandering the streets of Paris together. At the end of it all Ruby was ready to leave for Berlin, with Werner in tow.

....

The train rumbled sluggishly through the flat and colourless countryside, having slowed measurably since they crossed the border into East Germany. Ruby chatted with Werner and with a young West German couple sitting opposite them. They all laughed at her attempts to pronounce the few German words she knew, the language sounding rough and angry to her untrained ear. Often she would open her eyes to see the young man and woman necking, hands caressing each other's bodies without a care in the world.

Werner carried on trying to drill some German words and phrases into her, but Ruby was only half-interested. Then he said, "I think you should stay with me. Let's take a chance on each other and see how it works out. Anyhow, where else are you going to go?"

"Well, I would have stayed in a youth hostel for a while. But thank you for asking me to stay with you." Her first instinct was to go with the flow and say yes. It would be ideal for her, she thought, more than she could have asked for. "This will be true immersion in more than one sense," she said as she smiled at Werner, who seemed both nervous and pleased about her answer. They pressed rather uncomfortably into each other and let the night fall upon them.

Morning arrived cheerless and dim; whistles blew and the train jolted to a stop. Ruby saw guards perched on towers, rifles slung over their shoulders.

"We're here," Werner said, yet there was no station or city to be seen.

Ruby leaned out the window and spied a group of soldiers

in grey uniforms that seemed to match the countryside walking purposefully along the side of the train, reining in large German shepherds on leashes. The dogs sniffed at the underbelly of the train.

"What on earth are the dogs for?" she asked Werner.

"To check if anyone is hiding underneath," Werner replied a little curtly.

"Anyone . . . ?" Ruby asked.

"East Germans, of course. We've been passing through East Germany and are about to enter West Berlin and no one from the East is allowed in. Some people will try any means to escape to the West."

"Do they always do this?"

"Yes." His voice betrayed exasperation with her naïveté. It was ironic to Ruby that she, for some strange reason, was taking a reverse escape route, from West to East.

A voice rang out. *"Halten Sie bitte die Pässe bereit." Get your passports ready.*

The East German officers came through first, silently checking everyone's papers. Then came the West Germans, in dark olive-green uniforms, looking every inch as dour and authoritarian as their Eastern counterparts. They asked Ruby which baggage belonged to her, and after Werner translated, she pointed to the blue knapsack on the rack above her head. Only when they had finished carefully thumbing through her passport and returned it did she realize she'd been holding her breath.

As the train took off again, she noticed a grey slab of concrete looming behind a tall barbed wire fence.

There it was. So plain, so simple, so ugly.

They chugged along parallel to the Wall for a while and then snaked towards the city through a dense forest. The leaves on the trees were a vibrant shade of green, and tree branches stuck out from every which way as they coursed along the rails towards the city.

"This is the Grunewald," Werner told her. "Berlin has the largest urban forests in all of Europe."

Ruby felt this was most appropriate for a city enclosed by a wall. Soon she was taking in the beauty of the cityscape that was gliding by her window, so different from the harsh regime that surrounded it. Church spires, intricate and colourful facades adorning tall buildings, a gilded palace. Against the grey hues, the place radiated a melancholy elegance.

The train screeched into West Berlin's downtown station, Zoologischer Garten. Werner was telling her that he didn't believe in phones or televisions and she would have to place any calls from the public phone down the road from him.

The long train ride had taken its toll, for her whole body ached as she lifted her knapsack onto her shoulders. She stepped onto the platform with the throngs of other passengers, Werner following her and offering to take her knapsack.

"We made it," Werner said and smiled at her.

"That was quite some trip . . . and wow, I saw the Wall up close."

"You'll be seeing plenty of that while you're here—it's everywhere."

Werner led her into the heart of the bustling station. He

35

walked very quickly and she had difficulty keeping up with him. The subway was dirty and worn down, full of old men and women. They passed a group of young punks wearing studded leather bands, heavy black army boots, dog collars and safety pins hanging from their ears. Strips of hair split their shorn, shiny scalps in half. Two careening drunks waved bottles of beer like flags, shouting loudly at everyone and no one in particular.

As Ruby and Werner squeezed out the doors with the other passengers, an older man jostled Ruby and sneered something under his breath.

"What was that about?" she asked. "That guy bumped into me and then sounded really angry."

"Oh, don't worry. Our language always sounds harsh. It was nothing. Besides, Berliners are known to be grumpy."

"Just what I need when I'm striking out in a new place."

"Don't be silly, you'll be fine. But if you end up staying, you'll have to learn German."

The cool spring air had a peculiar sharp scent that Ruby couldn't identify. The buildings were tall, grey and close together, blocking an easy view of the sky. Not far from the station, Werner steered the way to a sombre six-storey building with a crumbling facade. Through the entryway, a wide corridor led into a cement-paved courtyard surrounded on all sides by more decrepit buildings. As she looked up at the high windows, she imagined countless pairs of eyes staring down on her.

"I live in what's called the Hinterhaus, or the backhouse. These courtyards were originally built so that a horse and buggy could come in, turn around and go back out. These houses are particular to Berlin—you won't find many of them anywhere else in Germany. Come, let's not stand here for too long," he said, pushing her on. "My place is very small and there are some things you'll have to get used to."

Ruby didn't consider herself a fussy person, but she was still surprised by the little closetlike chamber on the second landing, just large enough for a toilet, but no sink. When they reached the third floor, she was out of breath. As Werner unlocked the door to his apartment, he apologized that there was no shower or hot water; they would have to go to the public bathhouse down the road to wash.

"Of course I take sponge baths in the kitchen all the time, but every few days I go down the road and pay for a bath."

Ruby laughed and said, "I know a few people back home who would have a problem with that."

"Yes, I've heard that Americans are really obsessed with being clean and take baths every day."

It occurred to Ruby that the meticulous, uptight German was just as much of a stereotype, yet she was too tired to ask whether that was just a myth. Inside the apartment, a short, dark hallway led to a kitchen barely wide enough for a table. From there, a door opened to a bed-sitting room with high ceilings. Werner had built a loft bed, leaving space below for a desk and sofa. Over the desk hung a print of Picasso's *Don Juan*. In the corner stood a seven-foot-tall ceramic structure with two metal doors at the bottom and a third one in the middle. When Ruby touched it, the heat singed her fingers.

37

"What's this thing? An oven?"

"That's what heats the rooms in most of the old buildings like this in Berlin. You put bricks of coal on the grate inside that second metal door, light them and let them heat through. The ashes fall down below and have to be scraped out into a pail. That'll be your job."

"Jesus H. Christ. Now I'm Cinderella. Just what I always dreamed of."

"Actually, it's a great way to heat the room, even if it is a bit messy. People used to bake things on the shelf inside that middle door. I'll bake you into gingerbread in there if you misbehave."

"Don't you be telling me how to behave, or else I'll be the one shoving your head in there for some roasted Werner. Coal, huh? Is that what makes the air smell outside?"

"Yeah, this is mainly brown coal from East Germany, full of sulphur. You have to be careful when you light it that it burns properly, or you can generate poisonous gases."

"So I might die while I'm sleeping?"

"Not too likely, but it's possible."

The rest of the walls in the flat were covered with shelves stuffed with hundreds of books. Most titles were German, but Ruby recognized the names of many authors, including a whole row of works by Marx and Engels and anarchist writers like Kropotkin and Malatesta. On the top of the shelves were several intriguing postcard-sized prints.

Werner saw her studying them. "Those are reprints of woodcuts done by various artists," he said.

"What's a woodcut?"

Ruby's parents were all about music and the civil and human rights movements. Their children had not been exposed to the fine arts very much, though Ruby had a flare for all sorts of crafts.

"You don't know? Where have you been all these years? How could you be so uninformed?"

"Werner, don't be such a snob. Not everyone has had a chance to learn about and experience the arts in the same way."

Werner shrugged. "I am not a snob—it's simply a special technique where you carve out a design on a block of wood and use it for making prints. I can show you in some of my encyclopedias. Or better yet, we can check some out at one of the museums."

"Sounds good."

"So, what do you think?" he asked, gesturing out into the room. "Does it measure up to your standards, my princess?"

"It's fine. A little dark, maybe," she said.

"The other buildings tend to block out the sun unless you live very high up or in the front house, facing out on the street."

It hadn't escaped Ruby's notice that he had been quick to close the blinds as soon as they arrived, leaving the flat very dark.

"Do you want to stay? Try it out?"

Ruby pursed her lips and thought for a bit. She didn't feel that she had anything to lose by giving it a shot, and she liked that Werner looked nervous waiting for her answer. "Well, I think we should just go for it. Why not?"

"Great. I'm so glad you'll stay." Werner's smile lit up the dark room. "What would you like to do next?" he asked as he placed her knapsack down on the floor.

"Sleep."

"I thought we might go out for a walk."

"Can we do that a little later? The train ride was unbearably long and I didn't sleep much."

Werner seemed a touch disappointed but said, "Sure, sure, go ahead and lie down."

Ruby climbed the ladder onto the loft bed and sank under the duvet.

When she woke an hour later, Werner was lying on the bed next to her, his eyes straying over her body. They snuggled close together. Ruby stretched herself out like a cat and began to take off her clothes. Werner practically jumped on her and was all over her and then in her in no time. Ruby was hot and bothered at first, but when they came to the finish line she began to imagine them rolling frozen grapes and ice cubes across each other's bodies, with a squirt of chocolate sauce here and there. She remembered Pierre at university introducing her to frozen grapes. She loved it because you could eat them and they were so deliciously crunchy and sweet and would soften slowly in your mouth.

Werner interrupted her daydreaming and said, "How'd you like that?"

"It was fine, but . . ."

"But what? What's wrong?"

"I would have liked some warm-up exercises first."

"Warm-up exercises? What on earth do you mean?"

"Most women need a little more time and maybe even a few props to get going."

"Ruby, I didn't sign up for a cooking course, I signed up for you!"

"Well, you did such a good job on my toes before, I had different expectations of you. But we're still just getting to know each other. Anyway, keep your mind open for me."

Werner smiled. "Then, keep yours open for me as well. Just because you're here doesn't mean I won't see other women."

Ruby raised her eyebrow as she looked at him.

"I mean I have other friends. Women friends. We go out, and sometimes we sleep together, and I expect to be able to continue. Not that you can't come along sometimes . . . I do want you to meet my friends. Anyway, the whole thing could be fun for both of us."

"Well, thanks a lot! What you mean is we're going to have an open relationship. Do I get to come along for the sex?" She laughed. "It sounds a little risqué, but I'm not really the possessive type and I'm pretty open-minded." She was already having more of an adventure than she'd anticipated. "All right, let's try it. Should we set out some rules?"

"Yes. We remain primary partners and we don't bring anybody home with us."

"You sound as if you've done this before. What happens if we fall for someone else?"

"No falling in love. This is strictly for fun."

"It's hardly something you can decide arbitrarily!"

"Do your best. I don't mean that we'll be out sexing every person we meet, but we shouldn't have to turn down an exciting opportunity."

"Right. I'm all for exciting opportunities. But do you really think this will work in the long run?"

"Of course. Just remember not to bring anyone here," he insisted. "I need my privacy."

"Yeah, right."

"I'm serious. Don't try to mix with the people here in the building and don't hang around in the courtyard. The landlord is a fascist pig and there are quotas for foreigners in this part of Berlin."

"Are you telling me I have to hide? I didn't come here to be holed up in some shitty flat."

"You should be okay because you're Canadian. Even so, you look more like a Turk, and they're the ones who have a lot of problems. The landlord treats the Turkish tenants like they're ignorant, filthy children. Just try not to get involved with anyone. Anyway, I'm looking for a new flat, so maybe we'll be out of here soon."

Ruby mulled over the idea of an open relationship. Could she share Werner without getting jealous? Would he really let her wander, too? It would probably be harder in reality but she was willing to give it a go. This is what she had wanted, after all: to be free and have adventures.

Two days later, as they were heading out into the city,

they met the landlord huffing and puffing up the steps, his fat cheeks bulging out of a purply-red face.

"Und wer is denn das mit Ihnen?" Who have you got with you here?

Werner smiled coolly. "Just a friend visiting from Canada."

He said something, plainly rude. Ruby nudged Werner, who translated under his breath. "Since when did they make them like that in Canada?"

Ruby squirmed under the gaze of the landlord's wormy eyes.

"Never mind, excuse us please. We're on our way out."

"Canada. Not likely," the man harrumphed, squeezing his bulbous body flat against the dingy brown walls to let them pass into the courtyard.

"Whew. So that was him, huh?" Ruby said.

"Yeah, don't worry. He can't touch you. Just stay out of his way."

"Damn right I will."

They strolled through the side streets of Moabit and along the River Spree, passing countless buildings with banners hanging from them. Angry words were scrawled in red and black, punctuated at either end with an encircled capital *A*. Werner explained that the *A* stood for anarchy and that these abandoned buildings, marked for demolition, had been taken over by squatters. A massive housing shortage plagued West Berlin; many building owners wanted to renovate, and the ensuing increase in rents forced tenants out. People were rising up in protest.

Ruby and Werner crossed over the river and entered the Tiergarten, a vast park in the middle of the city with wide, rolling lawns, plenty of beautiful old trees and bike paths galore. They threaded through the English Gardens and then the Hansaviertel, a little community built around a square in the late 1950s that featured buildings by Le Corbusier, Gropius and Mies van der Rohe. Continuing along the path of the Strassenbahn tracks that passed overhead, they reached the Saturday flea market on Strasse des 17 Juni. As they passed stalls selling bratwurst and knackers on buns with hot mustard, the smell of cinnamon and other spices wafted through the air. Well-dressed people slurped hot mulled wine, taking a break from the crush of the crowd.

"This is the market that all the American tourists and soldiers come to and that's why the prices are inflated," Werner explained. "They don't realize that what they are buying isn't as antique as they believe."

After much poking around, Ruby found some nice earrings.

"They're lovely," Werner said. "Do you like them? Here, I'll buy them for you."

She was pleased and put them on immediately. They stopped to get some mulled wine and she felt its warm spiciness flush her face. As they strolled arm in arm towards the end of the market, Ruby said, "What a beautiful day." It was still early in the afternoon, so Werner suggested they head over to another market near Potsdamer Platz. They doubled back into the Tiergarten. Werner moved quickly, and Ruby struggled to keep up with him.

"We could have taken the U-Bahn," he said, "but in this city you'll learn to walk a lot with me. My father used to take my sister and me out hiking in the hills every Sunday for miles on end, so I'm used to it." Twenty minutes later, they arrived at a circular intersection in the park marked by a large golden statue of a man riding a horse. Four wide avenues branched off from the circle.

"That is the symbol of Bismarck defeating the French during the Franco-Prussian War, which happened on June 17," Werner explained. "That's the name of the avenue that the flea market was on."

For a moment, Ruby felt she was being lectured by her father.

They continued through the park. Not even the Bois de Boulogne in Paris felt this big. After another thirty minutes, they came out of the park and walked along the Landwehrkanal. They left behind the trees of the park and approached a flat and dusty square filled with merchants. Turkish music blasted from tape decks as tattooed and pierced punks flogged metal-studded leatherwear and long-haired hippies offered flowing skirts and beaded chains.

Mixed among the punks and the Turks, Ruby noticed, were people milling around in red and orange garb topped by long necklaces. The necklaces held a picture of a man with frizzy grey hair worn down past his shoulders and an even longer beard. Henna-haired women wore skirts that reached the ground, while the men had matching flowing pants.

"Who are those people?" Ruby asked.

Werner laughed dismissively. "My god, haven't you seen them before? How could you not know? They're all over the place. The Bhagwan nuts. Followers of an Indian guru named Bhagwan Rajneesh who sucks their wallets dry."

"Werner, would you stop talking to me like this? You're treating me like a child. I've only been here a short while. I can't know or have seen everything." She doubled back towards where they'd come from. When she arrived at the park entrance she was unsure which way to go—it was all so foreign to her with streets that turned every which way, and they all looked so similar. She started down the road to her right and figured she'd ask some other pedestrian for help. But she knew it had been a convoluted walk they had taken.

Before long Werner had caught up with her. "I'm sorry, Ruby. I didn't mean to be patronizing. I just feel like I have to look out for you. Berlin is a big city and it can be dangerous. Also you don't speak any German—yet."

"Werner, I'm a big girl. I don't need another father. And it's so hypocritical. One moment you're suggesting a relationship without restraints, and the next, you're trying to control me."

"I will try to let go. I'm just a little protective, I guess. I'll work on it, I promise. Now let's go grab a *Kaffee und Kuchen* somewhere." At Ruby's look, he laughed. "Sorry, some coffee and cake."

Ruby allowed a small smile in return, and as they walked down the street he began again to explain the sights along the way.

....

In those first days, Ruby felt as though she had stepped back into the early seventies. While most of the men she had known back home had already cut their hair short, so many men and women in Berlin still sported the long-haired hippie look. But she had to admit, she had also never seen so many punks, skinheads and new wavers colliding in one place.

Ruby's explorations of the city were haphazard in those first few weeks. She was somewhat intimidated by her lack of German and spent as much time lying around and reading books as she did wandering the streets. Her great-uncle was ever-present in her mind when she was out wandering. She thought to be gay in the twenties and thirties must have been very difficult. Berlin, with its sexual openness, would have seemed very welcoming. Had any of the places she passed by been there at that time? She promised herself she'd find the places her uncle had mentioned in his letters. She quizzed Werner about older buildings of interest in Berlin.

"You might try the Gloria Palast theatre. There's not much left of it, but in its heyday it was supposed to have been marvellous and was a very popular place to go."

"Where is it?"

"On Kurfürstenstrasse. From there you can easily walk to the gay village and take a look around. In fact, you mentioned the Eldorado nightclub. It used to be on Motzstrasse, right nearby. I'll take you to the library and we'll pull out a few books and maybe find an address. But you can visit the foyer of the theatre any day."

And indeed at the library they found many books with

photographs showcasing the theatre. It had been built in a Neo-baroque style, with a mirrored winter garden and writing rooms inside, marble steps, crystal chandeliers. She tried to imagine the elegance of it all. It was bombed in 1943, and now a new cinema stood in its place, still trying to be grand.

"Who was this uncle of yours, anyway?"

"Great-uncle, on my father's side. Don't know much, except that he was gay and he studied here for a few years in the early thirties. When he returned home he and his German lover were practically driven into seclusion in his sister's basement. He died young—of cirrhosis."

The next day, Ruby took a bus downtown to go looking for the theatre. She was minding her own business in the almost empty bus when three muscular young men lunged on board. Ruby noticed the emblem of the Berliner soccer team on their jackets. She suddenly wished she were invisible. She had heard from Werner about racist soccer fans. Hair shorn to within an inch of their scalps, the trio belched and swaggered their way to the back of the bus and slouched down on seats directly opposite Ruby, blocking her view out the window. Ruby crushed the bag of doner kebabs into her lap with tight fists. She scanned the ceiling, then decided that staring at her feet was safer.

"I smell a Turk," sneered the one in the middle, thumbing his nose.

"Smell?" said the guy on his right. "I *see* a Turk."

The first guy snivelled, "*Verdammte Türke*—smell, see, what does it matter? If you can't see them, you smell them. If you can't smell them, you see them."

The air burst with harsh laughter. Ruby looked up quickly towards the front of the bus. Just a few older women and a thick-set man, standing by the centre exit, his head turned away. No one who could help her. She took a deep breath and decided to stare them down. In their faces she saw grim mockery, eyes that avowed hatred for her and everyone like her. Ruby got up quickly, thinking, *Move, just move*.

"*Kuck mal*, Hans. Catch that, she walks. *Scheisse*, maybe she even dances. I like it when they dance."

Ruby whirled around and yelled, "You little Nazi piss-heads, what the fuck would you know about anything?"

Swaying towards the front of the bus, she clamped a hand over her mouth, hoping to stop the surging of her stomach. The three punks erupted into a chorus, chanting, "*Deutschland, Deutschland über alles.*"

The driver looked up into the rear-view mirror and barked, "Quiet or you're off the bus."

Ruby grabbed the pole next to the driver's seat, the steel like ice in her hand. Next stop was hers. As the bus lurched to a halt, the driver apologized. She nodded bleakly and stepped off the stairs. She felt like throwing up and stood where she was for a few minutes, trying to calm herself down. There was a bench down the road and Ruby went to it and sat down. She pulled out a cigarette, placing it between her still-quivering lips. She drew in the smoke and held it for a long time, just sitting there. She had never been exposed to such blatant racism, not even in Toronto. She didn't think this would have happened had she been with Werner. With him she was like an exotic appendage, to be stared at but not approached. Ruby sighed and tossed the cigarette butt to the ground. She still felt unsteady but got up anyway and set about on her way to the theatre.

There was not much left of the original building at all, but the facade and foyer had been maintained. She thought of the photos she had seen and imagined her uncle streaming in among all the others to see Germany's first major talkie, *The Blue Angel* by Joseph von Sternberg, or René Clair's *Sous les Toits de Paris*. Next she found the building where the Eldorado used to be. There was nothing there to suggest the hub it once was. But Ruby fancied watching her uncle come out of the club with his friends. He would have stood out with his brown skin, and Ruby wondered what tips he could have had for her about being a foreigner among Germans. She wondered if he, too, had been spat at and yelled at like she had and what he had done. She wished she could turn to him for answers.

When Ruby got home that afternoon, she was still feeling shaky.

"How'd it go?" Werner asked.

"Well, that depends on what you mean. The theatre was fine, but . . ." Ruby slumped into a chair and told him her story.

"I can't believe that actually happened. That's awful! But I told you that you'd meet all types here. There are lots of neo-Nazis floating around, so you better get used to it. That wouldn't have happened if you'd been with me."

"Is that all you can say?" Ruby stuttered. "Just 'Get used to it'? Those guys almost trampled all over me. Don't you have any kind of office where you can report racist incidents? Like a human rights commission or something?"

Werner laughed and shook his head. "Nothing like that here," he said.

It was Ruby's turn to express disbelief. Maybe there would be some agency working with foreigners and newcomers that knew about these kinds of things. She would have to find out.

Ruby enrolled in night school language classes, hoping not just to improve her German but to make some friends. Her German teacher was a laid-back young guy with cascading brown hair who wore flowing pants and loose cotton shirts. On the first night, she met Emma, a young British woman with spiky, copper-coloured hair who lived in the same neighbourhood. They chatted as they ambled back home after class. The next week, Ruby went home with her and met several Brits who were hanging out in her apartment. The place reeked of stale beer, curry and dope, but the conversation was sharp and cutting. Punk music rocked the air waves with an occasional interlude by Lee "Scratch" Perry and other reggae dub masters. She met Emma's neighbours, two men, Smithie and Jack, who ran a bar nearby. She met Lina, decidedly waif-ish, with raven hair and black clothes to match.

"The most important thing you need to know about me," Lina told her, "I think in Italian, I dream in Italian, I eat in

Italian, but I love the words of Apollinaire. The second most important thing—I am a follower of Leon Trotsky. Are you a capitalist? I am not. If you understand this, Miss Canadian, we can be friends."

Despite the mournful clothes, her liveliness was a welcome relief from the uncommonly morbid and sarcastic quips swirling out of the mouths of the others. The unfamiliar humour seemed raw, but Ruby soon grew comfortable among her new British friends.

It was not as simple with Werner. Ruby knew that he was attracted to her because of her biracial background, and she resented his tendency to patronize her, often downplaying her experiences and those of her family. Despite growing up in white-bread Don Mills, she had been schooled in Black American literature and the politicians, activists and leaders of the civil rights movement. And jazz music flowed like a river through their house. But outside of family and friends, there was little tangible exposure to Black people beyond books and discussions. She had always related more to the Black side of her "split identity." Yet here she was, out of sync with her raciality, slowly fading and subverting itself as she steeped herself in the Berliner culture and her relationship with Werner.

One day when he caught her humming a Marvin Gaye tune, he shrieked: "Oh my god, you don't like that Motown stuff, do you? It's not the real thing!"

"What on earth is, then, the *real* thing?"

"More obscure stuff than that. Like Stax. Motown was all just commercial trash."

Ruby wondered why there couldn't be a lot of "real things," and knew at the same time that he was expecting her to know about all other artists out there. He seemed to have studied Black music and literature, but when Ruby asked him if he knew any actual Black people besides her, he shook his head uncomfortably. Ruby stopped singing Marvin Gaye, Tammi Terrell or the Four Tops in front of him, but carried on just the same when she was on her own.

She regularly met with the Brits, and Werner went along with her from time to time. But while he enjoyed their company, he wasn't willing to stay out late partying, even when Ruby decided to remain with her friends rather than return home with him.

"I don't like you staying late on your own," he said sternly.

"Why not? What's the harm?"

"I'd hate to see you start up smoking dope, or anything else, god forbid."

"What's wrong with dope?"

"It will make you paranoid and make your mind lazy so that you can't do anything else."

"Jeez, Werner, you should have been in *Reefer Madness*— you'd be a good propagandist for the government. How does that sit with your anarchist ideals?"

"How can you possibly mix these things up?" he blustered. "They don't have anything to do with each other."

"Well, *I* think it's a major contradiction, but you'll have to figure that one out. Just go on home. I'll be along later."

When she got home later that night, Werner was pacing

restlessly. But rather than say anything more, he just hugged her like a bear and they went to bed.

The next day, Ruby went to the Beate Uhse sex shop near Bahnhof Zoo. It was time to spice things up with Werner. She stood outside to look in the windows for a long while. Once in, she was like a kid in a candy store. There were a couple of men in the store, but mostly it was women oohing and aahing over all the goodies. She herself was looking for handcuffs and anything else that might catch her interest. She found a few hanging on the far wall, but they were all furry and fluffy. She went to the counter, her voice shaking just a little. *"Ich suche . . . Hand . . ."* Ruby made a gesture, interlocking her hands.

"Möchten Sie die Handschellen sehen?"

"Ja, handcuffs," said Ruby.

The clerk, a young brunette with long, silky hair, nodded with a smile and took her back to the same wall.

"Da sind sie."

"Nein. No fur . . . *Metall,"* said Ruby.

The clerk was unsure of what she meant. Ruby tried to pronounce the word *metal* like she imagined it would sound in German. It worked.

"Ach, vielleicht meinen Sie diese?" Maybe you mean these? A little farther along the wall, below Ruby's sightline, hung some plain metal handcuffs.

Ruby grabbed a pair and smiled at the clerk. *"Ja, diese. Danke sehr!"*

She kept poking around in the store. She heard two

women guffawing and she followed their voices so she could see what was so funny. The young women were comparing different types of Thai balls to put in your vagina. They came in several different sizes and materials. The women were holding a set of wooden balls. Ruby thought she understood one saying to the other, "These would get lost inside me, or maybe they'd just fall out."

She reached in between the women and took a set of silver-coloured balls the size of large grapes. "You gotta squeeze really tight," she said slowly in English, "walk around and exercise your muscles. Like Kegels." She didn't know if she would be understood, but judging by the snorting and giggling that ensued, she had been.

Ruby was on a roll and so she looked around and found a small black leather whip, a chocolate-coloured vibrator and a butt plug. Thoroughly satisfied with her extravaganza, she left the store fantasizing about how she'd use these new acquisitions. Her uncle would be proud of her, exploring her sexuality. Werner wasn't home when she got there, so she got the Thai balls out of the bag and climbed up on the loft bed. She took off her jeans and popped one inside. She lay there for a few minutes just trying to see how it felt and if she could move it easily. She moved it up and down and then side to side. She popped another one in. Her body was getting tingly all over and she felt warm inside. She climbed down the ladder and stood doing Kegel exercises to hold the balls in. She was prancing around the room, bottomless, when Werner walked in. She stopped, let go, and the balls slid out.

"What the hell is that? What are you doing?" he yelped, a mixture of distress and bemusement on his face.

Ruby laughed. "Come on, baby, I have some presents for the two of us."

Werner gave her a quizzical look. "Before you take one more step, tell me what those balls are and why they fell out of you."

"They're Thai balls—good for exercising your pelvic muscles. I bought some fun things today for us. Come see."

Werner approached her hesitantly.

She shook the bag of goodies in her hand. "Reach in there and pull something out."

He took out the whip and cracked it in the air. "I see. So now you're my slave?"

"Don't even go there. No slaves here. We'll share it. Just fun. We'll alternate with spanking," she said with a twinkle in her eye. Werner reached in again and pulled out the handcuffs. "Wow, you really went on a spree. Yeah, we can try these."

Ruby slipped her hand into the bag. "Ta-da!" She waved the vibrator in the air.

Werner fell silent for a moment. "It's brown," he finally ventured.

"Yup. So it is."

"Do you have a problem with the colour of my dick?"

"Oh god, no, Werner. Of course not. This is just a little affirmative action at play."

"What?"

"Oh, never mind," said Ruby. "I thought it would be fun to have a Black penis to play with. It's just a toy." She was hoping he would just say "Whatever turns your crank" and get on with it.

"Well, as long as it doesn't take precedence over me . . . I guess," he said.

The last item was the butt plug. Werner gasped in mock horror as he examined it and then said in a serious tone, "You are not putting that thing anywhere near me."

"God, Werner, if you can put your thing up my ass, why can't I try this in yours? Affirmative action and sexual equality, that's what I want."

"No, no, no. You'll have to tie me down."

"Ooh, bad idea. I've got handcuffs right here." She picked up the butt plug and pointed it his way, bobbing it up and down in front of him. He scrambled away, and she chased him around the room waving the handcuffs and butt plug in the air. Finally, Werner collapsed into a chair, and Ruby climbed on top of him. "Shall we start now? There's no time like the present."

"Oh my god, you and your sayings." Werner pulled her down and kissed her mouth. "Here's to expanding our sexual horizons," he said.

Ruby clapped her hands in glee and twisted off her top. Werner, wriggling underneath her, did the same with his pants.

An hour or two later Ruby whispered in Werner's ear. "Do you know why I like you?"

"No, why?"

"Because you are funny. But mainly I know that you have a big heart, a good heart. I always think of little old

Frau Menzer. Almost every night you're out there helping her down the steps to the toilet. Or you're cleaning up after the drunks who piss by her door. Very gracious and thoughtful."

"My parents taught me well."

"I like you because you are articulate and intelligent and thoughtful."

Ruby cared a lot for Werner and she knew that he looked after her well, despite his foibles. But was it love? She couldn't say for sure. Not yet. She would stick it out, though, and see how far and how long they could go.

They spent much of their free time walking across town to weekend flea markets and checking out the plentiful all-day and all-night repertory cinemas where popcorn was replaced by beer and boisterous crowds. The crowd seemed to be there as much for the infamous Marlboro Man cigarette ads as for the movies. The ads played before each screening, and sometimes there was the Camel guy, too. One always seemed to be trying to best the other with new and ever more dangerous escapades. As the audience watched the Marlboro Man gallop across canyon floors, muscles always bulging and ten-gallon hat on tight, they whistled and howled and chortled loudly. Ruby was surprised at the intensity of their hilarity, but it was clear that to them this was merely yet another representation of American society—modern, macho cowboys hustling after the American Dream.

The weeks flew by and became months, until suddenly

it was December. Ruby's first Christmas Eve away from home was spent sloshing back a tall bottle of yeasty beer while watching flesh-eating zombies feast away in *Night of the Living Dead*. Christmas Day she wrote a long letter to her parents, telling them how much she was enjoying Berlin. She didn't linger too much on the fact that the weather was so grey and depressing, or that she missed them. Then she took her collection of coins to the phone booth down the road and called them.

"Mom? Put Dad on the extension. Dad? Merry Christmas! I love you and I love Berlin, too. It's fantastic here, so full of history. I've met a man. I think you'd like him. He's very sweet."

"That's wonderful, Ruby," said her mom.

"When will you bring him here?" asked her dad.

"Well, I don't have money for more travelling just yet. I hope to find a job soon."

"What will you do there?" her father asked.

"Oh, there's all kinds of odd jobs to be done. I'll find something."

"I miss you, Ruby," said her mom. "So does your dad."

"I miss you, too. I just wrote you a long letter. Write me back. Gotta go, my change is running out. Love you."

She hung up and was surprised to feel a tear trickle down her cheek. They were so far away and she missed them more than she had expected.

Ruby's German was quickly improving under the tutel-age of her charming night school teacher, so she felt confident enough to look for work. She had no official visa, so whatever she did would have to be paid for under the table. Scanning the ads in the city's newspapers, she found the most common unskilled labour for women was cleaning houses or apartments. Within a few days she found a cleaning job.

Her employer, a wiry woman of seventy-six with a voice as deep as Marlene Dietrich's, lived in a grand old home in the southern reaches of the city, replete with an indoor winter garden, a library and a huge kitchen with a walk-in pantry. This was a Berlin full of old women, their men lost to the ravages of two wars, and Frau Herzog was no exception. Ruby could tell that she had been a beauty, despite the wrinkles that now crisscrossed her face. She dressed stylishly and she seemed friendly; however, suspicious whether a young Canadian could keep up with German expectations of cleanliness, she gave Ruby specific orders and closely monitored her work. Windows were to be cleaned with rags soaked in vinegar and water and dried with newspaper and then again with soft leather cloths so no streaks marred the ingress of sunshine.

Ruby loved the winter garden. She had never seen anything quite so big. The room was wide and very long and on three sides it was glassed in, ceiling to floor. Plants of all species, sizes and colours covered much of the floor, with two pathways dividing the room. There were philodendrons, jades, crotons, ficus, pineapples and all manner of ferns, with their gentle tendrils swirling every which way. The different shades and hues of green held her fascination. But most of all she loved the flowering plants—bougainvillea, hibiscus, azalea, amaryllis and wonderful orchids galore. It was basically a greenhouse within a house—it reminded her of watching her mother's svelte body bend and swivel in her garden back home, and she felt happy in there as she washed the cool ceramic floors and the windows. The air felt humid and lush. She hummed her mother's favourite songs and sang to the plants as she dusted their leaves and spritzed them and checked the soil. One time she was singing "The Surrey with the Fringe on Top," her voice growing louder and louder without her noticing. Suddenly Frau Herzog stood in front of her, arms crossed.

"Ruby, what are you doing?"

"Oh! Oh, I'm sorry, Frau Herzog, I just got carried away."

"My dear, you have a fine voice, but we're not in the theatre and I didn't hire you to sing for me. There's no need to bellow. Please, just pay attention to your work."

"Yes, of course," Ruby mumbled.

She had gotten off lightly that time.

Week after week, Ruby mopped floors, cleared and dusted attics and picked cherries from atop unsteady ladders. Then one day, Frau Herzog ordered her to climb out the window of a third-floor sitting room onto the roof and scoop the leaves from the eavestroughs.

"Here, we'll just tie some rope around your waist and attach the other end to the tree trunk over there. Don't worry, I know my knots," she said, smiling at the dismay that crossed Ruby's face.

Despite the trunk's apparent sturdiness, Ruby had visions of crashing through the window, flattened like a coyote in a *Road Runner* cartoon. Nonetheless, out the window she went, and she inched around the roof's edge, trying not to peek at the ground far below, grabbing and bagging leaves and cursing her inability to speak up for herself. She needed the money, and as an illegal worker she felt she had no rights.

The following week, Frau Herzog insisted she clean the living room windows from the outside. She tied Ruby to a chair in the dining room, from which she was to climb out onto a ledge that overlooked the driveway two storeys below. But the chair was not anchored to anything, and again it seemed she was placing her life in the hands of Frau Herzog.

When Ruby told Werner about her day at work, he exploded.

"How could you let yourself be treated that way? You have absolutely no insurance, nothing to protect you if anything happens. You're such a fool!"

"Maybe so, but she can be like a Nazi sometimes . . . Is that it? Are all older Germans former Nazis?"

"Well, many were at least part of Hitler's machinery. But you know, many Germans did not want to fight a war, but they felt there was no choice. People did fight against the Nazis, in the resistance. Still, in the end many became enmeshed in the regime."

Listening to Werner, she thought of her own parents, and what they would think of her job. Her father would say of her time in Berlin that she was aimless, rather than getting a global education. She was simply sponging up all that the city and Werner had to offer. But it was all so new and different and exhilarating. Work was difficult, but she knew she would eventually find something better. Her uncle was with her in spirit, and he was right: there was something special about this city, and she wanted to open herself up to it. It was as if within the Wall someone had put a 33 LP on and then changed the speed to 45 rpm. Everyone was dancing to a song that had no end while the rest of the world looked on. She wondered about life on the other side.

As the day receded into the blackness of night, she dreamed of walking the length of the enormous wall that enclosed the city, climbing to the top, stumbling along its concrete edges, discovering how it felt to balance West against East.

CHAPTER THREE

Train

AT THE NATIONAL GALLERY, RUBY FOUND HERSELF standing in front of Fernand Léger's "The City." The primary colours vibrated off the canvas; bold, cubist shapes that only vaguely resembled a skyline. She had been in Berlin for over a year and was thinking it was time to make some changes—to find a better job, for starters. She and Werner had moved to Wedding in the summer, where they had two similar flats in the same building complex. Ruby lived on the third floor of the first backhouse and Werner was on the fourth floor of the second backhouse. This arrangement was working out well, as they could choose to enjoy some freedom from each other or, conversely, spend as much time together as they wanted.

While Ruby was standing in front of the painting, thinking about her situation, she felt a sharp pang in her abdomen that took her breath away. The cramps worsened until finally she was crouched on her knees, head hanging forward. As she moved to stand up again, a guard came up to her. "Miss, are you all right? Can I help you?"

"I just need to find a washroom and then call a taxi."

He walked with her to the washroom, holding her arm ever so lightly. He told her to come see him about the taxi when she was ready. Ruby felt as if a knife was slicing through her abdomen. She stayed, doubled up, in the washroom for half an hour, and when she came out she found the guard, who called a taxi to take her home. She spent the night in the bathroom, alternating between vomiting and diarrhea. Werner fixed her pots of chamomile tea, which she disliked intensely, but she knew it was good for her. It made her think of Beatrix Potter and the stories of Peter Rabbit.

Over the next three weeks her symptoms didn't let up much.

"Werner, what am I going to do? I'm really scared—I've lost twenty pounds now."

"I don't know what to suggest, but you're not getting much help here."

Werner talked to his father, who suggested that she come to Stuttgart, where he had connections to one of the hospitals and she could get some tests done. Ruby had met Werner's parents in Stuttgart over the Easter holidays. Werner's mother, Heike, was a sculptor and his father, Hermann, was a graphic designer. She knew that his father was an ethnic German who had come to Germany after being expelled by the Russians from his home in Sudetenland, Czechoslovakia. She also knew that his parents were disaffected Communists.

Werner suggested she leave on the weekend, but said that he wouldn't be able to accompany her. He would come a few days later. Ruby was terrified about making this ten-hour trip on her own in her state. But Werner was busy with his studies. She packed a small bag, and on Sunday they went down to the train station. Ruby found herself a seat in a compartment with two other people—a woman in her forties and a young guy. The man was flipping through a magazine, and the woman, who was at the window, was deep into a book. Ruby sat on the same side as the woman, but up against the door. People were still milling around on the platform, but Werner had already gone. Just like him to leave her without a reassuring word.

Ruby felt faint. Her head ached, and her abdomen was cramping again. Although she had brought along a couple of magazines, she didn't feel well enough to read. She pushed herself into the corner of her seat, which looked out onto the corridor. She rested her head against the metal and glass. Beyond the window, the light was spreading barren, grey, indifferent. Ruby could feel her heart pounding as the pain sliced through her stomach.

Just before the train left the station, another man, balding and bulging at the waist, took a seat across from her, next to the young man. An elderly woman squeezed in next to Ruby, sandwiching her rail-thin body between the window and door seats. Ruby watched the man on the other side as he took out a wooden box and placed it on the seat beside him. He opened the box and took out a knife, a napkin, some bread, a piece of cheese and an apple. He spread the napkin on his lap and placed the bread there. After watching him dig into his piece of bread and passing a cursory smile, Ruby closed her eyes, trying to shut out the light and distraction.

The woman sitting next to her gave her a nudge. "Young lady, do you know what time it is?"

Ruby opened her eyes a little and responded that it was noon. She continued, "Do you know what time we arrive?"

"Uh, I'm not sure. Evening, I suppose."

The man with the lunch spoke up. "We arrive at ten p.m. on the dot."

"Thank you, *mein Herr. Danke.*"

Ruby tried to go to sleep but was haunted by her thoughts. Her mind swirled around, trying to imagine what was wrong with her. Maybe it was all in her head. But she didn't think that losing twenty pounds in three weeks could be all in her head. Werner had been concerned but was often short with her—he too was baffled.

The little old lady poked at her again. "My dear, where are you from?" She spoke in a low, clear German that Ruby could understand easily.

Ruby sighed. "Canada."

"Then I bet you don't know much about this trip you're making. We will be travelling through the eastern corridor. Ever heard of that?"

Ruby nodded in silence. A sense of panic began to spread slowly through her body and she wondered what awaited her at the hospital in Stuttgart. Why had Werner left her to make this trip on her own?

"Those nasty East Germans. They have ruined everything.

Do you know that my youngest son is stuck in the East? Do you know what that feels like? I've lost him to the Communists. Young lady, you're not listening to me."

Ruby felt a tightening wind its way like a vise around her throat. If she was just imagining things, why did she feel so awful?

"Are you all right, missy?" said the man across the aisle.

She shook her head. Her heart began to race. She twisted and turned in her seat, but tried to keep her face turned away from the other passengers so they wouldn't see her fear. Tears began to trickle down her cheeks.

The little old lady shook her arm this time. "Why, whatever is wrong? Why are you crying? You're not all right, are you?"

Ruby sniffled and turned to her, and without being able to say a word she broke down into sobs. Her abdomen was pounding; she felt as if it were on fire. The woman rubbed her arm gently and asked if there was anything she could do. Ruby shook her head listlessly. She bunched herself up in the corner again. She could barely breathe. She started gasping as she became more and more agitated. Her heart was bruising her chest with its mad strumming. She wanted to get off the train. What was going to happen to her at the other end? She didn't know Werner's parents that well. What could they do? She tried to stand up but crumpled back down on the seat.

The young woman stood up. "I'm going to find someone to help you. Hang on there."

It felt like quite a while before the woman returned with a conductor. They hadn't been able to find a doctor on the train.

The man bent down and said, "Miss, what's wrong?"

Ruby could barely open her mouth but managed to squeak out, "I don't know what's wrong, but it hurts terribly."

The man told the younger woman to stay in the compartment with Ruby. Ruby felt like an hour passed as she quivered and turned in her seat. Then the train began slowing down, the wheels finally grinding to a complete standstill in the middle of nowhere. Outside were empty fields, no houses. Everything looked like a wasteland.

Everybody in the compartment was looking at each other. They were not yet near the border.

"What's going on?" the fat man grumbled. "I feel bad for her, but do we really have to stop here?"

Eventually a woman and a man arrived at their compartment and asked the other travellers to leave. They bent down by Ruby, who was still huddled against the wall. "Ma'am, we're with the Red Cross and we hear you're having some trouble. We'd like to try to help you. Can you tell us what's wrong?"

Ruby couldn't stop hyperventilating. The woman kept tapping her hand gently, but Ruby couldn't revive herself enough to speak. Gentle, probing fingers directed a stethoscope to Ruby's heart, then took her blood pressure. Shaking violently, she was on the verge of passing out from the unforgiving pain.

"Miss, you are obviously in great distress, but we can't really tell what's going on. Tell us a little more about your condition."

Ruby stammered on about the events of the past three weeks as best she could. She explained that she had terrible pain in her abdomen. As the paramedic kneaded her abdomen, she sucked in her breath. "Get me out of here! I can't breathe."

"We're going to give you some painkillers and a sedative till you get to hospital."

Ruby accepted their offer gladly. Only then did she notice the grey East German Red Cross uniforms; only then did she fully realize that the train had indeed stopped for her deep in the narrow Communist corridor, West Berlin's umbilical cord to the free world.

The others were allowed back into the compartment. Back in her seat, the little old lady took her hand. "Now, now, my dear. They're gone. Everything will be fine. Ach, especially since the East Germans were here. Bastards!" The other woman hushed her. As the drugs kicked in, Ruby began to relax a little. In a short while, her eyes drooped shut and she managed to sleep through the last hours of the trip to Stuttgart.

When she got off the train, Werner's father was waiting for her. They took a taxi home, to a row of studio-houses built by the city for artists.

"*Komm doch essen*. Come have some food. There's plenty of it." And indeed the table was laden with meat, potatoes and salads.

"Thank you very much, but I'm really not at all hungry," Ruby said, worried about how her stomach would react.

"How about a cup of tea, then?" said Heike. "Peppermint tea might do you some good."

Ruby said she'd try some. Hermann motioned to her to take a seat wherever she liked, and she chose to sit on the sofa. He sat down next to her.

"I hope this isn't anything serious," he said in halting English. "Let's wait to see what the doctors have to say."

Heike brought her tea in a beautiful old cup with matching saucer. She placed it on a rickety little side table that sat next to the sofa. "You mustn't worry," she said, her English much better than her husband's. She pulled a chair over from the dining room table and sat down in front of the sofa. "You're probably just going through an adjustment phase, living in Berlin and all. Where is your family? Are you in touch with them?" Her tone was bright and cheery, and she leaned over and placed a hand on Ruby's arm. "You must make sure you can see them soon. They can always stay with us if they come by this way."

Ruby said that she hoped to see her parents when she was back in Berlin. Soon after, she lay down on the sofa and Heike covered her up with a blanket. Before long, her heart was racing once again and she began to feel very agitated. She jumped up from the sofa and paced around, not able to slow herself down. Soon the driving pain was back and she crumpled to the floor.

Werner's parents took her to the emergency room right away. Hermann had a chance to talk to the nurse on duty, and only a few minutes later several doctors arrived and Ruby was taken away for tests. A few hours later she was in a room with one other patient. The doctors didn't say much to her, and this compounded her embarrassment at succumbing to such fits of anxiety. She was asked to remain in bed and was told that she had been put on a diet of watery oatmeal, rusks and chamomile tea.

Ruby spent the next ten days being tested for all manner of things and generally resting up. The doctors could find nothing wrong with her. Looking up at the doctor one day, Ruby said to him, "I feel like the rest has finally restored my body."

The doctor nodded. "Sometimes nature does the best job of healing. You will be released to go home tomorrow. Just watch your diet for the next little while."

Werner came in that day. "Why don't you spend the next couple of weeks with my parents? You know, just to make sure you're really better. It'll be Christmas in a few weeks and we would have come down for the holidays anyway." That was the one and only day that she was allowed to choose something to eat different from her prescribed menu. Spaetzle, served with mushrooms. She enjoyed it so much, Werner promised to take her on a mushroom-picking expedition in the neighbouring forest when spring came. At the family home, Werner's mother and sister hovered over her, lavishing her with food and warmth. Now that she was able to eat again, Ruby wondered why her gut had caused her so much pain. She thought about Heike's earlier comments about adjusting to life in Berlin. Was that it? The change of cuisine, a new language and culture to learn, abysmally dark and wet winters and living with a partner for the first time?

Ruby joined Heike in the kitchen, where they baked cookies and stollen and made mulled wine to get ready for the holidays. She remembered Christmas at home with her own family and all the baking she did with her mother. She felt a little twinge of regret and she knew that she was missing her folks back home. Ruby watched with wonder as the family clipped real candles onto the Christmas tree branches and lit them. Everything on the tree was handmade, topped off by garlands of cookies. The house smelled of pfeffernüsse, and Ruby added to the German traditions by baking sugar cookies, shortbread, tea balls and a Christmas cake topped with rolled-out marzipan.

"You're supposed to be watching your diet and here you are going crazy in the kitchen," scolded Werner.

"Oh, leave the girl alone!" his mother replied. "She's having so much fun and it's all so good. Besides, she's not eating much of it. We're saving it for the visitors."

Ruby secretly watched everyone and wondered what they thought of her. Did they like her? Had Werner brought many other girlfriends home? Did they think or expect that she and Werner would marry?

People were always dropping by, bringing gifts of homemade fruit wine and plum schnapps. In contrast to the commercial frenzy back home, presents, if any, were simple: a book here, a framed photograph there, a box of cookies and treats. Aware of how different their festive traditions were, Heike proposed that they roast a turkey in Ruby's honour.

The days at Werner's parents' house were generally cheery. However, Ruby was not feeling cheerful about Werner. He continued to be demanding, and she squirmed more and more under his restricting influence. In addition, she hadn't been able to let go of the feeling that he had deserted her when she needed him most and that she wouldn't have faced such turmoil if he had travelled with her. She kept emotionally and physically distant from him, and when he asked what was wrong, simply said, "You know what is wrong." Her family had done a good job of teaching her not to wallow when ill; to pick herself up, dust herself off and carry on.

Finally, one day she started crying, and told him all that she felt. After listening to her he said quietly, "I'm so sorry that you have had such a hard time. But Ruby, you are not a baby, and I can't hold your hand through every situation you face."

Ruby was furious. "What do you mean? You try to hold my hand literally and figuratively all the time! You treat me like your child when I don't want you to! So why can't you help me when I actually *need* you?"

"I'm just telling you, I can't always be there for you."

Ruby left the bedroom with nothing more to say.

Christmas came and went relatively quietly. On the twenty-sixth, Ruby, Werner and his sister Ulli hiked up the mountain to a restaurant where they drank wine made from rosehips and gorged on schnitzel and spaetzle. Visitors continued to stop by the house in a steady stream, the tinkle of laughter and happy voices filling the soundscape. During all these activities Werner was there, watching her every move, giving directions all the time. She was irked, but decided it was just one of his things about being in control around his family and chose to ignore him.

Before going out on New Year's Eve, family and friends gathered at the dining room table for *Bleigiessen*, the annual ritual of pouring lead to predict the future. The talk was lively as everyone was given a small, rugged piece of unformed lead cast off from Heike's sculptures. Each person melted their piece on a large spoon held over a Bunsen burner until it was liquid and almost glowing. Then the lead was poured into a cauldron of cold water. It hissed and whistled and sputtered until a new shape floated atop the water. Everyone else around the table would take the piece in their hands and make a prediction based on the shape of the lead. Ruby's piece of lead looked much like a little pig, and Hermann exclaimed, "Good luck—that means good luck for you!"

The conversation turned to a new movie, *Das Boot*, just out in the cinema, and from there it turned to talk of war. Hermann asked Ruby if her father had fought in World War II. Ruby said her father had been in the army and he had been in combat in France. His foot had been shot badly within the first two weeks of his being there, so he was sent home. But he had had a chance to see the devastation all around him.

"There's a funny thing about war," said Hermann. "Sometimes both sides do terrible things. My father was a Nazi, and what he and all the others did was despicable. But when I was nine years old, the Russians came and made me and my family watch while he was executed in public. That was also wrong. A child should never have to see such things."

Ruby looked down. "I'm so sorry." A pang surged through her as she imagined losing her own father in such a manner.

She couldn't fathom the sense of loss it would beget. The relentless questions a child would grapple with unforgivingly. She had already been learning that there was more than one side to the story of World War II, things she had never heard about before, like the bombing of Dresden.

Ruby was surprised at how comfortable she was with Werner's mother and his family and how easily she fit into their life in Stuttgart. Her stereotype of a German family had been shattered. She wondered how they had produced someone as hard-nosed as Werner. He was so different from the rest of them.

Chapter Four

Harvest

RUBY RESUMED HER LIFE WITH WERNER IN BERLIN with a cheerful forbearance. But she still couldn't get a work visa, and she wanted to move on from her cleaning jobs.

"You know what we have to do, don't you?" said Werner.

"Yeah, but I'm not sure how I feel about it. Getting married, I mean."

"Listen, I'm not jumping up and down about this either, but if you want to get a decent job, we'll have to do it. We can both work for a few years and then I'd be able to go to Canada with you."

"That's what you're thinking of doing? Going to Canada?"

"I've always wanted to go there, you know that," said Werner.

"But I'm just beginning to like it here. I've found my groove—aside from work, that is."

"That's just the point, Ruby—you need to find a better job. And you can't do that unless we get married."

"What else would change? I don't know much about your laws here."

"You'd have to change your name," said Werner. "Or hyphenate it."

"Never. I will not change my name. I'm not your chattel, Werner. And besides, I like my family and their name. It means a lot to me."

"Who knows, maybe they'd make an exception."

"They'll have to. I'll argue that since I'm a Canadian, Canadian law should be considered. I absolutely refuse to change my name."

"Okay, Ruby. Just give it some thought."

After a week of hemming and hawing, Ruby agreed to tie the knot on the conditions that she could spend the end of summer picking grapes in France with her friend Emma, and that she be allowed to keep the name Edwards.

Emma was her closest friend, whom she'd met in her German classes. She was a little on the wild side, but Ruby loved her. She was a great conversationalist and had a fine sense of humour, and Ruby knew that they would have a lot of fun travelling together. As a francophile and someone who loved to cook, Ruby was ecstatic about the trip. The rain had been unrelenting so far that summer in Berlin. She was determined to find a change of climate, and with it, perhaps, some peace of mind.

Neither she nor Werner thought of marriage as sacred. It was a practical way to further their plans. So instead of thinking about her upcoming wedding, over the next few weeks

Ruby busied herself with gathering things for her trip and packing up her knapsack. Werner hovered around her all the while. Although he wouldn't say it, he was unhappy.

"It's harder than I thought, to let you go off without me," he said to her. "I'm afraid you'll get involved with other men. You know I haven't had sex with anyone else since we've been together."

Despite his early statements that he wanted his freedom, the issue had never arisen. But she was hoping that would change while she was in France, if only to give her a little breathing room in the relationship. Still, she tried to reassure him.

"Werner, I'm coming back, I promise. We're getting married, remember? I *have* to come back!"

"I'm just worried about what kind of trouble you'll get into while you're there."

"No trouble at all, just lots of fun and exercise," said Ruby.

"Do you love me?"

"Yes, I do," said Ruby. "Of course I love you."

Werner stood looking at her, shaking his head. "Yeah, well, think about this relationship of ours some more while you're away," he said before walking away.

Emma slept over the night before they left, and both of them were brimming with excitement when they took the subway and the bus at dawn down past Grunewald towards the highway and check point. They planned to hitchhike to France to save money. They figured they could make it to Alsace in ten hours and then to Burgundy in another three or four hours. Ruby was carrying a can of mace. They agreed, somewhat naively, that the safest rides would be with truckers; because the drivers were working, the girls assumed that they were somewhat less likely to commit a crime.

They got their first ride after an hour with an old man in a beat-up Benz. He asked them a lot of questions about where they were going and poked fun at their German. He was heading for Frankfurt. That would take them close to Alsace, a few hours from Strasbourg. He dropped them off at a rest station outside Frankfurt, and there, Emma flagged down a couple in a red Audi with French licence plates who agreed to take them to the border. When they hit the autobahn, Ruby lay her head down on Emma's lap, she was so afraid of the speed and the lane-swerving. She almost threw up when they got out at the border, still a ways north of Strasbourg. Pretty soon after that they caught a lift with a truck driver. The going would be slower, but Ruby was happier. From Alsace to Burgundy, low-lying, densely forested hills grazed the sky as the river Oise flowed alongside, and relief bubbled up now that she was in France. Here she was escaping Werner, her surrogate father. No one would tell her what to do every day, and she would be able to speak and hear her mother's language once again.

After arriving in Mâcon in the early evening, they stood in line with a motley assortment of people seeking fruit-picking jobs. One African fellow didn't have all his papers, and the official at the desk began yelling at him. Then a tall man around forty years old, with straggly red hair and beard, stepped out of the line. His sly grin revealed several missing front teeth.

"Mais qu'est ce que vous faites? Vous devez avoir honte de traiter les gens comme ça!"

When several others echoed the tall man, saying the official should be ashamed of treating people like that, the official shrugged and simply asked the African to come back the next day with all his papers. The redhead remained boisterous in the line, complaining constantly about the wait to his much quieter companion, a brown-skinned, black-haired teenager wearing a David Crosby–type fringed suede jacket. It seemed so seventies and out of place in this new era.

When Ruby and Emma turned in their papers, they were told that there was a potential job for them if they returned the next day. They were handed tickets to use at a campground half an hour away by foot. As they stood mulling their options, the tall redhead began speaking to Emma, also a redhead, in broken English.

"Ladies, I ask you, where are you from?"

"Canada . . . England," was their joint response.

"Well, well. Pleased to meet you. I am Jean-Claude and this"—he gestured to his friend—"is Willie. May we take you to the campground in our car?"

Ruby wasn't sure about these two characters, but Emma jumped at the chance. As the foursome walked over to the road, Ruby recoiled when she saw a bright red sports car with a sprawling naked woman spray-painted in silver across the hood. The side and rear windows were covered in foil.

"Emma, no, we can't go anywhere in *that*!"

Emma replied rather testily, "We're just getting a ride. Nothing's going to happen."

Ruby climbed reluctantly into the back seat with the teen-ager. In the front, Jean-Claude and Emma hit it off instantly, nattering endlessly, while Willie and Ruby did not speak a word. At the campsite, they pitched their tents and shared some fruit and cheese, sausage and bread. Jean-Claude and Willie supplied a few bottles of red wine and brandy. Willie loosened up enough to tell Ruby that his father was an indigenous Peruvian and that his mother was French. Ruby told him about her own mixed background, but she still felt strangely awkward.

Things worsened as the night wore on. Emma and Jean-Claude were all over each other, while Willie cast longing looks at Ruby. She felt sorry for him, but not enough to invite him into her tent. He was only eighteen and looked sixteen— too young for her. Willie eventually retreated to sleep in the red car, where he was less likely to hear the grunts and squeals emanating from the tent where the redheads were busy.

The next day, Jean-Claude and Willie left for town, prom-ising to look for work for the four of them. Ruby wasn't too sure about letting these guys—one loud and obnoxious, the other quiet and unassuming—take charge of their working future in France. But Emma was game, reasoning that being French, they knew the ropes. Hours later, they were back: they had secured a job on a pear farm about thirty kilometres down the road.

The next morning, hung over, Ruby was still feeling uncomfortable about riding in the car. Jean-Claude sped through Mâcon, running red lights and almost running down several pedestrians. Ruby yelled at him to slow down. But he just laughed. "If you're anarchist, this is the only way to drive."

Ruby could have told him that her lover was also an anarchist but would never drive so recklessly, but she knew it would fall on deaf ears. The car careened through the streets of the town and eventually onto country roads, the high speed reducing Ruby to a huddled ball in the back seat. She hated the smile on Emma's face.

Willie only talked when Jean-Claude addressed him directly. Then he would babble about how his father had led his people into rebellion in Peru many years ago and how he too possessed the ability to rouse people to revolt. Jean-Claude talked about his experiences in the 1968 student uprisings in Paris and how he hoped to repeat a similar situation, this time enlisting workers from across the country.

How different they sounded from Werner. He was an intellectual who lived through his books, his days of fighting in the streets a thing of the past. He had wanted to change the world; however, he had told her that he gave it up when he realized that it had become more about the excitement than about the cause. Now he was only involved in his books, studying German language and history. She tried to picture Werner dressed in black, from balaclava to boots, setting barricades on fire. What a different person that would have been!

Arriving at the farm, Ruby gazed over a vast expanse of

woods and fields; at the top of a ridge, she could see row after row of pear trees. They were immediately approached by a man who introduced himself as Monsieur Ranier. Short, pudgy and balding, he perched his sunglasses atop his shiny head as he looked over the group.

"I hope you all know that this is hard work. You'll get a break for lunch at one and then work until dinner at six. Pitch your tents and then come back ready to work."

They found a beautiful little lake surrounded by trees and rocks and a little sandy tract of beach. Just above the beach was flat ground where they pitched their tents.

"This is heaven," said Ruby. "I can swim!"

Heading back up the hill, they found Ranier waiting for them with the others. Ranier hooted when he found out that Ruby was Canadian.

"You are a cousin of ours, after all."

Ranier teased her about her slightly Québécois accent. From then on, everybody referred to her as "*La Canadienne.*"

Ranier sent Emma, Jean-Claude and Willie off to the pear trees to start picking. Then he said to Ruby, "*Eh, la Canadienne! Venez ici.*" *And, you, the Canadian! Come over here.*

Ruby was told to drive a tractor that held dozens of wooden flats of pears. "*Mais, vous vous moquez de moi. Je n'en sais rien,*" Ruby said. *You must be joking. I don't know how to do that.*

"*Ça ne fais rien. Venez avec moi.*" *Doesn't matter. Come with me.*

Ruby said, "But I don't even know how to drive a stick shift."

As Ranier continued to insist, Ruby thought he was trying to humiliate her. They walked up a long row of pear trees. The tractor at the top of the hill seemed like some mythical beast. Ranier made her climb onto the shiny red tractor and told her she was to back it slowly down the row, stopping every few metres so that more flats could be loaded. Each flat was about a metre square and would be filled with rows of barely ripe pears. Ruby was terrified. What if all the pears fell off? She fumbled nervously with her feet, trying to figure out the clutch. Finally she decided to shift into first gear without it and see what would happen. The gears screeched and groaned as they tried to find their place. As she heard the flats shifting behind her, she started shaking.

"Mais arrêtez donc," Ranier urged, telling her to be more careful. *"Tout va tomber. Vous foutez la transmission. Lentement, lentement!"*

Ruby finally managed to move the machine backwards with a bit of a lurch, not enough to make the fruit fall off. But how was she going to keep this up? The tractor stopped with a shudder, and two guys grabbed the flats that the pickers had filled with fat, ruddy pears and stacked them on top of the others on the tractor. Ruby felt her heart in her mouth each time the tractor stopped, afraid of losing the precious cargo. But as the hours passed, she learned to move her feet in sync and felt less shaky. The tractor's transmission had been spared.

By the lunch break Ruby was famished. She washed up and found her way back to the farmhouse dining room, where there was a long table with many chairs. Soon she was joined by Emma, Jean-Claude, Willie and another young man of stocky build with wavy brown hair and dark brown eyes. Ruby thought he was cute. She caught his eye and said *bonjour*. Introducing himself as Jean-Pierre, he smiled and sat down directly across from her. Ruby sighed and thought: *Not another hyphenated Jean!*

Slowly people took their places around the table, a dozen in all. The room buzzed with conversation. In the middle of the table was a platter of peppery veal loin chops with mush-room sauce, another large plate chock full of roasted potatoes, and several dishes of green bean and tomato salad. Ruby's mouth was watering and she dug in, chatting through the meal with those around her. Then, from the other end of the table, an elderly man called out to Ruby, *"Eh, vous, la Canadienne! Contez-nous une histoire de votre pays, une histoire de Québec."* *Canadian! Tell us a story of your country, a story of Quebec.*

Ruby was caught off guard. She had no real stories to tell about her country and felt ashamed, as if she'd let her family, especially her father, down. Her father and her sister were con-summate storytellers, but that gift hadn't been passed down to her. She was habitually shy about speaking in public.

Everyone started to call out to her. *"Oui! Oui! Contez-nous une histoire!"* *Yes, yes! Tell us a story!*

Ruby finally decided to tell them about her idyllic summers spent in Trois-Pistoles, Quebec, where she had learned French.

When she was finished, Jean-Pierre said, "I hear that you handle a tractor pretty well."

Ruby blushed. "I tried my best."

The farmer's wife put down several warm pear tarts on the table, with lattice crusts and what looked like an apricot glaze. Ruby was stuffed, but she knew she couldn't leave without trying dessert.

As she and Emma prepared to leave, Jean-Pierre said, "After dinner I'll show you around the farm."

"Sounds good."

Emma snickered. "Good. It's about time you were getting some."

Back in the fields, the sun blazed high above the surrounding hills. Leaving the tractor to someone else for the afternoon, Ruby joined the others in gathering fruit. Picking pears was simple enough: strap on a flat with a wide, beltlike contraption that hung over the shoulders, scale a stepladder and snap the barely ripe fruit from the branch.

They climbed up and down the ladders and moved up the rows. The trees looked beautiful, covered with small gifts of sweetness. Though Emma was working in the same row, she was too far away to carry on a conversation. When they loaded their flats onto the back of the tractor, they usually saw Willie and Jean-Claude working the other side of the row. Jean-Claude was often grumbling something about "the fascists and their work ethic" and then smacking Emma on the bum.

At dinner that evening, Ruby took her place next to Emma. Then suddenly Jean-Pierre sat down on her other side.

Willie and Jean-Claude sat on the opposite side of the table. Jean-Claude shouted out loud for everyone to hear, "Watch out. You're not likely to get much out of her. My boy Willie has tried already. Don't waste your time."

Ruby wanted to kick him in the groin, but he was too far away. Jean-Pierre smiled but kept silent. Willie's smooth face contorted with anger and embarrassment.

After they had all finished their main courses, a man named Jacques stood up and announced that he had some songs to sing and would love some company. He singled out Ruby, who blushed and demurred, claiming her voice had rusted over the years. Jacques began to sing with great fervour, moving from person to person around the table, addressing each one with a song. To Emma he sang, "You are the bright English redhead that loves French men, but who will leave them far behind." To Ruby he crooned, "To the Canadian who doesn't look Canadian, come from afar to steal our men."

Soon a wondrous array of cheeses spread across wooden platters arrived at the table, accompanied by samplings of the farm's own poire Williams spirit. The singers calmed down long enough to eat again, but when the drinking began, voices lifted into the air once more, this time in unison, and Ruby felt confident enough to join in.

"I never knew you could sing," Emma whispered. "Your voice is so sweet and pretty."

"Oh, I love to sing to myself, but to others not so much," said Ruby.

She mulled over her meagre repertoire of French-Canadian songs. She recalled an Acadian song by Zachary Richard, "L'Arbre est dans ses Feuilles," that was easy to sing. She gulped down her wine, hoping to calm her nerves. As she opened her mouth, the first sounds were squeaky and engulfed by a cloud of breath. She closed her eyes to focus on her breathing. Then her voice opened up and she felt the warmth of other voices joining in. As she signalled everyone to repeat the verses, her quaking subsided and her voice flowed out strongly in the company of others. Her face flushed and a feeling of elation washed over her.

After dinner, Jean-Pierre slipped his hand on Ruby's shoulder. "C'mon. Let's go for a walk," he said, grabbing her hand and squeezing it. "You're very sweet, you know. But I detect a little mischief behind all that sweetness. Anyone who can sing a song like that—so goofy, but loads of fun."

Ruby laughed. "Yeah, that's true. I take after my father. A part of me likes to do really silly things."

Suddenly she kissed him on the lips. They lingered for a few moments, tasting each other's mouths. Then Ruby broke away and looked at him. "You don't have a girlfriend?"

Jean-Pierre hesitated, and then confessed he did. But she was away for the summer and this was just for fun, he said.

Ruby nodded and said, "Same here."

"Where's your boyfriend?"

"In Germany."

"What? Do you live there? Is he German? I don't like Germans—never have. Nobody here does. Not since the war."

They wandered down towards the tents. Ruby said, "Well, it's true it's not always easy living there, but they're not all bad. There are lots of interesting young people, and the scene is politically charged."

"I don't care much about politics. It's all lies anyway."

"What about Vichy?" Ruby countered. "The French collaborated with the Germans right here. That's part of your history, too."

"Yes, it's true, it was a shameful thing."

Ruby took his hand and led him down to the water. Jean-Pierre cupped her face in his hands and kissed her cheeks and forehead.

"You are very beautiful."

Ruby blushed and stirred a little, uncomfortable with the flattery.

"So, *ma chère*, why don't we go for a swim?"

It was a warm, quiet night and Ruby was still aching from the day's work. "Are we going to strip right here?" she asked.

"Where else? Come on, what have you got to lose?"

They stripped down quickly, and Ruby ran into the water. They splashed playfully at each other, laughing, held each other's heads under the water, swam around each other, kicking up sprays of water. They kissed and fondled and licked while the water lapped at their skin. They decided to race each other across the lake. Ruby was a strong swimmer, but she preferred to swim on her back. She closed her eyes and let the rhythmic arcing of her arms and the kicking of her feet propel her smoothly forward as the water coursed over her naked body. She beat Jean- Pierre effortlessly.

"You were just lucky," he sighed.

They stepped out of the water, grabbed their clothes and made a dash for the tent. They dove inside, rolling around to dry off and then tumbled on top of each other. Willie slept in the car once more.

When Ruby woke the next morning, Jean-Pierre was gone. She felt a mild pang of guilt at her infidelity to Werner. But it was he who had insisted that their relationship be an open one. And because she hadn't taken advantage of that possibility before, she was determined to do it now, before she was officially married.

One Sunday about a week later, Ruby had an afternoon off and decided to venture into the kitchen and talk to the chef, Bruno. She was hoping to get in on some cooking action. Bruno was a tall, blustery man with a very big heart. He often stopped to chat with her when he saw her in the dining room. He immediately agreed to let her help.

"We're making onion tarts and tomato salad for tonight. You can help slice the onions for now. Make sure they're nice and thin. You'll find the knives over there." Bruno busied himself getting out cast-iron frying pans and tart forms. Then he rummaged on the shelves for the flour. Ruby peeled and sliced away and soon tears ran gloriously down her face as she cut the onions and made mounds of slices on the wooden board. Her sleeves were wet from wiping away her tears. Bruno instructed her to use butter and oil in the frying pans. He said they would let the onions cook for about an hour. Ruby hummed to herself while the onions sizzled lightly on the stovetop.

Meanwhile, Bruno was preparing the pastry. "I will make four large pies," he said. "We will have tomato salad, a green salad and plenty of bread to go along with it all," he continued. "Come watch while I do the *fraisage*." Ruby had read about the art of blending butter and flour in her *Larousse Gastronomique* at home. She loved making pastry and was thrilled to watch Bruno in action as he tossed bits of chilled butter with the flour, always lifting them in the air as his fingers moved quickly to break them down.

"Here, Ruby, why don't you try? The pastry needs air—just use a constant motion of lifting as you lightly squish the bits with your fingertips."

Ruby put her hands into the large stainless steel bowl and started in. She couldn't believe she was actually working in a kitchen in France. It wasn't long before her hands tired of the repetitive motion, but she kept going, lost in her thoughts.

"Ruby! Stop dreaming. You must be quick and not over-work the dough and let it get too warm." Ruby watched, impressed, as Bruno took over again and added a dollop of Dijon mustard to the mix. "It's all about flavours," he said. "Next we will brown some flour to mix into the onions. Find the caraway seeds in that corner there with the spices and then

92

grab the mortar and pestle and grind some up for me. Toast them first."

Ruby toasted the seeds in a small pan, fanning their scent into the air to breathe in. Then she crushed them and put them aside. Bruno put the pastry aside in the fridge to rest and then came to the stove, where he placed three tablespoons of flour in the pan Ruby had just used. "You have to be careful not to let this burn. We just want it light brown and nutty in flavour." Bruno kept careful watch over the flour, which was on medium heat and was ready in five minutes. Then he divided the caraway seeds and the flour between the three pans of sweet caramelized onions.

Half an hour later they took the dough out of the fridge. Sighing with pleasure, Ruby dusted the work table with flour. She flattened the dough with the heel of her hand and then took the rolling pin to it, gently moving the dough in a clockwise fashion. She loved the feel of the rolling pin as it barely slid across the surface of the dough, lifting at the edges, stretching it just a little more each time. She slipped it into the tart pan, crimped the edges, pricked the pastry and brushed it with egg white. Bruno cooed, "You do this very well. You've had practice, I see." Then Ruby repeated the steps, till all four tart pans were filled. Bruno slipped the onions into the pastry shells. Then he whisked up some crème fraîche, eggs and Gruyère and poured it over the onions, topping off each tart with more Gruyère. He slid them into the oven. "Voilà! There's dinner. Now let's get those salads done." The two of them went out to the garden to get lettuce and tomatoes. Few things made

Ruby happier than cooking with friends, and when the friends were French, it was perfection indeed.

One evening after supper, about a week later, as Ruby and Emma were wandering back to the tents, they passed by Jean-Claude, who was arguing fiercely with Ranier. The deal was that the workers were to be paid every two weeks, but Jean-Claude said he needed an advance to take care of some business.

"That's the deal!" Ranier shouted. "No work, no money."

Jean-Claude shot back, "No! No money, no work!" Then he gave Ranier a shove.

"That's it. Tomorrow morning you must be gone. You want your money, you will get it now."

Ruby was pissed. Jean-Claude's behaviour tainted them all. If he left, they would all have to leave. She snarled at Emma, "Do something about him. He's nothing but trouble."

Emma shook her head and said, "Listen, you do what you want, but I'm with him for now."

Ruby felt deflated. If she wanted to get away from Jean-Claude, it would mean leaving Emma behind, and she'd have to look for another place to work on her own. Emma put her arm around Ruby's shoulder. "Ruby, you should stay with us. You'll see, it'll be fine. I know he's a bit of an arse, but we'll find more work."

"I'm not as sure about that as you are, but I'll stick it out with you. I'm not ready to go home yet."

"Not ready to be married, perhaps? Are you stalling for time?"

"I don't think so, but I have to admit that I *am* uneasy about getting married. It's just not something that I ever wanted to do. And Werner isn't always easy to be with. On the other hand, I care for him, and I can't stay in Germany unless I marry him."

"And you don't think he'll mind you fooling around with other guys while you're here?"

"Come on, Emma."

"I want you to have a good time. I'm just wondering how you're feeling about it. If you're really comfortable."

"I am, pretty much. I do think of Werner and feel a little guilty, but not enough to stop me. Anyhow, he always said he was open to this kind of thing."

Ruby scouted around for Jean-Pierre to say goodbye. He was very hesitant about talking to her and it turned out that his girlfriend had arrived for a few days. He was embarrassed and distant, and Ruby knew that all she would have was a fond memory of their late-night skinny-dip.

The next morning, the foursome drove north to Champagne, in search of new work. In the back seat of the crazy red car, Ruby fell silent, wondering how she was going to survive with Jean-Claude at the wheel.

The red car wound its way northeast over several hours and endless rolling hills until they reached the town of Épernay, where they quickly found work at a vineyard just outside of town. With no place to pitch their tents, they had to sleep in the dormitories. Because there were no other women, Ruby and Emma were assigned separate quarters from the men. The fields were densely planted with rows of grapevines with yellowing leaves. The manager, Monsieur Tellier, a short, lean man wearing a bright red cap, paid particular attention to Ruby and Emma, as it was their first time picking grapes. They were each given clippers and a bucket, and Tellier supervised them for the first half-hour.

"Be careful when you're reaching deep into the vines," he warned, "as you may clip the hand of the person working on the other side. If you see any rotting grapes, leave the cluster behind. They will be collected for making vinegar later on. When your bucket is full, put it under the vines and a gatherer will come around to pick it up."

Ruby found the work strenuous. A few minutes after she'd placed her full bucket under the vines to be picked up, another one was tossed down the row. Gatherers came along with twenty-gallon tubs strapped on their backs into which they emptied the grapes from the buckets. From there they would take the full tubs to a tractor waiting at the end of a group of rows. The tractor had its own vats placed on the back, and the gatherers would empty their tubs into the vats. From there they were hauled down to the pressing station. After an hour's work, Ruby's back started to ache, so she tried stretching for a minute.

At lunch back at the dining room, Ruby watched a beefy guy practically bury his face in his plate, gulping down mouthfuls at a time, then chasing them back with swallows of wine.

When he came up for air, the man said loudly, "Who has the crazy red car in the lot?"

"That would be me," answered Jean-Claude.

"You might want to get a new paint job."

"I don't take kindly to people telling me what I should or shouldn't do."

"People don't want to look at that naked woman. It's offensive. It doesn't belong on a car."

"Aw, shut up and leave me alone. I'm busy driving all these foreigners around the country. I don't need this shit."

Willie quietly interjected, "I'm French, Jean-Claude."

"Now don't be silly. I'm not trying to put you down."

None of the other men responded to the "foreigners" crack, but Ruby noticed that some were eyeing Willie and her with suspicion.

"Have any of you ever picked grapes before?"

"Many times," said Willie.

"So the others are all virgins?"

"That may be," Ruby piped in, "but we know how to work hard."

"Why all the questions?" asked Jean-Claude. "You'll see that we pull our weight."

Ruby moved away from the table. She had eaten too quickly and wasn't feeling well. A young man in a knitted cap who had been sitting on her right stepped out of the shadows in the hallway and joined her with a pleasant hello.

"*Comment tu t'appelles?*" asked Ruby. He said his name was Jean-Yves. Ruby choked on her breath.

"Are you okay? Is my name funny?"

"No, it's just that you're the third Jean-something-or-other that I've met on this trip."

Jean-Yves smiled into her dark brown eyes. "Can I join you outside?"

"Sure. Why not?"

In the evening air, they lit up cigarettes and stared up into the night sky.

"I can tell from your accent that you must be Canadian. But you don't look like a Canadian."

"Tell me, in your opinion, what does a Canadian look like?"

"Well, they don't have frizzy black hair and light brown skin."

"Oh yeah? The first Canadians were all brown-skinned."

"What do you mean?"

"The indigenous people were the first on the North American continent and they are brown."

"Maybe you're right, but that's not what I meant."

"Well, I'm just telling you that I am definitely Canadian and I'm not white. Look." Ruby grabbed his hand and held it up against hers. The difference in colour looked clear to her. When she let go of his hand, a big smile spread over his face.

"Any time you want to go for a walk, let me know," he said.

"How about tomorrow?"

He agreed and bid her goodnight.

When Ruby entered the little dorm room, Emma was stretched out on a bed, thumbing through a magazine.

"How are you?" Ruby asked.

"A little tired and a little bummed. I'm missing the pear farm."

"Aha! I knew it."

"You don't have to gloat about it."

"I didn't mean to gloat. I miss it, too."

"And Jean-Pierre, I guess."

"Yeah, he was nice. But I didn't know him long enough to really miss him. And there's a guy here now who's really cute."

"You don't waste any time."

"Well, that's easy for you to say. You've got someone lined up for the duration of the trip."

"Speaking of that, what's with you and Willie?"

"He's sweet, Emma, just way too young for me. I mean, what is he, sixteen?"

"He says he's eighteen."

"And you believe him? That's a stretch. Anyway, I'm way older."

"Oh come on. He's so lonely . . ."

"God, why don't you do him, if you're so concerned? I'd spend an evening talking to him, but he doesn't talk. Get up, let's go for a smoke," she said.

Outside they were joined by Jean-Claude and Willie. Jean-Claude wanted to plan a strategy for the next day, but Ruby didn't want to hear about it. Perhaps if it had been another person, she would have listened, for she came from a family that supported workers' rights and unions. But she resented Jean-Claude for taking Emma away from her, for his dangerous driving and his pseudo-anarchism. She didn't really know what anarchism was, except that Werner had tried to thrust it down her throat. But Werner's anarchism was all intellectual—reading books or going to movies. In practice, he pissed on ecologists and Germany's green-loving alternatives, insisting that she not associate with the "tree huggers" living in their building.

Ruby finished her cigarette and returned upstairs to the dorm. She lay down and pulled out Germaine Greer's *The Female Eunuch*. It had been her bible in her last year at university and she had brought it to Berlin with her. She had read only a page or two when she looked up to see Willie standing in the doorway.

"Will you go for a walk with me?"

"Sure—what's up?"

Willie suddenly dragged her up off the bed, grabbed her shoulders to pull her into him and kissed her. As Ruby struggled free, his lips brushed across her cheek. She pushed him gently away, shaking her head.

"Willie, usually you ask for permission before you kiss someone."

"I just wanted to taste your lips. I know you think I'm too young, but I'm not."

"'Taste my lips'? Are you kidding? What have you been reading? Willie, you're a nice guy, but I'm just not interested."

"Okay, forget it. This is a waste of time."

"Anytime you want to talk, Willie, let me know."

"Aw, just forget it."

Ruby sighed and went back to her book. Emma came into the room and closed the door.

"What the hell did you say to Willie?"

"I just said no. I'm just not interested. Can't you get that through your head?"

"For chrissake, he's crying. You must have done something."

"He tried to kiss me and I pushed him away. Now will *you* please back off?"

"You're a stubborn wench. For the life of me, I don't get you. We came here to have fun."

"Listen, Emma, I don't like Jean-Claude, but you can have him. I'm not interested in Willie, but I'm having fun with other guys, okay? Isn't that good enough?"

"Stop going on about me and Jean-Claude like it's the end of the world. You know it's just a fling. We both have other lives in Berlin."

"You got that right."

"Okay, okay. I just hope you figure something out with this new guy you've got on the go."

Ruby turned on her side, the book still in front of her, and closed her eyes. The next morning, both women woke up to aches and pains they'd never imagined.

"How are we gonna get through the day like this?"

"I dunno. We'll drink a lot at lunch and see if that kills the pain."

They got their wishes early. After two and a half hours in the fields, Tellier told everyone to assemble at the end of a row.

The sun was high in the sky and though clouds were drifting by, it was another beautiful day. The tractor stood at the bottom of the row, set up with pâtés, cheeses and baguettes for all. There was a bottle of crème de cassis and a couple of bottles of Champagne so that everyone could imbibe.

Jean-Yves came over to Ruby and said, "We got a date tonight?"

"Yup, we do."

"So, I'll see you after dinner, then?"

"Okay."

Ruby enjoyed the taste of the sweet fizziness in her mouth as she sipped at her kir royale. The Champagne and cassis mingled nicely on her tongue. But she didn't for a moment think it would numb the pain she was feeling all over.

Ruby and Emma resumed working on the other side of the row, with Willie and Jean-Claude behind them.

"You look beautiful in the morning light," Jean-Claude cried out to Emma.

"Why, thank you, kind sir. I'll take a compliment from you any day."

Ruby thought she would throw up. But she stayed quiet and listened as she picked.

"Your eyes are sparkling, your lips are glistening . . ."

"Aw goddammit, would you quit it," interrupted Ruby. "Save it for tonight when you're alone."

"You have no appreciation for love in the light of day," Emma retorted. "No one has touched your loins recently—your engine's getting rusty."

"Oh, please," Ruby flared. "Have some respect for the people around you."

"Oh, don't be such a spoilsport."

Ruby fell silent and concentrated on picking. She liked looking at the triangular clusters of grapes and feeling their weight in her hands, imagining them being squished in a press to turn out a bottle of wine like the one they had just drunk.

The day passed away and the pickers drifted into the dining room, stiff and sore. The table was laden with vegetable salads and a selection of quiches. The men gathered around the table, Jean-Yves sandwiching himself in between Ruby and Emma. Dinners here were much more sombre than at the pear farm—no Jacques to liven everyone up.

Someone across the table called out to Ruby, "Where are you from?"

Ruby sighed. *Ah, the never-ending question.* She looked up to face her questioner, a plump, ruddy-faced man who looked a little rough around the edges. "Mogadishu."

"Where on earth is that?"

"Somalia."

"You don't look African."

"Well, you don't look French."

"I'm not."

"What are you, then?"

"Belgian."

"Well, you don't look Belgian."

"What do I look like, then?

"You look like you're from Lapland. You just need a reindeer . . . I'm just joking. The truth is, I'm Canadian."

"I knew it. You have a Québécois accent. But you don't look Canadian."

Ruby shook her head. Back to square one. It shouldn't have been such a big issue to be asked where she came from. But it was the accumulation of questions over the years that bothered her. It never ended.

When dessert arrived, Jean-Yves nudged her in the ribs and said, "Let's get some fresh air."

"After I try some of that," she said, pointing at the plum cake.

Soon they were standing outside in the cool night air.

"Why don't I take you to the building where they press the grapes?" he said.

They walked down a road till they came to a barnlike structure surrounded by a thicket of plane trees. They pushed the door but it was padlocked. Jean-Yves pointed to a row of windows, some of them open. "Let's try to get in that way." On the grass was a long table with a few chairs scattered around it. They dragged the table under the window and grabbed a twenty-gallon tub from the tractor, which they placed upside down on the table. Jean-Yves climbed up first. He stepped on the tub, which was a little wobbly but seemed strong enough to hold his weight. Ruby stepped quickly onto the tub and then squirmed her way up Jean-Yves's back until she was kneeling on his shoulders. When she was finally able to stand up fully on his shoulders, the tub creaked under their combined weight.

"*Merde*, I don't know if this will work," said Jean-Yves.

"I'm praying already," said Ruby. Barely reaching the open window, she grabbed onto the ledge as her legs swayed against the wall.

"Goddammit, my arms aren't strong enough. I can't pull myself up!"

As Jean-Yves shoved her up by her dangling legs, Ruby was able to look in the window. Below her was a room with various sizes of presses and many vats for stomping grapes. Next to them lay a pile of hay.

Ruby managed to swing her legs through the window. The drop looked to be about fifteen feet. But she'd come this far, so she decided to just let go. She crashed down on top of the hay and let out a yelp. Her feet and her head went numb for a moment. She tumbled out of the hay and sat down on the floor. Jean-Yves swung over the ledge and landed with a thud next to her.

"Are you okay?"

"I think so . . . just wrenched out of place." Ruby was lying on the cold floor, breathing slowly in and out, still shaken from the drop.

"Good," said Jean-Yves. "Pretty soon it will be dark, so I want to show you this stuff while we can still see it."

In the middle of the room stood a large press with a metal base and a wooden-and-metal vat attached inside. The vat was lined with sackcloth that stretched out over the edges. A gutter ran around the perimeter.

"The grapes go in here," Jean-Yves explained. "The

sackcloth keeps out skins and seeds and such. The juice runs through here and comes out in the gutter. Then it gets placed in barrels."

He turned and ran his hand through Ruby's hair and then tousled it.

Ruby smiled and asked, "Have you ever stomped grapes with your feet?"

"*Bien sûr!* Every year they have a grape-stomping contest here."

"Why not put on a contest of our own?"

"You have to take off your sandals."

"What else?"

Jean-Yves looked at her to see if she was serious. "Whatever else you want."

"Mmm . . . why not everything?"

Jean-Yves reached in to kiss her lips and then murmured, "Okay, let's do it."

They lifted grapes from the vats into the basin until it was half-full. Ruby stood back and grinned. "Okay, you first."

"No way. Ladies first."

"Ah, but I am not a lady. Take your shoes and socks off. I command you."

As Jean-Yves bent over to unlace his runners, Ruby smacked him hard on the bum. Then she continued, "Now take off your pants."

He was about to protest, but he stopped as he saw the look of glee on her face. "Glad to oblige, glad to oblige."

As she bent over to take off her sandals, Jean-Yves, standing in his underwear and shirt, tried to nuzzle his face into her breasts, but Ruby said, "Work before play," and dropping her clothes, jumped into the vat. Jean-Yves followed, stripping as he went. They stomped and flailed their arms around and jumped up and down on the grapes like little kids. Every so often they crouched to lick off the juices that had sprayed up onto each other's legs. Ruby took a handful of grapes and popped them in her mouth and then kissed Jean-Yves again, using her tongue to swish the broken bits of grapes into his mouth.

"Mmm, sweet . . . just like you."

She grabbed his hand and they hopped out of the vat onto the cold floor. Again they embraced and then moved slowly towards a table that was pushed up against a wall. Jean-Yves backed Ruby up against the table. He sucked on her breasts and then let his hand slide over her stomach and then her crotch.

Suddenly the door flew open and the lights came on.

"Ruby!" exclaimed Emma.

"What the hell are you doing here?" demanded Tellier.

"Jeez, I thought you would have figured that out already," Ruby answered.

"We've been looking all over for you two," said Tellier. "Go get dressed."

Ruby turned away and fumbled for her clothes, taking a moment to shoot daggers at Emma.

"I'm sorry," Emma said. "I was worried that something had happened to you. What did you expect me to do?"

"Couldn't you have waited till morning?"

"It's after eleven. We're supposed to be in our dorms by ten. I figured even if you had been screwing around you would have been back long ago. I had to work on Tellier to get him to look for you guys."

"I'm surprised that you'd get so worked up over it. I'm not a teenager!"

Jean-Yves came up behind Ruby and wrapped his arms around her waist. He whispered into her ear, "Don't worry, we will make up for it."

"Yeah, we better."

When they stepped outside, Tellier said, "Come see me before breakfast," and walked away. When Ruby, Emma and Jean-Yves arrived at the dorm, they saw several men, including Willie, milling around, smoking. Jean-Claude smirked at them as they walked by.

"You bastard!" Willie yelled at Jean-Yves, punching his fists into the air.

Jean-Yves shook his head and smiled. "Get it through your head, kid—she doesn't want you."

Ruby shushed him, as she didn't want any more fuss, but it was too late. Willie threw himself on top of Jean-Yves, knocking him to the ground. Willie was small but wiry and he held Jean-Yves in place while he tried to pummel him. Jean-Claude watched with glee, but two other men ran over and pulled them apart. Jean-Yves got up, dusted off his pants and walked over to where Willie was being pinned against a wall.

"*Maudits étrangers,*" he spat. "*Ça pue des étrangers.*"

Ruby yelled, "Don't you dare say that it stinks of for-eigners—*I'm* the only damn foreigner around here! Willie's French, for chrissake!"

"He's not really French. Just look at him."

"What about me? I have brown skin, too."

"You're a woman. It's different. Women are *meant* to be exotic."

"Wow. I can't believe you said that! You can forget about us getting together again, Jean-Yves. I'm not some precious doll to be toyed with."

Emma pulled Ruby aside. "Let it go. He's not worth it."

They walked up the stairs to their room and sat down on Emma's bunk bed. Ruby leaned her head against Emma's shoulder and sighed. They held each other in silence for a while.

"Oh, what have I gotten myself into?" Ruby said. "And what am I going to do about Werner? It's not so easy to think of facing him, and yet . . ."

"You said it yourself, Ruby—he laid down the rules. So don't feel guilty about having fun. This is like one extended bridal shower for you. Sorry if I messed things up tonight."

"You're forgiven. Especially since he turned out to be a racist pig."

The next morning, Ruby and Jean-Yves met Tellier in his office, expecting to be fired.

"You two trespassed on my property last night and ruined some very good grapes in the process," he said gravely.

"Maybe you can still use them," said Ruby.

"Silence! The loss of those grapes will come off your pay. Jean-Yves, you've been here many times. You should know that building is off limits."

"Yes, I know, but—"

"But nothing! I'll have no more of this. I would have been liable if you had hurt yourselves. I can't keep you from fraternizing with each other, but do your funny business outside from now on."

Ruby got up and left before Jean-Yves could say a word. In the dining hall, Emma had saved her a chair. As she sat down, she felt like crying. All eyes were on her, and low voices murmured in tones of judgment.

"What?" yelled Emma. "None of you lot have ever been shagged before?"

Ruby looked down at the chocolate croissant and fruit on her plate. She picked up the croissant and pulled away from the table without a word. Back upstairs, she lay down on her bed and thought of going back to Berlin. She didn't really want to return to her relationship with Werner, but she wasn't ready to leave it either. In Germany she had work, friends, a lover—it was her home for now. France had provided a welcome diversion, and she would be sorry to leave, but Berlin was still her base.

She buried herself in the work for the rest of the day. Her back didn't ache as much anymore and she was picking as fast as anyone else on the team. The next day it drizzled constantly and the slopes grew hopelessly muddy and slippery, spoiling the communal mood. Ruby wasn't talking to Jean-Yves, who appeared sullen and restless.

As she walked, tired and wet, through the dining room at lunch, someone hissed, "Whore!"

"That's it!" she bellowed. "I've had it with you assholes! Just who do you think you are? Let me be, and go back to picking your noses."

She turned to Emma and said, "This is the end of the line for me. Are you staying on, or what?"

Ruby expected her to say she wasn't through having fun with Jean-Claude. But to her surprise, Emma agreed. By evening they were packed and ready to head off to Reims. From there they would catch a train to Paris and then carry on to Berlin. Emma lingered for a long time saying goodbye to Jean-Claude, their two red heads pressing together like kissing grapes. He drove them to Reims. When they got out at the station, Ruby took one last look at the crazy red car and smiled ruefully. As they walked away, Willie yelled from the back seat, "You'll never know what you missed!"

That's truer than you know, she thought. *Every time you make a choice you turn your back on other opportunities. I only hope I'm making the right one.*

CHAPTER FIVE

Mean's Motel

IT WAS HER WEDDING DAY. RUBY FELT SLIGHTLY queasy as she pulled on a cocktail dress she'd bought at the flea market and donned a pair of suede lace-up granny shoes with just enough heel to set off her calves. Tying the ribbons tightly, she knew that all she really wanted was to be able to get a proper work permit so she could stop cleaning old ladies' houses. All *Werner* really wanted was to be able to live in Canada one day. And this was a step they had to take to reach those goals, it was that simple. They had mocked the idea of a real ceremony and planned to treat this like an ordinary day with a little party at the end of it. They would carry on as before in their two separate apartments. There would be no honeymoon. Ruby's camera was broken, so there would be no pictures either. Would anything really change?

It was two o'clock in the afternoon. They were getting married at three. Ruby and Werner walked down the street to the subway, with Werner, as usual, walking a few paces ahead of her. The trains whizzed uneventfully through tunnel after tunnel until they reached downtown. Outside city hall her friends were waiting, all sombrely dressed in black. Ruby was not upset by the gloomy tone of their clothes; she glossed it over with a smile that said "Let's get this job done with."

The justice of the peace was a serious woman, all business and more than a little perfunctory. Ruby and Werner stood at the front of the room on a platform. They had given no thought to writing out their own vows and so they glibly repeated the phrases to each other as the justice of the peace read them out. Emma and Jack acted as witnesses. The whole thing took less than an hour. Ruby was relieved when it was all finally over; now they could go enjoy themselves.

From city hall they went to Jack and Smithie's bar. Ruby and her friends loved it, partly because it was so rundown. The bar was in a former storefront, a low building that stretched along a grey, almost treeless street. The building facades were decrepit, weary with the weight of an uncaring history, and the sidewalks were littered with refuse and dog shit. A bright neon-pink sign with black lettering screamed out "Mean's Motel" to passersby.

Inside, it reeked of stale beer mingled with the smell of curry. Jagged pieces of glass etched out a map-like piece of art on the back wall. The bar itself was shiny steel, and black and white tiles gleamed on the floor. There was one room for a pool table and another decked in red with a tiger-print blanket strewn across a black sofa. In the red room, all the tables were pulled together so the wedding gang could sit together for a meal, and red roses sat upright in a vase in the centre. Lina uncorked a couple of bottles of Veuve Clicquot and they started drinking. With R& B music blasting, they danced, taking turns as couples and then together as a group. They ate curry and continued drinking until the regulars started arriving. At the end of the night, the newly married couple stumbled back to Ruby's apartment, too drunk to make out, and fell into a noisy sleep. Ruby was right. Being married didn't change anything.

That night she dreamed of a long-forgotten memory. Ruby sat on the stairs in her teddy-bear pyjamas, chin cupped in her hands. She let the music wash over her. Her eyes were transfixed on her parents, as the big Basie beat swung them around the crowded room. She had watched them dance so often, always lingering to mimic their steps. Her father didn't let his bad foot stop him and he still stomped out a rhythm in his own way. She skipped down the stairs and waded through bouncing, swaying legs.

"Please, Daddy, Mommy, let me dance with you."

"Okay, sugar-pie."

She sashayed between them, swishing her thin little hips from side to side.

"Girl, who taught you how to dance like that?" her father asked in a playful tone, eyes wide open with proud surprise.

"You did! You and Mommy!"

Her father roared with laughter, and then, as if remembering himself, he bent down to whisper with gentle sternness in her ear, "You better not take those moves out of this room, you hear!"

....

One evening a month later, Ruby went to Mean's on her own, without Werner. It was later than she usually went to the bar, and the room was edgy. People were dressed from head to toe in black, with mohawks or gelled and spiked hair, piercings erupting all over their faces, the requisite Doc Martens boots on their feet. Ruby's ears started to throb as the music pulsated in and out, punctuated by yelling voices. She stood in the room and could almost feel the shards of glass on the wall sticking into her skin. She was beginning to shake a little from nervousness, and needed some alcohol to quiet her nerves. This wasn't really her crowd.

Jack and Smithie were working behind the bar. She ordered a whisky sour.

"Hey there, Miss Canuck! We're just chatting about events back home," said Smithie over the music. "You know our Dickie Mountbatten was assassinated last year. Well, now the government is tearing apart the IRA."

"Who's Mountbatten?" Ruby sorely regretted her question as soon as it slipped from her lips. There were guffaws all around.

"Lord Mountbatten of Burma, the overseer of the partition of India. What on earth do they teach you over there!"

Ruby countered, "Not as much colonial nonsense, that's what!"

"Oh, low one, low one," muttered Jack.

Now Ruby knew that was a bit of a lie. Her education had been focused on Europe, particularly England, not on Canada. It was not the first time that the Brits had put her in her place in terms of her knowledge of world history. She had the feeling that her North American education had short-changed her.

Luckily Smithie said, "Oh, don't be getting all serious and spoiling our fun. Lighten up, would ya?"

Ruby turned away from the bar to look into the crowd. At the doorway, she could see Emma wrestling off her coat. She looked forward to telling her about the new job she'd found as a translator at a language institute, and remind them both that the marriage had been worth it. She waved her hand in the air, and Emma smiled and nodded. As she turned back to the bar, she accidentally elbowed the young man standing next to her.

"You almost knocked my drink out of my hand!"

Ruby blushed and apologized profusely. He was fairly tall and had sharp features, with flinty grey-green eyes. His brush-cut hair was dyed black; if he hadn't been in this bar, he could have almost passed for a military man.

Ruby smiled winsomely and said, "Can I buy you another, to replace the one you almost lost?"

He smiled and said, "Yeah, sure. Go right ahead."

"What's your name and what are you drinking?"

"It's Dominick, and I'll take another Pilsner."

Ruby turned to Smithie. "Another Pilsner for Dominick here. It's on me."

Smithie eyed her. "What are you getting up to? And where's Werner?"

"He's out with his friends and I'm just having a little chit-chat here."

By this time Emma had come along and wedged her way between Ruby and Dominick. "Hey you."

Dominick pulled up against Ruby and whispered, "Your friends are here, now you're safe." He grabbed his beer and stepped away. "Thanks. Catch ya another time?"

Emma shook her head and said, "I'm glad I saved you from him."

"Why?"

"'Cause drug dealers aren't a good catch."

Ruby nodded, but she knew she was already taken by him—his undulating voice and knowing eyes, his cockiness. She wanted to see him again, no matter what he did.

"Girl, what's gotten into you? Gone all goo-goo-eyed. Snap out of it. Where's Werner? It's past your curfew."

Ruby winced.

Emma said, "Come on, let's go dance."

Ruby spied Dominick off in a corner chatting with a blonde in a revealing V-neck sweater. He saw her looking and nodded at her. Then he waved her over. Ruby turned to Emma and said, "See you in a bit."

"Right, right, that's the way," Emma said and gave her the finger.

Ruby pushed through the crowd towards Dominick and his woman friend.

"Let me introduce you to Franka," he said.

Franka's lips curled into a smile as she leaned in to Ruby, saying, "My art, you know, is stripping. What's yours?"

Ruby tried to find a witty retort. She pushed up her breasts with her hands and said, "Do you think they're big enough? Maybe I could join you."

Franka simply continued to smile while Dominick chuckled under his breath.

Ruby felt lost. She couldn't keep up this sort of thing for very long. While she felt lucky that she had found something clever to say this time, she knew it would only be a matter of time before she struck out. And she wanted to impress Dominick.

"I hear you don't learn much British history back in Canada," he taunted. Apparently he wasn't going to be easy to impress.

Ruby sighed. "We learn Canadian history, we learn a bit of American history. We learn a bit of British history, too. But by my thinking I'd rather learn the history of the world's indigenous peoples rather than that of former slave masters."

Dominick's smile disintegrated, floating off his face into the air. "Are you calling *me* a former slave master? I'm *Irish*. We were the first victims of the British Empire."

Franka had turned to face the broken mirror on the wall and was playing with her hair. Dominick excused himself and stalked off towards the back room. Ruby followed him; she was worried that she had offended him and wanted to apologize.

The back room contained a pool table where there was usually a game going on. Tonight, however, the lights were dimmed and a young couple lay naked on the table.

"Whoa," yelped Ruby.

The young man cranked his head back towards her and yelled, "What are you staring at? Get outta here."

The door to the kitchen swung open and Dominick stepped out. "You guys at it again?" Looking at Ruby, he shook his head and said, "You never know what's gonna happen in this place. Come on, let's get out of here." He slipped his arm under Ruby's and they glided through the crowd and out the door. "There's an all-night café just around the corner."

"Thanks, but I really have to go home soon," she said, surprised by his sudden change in attitude. Before he had seemed shaky and on edge; now he was good-humoured and seductive.

"Oh, yes. I've heard about him. Keeps you wrapped around his finger, doesn't he?"

"Clearly not. I'm here, aren't I?" After they sat down at the café table, Dom took her hand and pretended to read her palm. In a low voice he intoned, "You will be successful late in life."

Ruby laughed and leaned in to him from across the table for a deep kiss full of longing. Then she said, "I have to go, but I'll be back for more soon," and slipped out the door.

When Ruby got home, Werner was waiting up for her. "Where have you been?" he asked.

"I told you I was going to Mean's."

"It's so late. I was out, too, but I've been home for a while, waiting for you."

"Werner, I detect a note of aggravation in your voice. What's up?"

"I just don't think you should be going there so late by yourself. It's not safe."

"What are you worried about? After all, didn't you say we should allow ourselves some freedom? You're treating me like a child again."

"I have to look out for you."

"Listen," said Ruby, "I don't need another father. One's plenty enough. I'm going to bed."

"Wait," Werner called out. "I'm sorry, but I'm anxious because I feel responsible for you. And . . . I don't want to lose you already."

"Aha, so that's what it's all about. Lose me? Werner, I'm right here. Why do I have to remind you that you were the one who said we didn't have to be monogamous?"

"Well, maybe I've never felt as strongly about someone as I do you."

"Thank you, sweetie." She stepped towards him and gave him a kiss. "But don't push me into a corner and step on my toes." They went to bed and Ruby let Werner make love to her, but she wasn't really present. She fell asleep feeling confused and with her stomach in knots.

A week later Werner and Ruby went to Mean's at their usual early time. Dominick was playing guitar in the band. Noticing her watch Dominick, Werner asked, "Who's the junkie?"

"He's a regular around here. Let's go see if Emma's in the kitchen."

They walked through the bar to the back and pushed

through the kitchen door. Two guys were huddled over a table, scoring some kind of deal.

"Hey, we're not open for business back here," said one, his sleeves rolled up and scarred arms naked to the eye.

"Sorry, we're just looking for someone," said Ruby as they backed out.

"They're selling drugs in there," Werner told her. "Now you see why I don't like you coming here on your own."

"Oh, come off it, Werner."

"I don't think we should stay too long," he said. "I don't want to hear any music tonight. Please come home with me."

"Werner, I'm staying."

"You're a real piss-off, you know. I don't want you to stay. I don't want you watching that junkie all night."

"Werner, stop being such a child. Now leave me alone."

Werner's eyes flashed in anger. Finally he said, "Okay, to hell with this. I'm leaving."

Ruby watched him exit through the door, annoyed and confused by his jealousy. On the one hand, she didn't want to feel like a puppet with Werner holding the strings; on the other, neither of them had been able to talk about their earlier deal since they got married. Her hands twitched at her sides and she kept circling around the bar stool, not knowing whether to sit or stand. She didn't want to hurt Werner, but still she found herself looking around the bar for Dom.

Emma grabbed her hand and said, "Look. Here he comes. Your would-be lover."

"Would-be?" said Dominick. "I'm not would-be anything."

"Can you settle for lover?" asked Ruby. She got up off the stool and placed her arm around his waist. He was tall, so her head only came up to the top of his chest. He was wearing an electric-blue shirt and skinny black jeans and looked mighty fine. "Were those guys in the kitchen with you?" she asked.

"Don't ask," he said.

"I want to get to know you, so I ask questions. Isn't that normal?"

"Yeah, but I'm a private kind of guy. Don't like it when I think people are snooping around in my business. Anyway, I'm fine. Psyched up for playing tonight." He went back to the stage.

There were three others in the band. Ruby was particularly interested in Isaac, on the drums. He was a Black guy with a giant afro. She was stunned to see him at Mean's—everyone else was very white—and he gave her a nod and that smile of recognition that Black folks save for each other, especially in such situations. She remembered that her father would always point out any Black person he saw, and if it was on the street he would always wave or say hello. There seemed to be an implicit understanding that you acknowledged one another.

"Ruby, I think you should know that Dom is a user," Emma burst in.

"What do you mean? He does drugs, I know."

"Girl, he uses heroin. That's a little different from smoking a joint."

What did a heroin addict—was he an addict?—look like after all? Certainly she had noticed the shakes, as well as his ultra-nonchalance. She didn't know what to think, so had chosen to be silent. There was something that drew her to Dom that she couldn't put her finger on. She knew that she would be going home with him this night, but she was worried less about betraying Werner and more about whether Dom was truly a junkie. What was happening to her? Ruby shook off her many questions and grabbed hold of Dom at the end of his set and wouldn't let go. Eventually, he said, "Let's get out of here," and pulled her towards the door.

Dom lived near Hermannplatz. From the subway they walked a few blocks to his apartment. As they climbed the flights up to the fifth floor, the rank odour of urine lingered on the landings. Dom led her down the hall to his room. One wall was painted black, with the Irish flag hanging on it. Photographs and maps were pinned up on the other walls.

Dom lay down on the bed and pulled Ruby down beside him. Finally, he slipped off his shirt and mumbled, "This is what you want to see, isn't it? My tracks? I saw Emma talking to you and somehow I knew . . ."

"Yes, Emma did tell me, but before that I had no idea. Your arms do look pretty rough." She couldn't bring herself to touch them.

"So, you like asking questions. Fire away."

"How long have you been hooked?"

"Two years. Not so long, really."

"Are you really addicted, or just an occasional user?"

"Does this look occasional to you?" he said wearily.

Ruby didn't want to ask any more questions. She didn't

know what to do with the information, what it meant to her, how to process it. "You're going to get sick, Dom."

"Don't condescend to me. I know what's in store."

Ruby curled her body into his and she lay touching his chest, his face, tracing her fingers over his lips. They lay there, breathing quietly, not talking for some time. Eventually they undressed each other and made love for an hour before falling asleep.

When she woke at ten the next morning she thought that she could go back to her own place without worrying Werner. But he was in her apartment when she arrived.

"What are you doing here?" she asked.

"What else? I'm waiting for you. I guess you were out all night? Tell me, Ruby, did you go home with someone?"

"Oh, Werner, I don't get you! My god, you practically announced the rules of the relationship to me back on that first night. We fall in love, but we come and we go as we please, more or less. Wasn't that about it?"

"That is the way I've done things till now," he said, looking down at the floor. He looked beat. "But, I just can't let you go. It's not the same . . . it's not the same. I've told you already, you're naive and so trusting. I can't let go of you—it's as if you might break. Then what would your father say? I'm asking to change this deal."

"Right, bring my dad into it. You're both the same. Werner, I want to stay with you, I do, but you have to give me space, let me come and go. You started this, you can't just stop it. Why change now? Because I'm having fun and you're not?"

Werner cursed under his breath. "I want to know if you went home with someone last night."

"If you have to know, yes, yes I did. And that's all I'm saying."

Werner shook his head, a grimace contorting his face. Then he stormed out the door.

Ruby and Dom continued meeting up at least once a week, and Ruby thought she was avoiding Werner's watchful eye. She was becoming extremely fond of Dom. He was funny and raucous, yet gentle when he needed to be. He had a musical soul and Ruby loved this about him. She loved to watch him play, his fingers lost between the frets, his mind at ease. He was a thoughtful lover and paid careful attention to Ruby's desires and whimsies. But she worried incessantly about his addiction. She had seen him blow up on occasion, when he hadn't gotten his fix. He was a different person then. She couldn't talk to him about it; he would just shut her down.

A month after her blow-up with Werner, Ruby was visiting Emma in Moabit. Smithie and Jack crashed the party, bringing beer and vodka in tow. The two men settled in quickly, discussing the Pogues, a band they had all recently seen in concert. Jack watched Ruby and tilted a bottle of beer to his lips. "I hear you're getting into Dominick's pants," he said.

Ruby gulped, came up for air and whooped, "What the hell is going on? Why does everyone know or care about this?"

There was a knock at the door. Emma went to open it and muttered, "Speak of the devil." Dom stood before her.

"Is Ruby here?"

Emma nodded.

"I thought so." He stepped into the apartment and waved Ruby over to him. "Been trying to reach you," he said.

"Why?"

"I've come to take you for a ride," he said, beaming at her. "I've got a car for a couple of days. Come on."

Ruby didn't hesitate. As they left the building the skies were darkening. Streaks of neon orange and pink crested the horizon. Dom pushed her towards a bright yellow Mustang.

"Wow," she said. "Those are some wheels. Let's drive down to Wannsee. I've never been there in winter before."

Dom drove south and in no time they were in the Grunewald. As Dom kept her laughing with an array of new jokes, Ruby was mesmerized by lights that flanked the road, by the stark silhouettes of the trees, which were beacons in the night. They reached the lake and pulled into a parking spot. Stepping out, Ruby could see little waves frozen near the edge of the lake, looking like someone had dipped them in frosting. She sighed and thought of Uncle William's first letter to Ella. Here was his beloved Wannsee, and she wondered if he had ever come here in winter. She grabbed Dom's hand and ran down to the water. After walking along the shoreline for a bit they turned back to the car, and Dom crawled into the back seat, motioning for her to follow. They pulled off their coats and began a furtive game of kissing and touching. As things became more furious, they heaved against each other, grasping for bare skin and more kisses.

Ruby's face was turned to the window, and she noticed someone skulking across the parking lot, headed their way. He had a dark mask pulled over his face and was waving something in his hand. "Oh my god, Dom. Dom! Someone's coming."

Bam, bam, bam! A fist rammed against the back window. "Get out of the fucking car" came a voice, muffled somewhat by the mask. He pointed a gun up to the window. "Get out or I'll shoot."

Ruby pleaded with Dom to not open the door, but he rolled the window down a notch and looked at the dark silhouette facing him. "Whaddaya want, buddy?"

"Ha! Good question. Let's see—what do I want? I want the woman, that's what. Both of you get out of the car," the stranger yelled as he cocked the gun.

Ruby's heart was leaping against her ribs. "What does he want with me, for god's sake?"

Dom said, "Put the gun down and we'll get out."

"You've got some nerve, mister. Okay, down goes the gun." He lowered it onto the icy ground.

Ruby and Dom crawled out of the back seat.

"That's more like it," said the man. His voice struck Ruby as being eerily familiar.

"Werner! Is that you? Are you fucking crazy?" She tried to grab at the balaclava covering his face. "Oh my god, it *is* you. Just what the hell are you doing, trying to pull off a stunt like this? Jesus!"

"Damn right it's me. I followed you. I don't want you making a fool out of me with this junkie. You're coming home with me."

Dom dove for the gun. Werner kicked at him as he went down. Ruby yelled, "No, Dom!"

Then a raucous laugh slipped from Dom's mouth. "It's fake, it's a toy," he said with a look of disdain and relief.

"Werner, how is this supposed to make me want to go home with you? Did you think stalking me would bring us closer? And how did you find us, anyway?"

"I followed you from Emma's in my friend's car. Now come with me," he said, reaching to grab her hand.

Dom shoved Werner away and planted himself in front of Ruby. "You're one sick puppy, man. She's not going home with you."

Werner was floundering. Dom was bigger than him and wouldn't be easy to intimidate without a gun. Meanwhile, Ruby had slipped around to the other side of the car and slid into the passenger seat.

Werner kicked the side of the car several times. Dom just got back in, started up the car and drove off. Ruby looked back at Werner, who was shaking his fist at them, raw fury sweeping across his face.

As soon as she was home, Ruby went into the kitchen and poured herself a shot of brandy. She downed it in one go and walked down the hall to the bedroom. She threw herself onto the bed and without taking off her clothes, pulled up the duvet and closed her eyes. Her sleep was fitful. She woke in the night to the sound of dishes clattering on the kitchen floor. She got up and went down the hall. She could hear Werner cursing her as she neared the kitchen. Ruby stood gawking as she watched Werner smash plate after plate, glass after glass on her kitchen floor and against the walls.

When he saw her he yelled, "You bitch! I do everything for you—I even married you so you could stay here and find work. I don't care what we said about having an open relationship. I want this to stop. I can't handle it."

"Why? This is exactly what you asked for. An open relationship with no chance to get bored . . ."

"It's one thing for you to go off and screw your way around France. But not in my backyard. That's different. I'm not seeing anyone else, Ruby, and I don't want you to either. This whole thing was a mistake."

"Oh, come on," she said. "You can't expect me to believe that! What about your friend Ana? You have something going with her."

"No, we're just good friends."

Ruby was floored. Werner had lots of female friends so she had just assumed that he was getting it on with one or the other of them, as he had warned her he would. Then she got angry.

"This is not okay, Werner. You started this. You said that you need to be free to see other women. Now I'm finally having some fun, you can't just stop me. My god, you think you're allowed to follow me and hold me up at gunpoint? And then you have the nerve to trash my kitchen? Get the hell out of here. I have nothing to say to you."

Werner slammed the door behind him and she could hear his footsteps heavy on the stairs.

In the morning when he came by to apologize and offered to help clean up, Ruby told him, "I don't want to see you for a while. I need a break."

"Why are you walking away from me? What is wrong with you?"

"Are you crazy? Look what's happened over the last few days. This is not working for me. I need some time to think."

He stomped his foot on the floor, and she could almost see the flecks of fire exploding in his pupils. "*You're* the problem, Ruby—not us, not me. You have no sense of direction, no sense of purpose, no sense of loyalty."

Ruby looked at him and said quietly, "I am very sorry if this is hurting you. I'm feeling squeezed on all sides now and I need to take a breath. You won't let me breathe. I'm not saying it's over, I just need a break."

Werner stormed off without another word. Ruby lay low for the next three weeks. He came knocking at the door a few times and left her a few pleading notes, but she managed to avoid him by keeping the chain on the door and by ducking in and out of the building only when she thought he would be busy with work or school.

One morning she woke up sick as a dog. She continued to feel shaky and queasy for several days. Finally she went to the doctor. He confirmed her suspicions. Ruby was pregnant.

Ruby told Emma the news.

"Oh my god, no. What are you going to do? I wouldn't

tell Werner if I were you. You have a big decision ahead of you. Like, are you going to keep it?"

"I don't know. I don't think so. I don't know whose it is. Werner and I use condoms and so did Dom and I. It's a crapshoot. Impossible to tell."

The doctor had told her that she was only seven weeks along. She could still have an abortion if she wanted one.

The next morning she stopped by Emma's, hoping she was home. When she got upstairs, Dom opened the door, and Lina stood behind him in his shadow. Ruby almost fainted. She hadn't expected him to be there.

"Where have you been lately?" he asked.

"I've just had some things to take care of, things to mull over."

"Well, I'm glad you're okay," he said.

Emma put on a pot of tea. Ruby was really stuck now, weighing what to say to Dominick. She wished he weren't there, so that she could talk to Lina and Emma in private first. Finally, unable to contain herself any longer, and wanting to know how he would react, she asked Dom to come into the kitchen. There she blurted out, "I'm pregnant. I don't know if it's yours. I mean, I've been having sex with you and with Werner, too, occasionally. But I'm pretty sure I'm going to have an abortion."

"Oh my god, Ruby, no. Jesus! Don't make any decisions too quickly. What about keeping it?"

"I'm not exactly mother material right now."

"Look, Ruby, take some time to think."

"Christ, Dom, that's what I've been doing all week. Feeling sick and thinking."

"If you've made up your mind already, go ahead. You know what's best."

"Oh, thanks."

"I don't know what you want from me, but I'll do my best."

Ruby and Dom settled back down in the living room, but sat apart.

Emma studied them, and then stood up. "I'm gonna rustle up some potatoes and quark, if anyone's interested."

Ruby wasn't feeling very hungry, but as usual, she found consolation in food. This was one of her favourite German meals. Werner made it for her all the time: waxy potatoes covered with a thick and creamy fresh cheese with linseed oil drizzled over top and some fried onions on the side. Simple and absolutely delectable. Thinking about it made her feel a little better right away, though the reminder of Werner stabbed.

She made an appointment for the following Thursday at the Turmstrasse Hospital. She had ten days to steel herself for the abortion. Emma came by for tea the day before her appointment, and in the evening they decided to go to Mean's. Ruby ordered a beer for a change, wanting something cold and frothy to soothe her throat and quench her thirst. Then Dom stumbled through the door, and Ruby suddenly noticed just how thin he had become, and how dark the circles were under his eyes. He had put gel in his hair, and it was standing on end, all askew. He was drunk and frayed around the edges—shaking, his face drawn tight. He sidled up to

Ruby, slurring his words as he locked his hand around her arm. "I have no time for you and your baby, you hear. I've got my own life to live."

Ruby sighed and started to leave. Emma grabbed her hand and said, "You go on home, but you can count on me to come with you tomorrow if you need it. Just come by ahead of time."

At home, Ruby lay down on her bed. She placed her hand listlessly on her belly and mused to herself whether it was a boy or a girl. Then she said a little prayer to her child, asking for forgiveness, and fell into a fitful sleep.

Muffled grey light slipped, barely noticed, through the curtains. It felt like the sun would never round the corner of the sky to come awaken her. In German, Thursday was *Donnerstag*: the day of thunder. She felt she had no other choice than to let herself be pummelled today. She rose quickly and showered in the stall that was built into the pantry in her kitchen. She was sure she was supposed to fast, but she drank a glass of juice anyway. As she dressed, she heard the key turning in the lock and then Werner stood before her. He tried to lead her playfully to the bed, but Ruby pushed him firmly away.

"Werner, I'm not interested. I have a lot on my mind."

"What are you so busy with that you can't spend some time with me?" he asked, looking doleful.

"I'm trying to find a purpose in life, remember? You need to give me space."

"Why can't I be involved? You need help finding yourself here in Berlin."

Ruby threw her hands up in the air. "Stop trying to protect me from life! I've had it."

Wheeling around, she grabbed her bag and ran out the
door. She still had plenty of time, so she decided to walk
down to Moabit from Wedding. She passed the square at
Leopoldplatz just as the church clock was chiming. Ruby loved
that she never had to wear a watch. The city was full of old
squares with churches and their clocks. Time was everywhere
and belonged to everyone—not just those with watches.

It took Ruby forty minutes to reach Emma's street. She
climbed to the second floor and knocked on the door. Emma
opened and said, "Gimme a second, just got to pull my sweater
and boots on. You know, I've been there before, too. I'll bring
you home after and feed you. You can stay as long as you like."

Ruby just wanted it to be over, to stop thinking about
babies and what this one would have been like.

She felt groggy and nauseated when she woke up, but Emma
took hold of her hand as she sat up in the narrow bed.

"You should stay here for at least half an hour before we
go home, just to get your bearings."

"Good idea."

"Do you want me to call a taxi?"

"Do you mind if we walk a block first? The fresh air will
do me good, I'm sure." Ruby was hoping to slow the rush of
thoughts pouring into her head.

"Of course, but rest first. You shouldn't get up yet."

Eventually they got up to leave. Ruby felt tired and sore but was determined to walk the distance. When they arrived at Emma's, Smithie was already there. As soon as Ruby sat down on the couch, he grabbed Emma and pulled her into the bedroom. Ruby barely noticed the hushed whispers taking place in the next room. She lay down and covered herself with a blanket. A moment later, Emma came back into the living room, looking as if she carried the weight of the world on her shoulders.

"Ruby, I don't know how to say this, and I'm so sorry."

"What? How to say what?"

"I have some bad news for you—Smithie just told me. Dom overdosed at Mean's last night. He didn't make it. He's gone."

Ruby gasped and struggled to get up. She knocked over her tea. "What do you mean? Emma, please say it's not true."

Emma looked at her with pity and shook her head. "I'm sorry, Ruby. It's not nice to tell you when you're like this, but I didn't want you to find out on the news."

Ruby collapsed back on the couch and buried her face in her hands. She was unable to catch her breath. Emma sat down beside her, put her arms around her and just held her, rocking her back and forth as they both cried. Ruby finally lay still in Emma's arms. She put her head in Emma's lap, and Emma stroked her hair gently.

When Ruby woke up several hours later, she felt numb, and a flat greyness had settled down on her. Despite Emma's invitation to stay, she felt an urge to go home, where she could sequester herself, so she took the bus to Wedding.

Alone on the bus, she began sniffling into her sleeve. When she came to Leopoldplatz she got off the bus and went into the church to rest. She sat on a pew at the back and soaked in the beauty of the stained-glass windows and the high, arched ceilings, thinking about how God could be so heartless as to take away so much in this world. It was all too much. She ran out of the church and continued running till she was out of breath. That night she sat up in the kitchen with a pot of tea, writing in her journal. *Dead. Gone. Two down, one to go. I am so exposed. My head feels like it's opening wide. So many thoughts coming in. Dead souls. Where's Jessie? Please come save me.*

Finally, as light strayed in through the window, she lay down on her bed to rest. Her head was filled with a jagged stream of words that gnawed away at her soul. But she couldn't stop the *click click click* of her mind. Dom's face flashed in front of her over and over again. *I'm so sorry, Ruby, I just had to go. Nowhere else to land safely in this world.* And then there was Werner's stern countenance. His words seemed to merge with an image of her father shaking his head. *I told you so. You have to be protected. You are not safe or capable. This is my world. You follow my rules.* Both of them were talking rapid-fire.

Emma came by to visit a day later and walked into the bedroom with a tray laden with teapot and mugs.

Ruby said to her, "I've been talking to Dom. He's apologized for rejecting me and the baby. He's sorry."

Emma looked at Ruby quizzically, and poured their tea before she spoke. "Ruby, I'm sorry, but Dom is dead. Nothing you do is going to bring him back. Of course you can talk to him in your dreams, hold him in your thoughts, but beyond that . . ." Her voice quavered. "I think we should get you back to my place where we can all watch over you."

Ruby was beginning to slowly lock herself up inside her mind. More and more people were prying their way into her head, talking to her. *Ruby, come home, Ruby, come home. Don't go. Eat chocolate after your meals. Always walk with your right foot first when going south. Turn your head to the right to delete a thought. Lie on your left if you want to be close to him. Get up move around clean the house.* She became entranced listening to all their voices, searching for some truth in their words. Emma's voice broke through occasionally from the outside, but her presence was beginning to make Ruby feel paranoid.

"Ruby, help me out here. What can I do for you?"

"Nothing, Emma, just let me be."

When Emma left, the voices became more insistent, and Ruby found it harder to ignore them. Why were people talking about her? Why were they saying these things to her? When she lay down they all came out of their hiding places, all trying to talk to her at once. She could hear her own voice respond-ing, but she couldn't understand her own words and therefore didn't know what she was saying. Her father, Werner, Jessie: everyone was talking at her and it was all negative. She didn't know how to defend herself or if she even had to.

All her life she had felt like she had done something horribly wrong, though she truly didn't know what. She thought of the recurring dream of the man lying on her and smothering her. It had plagued her since she entered puberty. What did this mean? Now she cried and cried, for all those years of failure. Her father was telling her that she was mean to leave Werner behind. Her mother was telling her to come home. Jessie told her she was too free. Dom was still whispering in the background: *Come get me, Ruby*. Some voices were clearer on her left, others on her right. If she wanted to stop hearing certain voices, she just turned the other way. But inevitably there was negativity on the other side, too.

Another day Emma returned to take her to the greengrocer's. Emma hung on to her arm all the way there. Ruby picked out some apples, oranges and vegetables, and the cashier cast his head to the right as he was ringing up the produce. Ruby looked right, too. She started sorting people depending on whether they were on her left or her right. Her mother was left-handed and left politically, so she was on Ruby's left. Her father was more conservative and represented the past and family history, so he was on her right. On down the line she went, dividing up family, friends and acquaintances. That way she could tell who was working with whom. There was some kind of conspiracy against her and it was her job to figure it out. But it was too labyrinthine a task.

Ruby almost ran home, leaving Emma trailing behind. She didn't want to see any more people, didn't want to keep classifying them. She shook her head ferociously over and over, starting to feel crazy and out of control, then clambered up the stairs, flung the door open and ran to the kitchen. Emma followed her in.

Ruby got out her journal and started scribbling furiously. Her thoughts were broken. *Who is on the left? Who is on the right? Left is future. Right is past. Where's the present? No, I can't keep my head in the middle, there's someone there, too. Everyone is against me and I don't know why. How is it that they can read my mind, but I can't read theirs?* Page after page, she wrote down the thoughts that jackknifed into her head.

"Emma, people are out to get me. Everybody was looking at me outside, like they knew me, like they knew my thoughts."

"Ruby, you're just imagining things."

"That's the point. Maybe I *am* imagining things, but I can't not think about them. I can't control it much anymore. It helps when I see people one-on-one, though. It forces me out of myself a little when I can talk to someone like you."

"Ruby, I'll do whatever I can to help. But maybe you should go to a doctor."

"Oh Christ, what can they do? Lock me up?"

"Let's hope not," said Emma.

There was a knock at the door. Ruby hissed, "It's Werner!" Emma told Ruby that she better finally talk to him and went to open the door. Werner rushed into the kitchen. He stood eyeing Ruby for a few moments.

Emma picked up her bag and hugged Ruby goodbye. "You'll be okay," she said.

Ruby didn't lift her head and continued to write.

Finally, Werner grabbed her arm and said, "Don't write that garbage, Ruby. What's wrong with you? Are you on something?"

Ruby shook him free and got up to wander around the apartment. She couldn't stop moving. Ruby didn't sleep that night and by the next day, she was only worse. Gibbering away, always writing, moving around or crying, unable to sleep. Werner called the doctor and then he called Ruby's parents. He told them that depending on what the doctor said, he planned to take Ruby away for a week, for rest and a change of scenery. Ruby sat listening to the conversation, as Werner did not want her to talk to her parents. She started humming a little song as she squirmed in the chair, unable to be at ease. Werner shushed her. She moved to the bed to lie down but felt as though a snake was slithering around her, tightening its grip with every turn. Over and over the scenario repeated itself until Ruby jumped up and ran down the hall and started beating Werner with her fists. "It's time to let go. You have to let go!"

"Ruby, I'll do no such thing. I'm taking you away for a while."

The next thing she knew they were racing through the night in a taxi. Ruby thought they had crossed over to the East and that Werner was going to trade her for some spy on the Glienicke Bridge. Then came the glare of an office and a man in a white coat pulling down her pants to put a syringe in her ass. Within an hour her brain was on lockdown. They took a taxi home and she stared morosely out the window, her hand in Werner's. At home she could still feel the lockdown closing in on her like a vise as she sat trembling quietly at the kitchen table.

CHAPTER SIX

Breaking Through

RUBY SLIPPED OFF HER CLOTHES AND WATCHED AS they fell to the floor. She let the cloud-coloured hospital gown unfold its worn cotton threads slowly over the tan curves of her breasts, her belly, then her hips. She sat down on the edge of the bed, bending over to feel if there were any straps hiding underneath. Curling up into a ball on the crisp sheets, she frowned at her ashen kneecaps. She thought of how her grandmother would have disapproved of their greyness and would have scolded her father for not teaching her how to lighten them up with the juice and rind of a lemon. In her mind she cradled this vision of her grandmother and her father, letting their comfortable sepia images rock her back and forth in sleep's lullaby.

Ruby woke with a start. She heard words hurtling out into the night, then a rush of feet stampeding off in the direction of the distressed voice. Then silence. The vastness of it engulfed her. She had dreamed about the faceless man again, but this time he actually raped her. There was something about his voice that seemed vaguely familiar. She tried to sit up, to escape it, but her body kept shaking violently. She began plummeting down a tunnel of darkness. She tried to still her frantic hands long enough to grab on to the rails of her bed. If she held on, maybe she could stop this sudden, mad descent. But she felt her spirit seeping away, leaving her bones and flesh wide open for the demons. In they came, piercing and penetrating what was left of her. A thousand different faces from her past erupted into her brain and just as quickly as they appeared, eyes that had laughed with her, lips that had kissed her, arms that had held her became disfigured. Ruby watched in horror as the flurry of faces flashing before her transformed into one massive heap of rotting flesh on the floor by her bed.

Then she saw his feet. Brown shoes, perfectly shined. Clad in a pale doctor's gown, Werner approached steadily. Ruby stared at his feet, transfixed.

Werner began to whisper. He swung an iron swastika tauntingly in his hand, its points sharpened like daggers. Ruby began screaming silently into her pillow, her arms pummelling the sides of the mattress. Her chest was heaving furiously; the air was being choked out of her lungs. In a low, halting groan she begged, "Go away, go away and leave me alone. Please," but his cold breath closed around her.

Rat a tat tat tat tat tat tat tat! Ruby thrashed free of Werner's hold. Hanging on to the bed rails as tightly as she could, she listened for this sound that played insistently on the edge of her mind. *Rat a tat, rat a tat, tat tat tat!* Her right hand loosened its grip and slammed against the wall in response. *Rat a tat tat, rat tat tat, ta ta ta tat!* She heard the door to her room fling open and a shaft of angry light bathed the wall where her hand was drumming ferociously.

"Frau Edwards! *Was machen Sie bloss?* What on earth are you doing?"

Footsteps neared the bed. Ruby felt a hand on her back, cold breath on her shoulder. Whirling to push the white blur away from her with all her might, she screamed, "Go awaaaaaay!" It went crashing to the floor. More footsteps thundered down the hall. Voices hissed like vipers. Ruby felt herself being shoved back down on the bed. She listened desperately for the sound of the drums. Instead all she heard was a voice yelling, "Give her the goddamn needle!"

Ruby wound her body up into a tight ball, and the doctor twisted her arm flat against the mattress. She waited for the steel to bite her flesh; she waited for blackness to come.

When she woke, she could feel the rays of morning sun streaking down her back. Rolling over to look out the window, she felt as if lead weights were attached to every muscle, every bone. With a slow, sickening realization, Ruby recalled the scenes from the previous night. She tugged hold of her pillow and crushed it against her body. Tears spilled over her face; anguish surged with every breath she expelled. When no more tears came, the cool silence of the room lapped over her.

It was not the first time Werner had tormented her in her visions. But she didn't want to think about him. She couldn't dig down below the surface. So she thought about the drums. She remembered how days before her hospitalization she had spent a whole day hallucinating that she was travelling across other continents. As soon as she had stepped out of bed that morning, she found herself thinking, *If it's six a.m. here, it'll be around midnight in Brazil*. She mumbled the words repeatedly to herself, until she had willed herself into the heart of Bahia. Her feet shuffled around the apartment to a samba beat. All day long she hummed what Portuguese words she remembered from all the bossa nova songs her mom had played when they were children. Werner tried to shut her up, pleaded with her to lie down and rest. He finally gave up, conceding that her antics were harmless, even if they irritated him to no end.

In the evening, she had looked out her fifth-storey window to find the air blackened with the buzz of insects. Bees, scorpions, flies, giant moths clamoured against the screen, wings flapping in a wild symphony. The buzz droned louder and louder in her head. Words fluttered in her ear. *Africa. The whole world will return here*. The flapping transformed into a steady drumbeat. Dark bodies swayed around orange firelight. Propelled by the rhythms, Ruby whirled around the room. Flinging her head from side to side, thrusting her arms out in front of her, she stamped her feet on the floor.

Someone coughed. Ruby realized she was no longer alone in the room. A woman with greying hair and a wrinkled forehead lay on the bed next to the wall, staring sullenly at the ceiling. Ruby wondered if she had been there during the night.

The woman glared back. Words percolated out of her thin mouth, hot and angry.

"Was guckst du denn so an?" What are you staring at?

The word *du* hit Ruby like a slap in the face. It was unusual for an older woman, a total stranger, to speak to her in this informal, familiar way. She got up to use the washroom.

She sat on the toilet, her legs spread wide, and watched the stream of warm, yellow liquid form a puddle on the platform inside the white bowl. She giggled at this Germanic need to inspect every aspect of their lives, inventing thrones for their shit and piss to rest on. All in order to check out its size, colour, texture. Werner bemoaned the toilets he had seen elsewhere. Of course the German toilets were superior!

Thinking of him, she dipped her fingers into her steaming excrement and brought the brown filth to her lips.

Someone pounded on the door. *"Beeilen Sie sich, bitte.* Hurry up! You're not the only one in here."

Ruby jumped off the seat with a start. Shaking, she slashed an arm across her mouth, wiping the shit from her lips onto her wrist. She turned on the taps, spat into the sink and let hot water stream over her hands.

The pounding started again.

"Okay, okay, I'm coming out!" she hollered.

When she opened the door, the woman brushed by her without a word and slammed the door shut. Ruby looked at her shaking hands, hands that no longer belonged to her. She flattened herself down on the mattress and pressed her hands under her body to still them.

She convinced herself that she almost felt safe. At least here her movements could be confined. At least here she couldn't step out into a street, oblivious to the screeching cars around her. Only one thought continued to stalk her. The words to frame it slipped backwards off her tongue, tumbling down her throat to toss in her stomach until they were carried out of her body again. *Home.*

Would she ever go home again?

Metal carts rattled down the hall. An aide came in and handed her a tray of breakfast. As Ruby balanced it carefully on her lap, she heard the aide call her roommate's name gently.

"Frau Elke Jungblut, *Ihr Frühstück ist da.*" *Your breakfast is here.*

"*Ich will es nicht*" came the voice from the bathroom. *I don't want it!*

The aide persisted. "You have to eat something."

"I said I don't want it!"

The aide shrugged and left the tray on the night table before leaving the room. Elke opened the bathroom door and peeked out. Seeing only Ruby in the room, she slumped down on her bed, ignoring the tray.

Ruby slapped the cheese and wurst on a piece of bread and chewed noisily on the rubbery bits. When she was finished, she sucked at the seeds from the grainy bread that had stuck between her teeth.

Frau Jungblut snapped: "Didn't anyone ever teach you any manners? Cover your mouth with your napkin when you do that!"

A jet of anger shot up out of the white nothingness that enveloped Ruby like a blanket. "This isn't exactly Café Kranzler." The hunched old women that filled the Ku'damm *Kaffeehaus* on Sunday afternoons flashed before her. Carefully slipping forkfuls of Herrentorte into their mouths, taking tiny sips of coffee, blotting their lips with folded cotton napkins, they reminisced about the good old days before the Wall, before Willy Brandt, before the Turks.

Frau Jungblut's voice burst through the flow of images: "Why, you rude thing, you. Just who do you think you are? You're not German. What are you doing here anyway? All you people, stealing from us, using up our money, our resources. Why don't you go home!"

Ruby looked at the woman lying in the bed next to hers and wondered where she had been during the war. She snarled. "Ach. You're so right. This place should really be reserved for Germans only."

The ferocity of Ruby's words stunned the old woman. She sputtered, "Well, well . . . I didn't ask to be here, my husband put me here. I didn't ask to come here."

Storm clouds closed in on Ruby again. She shoved the tray and sent it crashing to the floor. When someone came to clean up the mess, Ruby laughed at their tsk-tsking. A nurse came with more pills.

People floated in and out of the room, holding clipboards, jotting notes, whispering secrets to each other. Ruby closed her eyes and let the waves of darkness roll over her. Night came early.

....

Werner had taken her away to Corsica after Dom's death. But she hadn't gotten better. Every day they trudged for an hour up the dusty road. The yellow and orange flashes of the fruit trees interrupted the monotony of the dirty brown September hills, the craggy bushes that marked their way. She was careful to watch out for the scorpions that seemed to dart out from under every rock. At the village market, she picked over grapes and oranges. Her fingers finally rested on fresh figs, bursting with juice and seeds, to bring home. She smiled at Werner and thought he knew. They filled their baskets with lemons still graced with their dark shiny leaves, artichokes, olives, bread and cheese. And figs. She hummed an early Ella tune on the way back down the mountain. It was part of a collection of her father's old jazz 78s. Werner knew the song: it wasn't too highbrow for him. As he chirped along with her, she smiled and held his hand tightly.

That night the owner of the house they rented brought them wild boar. On his way up the path, Ruby saw him stop to pull fresh bay leaves from the laurel tree that shaded the courtyard. He showed them how to cook it the Corsican way. Wine, garlic and bay leaves, braised slowly in the oven. A celebratory feast. Ruby smiled at him and lifted her glass of wine to her lips.

She left the men and wandered out into the dusk, staring at the stars blinking in the early night sky. The pungent smell of eucalyptus filled her nostrils. It all smelled so new, so clean. She pressed a hand into her belly and thought, "Daughter of the southern stars."

Those late-September days were filled with dark clouds that burst across the skies, crowding out the sun momentarily. She missed their drama when they returned to Berlin ten days later. The city was a blanket of grey. Werner called her sister and asked her to come. She heard him whisper, "It didn't help. She's not getting any better."

Ruby spent days staring out the window, waiting for her sister to arrive, waiting to be admitted to hospital. Four flights up, on the other side of the courtyard, she watched her neighbour knotting the muslin curtains that hung in her windows. Two knots hanging in the window. Ruby pressed her hand into her tummy, feeling around for life. "Twins," she whispered to herself.

That afternoon, she lay on the bed, fighting to keep the voices out of her head. They were getting louder and louder and she couldn't hide from them anymore. Werner turned on the vacuum. He pushed the machine all around her, zig-zagging over the floor by her feet. Suddenly she felt the air-sucking nozzle buzz up between her legs. Then it was inside her, shoving, sucking, shoving, sucking. One fetus after another being ripped right out of her.

"No!" she screamed. "No!"

She ran over to yank the cord from the outlet. But it was too late. She saw the blood streaming down her legs. She grabbed a T-shirt from the dresser to wipe off the blood and plug up her vagina so that nothing more would come out. But when she wiped the inside of her thighs, there was nothing. Nothing. Werner stood shaking in the middle of the room, still holding on to the nozzle. He let it drop with a thud on the floor and came over to where she stood. She screamed at him to get away. He stomped out of the room. She could hear him picking up the phone in the hallway, dialing. He had betrayed her. Yes, he had told her that he wouldn't bring children into this godawful world, but she thought all that had changed. After all, he had sung the song with her. He knew. She crumpled up on the bed and wailed. Half an hour later they were in a cab, racing through the city. Another needle.

Ruby opened her eyes. Cold sweat dripped off her body onto the sheets. She was shivering. She looked at the clock. Seven a.m. A young woman, dark hair flying about her face, burst into the room. She surveyed the cold, rectangular space with a disdainful eye. It was as if she knew the place well and wanted to be sure she had the best room possible. She stepped back out into the hall, talking loudly in a language Ruby had never heard before. Every so often a turn of phrase caught her ears, lilting with the sounds of something vaguely French, vaguely Spanish. When she returned to the room, the woman was dragging an enormous suitcase, ragged and bulging at the sides. Two other women lingered in the doorway, saying goodbye to her. Ruby looked in amazement at the suitcase, its tan leather streaked with wear, and somehow felt naked. She had brought so little with her.

A harsh peal of laughter vibrated throughout the room. The woman had let go of her suitcase and was laughing at her friends, inviting them in. Her whole body, round and full in its curves, echoed her amusement. She began speaking in German. "*Komm doch 'rein*. Come in, come in. Don't be afraid of them. They won't bite." She looked at Ruby and her room-mate and added, "Will you?" She eyed Frau Jungblut with a look that said, *Yes, I know you very well*. Then, resting her gaze on Ruby, she said, "You, you're not German. Turkish?"

Ruby shook her head.

"What are you, then? Where are you from?"

Ruby smiled at this old, familiar question that had fol-lowed her overseas. "My name is Ruby and I'm Canadian."

The woman did a double take, her eyebrows rising right off her forehead. "Hah, Canadian." She added brightly, "Well, they've captured quite a little corner of the world right in this room, eh? I'm Irina. I'm a Roma. From Romania." She broke out into that wild laughter again, slapping her stumpy thighs, pleased with the alliteration. Behind her, her friends were nod-ding, smiling shyly, still not part of the conversation. Ruby was turning the word *Roma* over in her mind.

As if reading her thoughts, Irina snorted. "Ah yes, of course. You Americans know nothing." She turned a cool eye on Frau Jungblut, now feigning sleep, and continued, "But maybe this is better than the Germans who know all but do nothing. Hah! Yes, Roma, we are what you call Gypsies. Roma, Sinti, Kale, Gypsy. Call us what you like, we are all over the world."

She picked up the strap of her suitcase, jerked it like a recalcitrant puppy over to the only empty bed in the room. The others followed. The mattress sighed underneath the weight of the valise. Irina whisked the zipper noisily along its track. Ruby watched eagerly as her new roommate unfolded the suitcase. First came the bottles, each carefully wrapped in black, red, pink panties, all satin and lace. Ruby strained to see the names but found it easier to make them up for herself. Dawn's Dew, Lascivious Lavender: the kind of scent that would wither your nose. Irina and her friends unpacked bottle after bottle. They were followed by slithery, slinky nightgowns that matched the panties that had snuggled the bottles so closely. Irina tossed these carelessly onto the bed. Next came shoes, spiky-heeled, shiny black ones, flat silver sandals, fuzzy pink slippers. Frau Jungblut sat up in her bed. Irina stopped fumbling with her clothes long enough to say, "Hi. I'm Irina. Who are you?"

Frau Jungblut sniffed the air, wrinkling her short, stubby nose. "What is that smell?" she demanded.

"Oh, it's probably these," replied Irina, her chubby, ringed fingers holding up a pair of satin undies. "I spray them with my perfume. I mean, even in here you gotta smell nice."

"Could you crack the window open? I feel a little faint." Frau Jungblut held her hand over her mouth.

"Why certainly," chuckled Irina, blinking thick black eyelashes at her friends.

"You didn't answer my question. This is Ruby. I'm Irina. Who are you?"

"Elke Jungblut" came the answer. Elke slid her body back under the covers, scowling at Irina's back as she watched her get up to open the window.

A man in a white coat entered the room.

Irina saluted him. "Hello, Dr. Heller. Nice to see you again."

Dr. Heller was short and fit, with wiry brown hair. Ruby thought he looked awfully young.

"Hello, Irina," he said kindly. "How are you?" Stepping up to her, he told her quietly that her guests would have to leave.

"Okay, Doc. I know the rules."

While Irina ushered her friends out of the room, Dr. Heller took Ruby's hand firmly in his and gave it a resounding shake. She was aware that her hands were clammy, her grasp clumsy. Werner had told her that Germans regarded a strong, firm handshake as a sign of a strong, firm character. She felt weak.

"Nice to meet you, Frau Edwards. I wasn't on duty last night, but I hear you had a pretty rough go of it."

"Yeah, I guess so." She paused before asking, "Did someone get hurt?"

"You knocked down a nurse. But you're lucky. She's okay."

"What's going to happen now?" Ruby's voice was hushed as she looked at the doctor.

"Well, the medication you were taking before you were admitted was obviously not strong enough. They had to give you a pretty hefty dose of Haldol last night. It's what we call a neuroleptic. And a much more potent antipsychotic than what you were on. We're hoping it will be enough to prevent the kind of hallucinations you were having last night. If you don't get better and you continue to pose a safety threat, we'll have to move you to the other ward down the hall until you improve."

153

"God, no," Irina gasped, "don't send her there!"

Ruby's eyes welled up with tears. "I never thought things could get so out of control," she stammered.

Dr. Heller took hold of her hand again. It was still shaking. "Listen, you're not alone here. I'm hoping we'll be able to help you. That's my job. Your job is to rest and take it easy on yourself. In the meantime, we'll start you on something that will help prevent the shaking. It's a common side effect of antipsychotic medication."

He picked up a book that lay on the table next to Ruby's bed. "What's this you're reading?" he said, turning the book over. "Ah yes, Langston Hughes."

Ruby had forgotten about the book. It was the only thing she had grabbed before leaving her apartment. She had left everything else. Werner could bring it later.

"Yeah," Ruby responded. "Helps keep me sane. Helps me remember who I am."

"Well, we'll do our best to get you out of here as soon as we can. I'll be meeting with you once a week in my office. We also have group therapy sessions that we like the patients to participate in, but you can take your time deciding about that. No rush. I'm here Monday to Friday, and every third weekend. If you have any questions, just come on down to my office, okay?"

Dr. Heller strode up to Frau Jungblut, who was sitting up in her bed, fidgeting.

"Doctor," she burst out before he had a chance to begin. "Dr. Heller, I don't think I should be here. You know my husband brought me here against my will. I'm really fine, just a case of bad nerves. Harald, the jerk, he's just worried about me spending all his money. I, I'm not like them." She waved a thin arm dismissively around the room.

Dr. Heller raised his eyebrows and reached for the file that was clipped to the end of her bed. "Well, Frau Jungblut, we'll have to see," he murmured as he glanced over the notes. "Hmm. Says here that you threatened to kill your husband and jump out of your condominium window. Then you took an overdose of pills after he cut up your credit cards. I think we'll need a little time to straighten things out here, Frau Jungblut."

Irina screeched, "Hey, way to go, Elke!"

Dr. Heller frowned at Irina and scolded, "I'll have none of that." Turning back to Frau Jungblut, he said, "We'll have to wait until your weekly appointment with me to discuss this further. You'll need at least a few days to recover. I'll be talking with your husband in the meantime."

Elke Jungblut's face had turned red as a beet. "Doctor," she whined, "you can't leave me here with these, these . . . madwomen! Foreigners, stinking foreigners. And down the hall, the screaming. Please, I don't belong here," she wailed, her blue eyes full of fear.

Irina jumped up off her bed and shouted, "Hey! Who you calling a madwoman? Who you callin' stinkin'? You better watch your mouth, bitch, 'cause you're stuck with us now."

Dr. Heller stepped quickly to the door and signalled for a nurse. Then he clapped his hands together twice and said,

"Enough, Irina. Sit down right now or I'll have you removed in an instant."

Dr. Heller waved a male nurse into the room. Throwing Irina a last glance of disapproval, he returned to Frau Jungblut's bed. "Frau Jungblut, you are being unreasonable. You must not upset yourself and the other patients like this. It will get you nowhere. I don't want to have you restrained, but if you force my hand, I will."

The old woman was now sobbing uncontrollably. Ruby rolled her eyes and looked over at Irina, who caught her glance and tossed back a wry smile. Dr. Heller ordered the nurse to give a sedative to Frau Jungblut. He watched while she swallowed her pill obediently and then rolled over to face the wall, sobbing. Ruby was relieved, though she also felt sorry for her. There was something ominous in other people having the power to control your pain.

Dr. Heller went over to speak quietly to Irina now. There was a certain sorrow in his voice as he spoke, and she too was subdued, listening and nodding. Ruby wondered how many times she had been in and out of this place. Then Dr. Heller announced that a nurse would come in right after breakfast to tell them when their weekly appointments would take place, and left the room.

A feeling of numbness began to wash over Ruby. She knew it was from the mega-doses of drugs the night before. Sure, she was back in the real world for now. But it came with a vast feeling of emptiness that swallowed her up.

Irina's voice interrupted her thoughts. "Y'know, you just

gotta learn to go with the flow here. It's like Pavlov's dogs—you'll get rewarded for good behaviour and deprived for bad. You hear those screams down the hall earlier? Well, that's the other wing. Only it's not so far away. Got the real bad cases over there. You wanna make sure they don't send you down there. You won't get out too soon."

"Yeah," Ruby mumbled, "I was wondering what that was all about."

"Listen, take some advice. I don't know what you're in here for—I don't care really. But you just try to get along, and pretty soon you'll be taking strolls out on the grounds, meeting up with friends in the Schlosspark for a bit, and a few weeks later you'll be out on weekend passes. And you know, you can still get away with having some fun in here. Just choose your moments carefully."

"Fun?" scoffed Ruby. "I didn't come here to have fun. Just to get better." She looked down at her hands.

"*Meine Liebe*, there is no quicker way to get better than with a little fun. Hey, I bring my guy down here all the time. You know, nooky-nooky here, nooky-nooky there."

"I wouldn't know what that's all about anymore," Ruby said.

"So why you here? You got a bad husband, too?"

"No! I don't know. Lots of things went wrong at the same time. My mind was like a closet with too many old clothes stuffed up in the corners, just waiting to tumble out. Then I couldn't sleep. My brain was going *tick tick tick* all night long, all those thoughts going round and round in my head. Telling me things, making me see things and hear things. Couldn't ignore them." Ruby started to choke on her words. "God, it gets so scary . . . something so simple as lack of sleep . . ." Her voice trailed off into nothingness.

Irina looked at Ruby as if to say, *Yeah, I've been there too*, but all she said was "Doesn't sound to me like it was just lack of sleep. When are we going to meet this husband of yours?"

"Oh, he'll be here every day, knowing him. He's a German guy. I met him when I first came to Europe, one and a half years ago. We got stuck on each other somehow."

"Goddamn Germans. They have a knack for making you fall for them. And look at what we have to put up with over there," she said, nodding at Frau Jungblut. "Another German. *Scheisse*, every time I've been in here, there's been someone like her around. Cursing the Turks or the Jews, talking about the good ol' days with Hitler when they all had work and dignity. Man. They're so intelligent, they had to go kill off everyone that didn't look like them. Look what they did to my people! Executed as many as they could. And those who're left? I know people who were born here, parents born here, grandparents born here. They still won't give them no German passport. Just call us stinkin' Gypsies."

"You're right," said Ruby. "All those old men and women on the subways. They just sit there complaining and hissing. It's like it's against the law to smile. And then the neo-Nazis and football fans storming down the platforms with their racist chants. But I'll tell you one thing. Despite the fascism, I've never seen people take to the streets anywhere else like they do here. I never saw anyone barricade streets in Toronto like they do in Kreuzberg."

Ruby heard Irina snort and she rolled over to look at her. She was fast asleep, snoring away. Ruby sighed and gazed back up at the ceiling. *I guess that's all there is to do here*, she thought. *Talk, sleep, wait for meals, wait for visitors, talk, sleep.*

She looked at the clock on her bedside table. Only eleven. Lunch wouldn't come for a while yet. She rolled over and picked up Langston Hughes's book and flipped it open. She began reading softly out loud to herself, letting the words glide over her tongue like honey. "My People" was her favourite poem, gentle yet melodiously insistent. Poetry was the perfect antidote, as it didn't require the extended concentration that a novel might. She closed the book when the last lines had crossed her lips.

Ruby had always yearned to draw out her blackness, to place it front and centre. Here in Berlin, without her family around, she struggled to keep in touch with this part of herself. Perhaps this ambiguity had helped lead her to the psych ward. But there had been so many years of questions even before this: "What are you, anyway? Where are you from? No, that can't be!" And it wasn't only the endlessly stupid reactions of white people that bothered her. She had recognized early in her life that many of them couldn't focus their lenses to include any landscapes beyond their own narrow borders.

What was worse was the disdainful comments of Black

people outside her circle of family and friends. She would return home with the words *half-breed*, *half-black*, *yellow bitch* seared in her brain. She knew the history of their anger. Her father had spoken often of the wretched comments of his own maternal grandmother, who advised her children to "marry light, but not white." And she remembered his singsong words, "The blacker the berry, the sweeter the juice." He had never told her the rest of the lines until she was a young adult: "But when they get that black, they ain't no use."

She had never thought of herself as more beautiful because of her light colouring. In fact, she had secretly wished she had been born darker, certain that this would have kept the questions at bay. Her father's words, the familiar rhythm of his speech, would shore her up, reassure her. He spoke to her as his girlchild: "Darlin', butterball, honeychile . . . Don't let them take away who you are. Being black isn't a mono-chromatic state. Just look at the rainbow of colours in our family. Being black doesn't mean we're all the same. We are many people, many colours, many cultures. And therein lies the beauty of it."

She loved her father dearly. Loved his wide open view of the world. She was enthralled when he took his children to the Japanese Canadian Cultural Centre and plunked them one after the other onto the knees of a Santa whose eyes looked so different from any Santa she'd ever seen before. She loved it when he took them to the traditional wedding of a Native Canadian colleague and spoke to them of their great-great-grandmother, an Algonquin woman who left her people to marry a Black man. He told his children that he himself believed in no god, but that they should accept other people's right to believe.

"Just tell them your mother's white and your father's Black" was his response to his children's need for a simple answer to the constant queries of the people around them. For years she dutifully repeated his words to all who asked. Only as a young woman did she realize that describing her *parents* did not actually define who she was herself. She wished he had not left her to struggle with that damn puzzle all on her own. And now here she was, stuck in a Berlin hospital, the blackness and the whiteness, the days and nights, battling like knights and dragons over her true self.

Ruby heard the carts rattling down the hall and checked her watch again: 11:30 a.m. Her thoughts drifted to easier questions, such as what lunch would taste like. She checked the card she had filled in at breakfast time, full of tedious little boxes lined up next to equally tedious selections: yogurt, porridge, cheese, white rolls, brown rolls, sausage, rice, soup. She had been given the option of deciding one day at a time what she wanted to eat, or selecting foods for a whole week at a time. She chose the soup and the sausage and rice, as she was tired of cheese and rolls and sticky porridge.

Emma poked her head into the room and waved. "Hiya!"

"Oh my love, I'm so glad to see you," said Ruby. They hugged for a long, long time.

"So, you're in the loony bin. How do you feel?"

"Tired and scared. Wondering how long I'll be here for, wondering when I'll have my mind back."

"Ruby, just so you know, I don't think you really belong here. I'm sure you'll get out soon."

"I wish I could just snap my fingers and it would all be done with."

The two women carried on together for an hour. Emma had brought wool and knitting needles with her and showed Ruby how to cast on and off and do a simple knit stitch. They chatted about their friends and about planning a trip to the East. When Emma was ready to go, she said once again, "You don't belong here, Ruby. Come home soon."

Ruby nodded and waved goodbye, sorry to see her friend leave.

The clattering food carts neared their room again. Irina and Elke began to stir in their beds, pushing sheets aside, rubbing their eyes. Ruby wondered if they felt the same panic she did every time they woke. "Where am I? Why am I here?" followed by the realization that she was adrift in this sea of strange faces, sounds and sights. Irina sat up, swung her feet out over the floor and stretched both arms up over her head. Thick, mottled scar tissue zigzagged around both wrists. She saw Ruby staring at them.

"Yep, these are my battle scars." She laughed. "Been here a few times."

Ruby looked down at her hands in silence.

"Hey, don't be sorry for me. Every time I've been in, I've

gotten out. Besides, my honey's coming to see me today. I bet yours will be here soon, too."

Ruby smiled at her, glad at the chance to talk about something else. "Who's your honey?"

"His name's Niko. He's a beaut. Just you wait and see. He'll be in here every day, bringing me things, taking care of me. I'll be out in no time. Mmm! Can't wait to get some more of his stuff." Irina thumped her hands down on the bed next to her hips and shoved her pelvis into the air.

Ruby blinked in astonishment and then laughed. She could see that Irina would breathe a lot of life into this place.

"Excuse me!" Frau Jungblut's voice exploded through their giggles. "Would you refrain from making such crude gestures in my presence!"

Irina shot off the bed and stamped her foot on the ground. Ruby shook her head at her and pressed a finger to her lips. Irina glowered at Frau Jungblut and marched off to the washroom.

"*Ja, sicher*. Of course, *meine Dame*. We'll just have to take it out to the hall."

Two aides pushed lunch carts into the room. Ruby lifted a tray off one cart and opened the lid gingerly. Three compartments divided the servings: sausage, rice, mixed vegetables. She pushed a slice of sausage into her mouth. Frau Jungblut took a tray, but left it resting on her lap.

"You should eat something," Ruby ventured. Although she didn't really care for her, she couldn't stand the thought of being locked up with this woman without being able to have a sensible conversation with her.

"I'm not really hungry."

"You'll feel a lot better if you eat. Try it. I've seen worse."

Ruby chewed slowly and watched Frau Jungblut hover her nose above the food on her tray, nostrils flared.

Just then Werner strode into the room. He held one hand behind his back, and with the other he brushed back a lock of Ruby's curly black hair as he bent over to place a kiss on her cheek.

"Ta-da!" He handed her a bouquet of red roses. As Irina let out a loud whistle from her bed, Ruby's face flushed.

"Thank you," she murmured. Lifting the roses to her lips, she kissed a petal. She let her fingers graze the tip of each flower, carefully avoiding Werner's eyes.

"Eleven," Werner said, interrupting her counting. "You always give an uneven number of flowers."

Ruby sighed and laid the bouquet beside her on the bed. "Yes, of course. You've told me that more than once already."

Werner's eyes narrowed. He grabbed her hand. "Come on. Let's go find a vase for these."

Ruby pried her hand loose and lifted the tray off her lap. She shifted her feet into a pair of paper slippers the hospital had provided. She moved to stand up. Her legs felt rubbery, as if they couldn't carry her weight. Werner took hold of her arm and guided her out of the room. He stopped just outside the door and took both her hands in his.

"What happened?" he asked, when no one could hear them.

Ruby looked at him. "What do you mean?"

"Last night. The doctor told me you had another fit."

"Oh. So you were talking to him already?"

"Yeah. Tell me what happened."

She thought about the visions she'd had and looked into the face that had stalked her at night. "Just like the doctor said. I had another fit. I don't really want to talk about it." She didn't like the way he was looking at her with such intensity. She couldn't shake the thought that he was really out to get her. Could all those visions be wrong?

She moved away from him. He pulled her back.

"Listen, it's better to talk to me than to some group therapy nuts."

"Werner, I just want to forget about it. Besides, I don't have to do the group therapy stuff if I don't want to. I can just see Dr. Heller."

"That's good."

"Werner, I'm still feeling pretty shaky. Can we go back?"

Werner shrugged. "Okay. Just wait here a sec while I get the vase."

Ruby leaned up against the wall and watched him march down the hall and disappear into the nursing station. He came out and waved a white porcelain vase in the air, his lips stretched into a thin smile. Back in the room, Werner put the flowers in the vase and placed them on the night table. Then he pulled a chair up next to the bed.

"I'm going to need a few things from my placc," Ruby said.

"I know. I brought some paper and a pen so you could write a list."

"The doctor put me on some stuff to stop the shaking, but I guess it'll take a while to kick in. Can I just dictate the list to you?"

"Sure." Werner printed at the top of the paper, in neat, block letters: LIST OF THINGS TO BRING TO THE HOSPITAL. Then he drew three columns, printing at the top of them *Toiletries, Clothes, Miscellaneous*. Ruby waited for him to finish organizing the page. Then, column by column, she rhymed off the things she thought she needed.

Irina was listening carefully. "Boy, are you guys ever organized! I just threw whatever I could find into my suitcase."

"Being organized is his specialty," Ruby said, nodding at Werner.

"Well, of course," said Werner, looking sternly back at Ruby. "How do you expect me to sort through all your things and know what to bring without a list?"

"Werner, give it a rest, okay? Anyway, it's finished. I can't think of anything else I need."

There was another knock at the door. Irina yelled out, "Come on in, don't bother knocking."

A short man with dark hair slicked back off his forehead came into the room. He wore a bright orange shirt unbuttoned to his navel, black pants and pointy black suede boots. Ruby stared at the thick mat of hair that covered his chest. Irina bounced up and down on her bed, shouting, "Niko, Niko, I knew you'd come. Darling, come here and let me kiss you!"

Looking a trifle embarrassed, Niko flashed a bright smile

at no one in particular and went over to Irina's bed. She threw her arms around his waist and shimmied up against his furry chest. Werner looked at Ruby and rolled his eyes in disdain. Ruby ignored him and smiled, enjoying Irina and Niko's reunion. The two lovers got up to leave the room. Irina turned to wink at Ruby as she passed through the doorway. She whispered, "Remember what I said about having fun?" Ruby laughed and said, "Go for it!"

"Did you see the clothes the guy had on?"

"Yeah, I saw. So what? They're in love," Ruby said almost accusingly.

"They look like a couple of wackos, if you ask me."

Ruby changed the conversation. "How's my sister?"

"Jessie's okay. Packing her stuff up. You know she goes back tomorrow?"

"Yeah, I know."

"But she'll be in to see you later today."

"Why didn't she come with you?"

"I don't know. I guess I wanted to see you by myself first. See if you're okay enough to have any more visitors."

"Werner, she's my *sister*. She's seen everything there is to see already, anyway." Ruby sighed. She remembered how anxious she had been about Jessie's arrival in Berlin. Werner had gone to pick her up at the airport. Tired from the long flight, her face had blanched when she first saw Ruby. The next day she had slept late. Ruby had stood over her prostrate figure on the mattress, listening to the high-pitched wheeze of her snore. She stared at her flared nose, thick lips, the tight kinks of her light brown hair. She wondered how it was that they had come out so different.

She had missed Jessie incredibly these years. Her father had always insisted that family was the most important thing in the world; she never believed him before, but now she understood. Despite having rejected them, having run away to Europe and married Werner, it was her family that she loved more than anything else.

Ruby wasn't able to talk to her sister much about anything, as fragmented as she was. But Jessie kept her company and held her hand and hugged her. She cooked for her and made end-less pots of tea. She made sure she didn't go outside. She was there. That's what counted. Once she asked if she could look at what Ruby was scrawling in her journal. Ruby had reluctantly pushed it towards her and said, "You won't understand."

Jessie read the journal thoughtfully, her head in her hand. She said, "You're right. I don't really get it. So much paranoia, Ruby. Where do all these thoughts come from?"

Ruby shrugged and said simply, "They're a part of me. I can't separate myself from the voices, the thoughts."

But it did open up the door for them to talk about Dominick and the abortion.

"You really took a gamble on him, Sis. And you put your relationship with Werner on the line. He must have been dev-astated when you told him."

Ruby nodded and gave a watery smile as tears rolled down her cheeks. "Yes, he was." She hung her head in her hands.

Werner's voice brought her back into the present. "Ruby,

you're in a safe place now. They'll look after you here. And I'll be in to see you every day, I promise. Besides, your parents will be here in a few days."

"You're right. Listen, I'm sorry I've been snappy. I'm just worn out."

"Yeah, I know. I'm going to go now anyway. I'll come back with Jessie tonight."

"Will you? I don't know what I'm going to do here all day long. I guess if you bring me those books, I can read some."

"I'll bring them." Werner leaned over and kissed her again. "I'll see you later, then. Don't go thinking any more funny things."

"Christ, Werner. It's not as if I can control it," Ruby said, looking up at him.

"Well, just don't go getting into any trouble with what's her name out there."

"Her name's Irina. And actually, I think she's gonna be a lot of fun."

"Uh-huh," Werner groaned. "Just take it easy, for my sake."

"Yeah, sure," Ruby muttered. Then to herself: "Everything's for your sake, my dear." Then she waved at him from her bed, watching as his perfectly polished brown shoes marched out of the room.

Ruby had forgotten about Frau Jungblut. She had been dead quiet while Werner and Niko were there. Ruby rolled over to see what she was doing. Frau Jungblut's head was propped up on her pillow and she was staring at the ceiling again. Tears were rolling down her cheeks.

"Hey, are you okay?" Ruby asked.

"It's hard to see you two with your husbands or boyfriends or whatever they are. But you should go on and enjoy yourselves."

"I'm sure your husband will be in to see you today," Ruby sympathized. "Is he working?"

"Yes."

"Well, then, maybe he'll be here at suppertime."

"If he shows up I'm going to make sure he gets me out of here today."

Ruby said nothing. Everyone was wondering when they would get out. Just thinking about it gave her a headache.

Irina and Niko came back into the room, arms wrapped around each other like a couple of teddy bears. After Irina sat back down on her bed, Niko leaned over and whispered something in her ear. Irina smiled and said, "Just make sure you come back tomorrow."

Niko smiled. "Of course I will."

There was something in the tone of his voice that made Ruby look at him. The muscles of his face were pulled into a tense smile, his body coiled like a spring waiting to be released. She remembered that he hadn't looked her in the eyes when he came in. He left the room a few minutes later.

Ruby smiled at Irina. "Everything okay?"

"Mmm-hmm," Irina answered, all dreamy-eyed. "What did I tell you? He's gorgeous, isn't he? My Niko."

"Yeah, he seems nice. Did you guys have a nice stroll?"

"Yup." Then in a conspiratorial tone, she added, "If you

go right down the hall and into the stairwell, you can have a bit of privacy, if you know what I mean."

"You're not serious," said Ruby, almost choking on her laugh.

"Of course I am! Just remember what I told you before."

"Yeah, right."

Frau Jungblut's bed creaked. She got up and began pacing the floor, back and forth. Irina nodded to Ruby as if to ask "What's the matter with her?" Ruby shrugged.

"Goddamn men," Frau Jungblut muttered. "You cook for them, you clean for them, you have their children." She stopped pacing and stared at Ruby and then at Irina. "And then, just when you're thinking it's about time for you to have some fun, they go and throw you in the loony bin, so they can sneak around with some young thing."

Irina stared at Elke coolly and said, "Some things are the same for everyone, it seems. But I wouldn't take any shit from a man."

"You'd think I'd have a right to go shopping after all I've done for him. It's just that the Porsche got smashed up, too."

"Who smashed it up?" Ruby asked. "You?"

"Well, yes. But we'd had it a long time."

Irina mumbled, "You must have been daydreaming about all those new things you'd just bought, huh?"

"It's the first time I ever had an accident," Elke snapped. "Besides, didn't I hear you cheering me on just a few hours ago?"

"You sure did. Like I said, I don't take shit from any man."

"But how do you think I'm going to get out of here, except through him?"

"Just sweet-talk him till you get what you want. Then take off. Divorce him."

Elke walked over to her bed and sat down. "I can't. I'm Catholic. We have children."

The three women sat in silence for a few minutes. Elke stretched out across her bed and covered herself up with a blanket. Irina slouched down on her pillow and began chewing on her nails. Ruby rolled over and picked up her Langston Hughes book. She opened it up to the last lines she'd read. She lay there reading the poem, quietly mouthing the words to herself until the book slipped out of her hands and her head rested against the pillow.

A few hours later, the touch of a hand brushing through her hair jolted her out of a deep sleep. Werner and Jessie were sitting on the bed.

"What time is it?" she asked, smiling sleepily at her sister.

"Five thirty. Dinner's coming soon. What's on the menu?"

"Oh, I don't remember. But you're welcome to share with me if you're hungry."

"No, we're okay. We're going out for a meal when we're finished here," Werner answered.

Jessie's presence comforted Ruby and she let her guard down. She began crying. "Damn, don't say those things around me. I don't know if I'll ever get out of here." She couldn't stop the rush of sobs. Jessie pulled her up close. Her long, full arms hugged her tight.

"Hey, you're already looking better than you did two days ago. You'll be okay, Sis. It's just going to take some time. Anyway, before we go for dinner you and I are going to go for a walk in the Schlosspark. It's beautiful outside. They'll let you go out for half an hour if you're with someone."

Ruby continued sniffling, but smiled a little. Immediately she thought of how wonderful it would be to put clothes on again. What freedom!

Werner was fidgeting, wringing his hands while Jessie talked. "Calm down," he said. "Stop crying, you're getting yourself all worked up. I told you I'd come to see you every day. They'll take good care of you here."

Ruby ignored him and held on to Jessie's hand as she pulled away from her. "You're leaving tomorrow," she said matter-of-factly.

"Yeah, I have to. I've been here for two weeks, Ruby. Now that you're here and settled—well, I've got to get back home. I have work to do. You are gonna be okay, aren't you?"

"Yeah, I guess. I'm sorry, Jessie. It's so weird being in here. It's enough to make you crazy!"

Jessie laughed and stroked her head. "You'll have some pretty good stories to tell when you get out."

The rattle of carts punctuated her words. Ruby threw her arms up in the air and said, "Here we go again, the major event of the day. Meal time!"

Werner picked up Ruby's dinner tray. "Let's see what we have here," he said. "And where are your roommates? They'll miss dinner."

Ruby looked around and saw that neither was in the room. "They must have gone wandering down the hall while I was sleeping."

Werner sat down on the bed and pulled up the table and placed the dinner tray on it. Jessie pulled up a chair. "Mmm, smells good," she said and laughed.

"Yeah, well, you can take some with you if you think it's so good," said Ruby.

She ate her food quickly. There was no point in taking time to savour anything; it was hospital food, mushy and tasteless. When she finished, she pushed the table away and got up from the bed. She went to the small dresser and pulled out some clothes: jeans, sweater, bra, socks. She went into the bathroom and got changed. She looked herself up and down and said, "How liberating! I almost feel myself again." She stepped back into the room and said "Ta-da!" Jessie and Werner looked at her and beamed, sharing in her happiness.

Werner said, "Maybe I should go with you? Can you manage on your own?"

"We'll be fine," said Jessie. "Don't worry about us. You'll be able to see us walking down the park path if you look out the window in the lobby."

Ruby grabbed her sister's arm and said, "Come on, let's go, no time to waste here."

The two sisters went out onto the floor and strolled down to the nurses' desk by the elevator. They put an armband on Ruby and told her that she had half an hour. She was looking forward to this walk with her sister, time with someone she loved. Once outside she held her head up to face the sun and yelled, "Shine on me. I worship you."

Jessie held her arm for a while as they headed down the path through the top end of the park. They could see the Charlottenburg Palace glistening in the distance. The beautiful gardens were modelled after those at Versailles, full of formal beds and symmetrical paths. The air was crisp and the sweet light of the late afternoon had set in. Ruby walked stiffly, her shoulders hunched over, her feet dragging one after the other.

"The medication has its side effects, doesn't it?" said Jessie, watching her sister. She took Ruby's hands in hers and said, "What about the tremor? How's that going?" Ruby's hands were trembling considerably.

"Same as usual. It got a little better when they added the second medication, but they still shake a lot. Just like Mom's."

"Yeah, it really does run in the family, doesn't it? I'm sorry, Ruby, I'm so sorry that this had to happen to you. Why you and not me? Why?"

"Lord knows. You know, I never saw this coming. Even with Mom being bipolar, it just never occurred to me. I just went blithely along, leading my life, never stopping to worry that I might get sick. And then wham! Now look at me."

"I used to wonder if I might turn out like Mom. But I didn't dwell on it much. Maybe it was just too scary a thought. But Ruby, just know you're gonna get better. The whole family's behind you. Mom and Dad will be here soon. And you've got Werner. I know you guys have your issues, and he may not be all that you want in a husband, but he's definitely looking out for you."

Half an hour had slipped by quickly, so Ruby and Jessie walked back towards the hospital at the other end of the park. When they got up to the room, Werner was sitting there with cups of coffee for everyone sitting on the night table. There were also two pieces of Sachertorte for them. "I had mine already," he said, gesturing at the cakes. "Enjoy."

Jessie smiled and said, "I'll save mine for after dinner. Listen, Ruby, I don't want to drag this out. You know how I hate goodbyes. I just want to tell you how important it is for all of us that you get better. Maybe when this is all over you can come home for a while."

Ruby sighed. "Yeah, I don't know how I would have made it this far without you being here."

Werner stood up and blew her a kiss. It was so typical of him that he would refuse to kiss her in front of her sister. Jessie pulled a small book out of her bag. "Here, I brought this for you as a present. Pushkin. I think you'll like it."

Ruby took the book and flipped through it. Jessie continued: "You told me about Alexandre Dumas and Napoleon's Josephine. Now I've got one on you." A slight grin crept onto her face. "He's mixed race, Sis. His grandfather was Black."

Werner's body almost bounced off the bed with the force of his "No way!" Ruby smiled at the thought of Werner not knowing something for once.

Jessie stooped over and planted an awkward kiss on her cheek. "Ruby, I love you. We all do. Take care of yourself."

She straightened up and walked quickly towards the door with Werner. She stopped to wave goodbye. Ruby thought she could see her eyes clouding over. Then she turned and disappeared down the hall.

Ruby could feel her heart knocking in her chest. She sat still for a moment, gulping in breaths of air. "Jessie," she called out. But her voice cracked. Her sister had gone.

She couldn't stand being alone with her thoughts. She got out of bed. *Maybe they're still waiting for the elevator.* She rubbed her hand up and down over her chest, over her heart, as she walked out into the hall. She could see the elevators straight down the hall but there was no one there. She walked in circles outside the room. She heard the noise of the television in the common room a few doors down the hall. She hadn't been in there yet. *Go there. Fill your head with other thoughts so the crazy ones can't come in.*

There were only a few people in the room; some slouched in armchairs, others sitting tensely on the couch. The face of J. R. Ewing was plastered across the screen. *Dallas.* God, even over here! She didn't have a television at home but she had heard about the show. She plunked herself down on a small wooden chair, still rubbing her hand back and forth over her heart. She couldn't break its rhythm. Her eyes followed J. R. around on the screen. He was arguing with someone. A door slammed, someone cried, another shouted, "Murder!"

Ruby sat on the edge of her seat and stared into the

screen. Another voice eased its way into her ears, sliding over the voices of the actors. She could feel its slippery tentacles sounding their way into her head. Her hand rubbed harder and faster over her heart. *Jessie, Jessie, Jessie, Jessie.* The chameleon voice rustled now like a distant wind. "Hush!" Ruby told it. She shook herself and squinted at the screen.

Werner's mocking voice droned on and on in her ears. "She's gone. She's gone. She's gone." She slapped her hands against her ears and threw herself on the floor. She crawled over to the TV and pawed the screen. Her voice railed out into the air, "Why are you doing this to me?" White blurs appeared in front of her again, lifting her, pushing her.

"Get her back to the room. Then get Dr. Heller. Quick!"

Ruby's body collided against the mattress. Bodies huddled over her. She heard someone say, "Take it easy, take it easy on her, will ya!"

Irina! Ruby flailed the space in front of her.

"Get the hell back! Get her out of here!"

Ruby fought to get a glimpse of Irina's face. Someone yanked on her arm. She knew the needle was coming.

"Come on, let it come, let it come," she ranted to herself. Heavy clouds puffed up in her head. Exhausted, she fell back against her pillow, waiting for the nothingness to come.

At two o'clock she got out of bed and prepared to go down to Dr. Heller's office. Irina and Elke were sleeping. She walked slowly out into the hall, her arms hanging disjointed at her

sides as if they no longer belonged to her. She stared at the
floor, watching her feet move, right, left right, left, in front of
her. She looked up only when she was at the nursing station.
An older woman was standing in a hospital gown outside the
station, drooling and babbling to herself. Down the hall a
young man was banging himself up against the wall, moaning
and pulling at his hair. "Christ," Ruby thought. "What am I
doing here?"

When Werner came to visit the evening before, he told her
that her parents would be arriving the next day, and that made
her feel better. The next morning he called, saying her parents
were on their way in. Not long after, her mother and father
poked their heads through her door and then came rushing up
to her bed. Ruby began to cry at the sight of them.

"My dear daughter, no tears, we're here now," her father
said, standing over her bed with a wide smile on his face.

Ruby's mother hugged her daughter to her chest and then
wiped Ruby's cheeks gently with her fingers. "Yes, we're here
now. What happened, Ruby, whatever happened to you?" her
mom asked. Her face was not wide open and beaming like her
father's but tired and drawn. Ruby did not want to go into
any stories about Dom and the abortion and said simply that
she was stressed out at work and that things slowly began to
cave in on her. Her mother looked sad as she listened, and
Ruby wondered if she blamed herself for her daughter's mis-
fortune. "I wasn't getting enough sleep and everything caught
up with me." She held her mother's hands and whispered, "It's
not your fault, Ma."

Two solitary tears trickled down her mom's face. "Maybe not, but I can't help feeling like it has to do in part with me. What can we do for you? What can we bring you?"

Ruby smiled at her mom and said, "You can bring me some chocolate and some sweets. Werner will know what to pick."

Ruby's father sat down on the edge of her bed. "We'll be in to visit every day. When you're better, maybe we can take you out for walks. What do they have you on?"

"Haldol. It's an antipsychotic."

"Your mother was never on anything like that. Will they put you on lithium?"

"So far they're just treating it as one episode, so no lithium."

"Hmm," said her father. "I hope the doctor will agree to talk to us."

"I'm sure he will. He's very pleasant."

"How are your roommates?" asked Ruby's mom.

"Well, as you can see they're still sleeping. Not much else to do here. They're fine. Quite nice, actually."

"We brought you a book," said her father. He tugged at the small bag at his feet and pulled out *The Color Purple*, by Alice Walker. "Your mother and I both loved this book and we thought you might enjoy it, too. Give you something to do with all that free time you have."

Ruby smiled as her father handed her the book and thanked her parents for the gift. "I'm so glad for anything to read."

After another thirty minutes, Ruby's parents got up and said they were leaving but that they'd be back to see her again the next morning. Ruby kissed them both goodbye and waved when they turned before going out the door. She was so happy to have seen them that she started to cry again.

That afternoon she went to see Dr. Heller for her appointment. She sat down in his office, squirming in her chair, and proceeded to skirt around every direct question he asked her. She avoided his eyes when he spoke to her, looking down at her nails or up at the ceiling, or commenting on paintings hanging on the walls. She remembered Werner telling her not to get caught up in a bunch of psychobabble with therapists there. He didn't want her to go to the group therapy sessions. Why should she divulge her life history to a bunch of total strangers? Forty minutes later she left the doctor's office and felt somehow cleansed even though she'd said very little. The old woman was still there, still babbling, still drooling.

Back in the room, Irina was sitting on the edge of her bed, knees pulled up to her chest, painting her toenails scarlet. Ruby heard water pounding against tiles in the bathroom. Elke was in the shower. A heavy smell of sweat mixed with the damp heat rushing through the cracks of the bathroom door and enveloped the room like a musty old blanket. Ruby could hardly breathe.

Elke emerged from the bathroom, wrapped in a towel. Her skin was silky with wetness, and shiny beads of water dripped with rhythmic precision from the tips of her hair. She looked at Ruby and scowled, nodding towards Irina. She whispered, "Can't you tell her that she should clean herself up? It smells awful in here."

Ruby sighed and thought, *Why me?* She went over to Irina's bed and sat down. "When is Niko coming?"

"I dunno. He didn't call yet. But I'm getting ready just the same."

Ruby nodded sympathetically and said, "Yeah, what else is there to do here anyway?" She added, "You know, Irina, if you're getting ready for him you might want to take a shower before you put on your perfume."

"Bah! Bodily smells really bring out the animal in men. Grrrr."

Irina's frank irreverence unsettled Ruby for a second and she shuffled backwards on the bed.

Irina threw back her head and laughed. "I've heard about you North Americans. Always showering, washing your hair every day. Why are you so afraid of your bodies?"

Ruby stammered, trying to find words to defend herself.

Irina continued. "Even the Germans with their crazy need to clean, clean, clean. Even they respect the nature of their bodies. Look at her." She pointed a painted toe conspiratorially at Elke and whispered, "Do you see the fur underneath her arms? Even she knows enough to let nature alone."

Ruby couldn't resist sneaking a look. Elke sat in her underwear on her bed, facing them. Her slim arms were raised, her hands ruffling her still-damp hair with a towel. Tufts of curly blond hair sprouted out from underneath the joint where arm met shoulder.

"What are you two gawking at!" Elke sputtered. "You're always up to something."

In between gasps of laughter, Irina said, "I'm just giving her a lesson in German Naturalism. I thought you'd be as good a specimen as any."

"I don't know what you two are going on about. But if you're not going to clean yourself up, you could at least have the courtesy to open the windows."

Elke pulled on a bathrobe and pulled the door wide open.

Irina snorted. "Looks like I'm giving lessons to the wrong person." She resumed painting her toenails.

Ruby shook her head and stood up by the windows. Looking down into the verdant colours of the Schlosspark, she watched people thread in and out of the palace and hand-holding couples stroll along the paths. The sight made her feel lonely, then edgy. She left the room and walked down to the front lounge. She hadn't spent much time there, except when she went for her evening smoke. The chairs were all full. People sat reading, sleeping, smoking. A young man was walking circles around the lounge, moaning loudly. Every few seconds he'd stop, shake his head furiously and throw his hands up in the air, and then continue his circling. His eyes fixed on Ruby a few minutes after she entered the lounge. He stopped pacing and stared at her from across the room, his hands on his hips. He started rocking back and forth on the balls of his feet, still staring at her. He stuck his tongue out at her. Ruby felt her legs grow wobbly. She thought, *Am I afraid of him?*

She leaned against the wall and looked away. Her eyes rested on a group of women who sat knitting. *Click, click, click.*

The whir of the needles brushing against each other entranced her. Out of the corner of her eye, Ruby saw the strange man snake across the room in her direction. His tongue darted in and out of his mouth. Her feet became glued to the floor. She flattened herself against the wall, closed her eyes and tried to will herself back to her room.

"Blaaagh! Blaaagh! Blaaagh!"

His gravelly voice blasted into her ears, making them pop. A hot, dank smell of rotten eggs breathed onto her face. Rough, leathery fingers dragged down her cheeks. His slimy tongue spat out at her nose and jabbed into her nostril. Ruby shuddered and squeezed her eyes shut tighter, and balled her fists, pressing them into the wall. Her body froze in fear.

Someone yelled, "Cut it out, Hans. Stop it right now!" Someone pried him off her. Ruby crumpled to the floor, her arms crushed up against her face.

"Aiyeeee aaaaaahhhhahahahah . . . !" His laughter turned into screams as the nurses dragged him down the hall into the other wing. A woman knelt down next to Ruby and patted her arm.

"It's okay, dearie, he's gone. He does that to everyone who's new on the ward. He's been here forever. Don't mind him. He's gone now."

Ruby opened her eyes. The woman was still there, still patting her arm. Irina sat next to her. She nodded at the woman and said, "Help me get her up." Then, whispering in Ruby's ear, she said, "Let's get you back to the room."

Ruby shuffled down the hall beside Irina, her head hanging down, her arms hanging limp and disjointed at her side. *Could that be me? Could that be me? Could that be me?* The words echoed endlessly in her mind. She closed her fingers tightly around Irina's hand.

She stayed curled up in bed for the rest of the day, not talking to anyone, not eating. *My god*, she thought, *will this never end?* Werner came in the evening, but she only opened her eyes long enough to shake her head at him and whisper that she just wanted to sleep. Her lashes fluttered shut. He shook her shoulder gently, but she didn't respond. His hand rested on hers for a while, his fingers curled up, locking into hers. Then they were gone.

Ruby's parents came the next day, and they all went to see the doctor first. He told them that he did not intend to put Ruby on lithium, and that the Haldol should do the job well. He explained that it took a while to settle on the correct dose and that Ruby had been having ups and downs, so they had increased the Haldol. She should react quickly enough.

Ruby spent the next week going for daily walks with her parents in the park. The weather played along, and while there were often clouds in the sky, the sun was never far away. Both her mother and her father tried to cheer her spirits with stories from Ruby's childhood, gossipy tales of their neighbours and updates of family friends. On their last day of visiting, they brought in a spread of food for Ruby to enjoy, followed by various cakes from the local bakery.

"Ruby," her dad said, "I've said this over and over again, but I do truly believe that you're going to be fine. It all takes some time, but you will get better eventually." Looking at his wife, he continued, "I have some experience in this field already, as you well know. Your mother has always come out of her troubles with flying colours, and you will, too."

Ruby's mother added, "We'll be expecting a visit from you soon. I never thought I'd be saying this, but you should come home for a while."

Ruby's parents lingered for a final walk in the park and they tried to draw out a plan for her recovery from her.

Werner visited as usual that evening, but he was not happy with her talk of going home.

Beady eyes bulged out at her through the darkness. A red tongue darted in and out of her mouth, in and out of her ears, flicking, hissing, flicking. Ruby lay still, her body pressed into the mattress. Slithering around her belly, he slunk down between her legs and invaded her, thrusting in and out. Ruby felt hot waves flush over her tummy. Her pelvis contracted with the involuntary orgasm that was rushing over her. She heard him laugh: "Aiyeeee ha ha ha ha!"

Ruby slammed her eyes shut and pounded against the bed. The thud of her fists on the mattress reverberated through her head. Werner's words exploded into her, flung themselves out at her, wrapping around her, tightening, choking, strangling. *Why do you people have to wear such stupid hats why i don't care if you're black i don't think you should ride a bike why the fuck would you go to a demonstration did you wear a balaclava why do you always blame it on me you don't know what to do with yourself why don't you ever listen to me close the blinds before you turn on the light these tree huggers here are fools think if they plant a tree it will change the world do you think your parents are the only ones who suffered because of their race the world's fucked why have children why is his english so bad if he's from ghana louis jordan not ellington that's the real stuff you can't leave don't you see it's you not me you're getting fat what does it matter whether you're black or white what does it matter . . .*

Ruby was panting. Her fingers flailed back and forth over her crotch. A thick, sticky wetness streamed out of her. She looked down and saw a head protruding out of her. She groaned and pushed. A tiny baby's body thudded dully on the floor. Ruby screamed. It had Werner's face. She reached down to touch it. It was cold, lifeless. Another voice. *My people, my people, my people, my people.* The rhythm of the words pounded like a drum in her ears. Ruby pulled her knees to her chest and rocked herself to the rhythm of the words that pounded like a drum in her ears.

When she opened her eyes the next morning, she saw Irina propped up on her elbows, her chin resting in her hands, staring at her.

"Jeez, you sure know how to have yourself some fun," she said, winking at her. "But I still think I could teach you a trick or two."

Ruby winced and pulled the sheets up over head. Irina's voice trilled through the stuffy air.

"Hey, don't be embarrassed. Everybody does it. I just happened to be awake at the same time. But you were so caught up with yourself you didn't even notice."

Ruby wept silently under the sheets. Irina was quiet. Elke sat up in her bed and reached over to pat her arm. "There, there," she whispered. "You know what she's like."

Dr. Heller came in to speak with her. He explained quietly that they were increasing her dose of Haldol because of her outbursts. Ruby rolled away from him and refused to answer any of his questions. He left her alone. Then he came back, as if as an afterthought. He suggested that Ruby join one of the therapy groups. She shook her head silently. He persisted. "If you don't want to go to group therapy, that's okay. But we have a hospital policy. You have to try something."

Ruby mumbled that she wasn't interested in making ceramic bowls or ashtrays. Dr. Heller said, "Well, we have music therapy. Why don't you try that?"

Ruby was too tired to put him off. "Okay, okay. I suppose I'll be able to sing my way out of here, then?"

Dr. Heller laughed and said, "That's the spirit."

Lunch came and went. Nobody talked. But Ruby heard Irina mumble into her pillow, "He's not coming back, is he? Niko's not coming back."

Ruby caught her breath. It was true. Niko hadn't come back since his first visit. Ruby got out of her bed, went over to Irina and knelt on the floor beside her bed. Her hand reached up to touch Irina's head. She knelt there silently for half an hour, stroking her fingers through her hair.

Werner came that day with another bunch of blood-red roses. The sickly sweet scent filled the airless room. Ruby was overcome with nausea. Werner spoke to her softly, rubbing her curls, stroking her arm. His eyes smiled lovingly at her. She tried in vain to separate them from the eyes that stalked her at night. As Ruby gazed at him, she realized nothing would ever be the same.

She didn't love him anymore, and indeed, despite the fact that he done his best to care for her, she felt intimidated and frightened by him. This was the beginning of the end.

CHAPTER SEVEN

Hello, Dolly

RUBY SPENT SEVERAL MONTHS RECOVERING AFTER her hospitalization. She managed to keep Werner at bay, much to his dismay, but remained sequestered inside her apartment most of the time. Werner would still come creeping around to her door, calling out for her insistently, but she had changed the lock and refused to open the door. He'd have to get the picture and stop sometime. She hoped that would be soon.

Her mood had fallen very low; she had decided that this must be the usual trajectory of mental illness—skyrocket, then crash and burn. What goes up must come down. She was still heavily medicated with Haldol, and was going once a month to the doctor's for a shot. She felt woozy a lot of the time and still suffered from stiffness in her joints, but "the Haldol shuffle"—slumped head, arms hanging like a gorilla, trudging pace—was gone. The language institute had been very generous and sympathetic and had given her another two months off work, so she needn't worry about that. In fact, there was scarcely any reason to go out at all. Ruby lay in bed all day tossing and turning and sighing. She would only come up from under the blankets when her lungs could no longer stand the closeness under the covers. A deep sadness lapped at her, like little waves pulling her away from her core, setting her adrift in a vast nothingness. Her mood was grim and she remained incommunicado, not wanting to reach out to anyone or have them reach out to her. She had lost her appetite, nibbling on crackers and cheese or a piece of fruit. Sleep was her best friend. She called out to death one day, wishing it would lay its blanket over her and extinguish the fire of life once and for all. But underneath all her blues she could hear her family calling out to her. *Be strong! Pull yourself up! Stand tall!* "I don't know how," she would wail. But she couldn't drown out their voices as they tried to coax her on.

After three weeks her mood finally began to lift a little in the evening and she would sit up, maybe even stand and stretch for a moment or two. She managed to sit in the chair in her room, but couldn't summon the interest to read a book. One evening she tiptoed down the hall and put on a little music— the lilt of the jazz horn made her cry. Someone knocked at the door. She knew it wasn't Werner because he always gave three knocks followed by two quick knocks. It was Emma, who had been trying to reach her for ages. Her friend was stunned at the mess in the house: dishes left standing everywhere, clothes strewn across all the surfaces.

"Ruby, you can't go on this way. You have to get some help."

"I have my doctor, that's all I need."

"But you don't even have a therapist or psychiatrist."

"I have my friends, like you. Why go to a stranger?"

"Oh Ruby, don't you see, I can only help so much. You're stuck inside your flat, and probably inside your head, too. How long have you been lying around day and night?"

"A while now. It's hard to get motivated. It's like I'm in the slow cycle of the wash, swishing back and forth in the darkness. Sleep brings relief."

"You need just as much help as you did before. You let yourself be helped then. Why not now? Just because you're not having delusions doesn't mean it's not just as important."

"I know, Emma, I know it's not right. I just can't bring myself to do anything about it. I'm like a rock stuck in a cave."

"Do me a favour, Ruby—call your parents and let them know what's going on. Maybe they can come over again."

Ruby mulled that over. She hadn't wanted to bother them again, but Emma was right. She should ask them if they'd be willing to visit again.

After Emma left, Ruby went back to her routine of wandering the apartment, lying down, wandering some more, jags of crying in between. She eventually picked up a book by de Maupassant. The coarse slang of the Normandy countryside reminded her of Quebec's *joual*, which had filled her ears in her university days. It was like comfort food, sustaining her for an evening. She played Marvin Gaye, Otis Redding and Solomon Burke on the stereo, alternating them with familiar jazz standards. Sometimes she cried while listening to the music, imagining herself to be the spurned lover in one of the songs, feeling the splintered blueness of her situation. In a way it all reminded her of home. Especially the jazz.

When she called her parents the next night, her voice was shaky. "Dad, it's me. How are you?"

"Ruby! I'm thrilled to hear from you. We've been worried. We tried and tried but we couldn't reach you."

"Dad, I'm calling to ask if you'd like to come over and visit again."

"Of course we would, but I have to discuss it with your mother. She's been through a rough patch herself in the last few weeks. But she's coming out the other side now."

"What happened to Mom?"

"Well, she got so busy worrying about you that she went off a little herself, got a little manic."

"Is she all right? How is she now?"

"They adjusted her medication. But she's a trooper and she'll be fine. Just like you, Ruby. Are you okay?"

"I'm a little low, but I'm doing fine," Ruby lied. "But I'd really like to see you soon."

"Fine, my ass. I can hear your voice quaking as we speak. We'll arrange to come over as soon as we can. Are you still seeing a doctor?"

"I see my GP, but no psychiatrist."

"Ruby, that's not good. Your mom's got a great shrink."

"I don't know any shrinks here. My GP is just fine."

"We'll talk about it more when we see you."

In the one week it took for her parents to arrive, Ruby tried hard to pull herself together. She cleaned up the apartment a little bit every day, but it was still rough around the edges. Which is exactly how she felt. One day Ruby put on her shoes and slipped out the door. She had decided to go to an animal shelter and look for a cat. There was an array of cute cats and dogs, kittens and puppies at the shelter. But Ruby saw one beautiful little kitten, white with swirls of grey, that hung back in the cage, shy and tentative. She bent down further and picked up the little thing by the scruff of its neck and pulled her out of the cage. It squirmed and cringed and tried to break free. But Ruby kept petting it and cooing at it until it sat still for a moment. She gestured to the staff that she wanted this kitten, and they prepared the papers for her. "I will call you Luna, which means 'moon' in Spanish. You feel electric and full of emotion, just like when the moon comes out."

Ruby took Luna home and set her on the living room floor. She folded up a blanket and made an indentation where Luna could nest. The kitten ran away and hid. Ruby looked for her for ages but couldn't find her and gave up the search. Finally at night the cat resurfaced. Ruby was lying in bed when there was a little thump. Luna came nudging her way along the bed to where Ruby lay. She reached out with her paw and gave Ruby's hand a pat. Ruby scratched and caressed the kitten and then lifted up the duvet so that it could crawl in. It wriggled up against her and promptly fell asleep. Luna would continue to hide much of the day and come to see her at night when it was quiet and dark. Ruby would make shadows on the walls with her hands and the kitten would lunge after the shapes with comic ferocity and pluck. Ruby was gratified for this little bit of company and touch, and a deep smile penetrated her being.

It was the day her parents were to arrive. Standing at the window of her apartment, Ruby looked out over the courtyard, watching for them. She had to admit she was thrilled by the prospect of seeing them again, even though she knew that her father was a man on a mission, crossing an ocean to retrieve his wayward daughter.

As Ruby turned for the door, an image of her younger, more innocent Canadian self flashed before her eyes. As she stood there, her hand, the colour of cardamom, wandered like her mind and ruffled her dark curls. She looked forward to some sassy repartee with her father and her mother, some juicy updates on the latest family gossip. She thought of her mother and father and could see them wrapped in each other's arms dancing around the living room, while she first watched and then joined in. *Tight-knit*—that is how she thought of them, with so much love in the air.

Ruby had just turned six. The new dress lay on top of her bed, where her mother had laid it out carefully for her. Her small, pudgy fingers gingerly traced their way over the soft red velvet, then round and round the shiny black buttons, up to the lacy collar, and finally slid down plushy sleeves that ended in smooth black cuffs. Oooh, wasn't it so pretty, pretty, pretty, she whispered to the collection of dolls and animals—a pink kitten, a spotted puppy, a cloth doll made by her grandmother, and a doll her father called Pocahontas, its head smashed in by her sister's baseball bat. Ruby had painstakingly coaxed what was left of the brown plastic head back onto the shoulders with a bit of adhesive tape. But it sat there lopsided, ready to fall at the slightest mishandling. They had snuggled up close together, and watched Ruby from their corner of the bed.

She slithered eagerly into the dress, then stood in front of the mirror admiring herself. Little brown-black freckles danced around her nose; chestnut eyes shone brightly. Two thick, black braids tumbled down behind her shoulders. She did a little twirl. And then again, round and round and round she went, arms flung high in the air. Breathless, she fell onto her bed and gathered up her furry friends in her arms. The voices of her mother and father wafted into the room.

"Aw, Louise, baby, I'm not sure it's a good idea to let her get up in front of people like that."

"James, nobody's pushing her. It's just for fun. You know she loves to sing."

Ruby flung her bedroom door open. "It's true, Daddy, it's true, I want to do it."

Her mother and father stood in the hall, arms locked around each other's waists. Ruby eyed her father's hand as it slipped down to pat her mother's bottom.

"Eeew, yuck! You guys, don't do that stuff around me."

Her mother brushed her father's hand away playfully. She

slanted her eyes down towards Ruby and said, "Darlin', it's called love. That's what people do."

Stooping down, she caressed a few curly threads back from Ruby's face. She turned Ruby around to do up her dress. "Listen, sweetheart, are you sure . . . ?"

"But I am, Mommy. Daddy, puh-leeze!"

Her father grunted. "I can't fight against two of you. Okay, go ahead."

Turning away from them triumphantly, her mother waved and said, "See you guys downstairs."

Her father picked her up and looked her over approvingly. "Well, my, my, my. You look beeyoootiful," he cooed, squeezing her in his grizzly-bear arms. The smell of his aftershave tickled her nose. He tossed her into the air. She squealed with delight, not wanting him to put her back down.

"Daddy, Daddy, tickle me."

He poked thick fingers into her ribs, this side, now that side. She wriggled away, feeling as if she'd burst, then came back for more.

"You're getting too big for this now," he said, catching his breath. He escorted her down the stairs, his hand wrapped tightly around hers. "Now be good. Company is here."

Ruby's parents were surprised to see how large her flat was and more than a little unnerved by the messiness they found. Ruby had tried to tidy up, but dishes were still stacked high in the kitchen sink, though the counters had been cleared. Papers and odds and ends were strewn over the coffee table, and a multitude of shoes lay piled up at the door. Most surfaces had something gathered upon them collecting dust.

"My dear, it looks like you're barely managing," her mother said. "That's not like you, Ruby. Tell me what's going on."

"I'm just a little out of sorts, Mom. It's been hard, breaking up with Werner. I don't feel like going out much these days. I guess my spirits are low."

"Werner called us and was very upset. Are you sure you're doing the right thing by letting him go?"

"Mom, I couldn't carry on—he was so overbearing, he left me no room to move. If we argued, then he simply insisted that I was in the wrong all the time. There was no way to seek a compromise."

Her father cleared his throat and mumbled something about young people today.

Ruby wheeled on him. "You had your time, too. Don't deny it, Dad."

Her father responded by saying they would all go out to dinner the next night at the hotel on Kleiststrasse and have a family meeting of sorts.

As a young waiter cleared their plates from the table the following evening, her parents ordered coffee. Ruby sipped on a crisp Riesling, washing down the sharp, smoky taste of the fish she had eaten. Raindrops sprayed the window of the hotel restaurant, and she stared out through the glass. Ink-black clouds hurtled across the skies, and in a far corner of the palette, rays of lemon-orange light burst through, dissolving the darkness around them.

"Honestly, Ruby, why don't you come back home?"

Her father's voice demanded her attention. She watched him defensively as he took another swig of his coffee.

"Damn, it's cold," he sputtered. He stood up, snapping his fingers to get the waiter's attention.

Ruby was used to her father's restaurant antics. As a child, she had always cringed when he returned food, demanding that it be brought back piping hot. Now she took it for one of those immutable traits that you just lived with. As she watched him chastising the waiter, she noticed he had thinned down over the last few years, but there was still something impressive, almost majestic, about his frame. It wasn't that he was especially tall, yet he seemed to loom over you with an aura of authority in his bearing. His skin was smooth and toffee coloured, his head balding. His dark brown eyes danced in his face, but they could stop and pin you down in a moment.

When he sat down, Ruby's mother whispered, "James, do you always have to be so insistent? It borders on arrogance, my dear."

Ruby egged her father on. "You were saying . . ."

"Well, yes I was. You know, Ruby, there are lots of good jobs at home for a bright young woman like you. Think about your future, about your security. What can Berlin offer you . . . ?"

Her mother piped up. "Your father and I disagree on this matter, Ruby. I think that if you're happy here, if you have a good job and you're healthy, then you should stay. But if you can't look after yourself, especially with this illness, you should come home."

"Thanks, Mom. God, Dad, I thought you told everybody I was a translator. Isn't that good enough for you?"

Her father winced. She had slowly returned to work at the institute, but only part-time. As a result, she did just about everything—translating, tutoring English, even modelling nude for desperate art students. Her father had stretched and eliminated truths, telling the neighbours that she was a translator in French, German and Spanish for some prestigious German company.

But the one thing she wasn't doing in Berlin was pursuing security. Why bother? Life was too short to worry about pensions. Besides, how could she explain to her parents that she was still infatuated with the city? How she loved its wild extremes, from tattooed punks and anarchist squatters to soaring public monuments to winding, winsome tree-lined canals. Where else could she pedal off to the open-air cinema to watch *Jules and Jim* in the twilight? And finally, where else could you knock on a neighbour's door and she'd open it up nice and wide and stand there stark naked and say, "Hello, Ruby, what gives?" She had not done any of these things lately, but she knew they were waiting for her.

The waiter carefully set the fresh coffee down in front of her father, then stood back and waited for his approval. Her father took a sip, nodded, and pronounced with sudden graciousness, "It's fine now, thank you."

Ruby smiled at the waiter, her thoughtful gaze resting on his tanned body, curly brown hair and sensuous mouth. Her eyes followed him as he turned away.

Her father chuckled. "You haven't forgotten how to flash that smile. Well, that's okay, as long as it's just a smile."

"Oh god," Ruby groaned. "And what if it wasn't?"

"Oh, go ahead and flirt," said her mother. "Enjoy it while you're young!"

Her father continued as if he hadn't heard either of them. "Ruby, you know, before I met your mother I did a lot of running around with all kinds of women. I hung with a guy, both of us just out of the army, blowing whatever money we had on the finest zoot suits and fancy drinks for the gals we chased." A childlike grin broke over his broad face. "Damn, I nearly drove your grandparents crazy. Maybe that's why they never said much when I told them I was marrying a white woman. They just wanted me married and out of the house."

Ruby laughed and shook her head. She'd heard different versions of the same story a million times, but it was still a stretch to imagine her flashily dressed father hitting the nightclubs years earlier.

"What are you trying to tell me?" she asked with a smile.

"Well, I know everyone has to kick about and enjoy life when they're young. But there comes a time when you just have to get it out of your system. Your mother and I have been married thirty-five years now. And I've never looked at another woman since I met her."

Ruby shuffled her legs impatiently under the table. She knew she couldn't expect her father to understand how she could love one person and still get a kick out of messing around with someone else. Especially since she didn't quite get it herself. Intellectually it made sense; she'd read all those books about Sartre and de Beauvoir, Hammett and Hellman, and the tyranny of marriage as a patriarchal institution. And she knew many Berliners who seemed to thrive in open relationships. But something else seemed to be driving her that she couldn't explain.

Ruby stared out the window, head resting in her hand, fingers pressed tightly over her mouth. She looked at her father, his hand stirring a brown whirlpool in his white porcelain coffee cup. She expected him to launch into another tale of how her great-great-grandfather rose up from the shackles of slavery to become one of Canada's first black dentists, how her great-aunt Rose had painted in Mexico with Diego Rivera, how Great-Uncle William had studied music in Berlin, how her sister was a productive, successful member of the community back home. But surprisingly he remained silent.

"Dad, I'm doing my best. I'm doing what I like, though it can be menial at best. I don't want to be trapped in the same old job for thirty years. And I won't stay tied to someone who doesn't understand me."

"I know, sweetheart. I guess I just want you back home, safe and sound."

Ruby reached over to touch her father's hand, his shiny

brown skin still smooth and supple. "I'll be back someday, Dad. You'll see."

Ruby's mother pursed her lips and said, "Ruby, we've been worried about you. I can't help wondering if you're still depressed."

"I have been kind of low, but I'm starting to come around."

"You look rather drawn to me, not as spunky as usual. You need to come home for an extended visit."

"I think you're probably right about that. I'll see what I can do."

"Please come home soon, darling."

"Mom, I'm sorry to hear that *you* weren't well either," Ruby said. "What happened?"

"We'll talk about that later, sweetie. Right now I want to focus on you. Can you get a recommendation for a psychiatrist from your doctor? It would be great if you could get some more help."

"I'm taking my meds already, Mom. I get a shot of Haldol once a month. I'm not big on psychiatrists. But maybe I can find some other kind of therapist. I'll look into it."

Her father took a last sip of his coffee, now cold, and grimaced. He stood up and said, "I'm going back to the room."

Her mother smiled and touched his hand. "I'll stay here with Ruby for a while." Her father nodded and slowly left the restaurant.

Ruby's mother reached across the table and grabbed her daughter's hands in hers. "Darling, I'm so sorry this has happened to you. I don't know what to tell you, except that I'm so worried that you have to handle it on your own. Are you sure you're done with Werner?"

"Yes, I'm sure. He was smothering me."

"You've always been so headstrong. I guess you're following your gut instincts, and if so, you know what's best. But being on your own means you have even more reason to look after yourself."

"Mom, while we're on the topic, let me get right down to it. How come you and Dad never gave Jess and me a heads-up about mental illness?"

"Goodness, you and your sister were very young when things first started going wrong. We didn't know *what* to say. I just did my best to get better with the help of medication, a psychiatrist and your dad." Her mother was looking deep into Ruby's eyes, searching for a little compassion.

"But all you had to do was describe what you went through, what it felt like and what you were doing about it." Ruby turned her gaze to the window again and chewed her lip. The sun was still inching its way across the moist sky.

Her mother twirled the cardboard coaster that sat in front of her. She waved the waiter over to order a martini. Then an almost imperceptible sigh slipped from her lips. Ruby watched her mother as she struggled with the words. "I didn't know you were so angry. But Ruby, how could I possibly describe what I was going through to a young child? There's not much you would have truly understood. I was just as scared as you, but in a different way."

Ruby thought about everything her mom would have

had to contend with and suddenly felt sorry for her. But she continued nonetheless. "You could have talked to us when we were a little older."

"You're probably right. I can't say why I didn't. We weren't consciously trying to hide it. I guess we just dealt with it as honestly as we could have. We were still young, and mental illness was very taboo at the time."

"Yeah, I know. It still is. And it's awful, being so out of control. Never knowing who or what to believe. Being so angry when the happiness and energy disintegrate. Did you ever have delusions? My head was full of them."

Her mother paused before answering. "Aside from feeling like I had a godlike strength, no, I never got psychotic, if that's what you mean. It was all rampant energy, feeling strong, creative and happy."

"But you were really cranky, too."

"You're right. I was getting to that. I was edgy. I wanted my time all to myself and not to have to share it with anyone else."

"And then you crash . . ."

"Yes, down, down, down."

"Do you remember when I came to see you in the hospital once?"

Her mom shrugged. "Umm, I'm not sure. Which time?"

Ruby leaned in towards her mother. "You hugged and kissed me all over. And then suddenly you jumped up out of bed and ran down the hall, yelling and crying." Ruby sat back again.

"I don't remember that at all." Her mom hunched over her martini.

"I thought I'd done something wrong. I didn't recognize you anymore. Who was this person? Not my mom."

Ruby's mom scraped her chair back and sat straight, as if collecting herself. "I'm so sorry you went through all that. And maybe somehow, when you and Jessie were older, we should have tried to talk to you about it some more. But it's not like other illnesses. It's invisible. There's no cure. There's so much stigma. And after all, just what is a 'broken' brain? It manifests itself in so many different ways. Your experiences are so different from mine."

"I told them in the hospital that my mother was bipolar, but they preferred to treat it as a one-off situation rather than permanently diagnose me."

Her mother's fingers tapped out a little song on the table. "I'm not sure if that's wise or not. I needed a diagnosis in order to get proper help."

"But this way I'm not labelled for life. I can get on with things. I know I'll only be on meds for a limited time."

"Ruby, I hate to say this, but don't fool yourself. You may well get sick again, you just don't know. And then you may need medication again."

"Yes, but maybe only temporarily, just like this time. Mom, what seems to bring it on for you?"

Her mother smiled at her. "Plain and simple—stress and lack of sleep. Maybe there are other factors, but those are the two biggies for me. The latest episode was when I was up a number of nights worrying about you. I had to increase my medication and lay low for a while. What sets you off?"

"I'd have to say the same. Stress. Troubles building in and out of my relationship with Werner. Other stuff." Ruby couldn't look her mother in the face. She was not about to tell her any details about Dom and her abortion, although she guessed that Jessie might have alluded to it already.

"How were you managing your so-called open relationship with Werner? I'll admit it's not my cup of tea. It must have been rather trying." Both women wriggled a little in their seats and glanced out the window. The final clouds had blown by and it was as if threads of gold were suspended along the lines of dampness still in the air.

"Perhaps more so for him than for me in some ways. For Werner it was all theoretical, a way of asserting his authority, but I needed to feel free and took advantage of the deal. He couldn't handle it."

Ruby's mother drained the last drops from her glass. The women stood up and embraced for a long time, then Ruby went back to her parents' room and lay down on the sofa for a nap. Such frank talks were rare between them, and exhausting. She thought of earlier days.

Claude Gauthier, Claude Léveillée, Félix Leclerc. Ruby's mother was playing the music of various chansonniers from Quebec, their haunting and mournful music filling the quiet Sunday afternoon air after brunch at the Edwards' house. Music was blending with food, food with music.

"Mommy, put on something French."

Her mom slipped a record on the stereo and sat down on the sofa with Ruby tucked neatly into her body. Her mom always smelled so good. Today she smelled of baked apples. Although Louise Edwards was not the housewifely type, she had a few tricks up her sleeve and today it was big Spy apples baked with cinnamon, brown sugar, butter and nuts. As Ruby uncurled herself after the song to look up at her mom, she saw eyes that glistened brightly as they drank in the music.

"Mommy, are you okay?" Ruby asked breathily. For she too was transported by the music, the rich voices, even though she barely understood the words.

Louise hugged her daughter. "It's just so beautiful," she murmured as she collected herself. They listened to *The Umbrellas of Cherbourg* and hugged each other knowingly as the songs reached their denouement.

"Mommy, is he leaving her?"

"Yes, he's going to war."

Ruby picked out bits and pieces of the lyrics.

"Mommy, Mommy. He's going to wait for her. But she can't wait for him."

"No, sweetie, he says that he will think only of her and that he knows that she will wait for him."

"Mon amour, je t'aime. Je t'aimerai jusqu'à la fin de ma vie."

Ruby smiled at the memory. She would always remember those dreamlike afternoons under the spell of *The Umbrellas of Cherbourg*.

....

Ruby told her mother she was going for a walk but instead went back to the restaurant and took a seat near the bar. She ordered a drink and took a pen and some paper out of her handbag, intending to record some of her thoughts while they were still clear. As she began scribbling notes to herself, a shadow loomed over her page. She looked up to see the waiter who had served her earlier. He handed Ruby her drink and sat down beside her. Broken English and German spilled forth. His name was Hans. They asked each other the usual questions. She felt the pressure of his hand on hers.

"*Fräulein*, we go get drink at another bar?" The restaurant was closing.

She nodded and emptied her glass, unable, as usual, to resist distraction. Unable to resist any man's interest in her. Crossing the street, Ruby turned to look up tentatively at the hotel windows behind her. Inside the new bar, the air was murky with smoke. The customers, mainly men, stared at them as they passed by. An hour later, back at the hotel, they rode the elevator to the top floor and stepped out, arm in arm. Hans unlocked the door to the restaurant and fumbled with a boom box behind the bar. Ruby's body jerked as Europop bounced off the walls and lights flooded the room, hurling throbbing streaks of red, blue and green around her head. Hans grabbed her hand and pulled her across the floor. She moved reluctantly at first, pushing the sounds away. Slowly she let go. They began circling each other. Ruby was losing herself to the music, but kept breaking the grip of his arms trying to direct her on the floor. The circles grew tighter and tighter, her body feeling freer, more fluid, more giving.

Ruby was downstairs in full regalia, standing in front of a crowd of her parents' friends. "Okay, Ruby, sing it!" yelled her dad, and the room became quiet.

With eyes closed, she listened to Louis blow his magic horn. Sweet, sweet horn. She stepped into the middle of the living room, puckered her mouth and started to growl, "Well, hello, Dolly . . ."

The grown-ups broke out into hoots and howls. When she finished singing, she took a deep bow and then ran over and dove into her father's lap. She buried her flushed cheeks into his chest. The world spun around her as she heard the people clapping. Her father hugged her with his big arms and planted a slobbery kiss on her forehead. "You were wonderful, honeybunch. You sounded just like Satchmo."

A door slammed. A tall, imposing shadow stormed over to where Ruby lay entangled with her lover.

"Get up off that floor, girl!"

A large brown hand grabbed her arm and yanked her to her feet. Hans melted swiftly into oblivion. Curse that old bear paw, she thought to herself, not yet daring to look into her father's eyes. She heard him shout: "Goddammit, there you go again!"

He pulled her into the elevator, and Ruby stared numbly at the numbers on the panel.

Back in the room, she found her mother in a distraught state. Ruby pressed her cheek into her mother's lily-white face and they hugged each other fiercely. "I tried to stop him," she whispered. "He couldn't reach you by phone at home, so went to look around the hotel for you in case you were still here."

Then she turned to her husband and said, "How dare you stalk your daughter like that. Surely it would have come to no harm. She's twenty-four years old. She has a right to have a life. What on earth were you thinking?"

Ruby decided it was time to go home. She said goodbye to her mom and ignored her father, who was standing in the doorway to the bedroom, his eyes on the floor. Ruby didn't know whether to laugh or cry. But already she envisioned sharing this story with her sister and enjoying the bittersweet mirth it would cause. She knew she would laugh, and then nod knowingly. Only Dad could pull off such a thing.

The next few days saw Ruby escorting her parents to various tourist attractions around town. Their mood was tense, and Ruby didn't speak much with her dad. On the weekend they went to the zoo and then wandered through the Tiergarten till they came upon the flea market, where Ruby wanted to look around. As the people crowded around the stalls, Ruby noticed a familiar figure a few steps ahead. She tried to turn around and shuffle her parents along another lane, but it was too late.

"Ruby, stop. Come here." Werner approached Ruby and

her parents. "I'm glad to see you again. But I must tell you your daughter has been awful to me. She refuses to even speak with me."

"Werner, you should know by now that Ruby has a mind of her own," said her mom. "There's no point trying to force her to do anything."

"Maybe we could go for coffee somewhere and talk a little more," said Werner.

Ruby turned to him to speak but her father beat her to it. "Young man, we only have a few days to spend here and I'd rather spend them with my daughter. Thank you for all you've done for her in the past. It was nice seeing you, but we have to go."

"Thanks, Dad. I really appreciated that," said Ruby.

But as the Edwards clan walked back towards downtown, Ruby realized that maybe her parents weren't so wrong after all. Ruby had come to Berlin to find herself, but instead she had lost herself in the process.

CHAPTER EIGHT

Café Babanussa

AFTER DOM'S DEATH, MEAN'S REPUTATION AS A haven for hard-drug users got it closed down quickly. Emma, Jack, Smithie and the gang needed a new place to go to. Tucked away in a far-flung corner of Moabit, yet still within walking distance of their flats, was Café Babanussa. The best falafel in town, and plenty of joints and parties that lasted till dawn. Emma persuaded Ruby to come along one Thursday night. "You'll meet the best guys in town here," she had gushed, brushing wisps of hair back from her face. "Just your type."

They met on the subway platform at Turmstrasse. Emma's long legs covered in fishnet stockings thrust out from under a miniskirt that hugged her ass, visible under the worn leather jacket. The jacket hung open, revealing a lacy corset and a gap of soft pink-white flesh between it and her skirt.

Ruby looked down at her loose-flowing pantaloons upon which black Egyptian hieroglyphics were scattered over shiny, lemon-yellow cloth. She had topped them with a black silk blouse she'd found at the flea market a few weeks earlier. The silk had lost its sheen, but Ruby was attracted to the elegance of the high collar and the small, round buttons of carved ebony that ran up the front of the blouse. It seemed to wink out at her from a heap of old clothes, and she wondered who it had belonged to.

She had spent hours getting ready, mixing and matching practically every piece of clothing she owned. She had toyed with putting on something daring, knowing the way Emma dressed, but letting her breasts hang freely underneath the silk blouse was as risqué as she would get. Still, "You're looking bloody all right, aren't ya now!" her friend had said, and this cheered her up.

Chattering aimlessly, they strolled past shops and sports bars, past snack stands that boasted bratwurst with curry ketchup, with schnapps or beer to chase down the inevitable grease, and headed into the café. A young guy was working the bar. Thin, dark dreadlocks fell around his face, and a red-and-white kaffiyeh draped his shoulders. As he argued with some men at the bar, his voice fought to compete with Dissidenten's "Sahara Elektrik" blasting from the stereo behind the bar. The men seemed impatient with him as they stood shaking their heads.

"*Ciao, bella,*" he had said to Ruby when she came in that first night. He had one of the sexiest smiles she'd ever seen. "Emma, Emma, Emma!" he called out as they drifted by. "Who's your friend?"

Ruby looked him up and down. "My name's Ruby. And you?"

"Hey, I'm the barman," he said.

"Yeah, I kinda guessed that."

He grinned. "My name's Issam. What are you drinking?"

Ruby and Emma looked at each other.

"You got enough money?"

"Yeah, I'm okay."

"*Weizenbier,*" they said in chorus.

Issam turned to get the bottles. Ruby and Emma wandered over to the back room and sat down at a small, round table. Issam brought over two tall, narrow glasses with a thick, frothy head on them and plunked them down on the table. Then he sat down with them.

"Na, Emma, *wie geht's dir*? How've you been?"

"Okay. Yourself?"

"Pretty busy. Ali should be here soon, then I'll get a break."

"Ali owns the place," Emma informed Ruby.

"You'll meet him soon. He always comes around to talk to everybody."

"Where are you from, anyway?" Issam asked Ruby.

"Canada," she replied matter-of-factly.

Issam eyeballed her and said, "*Echt?* Really? How come you speak such good German?"

"You think Canadians only speak English?"

"Well, yeah. English and French, I guess."

"Well, you're wrong." Ruby looked at his wide-open eyes

and relented. "I've been here for two years now, and I lived with a German guy for a while."

"That'll do it. Well, if you stick around long enough, you can catch some late-night fun here."

Ruby looked at Emma, her eyebrow raised.

"Yeah," Emma said. "Sometimes they lock the doors around two or three, bring out the joints, and everybody who's left in the place gets pretty tight."

Ruby didn't smoke much dope but was thinking that a puff might not be so bad. Blow those thoughts of Werner to kingdom come.

Issam stood up and excused himself. A couple of customers had been trying to catch his attention. "Gotta get back to the bar. See ya."

Ruby's gaze followed his lithe form as he left the room, and then she looked at Emma. "He seems nice enough."

Emma laughed and said, "Watch out for Issam!"

"Oh, piss off, would ya!" Ruby snapped. "I'm supposed to be enjoying myself, aren't I?"

Within a short time, the café had filled up. Ruby glanced around and noted that there were a lot of Africans milling around. "Do you know any of these people?" she asked Emma.

"A couple. A lot of the guys are from Ghana, Sudan and Ethiopia. Plus the whole Turkish and Arabic crowd. And the Germans, of course. Then there's us lot of strays from everywhere else. Makes for a good mix."

"I'll say," agreed Ruby.

Two German guys had just finished a raucous rendition

of part of Brecht's *Threepenny Opera* at the piano, and people were still clapping their hands and laughing when the sounds of Om Kalthoum came over the speakers in the front. The voice of Egypt's famous songstress flooded the room, and for a moment the café seemed almost quiet. Ruby wiggled her shoulders and grinned mischievously at Emma and Lina, who had just joined them at their table. Ruby stood up and beckoned to them, saying, "Hey, it's time to practise those new moves."

Ruby was thoroughly pissed and stoned. Emma shook her head, but Lina got up to follow Ruby to the front room. The two of them had been taking belly-dancing lessons on Friday afternoons for a month or two. Ali and Issam were busy handing plates of falafel over the counter, doling out cups of coffee and selling booze.

Ruby stood still for a moment, eyes closed, waiting to tune in to the rhythms at the right moment. Slowly she began to swivel her hips, marking wide figure-eights in the air around her. As she worked her body into the momentum of the music, she added a little shimmy, shaking her ass quickly while her hips still swirled in slow circles. She kept her eyes closed; if she opened them too soon, she felt she might get shaken by the burning gazes of the men watching her and lose control. She heard Issam whooping from behind the counter and opened her eyes; she saw Lina sensuously twisting her svelte arms and wrists in different directions, drawing hands up over her face and out, as if to unveil it.

Issam whipped his kaffiyeh over the counter to Ruby,

who caught it and pulled it tightly between her two hands. She slipped her right foot in front of her left, heel up off the ground, leaned backwards and began shimmying her whole body very quickly from side to side. Issam had now jumped from behind the counter to join the two women, gyrating up to both of them in turn while the others in the room clapped them on. When the song was over, the three of them fell into each other's arms, laughing and panting.

Two hours later Ruby and Issam stumbled out into the grey light of the early autumn morning, leaving only Ali and a few desperate hangers-on to close up the place. Ruby wanted to trace with her fingers the capacious smile that brightened Issam's face. She was taken by his funky, artsy look and she loved the air of light that he had about him. She was aching to be with a black man again and wondered what would develop out of this encounter.

They headed towards the all-night bus stop down the road and hopped onto a bus packed with late-night partiers. At each stop, more people pushed their way onto the steps leading up to the second deck when there was no more sitting or standing space below. The bus driver drove carelessly, seeming as drunk as the passengers. At each turn, Ruby and Issam careened into each other with the swaying of the bus.

Half an hour later, they hurried down the street towards Ruby's flat, with only the footsteps of a few people starting off to work disturbing the stillness of the morning. Every few steps they stopped, enveloping each other, exploring each other's mouths, slowly mimicking the whirling dance of a few hours earlier, crushed so close that they could inhale the scent of the sex billowing up between them.

They stayed in bed for three days. Each morning, Ruby called in sick, going out only to buy börek and kebabs. They sat naked on the floor and ate greedily, licking crumbs from the other's chins, Ruby giggling wildly, slapping frantically at Issam's hand as his fingers roamed deep inside her. Their sex was heady, fogged up by the endless joints they smoked before and after. He liked to make love side by side; he would let his hands wash over her body, describing colour and shapes as he savoured the silky skin beneath his fingers.

"You are my canvas," he would whisper.

When they weren't making love, he talked of how men had to discover the female within them, of how he wanted to express this in his painting, for that was what he did when he wasn't working at Babanussa.

They continued to see each other regularly. In the following months their best times were spent dancing late at night at Satchmo's, a discotheque across the street from Babanussa. There the dance floor became their playground, where they twirled and teased, dancing to the sounds of Miriam Makeba and Nina Simone, oblivious to the people around them. When they were too enervated to dance any longer, they would slink back to Babanussa and sip coffee, talking to Ali until their bodies begged for the sweet release that only sex and sleep would bring.

Ruby became a regular at Babanussa, ducking into the kitchen to watch how Ali used a couscousière and made ful and falafel. For each plate of ful, they would mash cooked fava beans with garlic, onion, tahini and olive oil, adding cumin, coriander, cardamom and lemon juice to taste. The beans would be spread out on a plate and then topped with finely chopped tomato, feta cheese and parsley and drizzled with more oil. It was served with Turkish bread, much thicker than a pita. They would rip off pieces of bread and dip it into the ful. It was simple but sublime. The cooked chickpeas that they used to make falafel were ground up in a meat grinder along with onions, garlic and lots of parsley. Then Ali added cumin, baking soda and an egg before frying them. They were never too oily—crunchy on the outside, soft and flavourful on the inside. He made a sauce with yogurt, tahini and lemon juice to serve on top. One thing was for sure: you would never go hungry at Babanussa.

Issam's voice rang out from her phone almost every day, wanting to do things and go places. But Ruby liked having time on her own and with her friends, without a man around, and Issam let her breathe in and breathe out. He let her move where she wanted, when she wanted, catching her only when she was ready to return. They took in movies at the repertory cinemas as often as they could. He talked to her about the greats of African cinema, taught her about people she had never heard of before. She had never been this comfortable with a man.

Then one day he told her that he was married. "I have a German wife but we don't live together anymore. Most importantly, I have a son, Magdi."

Ruby was floored. "What do you mean, you're *married*? Where is she? How long have you been apart?"

Issam explained that they had met in Portugal and had come to Berlin to get married four years ago. His son was three and a half years old. He said they just didn't get along anymore, that he couldn't stand living with her and so he left.

Ruby was not impressed. "You mean you left her alone with your child? Where is he? Where are they?"

He said that they were in Berlin, and that he visited his son frequently. "In fact, I'd like to know if I can bring him to your place sometime soon. Maybe he could stay there with us for a while. What do you think?"

Ruby stuttered her agreement, but in truth she didn't like the questions that were beginning to surge. She felt caught in turmoil, because she knew she was falling in love with Issam. She wondered at her reaction, and this new-found love of hers gave her a little more understanding of Werner and his misgivings.

Issam would often play tricks on her at night, constructing grotesque creatures out of brooms, hats and pillows that would leer out of a corner of the darkened bathroom, forcing her to shriek when she went in to wash off the sticky milk that still clung to her thighs hours after their lovemaking. Late at night when there were no more games to play, no more stories to tell, no more smiles spreading over the horizon that was his face, she watched him secretly. She recognized the weariness that spilled out of him. She lay listening to this wind breathe its tired barcarole over her bones, calling to her.

....

Ruby and Issam raced each other from the subway to Café Babanussa. Laughing and out of breath, they flung open the doors and stepped into what had become a little corner of Africa for Ruby. They were hungry and ready to order lunch. It wasn't often that they found themselves there midday, and the place was almost empty. Ali was behind the counter, wisps of grey hair framing his face. On the other side sat a man on a stool. Plump, with trousers that were slightly frayed at the bottom and a plain, beige cardigan, he looked to be in his mid-fifties. Listening to his accent, Ruby thought he might be South African, but was unsure. He stopped talking and took his fill of her, his muddy brown eyes gazing up and down. Issam went to the counter to order some falafel, and Ruby sat down at a nearby table. She didn't like eating sitting on a stool.

Ali introduced Issam and Ruby to his friend. "This is Winston, Winston Mbeki, an old friend. We studied together in Moscow."

Winston looked point-blank at Ruby and asked, "Eh, where are you from?"

Ruby gave her usual perfunctory reply.

"Miss, if you don't mind, tell me what you are." His voice had taken on a harsh tone, and his once full lips were tightened into a tenuous smile.

"What—what do you mean?" asked Ruby.

"Exactly what I said. What are you?"

Ruby glanced around for help and squirmed in her seat. "I'm Black," she stammered. "Well, my father's Black and my mother's white."

"I didn't ask you about your parents. This is the problem with people like you. Diluting the race and then not admitting to your own colour."

"I said I'm Black. What do you mean, diluting the race?"

"People like you, mixed-race babies, turning the world into an unfortunate shade of grey. What do you know about blackness, really?"

Ruby chewed her lip in sullen silence. "I was raised by a Black parent, one who taught me to be aware of my forebears and their contributions. I am surrounded by Black people here most of the time, my boyfriend is African and I will eventually choose to have a Black child. And my skin colour doesn't make me any less Black. That's the external stuff, but that's gonna have to be good enough for you."

"A Black child, eh? That would make you feel better, I guess."

Ruby wanted to smack the sarcasm right off his lips. "My child will never have to suffer such an inane line of questions from the likes of you. Nobody will ask 'What is she?'"

"Ah, so you are choosing allegiances. Black over white . . ."

"Yes, I am."

Ali interrupted. "Enough. Ruby, you should know that in Sudan we are many, many different colours. Babanussa is a town in the heart of Sudan, and if you came to visit me there, as I hope you will one day, people would accept you as their sister just as you are."

Issam added, "Don't listen to Winston. You know every-body here sees you as Black and as one of the crowd."

KAREN HILL

Ruby was murmuring to herself, "I am Black, I am Black, I'm Black." She felt grateful for having been accepted into the club. The feeling of belonging to one race, as opposed to none, empowered her.

Soon Issam started begging Ruby to let him move in. He was roaming, staying with different friends night after night, and he couldn't see why they couldn't just live together. Ruby was scared.

She called Emma the next day to sound her out. "Issam wants to move in with me. I don't know what to do. I'm not used to sharing my space with someone. What do you think?"

"I think you practically live together already. Seriously, he's a sweet guy. He's really good with people at the café. He's got a job and he's an artist. What more could you want? What are you afraid of?"

"Well, it's pretty soon after the debacle with Werner. Even we didn't really live together most of the time. That saved me, too—having my own place. Where would I have gone, otherwise? So I wonder, what if it doesn't work out?"

"You can't always be wondering 'what if?' I know you really care for him a lot. You two fit together well. Go for it."

Later that day Ruby sat talking with Issam.

"Ruby, I'm not asking you to marry me. You won't have to worry about me—I cook, I clean, I look after myself. You know I have my friends, you have yours. We won't be together all the time."

Ruby looked at his sunny, smiling face and melted. She felt nervous about the situation, but he was a very easygoing man, and that might make it easier to get along on a daily basis. She cared so much for him that she couldn't turn him down. She'd have to trust that it would work out.

Issam was busy cooking in Ruby's kitchen with two Sudanese friends. They had the door closed and were singing loudly to some music on the cassette deck. But the singing was broken up by Issam's constant coughing. His son, Magdi, came tearing out of the bedroom at the far end of the apartment.

"Daddy, are you okay?"

"Just fine, son, just fine."

Their meal was quieter than usual that night, even though this was Magdi's first visit. She enjoyed seeing him running and exploring the apartment, but she wasn't sure if she'd feel the same way after a few days. Ruby was beginning to worry about Issam's health. He had been coughing a lot and seemed worn down. But he, in his usual way, tried to make light of everything. They sat in a circle on the floor, with several plates resting on the newspapers scattered before them. Dipping pieces of crusty white flatbread into the spicy-hot shatta and then alternately into the bean, meat and salad dishes, they talked about friends, about Babanussa.

Ruby couldn't look up from her plate, except to glare at Issam when he fussed at Magdi for the third time to eat his dinner. She carried the empty dishes back down the hall to the kitchen. She stacked them on the small counter, looked at the sink, sighed and returned to the living room. Issam said good-bye to their other friends and went off to bed with Magdi. Ruby followed an hour later.

Ruby undressed quickly and threw on an old T-shirt that had been slung carelessly over the back of a wooden chair. She went over to feel the tiles of the oven that reached to the ceiling, a rectangular ceramic tower. They were hot now. She grabbed the iron rod that was leaning up against the oven and bent down to scrape the ashes and clear the grid to let air pass to the hot coals that lay on it. The coals were glowing brightly, so she shut the larger of the two small iron doors, turning the knob tightly. She pulled over a metal pail that was already half filled with orange-coloured ash. Using a small shovel, she lifted ash and hot embers carefully into the pail, so as not to send the filthy dust flying into her face. She replaced the lid, screwed the bottom door shut and stood up fully, smoothing her hands out over her T-shirt to wipe off any dust.

Issam was lying next to Magdi on one of the mattresses that lay on the floor. Ruby bent down and picked up Magdi and carried him over to the other mattress a few metres away and covered him up. As Ruby crawled into bed, Issam rolled over towards her. The cat poked its head out from some corner, waiting impatiently for its nightly round of games with Ruby. Issam shooed it away. Then he started coughing. He couldn't seem to stop himself, and as he pulled his hand away from his mouth Ruby could see that there was blood on his hand.

"Issam, you're coughing up blood. You need to see a doctor right away!"

"Yes, I know. I don't think it's serious. Maybe I tore something in my throat."

"No, I insist. You must see a doctor this week. Promise me you will."

Issam nodded and then said, "Come here." Then, pulling the T-shirt up over her head, he said, "Let's take this thing off." Her large breasts flopped lazily on top of each other as she lay on her side, facing him. Issam pulled at her nipples for a moment and then kissed her neck, her ears and her cheek. Then he pulled away and cupped her chin in his hand. Shaking his head, he said "No, don't cry. I'm okay."

But through the night his cough worsened. Ruby felt his forehead and he was steaming hot. She spent the next hour or so carefully wrapping cold, damp towels around his calves to help bring down his fever. After a long while he dozed off. She stared at the ceiling for half an hour before falling asleep, wondering what could be wrong.

In the morning, when she got up to leave for work, Issam, half-asleep, was stretched out on their bed, arms folded over his face. Saffron threads of light squeezed through the slats in the blinds and zigzagged across his dusky body.

All day long at the institute typing letters, filing papers, deflecting her boss's assuming leer, doing the shitty secretarial work that her friends thought was a pretty good job for a Black chick from America, all bloody day long Ruby had worried about Issam.

She hadn't seen him for two days, not since he had been coughing up blood that night at her apartment. She recalled the image of him curled up with his son on the bed in her back room and how hot and dry his skin had been in the night. The next morning he had still been asleep when she rolled off the mattress and knelt on the floor. Magdi's tiny hand lay splayed across his father's dreadlocks, like a spider web on the white sheet. He had crawled back into the bed with them. Ruby was learning to like the kid and wished he would come to visit them more often. She had covered Issam and the boy with a cotton duvet. Later that day she got a call from their friend Ali that Issam had been admitted to hospital. The doctors said it was tuberculosis.

The insistent whir of the electronic typewriter interrupted her reverie. It was past five. Ruby made a quick call to Emma to let her know what was going on and then tidied up her desk and threw on her jacket, hastily pushing knobs of braided black ribbon through frayed buttonholes. She hurried out of the office down winding, carpeted stairs. She waved to the security guard and left the grey maze where for three days of the week she was only "Fräulein Edwards." She stopped at a corner snack stand to buy two doner kebabs before boarding the U-Bahn. Fifteen minutes later, the subway barrelled into Kurfürstendamm station. She took the stairs two at a time and caught a bus that wound through an endless circuit of downtown traffic, then along wide open avenues bursting with cafés until it reached the edge of the city. Staring wearily out the window, she watched as the tall, gracious buildings of Charlottenburg gave way to tiny houses.

Before she had known Issam, she would never have thought that two bodies could stay so entangled for the whole night, for nights on end. She had been pleased, almost proud, to find this African man with whom to spend her days and nights. Someone who understood why she loved and hated Berlin. Bombed-out shells of once glorious buildings crumbling on the edge of lush, ligneous parks; bicycles flowing past in an unbroken stream; young people playing out their politics riotously on the streets and partying all night with an urgency she had never known; bent, archaic women hissing at children who put their feet on vinyl subway seats; bimonthly visits to the Ausländerpolizei, "the police for foreigners," who scrutinized their lives with hawklike intensity.

Decrepit yet exquisite, anarchistic and fascist, the city had intoxicated her for years. She was just twenty-one when she arrived in Berlin. Now twenty-four, she had drifted in and out of relationships with men, searching for something. Men who loved the exotic but not-too-dark tint of her skin, the frizzy wave of her hair. Men who sucked at her sweetness like a candy apple and spit out the core. The last one had been long. Too long. She craved the vibrant feel of blackness around her again. Issam's soft-spoken assuredness soothed her, anchored her. He understood.

Ruby passed through wrought-iron gates onto the sprawling hospital grounds and walked down a winding path flanked

by chestnut trees in pink bloom. Midway down the path was a
bench, its paint flaked off to reveal slats of cracked wood. She
sat down, still clutching the soggy bag of doner kebabs, still
smelling of garlic, tomato and lamb. She couldn't bring herself to eat one, so she crumpled the bag and tossed it into the
garbage can next to the bench. To her right the grounds sloped
down to the edge of the lake. She contemplated the water's
jade veneer and the dull, grey concrete jutting out from the
far shore. She wondered how many people had tried to escape
over the Wall from that point and remembered hearing how
mines had been laid out on the floor of the lake. Flinching at
the thought, she stood up and followed the path to the front
doors of the hospital.

Inside, old men sat around the corridors in wheelchairs.
Others were clustered around a door at the far end of the hall,
smoking. Ruby felt the eyes of nurses on her back as she passed
the reception desk. In Room 19, she found Issam lying on a
bed. She sucked her breath in sharply. Tubes sticking out of his
chest drained yellowish fluid into a metal pan. Bags filled with
clear liquid hung from poles, and another tube was jabbed
into his arm. Fighting the urge to turn and leave, she sat down
at his side and kissed his cheek. She nestled her head between
his chin and shoulder.

His eyes were barely open but he touched her cheek and
whispered, "I missed you." He reached for her hand and held
it for a moment. Then, gently, he pulled it under the sheets,
moving it with slow, rhythmic strokes around the hollow of
his stomach. He was wheezing.

Her hand kept tracing slow circles round and round and she could feel a tingling spread up from her thighs. As she watched her hand draw circles, her head began to spin. She wanted to tell him she loved him, but the words refused to come. Instead, she slid her head just below his chest and rested it there, watching his stomach rise and fall with his breath. She could feel Issam's fingers running through her hair, down over the nape of her neck. She wondered about Magdi, if he was safe and whether both of them should be tested for TB. Nobody had said anything to her upon entering the hospital. Nobody had asked Issam about his close friends and partners. Again, she wondered if this lackadaisical attitude was part of the racism and xenophobia expressed towards foreigners. They were just left to stew there. She would call her doctor.

A tall and lanky woman, blond hair strewn about her sunken, anger-worn features, strode into the room. Ruby arched up off the bed and pushed her body into the back of her chair. Like an inflamed Valkyrie, the woman seized the metal frame of the bed. "So this is where you are. Serves you right," she said. "Is this who you're fucking now?"

Issam pulled the bedsheets up around him. "Hello, Ute. How are you?" he asked calmly. "How's Magdi? Where is he?"

God, it was his wife. Why now?

"I can't believe this. I come in here and find you with her and all you have to say is 'How's Magdi?' They wouldn't fucking let me bring him in, that's how he is. And he has to get tested for TB. Because of you."

Ruby winced as she realized that Issam had given his son

back to Ute before he was admitted. Ute turned her piercing eyes on Ruby; she seemed so sure of herself. Ruby squirmed in her chair and looked away. Ute sat down at the foot of the bed and turned to Issam again. She tried to make him uncomfortable with her presence, but he closed his eyes, shutting her out. She picked up a magazine and let the pages rush through her fingers. Suddenly the sound of ripping paper broke the air. Ute stood up and let the pieces of shredded magazine sift through her fingers to the floor.

"This is what I hope happens to you," she jeered at Ruby. "You're fucking with my man. Do you think he will stay with you? You? Sleazing around like everyone else in this town? Don't count on it."

Ruby grabbed Issam's hand. He squeezed her fingers gently as Ruby spat back, "You two-faced bitch. You're so fucked up! You've already hooked up with someone else. What else do you want?"

Ute measured her words through clenched teeth. "Get her out of here or you will never see your son again. Get her out."

Issam slammed a fist down on his bed, jostling the intravenous tubes. His eyes pleaded with Ruby to understand, but she was too unsure of her place in this crazy triangle. She felt terrorized by this woman whose eyes burned holes through her head. In that moment Ruby was flooded with a hatred for all Germans, for the power they wielded over her life. The swell of wet salt stung her eyes.

Ute rattled the bedrail again. "Do something about her!" she commanded.

Issam sighed. He turned to Ruby and whispered, "Think of Magdi. Go. You must go."

Ruby's body sagged. Slowly she stood up from the chair, leaning on the back as her legs began to tremble. She took a step towards the door, then paused to look back at Issam. Her thoughts flashed back to the day she first saw his face in Café Babanussa. Smooth, dark skin flushed against high, sculpted cheekbones, Asiatic eyes. They had reached out to her, sparkling with laughter and mischief. Now they were faded, expressionless.

She faced Ute angrily. "You can't touch what we have. You don't come near it."

She turned back at the door to gesture to Issam that she would call. He nodded slightly.

Outside, Ruby shivered while waiting for the bus. Her head pounded from the strain of holding back tears, from the voices raging inside. An hour later, she stepped off the bus and hurried past the bodies huddled together in the shadowy entrance to the Zoologischer Garten subway station. An old man tried to block her way and hissed, *"Raus, geh heim."* *Get out of here, go back where you came from*. She stumbled as she ran down the steps to the subway platform. A ragged body lay in a pool of vomit at the foot of the stairs.

"Einsteigen bitte. Einsteigen," bellowed the conductor. The subway doors slammed shut behind her. Ruby shuddered and leaned up against them.

Inside Café Babanussa the high-pitched wails of an Egyptian singer cascaded from the tape deck, casting a haze over Ruby as she made her way through the crowd, clasping hands, hugging friends. African, Arabic, English and Turkish words mixed in with the music and the din of the kitchen to form a swirl of noise around her. She could hear a voice booming over in the corner. She followed its rich tenor. Standing in a corner, head tilted down, one of the regular musicians, Joe, was running his fingers over the strings of his bass. His American blackspeak—jazzy, lyrical and fifties hip—charmed the people around him into a place and time they had only dreamed about. He looked up and called out, "Hey sis," as Ruby wove past him. The silky, syncopated sound of his voice, his bass, bathed her with their familiar soulfulness. She smiled and sank into a chair. She was home.

Ali was working the bar tonight. He came over and took her hands in his, his eyes searching her face. The flecks of grey she met in his eyes almost matched the silvery wire of his hair and beard. "Ruby, how are you? Come, have a coffee. Would you like something with it? It's on the house."

She asked for brandy and went over to the bar with him. He stood behind the counter, taking orders, chatting with people, pouring drinks. Someone was passing a joint around.

"How is he?" Ali asked gently when he had a moment.

Several heads turned her way, waiting for her answer. She took a sip of the steaming black liquid before her, swallowed, and said, "Not good. I didn't stay long. Ute showed up."

Faces looked at each other knowingly.

Ruby moved wordlessly away from the bar with her brandy and sat down at a table where some Sudanese friends were playing backgammon. They ordered food for the table and invited her to eat with them. Fingers grazed deftly together in the large platter of falafel, beans, tomatoes, tahini and crusty Turkish flatbread. More people joined their table. She got high. She laughed a lot and drank a lot. She cried on the shoulder of a stranger, a geologist on his way to Costa Rica. He wanted her to go home with him. She considered it, but decided to stay in Café Babanussa among her friends.

When Ruby went home the next day, she doggedly climbed the five flights to her flat, a haze of stale dope and booze still swirling about her head. In front of her door lay a wilting bouquet of red roses—exactly thirteen. The leaves were starting to crinkle and the petals had taken on the hue of dried blood. A note, written in perfect block letters, stated clearly: "Please come see me!"

CHAPTER NINE

Abena

RUBY FIRST SAW HER ON THE DANCE FLOOR AT
Satchmo's. Tall and slender, with hair woven in tight, narrow
braids that spread across the top of her scalp and spilled down
over her shoulders. As the hi-life music hummed brightly in
the background, she flung her arms, adorned with tinkling
African bracelets, to her sides just so, legs spinning out and
around from underneath. She definitely had her moves down.
Issam whispered to Ruby, "That's Abena. Isn't she gorgeous?
I'll introduce you."

Ruby was glad that Issam knew so many people from
working at Babanussa. It was a great way to meet people. But
she was still worried about him. He had taken just under six
months to recover in hospital, and now that he was finally
home he had had to hire a lawyer to try to get a divorce without losing his right to stay in the country.

As they approached Abena, she smiled. Issam introduced
her to Ruby.

"Are you new here?" asked Abena.

"Nope, been here about four years now."

"Why haven't I seen you around before?"

Ruby laughed. "Well, we must be just missing each other all the time."

"Let's put an end to that. Come on and dance with me. The music's great tonight."

Issam took off to search for friends while the two women hit the dance floor. As the music heated up, they stopped trying to yell questions at each other and heeded their own rhythms and the beat of the music. They teasingly gravitated towards each other, then sidled and swayed around each other, coming to meet in the middle once again, arms reaching out. Ruby was thrilled to be out dancing again, and it showed in her springing, carefree manner.

At one point, Abena stumbled. Ruby grabbed her arm, preventing her from falling. The music changed to something slower and the two women made their way slowly to the bar stools.

"Are you all right?" Ruby asked Abena.

"Oh absolutely, I'm fine. I guess I must have two left feet tonight," Abena answered. She leaned in to Ruby and said, "Actually, I seem to be having problems with my balance lately. Gotta get that checked out, I guess. I live in Schöneberg. You should come by sometime and I'll show you around."

Ruby knew that Schöneberg was a beautiful part of town, full of cafés and shops and restaurants.

"I'd love to. Let's make a plan."

Two days later, Ruby found herself wandering through

Schöneberg, looking at the beautiful gardens peeking up out of the spring earth, yearning to see some such colour on her own working-class street. Abena's building had a paternoster elevator. This was the kind that moved constantly up and down and where you crossed your heart and said a prayer every time you jumped on, hoping not to fall between floors. She lurched out onto the fifth floor and knocked at Abena's door. Abena answered the door in full African regalia.

"Wow, you look beautiful. So early in the morning, too!"

"Yeah, I like to do myself up and prance around town and get all the folks gawking. It's so rare to see people wearing African clothes here."

"I know. It's not very diverse that way here."

Ruby looked down at her grey sweater, charcoal pants and black lace-up granny boots and smiled. "No competition here."

Abena ushered her into a sunny living room that had a bright orange hammock stretched from wall to wall.

"So where are you from, Ruby? The States?"

"You're pretty close—Toronto."

"Ah, the north lands. Haven't been there yet. Come sit down and I'll bring out coffee and food."

Ruby stayed standing while Abena stepped into the kitchen. She surveyed the small room and was immediately taken in by the sunlight dancing off the millions of particles of sand that filled the ledges in between window panes, and all the sea creatures and shells she found on it.

Abena came back with a tray full of cheese and bread, jam

and boiled eggs and sausage and caught her fumbling with a seahorse.

"Aha! You've found my little treasures. Wherever I go in the world I collect sand and shells and such. This sand comes from South Africa, Kenya and Cuba, as do the shells."

"You've travelled a lot, then."

"Yes, I try," she mumbled as she put the tray down. "Now tell me about yourself."

In between mouthfuls, Ruby explained how she had chosen to come to Germany, and Abena leaned in and burst out in a fit of appreciative laughter. She told her about Werner and her early years here and that during that time she had been out of step with whatever Black community there was in Berlin, but that she was setting that straight now. She explained that she was living with Issam and hung out frequently at Café Babanussa, where she had friends from around the world. Then Ruby said, "What about you?"

Abena closed her eyes. "You know, my childhood sucked. But I really don't want to talk about it right now. I'll tell you about my life as it is now. I'm a dancer, but I'm getting ready to take off for Ghana in a month. I have a friend, a lover, who's from there, so we're going down together and he's going to show me around."

The women cleared the dishes from the table and carried things into the kitchen. Then Abena said, "And now, we are going out. Just follow me."

The women flew down the five flights, their feet clattering loudly. Once outside, they linked arms and strolled jauntily along, heading towards what Ruby could only guess was the subway. More clattering down steps and then finally they were on the platform. Fifteen minutes later, they rolled into Charlottenburg, where Ruby could see the striking grounds of the Charlottenburg Palace straight ahead of her. Ah, hospital days—these were her former stomping grounds. Ruby wondered whatever had happened to Irina and Frau Jungblut.

She had no idea where they were going. They turned down a quiet little street with rather plain buildings, and Abena pulled her into one very quickly.

"We're here!" she said.

Abena rang a buzzer on the main floor and a rail-thin woman with long braids opened the door, blinked and then smiled broadly. "Abena. Hallo!" she said in a thick West African accent. "I see you have brought me another customer. Who is this?"

"Ruby, this is Mouna. She's a great friend—and she does hair! She's the best braider in town!"

Mouna reached out and first tousled Ruby's hair and then felt it carefully, lifting her curls and then letting them fall back in place. "Ach! Girl, I don't know if I can do anything with this. It's too soft and fine."

Ruby smiled at the irony of having an African critique her locks. Considered "good" hair by Blacks in North America, her hair had garnered many oohs and aahs over the years. Ruby never quite understood all the attention because she had always wanted to have the lovely kinky hair that others so often seemed to shun.

Abena laughed. "Now, now, Mouna. You can work wonders with all kinds of hair. I've seen you work with Germans."

Ruby watched Mouna's face as she harrumphed and then
turned back into her flat. Several ragged scars etched themselves across the height of both cheekbones. "Come in, come
in. But don't take your things off, we're going down to the
corner bar to get beer."

Ruby was used to almost everybody drinking beer at all
times of the day in Berlin, so this came as no big surprise.
Still, she didn't relish the thought of stepping into the local
sports bar to pick up a case of the stuff. Mouna was ready in a
minute and the three of them stepped out into the crisp spring
air and walked down to the corner. Outside the bar it reeked
of piss, while inside the air was stale and smoky. Several men
were hunched over at tables scattered throughout the room
and two short, husky guys stood at the bar.

Abena had on a lovely African dress that hung down
below her knees under a lightweight jacket, and Ruby was
dressed comfortably but managed to look sharp nonetheless.
The women made a grand entry, and Mouna marched boister-
ously up to the counter.

"Hah, they know me in here. Hallo, you! I want beer,
please. Twenty Pilsner to take with us."

The bartender headed to the back to get a carton of beer.
The pasty-faced men standing at the bar stood gawking at the
three black women as if they were from outer space. Ruby
started to stir, feeling uncomfortable under their unrelenting
gaze.

"You all don't drink beer, you drink coconut wine or something like that," one of them finally snorted.

Abena turned slowly to face them head on. "What do you mean, 'you all'? Who are you to talk to us like that? Do you think I'm not German? I'm as German as you."

A chair screeched behind them as one of the men from the tables stood up. "Not looking like that, you aren't!" he shouted. "Get the hell out of here."

Ruby tugged urgently at Abena's arm. "It's not worth the fight," she said. "You're not gonna change any minds here. Let's get the hell out of here. Now!"

But Abena and Mouna didn't move an inch. The air hung like a sullen gauze about them as the bartender banged the carton of beer on the counter, breaking what seemed like an interminable silence.

Ruby swallowed and then swirled and glared at the men standing around her. "I'm outta here!"

Her two friends reluctantly followed, both of them exclaiming shrilly, "You can't fucking tell me where to go" as they stepped out into the bright afternoon sunlight.

Mouna looked dourly at Ruby. "What's wrong with you? Have you no courage? You have to stand up for yourself in this country."

Ruby stuttered, "I've been in this kind of place more than a few times in this city. I don't care for the same old battles anymore. Not with these types."

Mouna shook her head, her leonine tresses flying. Then she took her kaleidoscopic cloth scarf off her head and folded it in half. She bent her sylphlike body forward towards the pavement, picked up the carton of beer and balanced it deftly on her head. She thrust her hips forward and proceeded to walk with a rhythmic sway back down the street to her flat. Ruby was in awe of her stature and her perfect sense of motion.

Abena whispered to Ruby, "Don't be jealous. She's been doing that since she was a kid. And besides, she's also a dancer."

Back at the flat, they cracked open the beers and sat Ruby down on a cushion on the floor. Mouna placed herself on a chair behind her and began to part Ruby's hair into different sections and then swiftly and tightly braid together tufts of her hair with extensions from the base of the scalp. Mouna kept Ruby busy as her ebony hands glided at full tilt over her head, slapping her hand or shoulder to tell her to hold this piece of hair or these bobby pins, or that bag of hair. Ruby's forehead felt taut and her scalp stung with little darts of pain. Her eyes teared up more than once as she watched Abena, busy in the kitchen stirring up chicken stew and keeping fufu warm in another pot. Ruby had taken a peek at the fufu. She had never seen it before. It was made of ground cassava and plantain and looked like a giant dumpling. After an hour or two passed, they took a break to eat, all the while keeping up their drinking and chatting about their experiences in Berlin. Ruby felt she had to explain her inaction at the bar.

"You know, I don't believe it's my job anymore to convert all the fascists and racists running around Berlin. I've had people spit at me and Issam and call us monkeys—I always yelled back, and sometimes I spit back at them, too. But in the end it's a waste of time. There are no laws to help you out here, anyway."

Mouna argued that it was always better to say something than just stand idly by, but she forgave Ruby her transgression: "You're getting tired of it all, I can see."

Abena said, "Living my life here as a nothing, being put down all the time, even by my own parents, I know a little about racism. I prefer dual action—say something and then get the hell out. Ruby, you can't give up yet. I've got places to take you, things to do with you. Tonight, when you're all done up, I'm taking you out to meet some friends. You look great. How much longer till you're done, Mouna?"

"In another hour she'll be ready to go."

Ruby was tired of sitting and started to sigh and squirm a lot on the cushion while she waited for Mouna to finish her work.

"What's wrong with you, girl? Can't you sit still? You're acting like a child! You North American Blacks have forgotten your ways. Here, have another beer."

Ruby took Mouna's chiding in stride and pondered Abena's comments. "Abena, tell us what it was like growing up here."

Abena looked startled. She cracked open another beer and took a long swig as if trying to stall for time. "I don't usually talk too much about these things. They're better left for dead. But you two are sisters. And Ruby, I know you have gone through some rough spots, too. I think you will understand what I have to say. My mother gave me up as a baby. My father was African, from Ghana. He was here studying. She didn't want a nigger child on her hands. I guess she didn't think much about the implications ahead of time. She was young and uneducated and worked in a restaurant. She didn't know what to do with me so she gave me away. I have never met her. I never met my father either, though I have more information about him than my mother.

"I was adopted by a white German family. They thought they were doing me a favour. Throughout my life they treated me as if I wasn't clean enough. If I got a little dirty, they always said people would call me the nigger pig. Sometimes even they treated me like I was just that and scrubbed me down as if they were trying to wash off the black. They treated me like I had to be on my best behaviour every single moment of my life, because 'what would the neighbours think of the nigger child.'"

"They actually used those words?" Ruby said. "They said 'nigger' directly to your face?"

"Yes, they did. They tried to be good to me, too, of course, but always when they were angry or tired things would slip out and I'd be humiliated in front of the rest of the family, always because of my race. Even when they weren't angry, they used belittling expressions without knowing or thinking that they were wrong. They didn't know any better, but it hurt nonetheless."

"Are you in touch with them now?" Mouna inquired.

"I've seen my sister on occasion. But I recently changed both my first and last names. I took on my father's name,

Agyeman, and the name Abena means 'Tuesday's child' since I was born on a Tuesday. Anyway, my adoptive family is upset with me for changing my name. They don't understand. It's my way of acknowledging my African identity, and this was even more important since I felt so alienated from my family here.

"Then of course I was the only Black child in my school. Sometimes teachers paraded me around like I was some kind of exotic pet to be toyed with. When I did something wrong, it was always because of my race. I was always reminded of that. Everywhere I went I always felt different, like I belonged nowhere."

"Abena, you express your pain so beautifully in your dance," said Ruby. "I guess it is a brilliant way of symbolizing your anguish."

"Sometimes I think the trials I faced in childhood made me a stronger person, but I really don't know. It brought about so much sadness and confusion, too. Dancing does help a lot, but it's also about having good people around you to recreate a new family, a new system of support. I think I have that now, and that's what keeps me going."

Mouna suddenly stood up and said, "Enough sadness. I have a story to tell, too. I must show you this before you go. I am having a big fight right now." ,

She unceremoniously slipped off her top to reveal her breasts, small and firm like two lemons.

"Look what they have done to me. I had my breasts made smaller because of dancing."

She lifted up her breasts, one after the other, to reveal angry strips of swollen pus-filled skin.

"They have ruined me. The swelling is getting worse every day and the scar tissue is not healing. They know about black skin. It doesn't always heal very well because of, what do you call it—keloids! They should have known how to do a better job!"

Abena asked if she had been back to see the doctor who had performed the surgery, or if she had insurance or a lawyer. Mouna said simply that she was trying to get a lawyer to help her get them to correct it. Calm once again, Mouna sat back down to finish braiding Ruby's hair. In half an hour she was done. When Ruby asked her what she owed her, Mouna said simply: "This one's for free. I enjoyed getting to know you. You can pay me next time you come."

One day later that week, Ruby went over to Werner's place to see if he was home. Usually he didn't answer the door, but if she used his old three knocks plus two knocks, he just might open. And indeed, a minute later Werner was standing there looking like he'd seen a ghost.

"Why don't we go down the street for a coffee?" Ruby said. "I just thought we should talk."

"Did you get my roses?"

"Yes, I did. Come on out. Take a break from the books."

"Okay, hang on a sec while I get ready."

As Ruby and Werner walked down the street together an

awkward silence rose up between them. It had been six months since they'd last bumped into each other and a year since they'd split up. Ruby thought Werner looked well. Same blond hair tumbling off his head, same bright, inquisitive eyes. Werner tried to take Ruby's hand in his, but she pried her fingers free. He looked hurt, but said nothing. They were walking down to the Red Door Café, near Leopoldplatz. Ruby became absorbed in the shapes and colours of the cobblestones underneath her feet, and hummed a little song.

"Still singing, huh?" said Werner. "Remember, no Motown around me."

Ruby laughed and thought, *That's as good a reason as any not to be with you anymore*. At the café, they looked for a table for two where they could have some privacy.

When they sat down, Werner insisted on taking Ruby's hands again and looking her directly in the eyes. He said, "I miss you."

Ruby squirmed free and sat back in her chair. She looked up at the ceiling and then back down at him and said, "Werner, I don't know what to say to that anymore."

A server appeared to take their order. Ruby asked for black coffee and Sachertorte and Werner ordered coffee and a linzertorte. "Why don't you start by telling me why you left me? You meant the world to me."

Ruby scrunched her body up tight. She didn't know how or where to start. She had run through possible conversations between the two of them ahead of time, but she froze anyway.

"Come, come now. Are you saying you had no reason?"

"Werner, look. It was a confluence of things. There was so much confusion around the open-relationship issue." Her voice drifted off and she tapped the table lightly with her fingertips.

"We could have just opened it up for discussion again, to realign things. But you were stuck on having your way," said Werner.

"What are you saying? It was your idea in the first place."

"Yes, it was."

"Well?"

"You broke the rules. You became infatuated with that addict."

Ruby sighed impatiently. "That's exactly why it's not so easy. Someone's bound to break the rules. How can you say 'Go have lots of sex, just don't fall in love'? It doesn't work that way. Or it didn't for me."

"Did you still love me at that point?"

"Of course I did. With your ideas you should realize that it is possible to love two people at the same time."

"You didn't love him."

"No, but he was special to me."

"You put yourself in a very dangerous situation, and therefore me, too."

"The more you go on about how dangerous life is, the more I want to go out and play hard and fast. Besides, you're the one who threatened us with a gun."

"A toy gun."

"How were we to know? Dom could have had a weapon, too. Then where would we be?"

KAREN HILL

"Ah, yes, but he's dead now, anyway. You think you would have learned from that," said Werner. "No, but now you're with another fool, who just happens to be African."

"Learned what? That I should stay with you? What I learned is that you're a control freak and that I needed a break, to be free . . . and that just grew into something longer. And so fucking what if he's African."

"So that's it?" Werner thumped the table, his body shaking as he leaned forward. His eyes were steely and hard, and Ruby shoved herself back. The chair legs screeched on the floor and several people turned to look at them.

"I don't know if this is getting us anywhere. Werner, I really appreciate the fact that you stood by me when I was ill. You were always there for me. But I don't want a man who is going to hover over me every second of the day."

"Hover? I'm looking out for you. That's what people who love each other do. They protect one another. Why can't you accept that? You don't know anything about love."

Ruby sighed again. "You remind me too much of my father. I don't want to be married to my dad."

Werner stood up, his hands gripping the table so hard that his knuckles were turning white. "I'm leaving. I only have one final thing to say. I have a paper for you to sign saying you lay no claim to any of my belongings."

"Fine, that's easy enough."

Werner scowled at her and muttered, "This is not what I had hoped for."

Ruby said she was going to stay behind on her own and have a drink.

"A drink? I hope you're not on any meds!"

"Goodbye, Werner."

"Goodbye."

Ruby sat by herself, relieved that this conversation was over. It seemed as if Werner had finally grasped the surety with which she spoke when she said they were finished. She knew she must have been hard to live with, considering France and Dom and all. But she had no regrets.

Abena was no stranger to Café Babanussa, and Ruby soon introduced her to Emma and Lina, dragging them all out dancing in the wee hours of the morning. Similarly, Abena felt it was her duty to introduce Ruby to the small Afro-German scene in Berlin. She took her to friends' houses and off to meetings of the young Afro-German Society, where there was much talk about how they should name themselves and whether they should use the term *Afro* or *Black* in their name. Ruby was surprised to hear hesitancy expressed over using the word *Black*, but she knew to keep quiet. She was already sure she had heard people grumbling that Abena had brought an "American" to the meeting. She certainly didn't want to be seen as trying to be an expert on the subject because of where she came from.

Ruby was especially happy to have found Abena, now that Emma had announced that she would be returning to London soon. Ruby valued her relationships with women the most. Issam was a playful and fun man to be with, but it was very hard to hold a serious conversation without him changing the topic sooner rather than later.

Ruby felt that her friendship with Abena was a kind of kismet, they were so alike and so dissimilar at the same time. They could talk about Black music, Black hair, Black politics. They would spend hours in front of the mirror, choosing clothes and accessories as they got ready for a night out on the town. Abena was like a sister. One night she lay contemplating this fact, and her mind seemed more awake than usual and she felt a click in her body, a surge to a heightened awareness. From that night on, over the next weeks the adrenaline seemed to flow just a little more. Ruby felt on edge, but it was a feeling that gave her energy. Her mind was buzzing alive with thoughts of life's potential.

One day Abena approached Ruby and asked if she would attend a dance performance that she would be in. On the night of the performance, the theatre was crowded with people, some of whom Ruby had already met over the past few weeks. The performance was a modern dance piece in several acts that took a harrowing interpretation of the issues of blackness and whiteness. In watching Abena, Ruby could feel their struggle to face down the same questions: Am I Black? Am I white? What is this state of in-between? It gave her strength to know that Abena shared her history in many ways, searching to mould an identity as yet undefined.

By the beginning of the third act, Abena was looking a little pale and shaky. The next thing Ruby knew, her friend lay in a crumpled heap on the floor. The crowd was hushed at first and then everyone was rustling in their seats and many, including Ruby, rushed to the stage where Abena lay.

The next day, Ruby visited Abena in hospital. She was curled up in bed on her side, looking quiet and frail, and she didn't open her eyes when Ruby took her hand and held her long, slender brown fingers loosely in her own hand, waiting for the warmth they would bring. But Ruby felt only a brisk coolness as Abena shuddered and shook Ruby's hand off. Ruby sat down quietly beside her and settled herself in, not saying anything at all at first.

Then she whispered, "Abena, what happened?"

Abena whispered back a simple, "Ssh, I don't want to talk now. Come back another time, please."

Ruby sat for a little while nonetheless. Finally she stroked her friend's arm a few times, stood up, then lowered herself to Abena's level and spoke gently into her ear. "I'll be back soon."

Ruby went back to see Abena another two times and always got the same response. Ruby had heard in the meantime from two friends, Kwame and Mahmoud, that Abena had been diagnosed with a particularly severe form of multiple sclerosis. Finally her friend was released, and Ruby rode her bike from Wedding to Schöneberg to pay Abena a visit at home. She sailed through the streets and along canals, the rush of the air swooping in to fill the spaces around her. The ride left her giddy and pumped for her visit. Abena let her in, wearing only a long T-shirt, but turned away from her immediately and sank into her bright orange hammock in her living room. Ruby crisscrossed the room to where the sand and shells lay in between the panes of glass. She opened up the inside window and let the sand whoosh through her fingers as she said, "You're not going to Ghana after all, are you?"

Abena looked at her dully and replied, "No. Not now."

"Abena, you have to get better first. This is just a temporary phase, and you'll recover. Then you can go."

Abena just nodded her head and lay there rocking quietly back and forth on her hammock, refusing to say a word.

Over the next month Abena gradually regained some of the sunshine and warmth that used to spill out of her so easily. Ruby as well started feeling more expansive and joyful and became much more talkative than usual. Increasingly, as the weather warmed, Abena would ask to go for walks outside, and Ruby helped her, only too happy to walk off the extra energy. Eventually, Ruby asked her to go to Café Babanussa one afternoon.

"Maybe Issam will be working, or maybe Ali. Either way, they'd both be thrilled to see you."

"I'm not sure if I'm up to that kind of thing right now."

"Oh, come on. Just change your clothes, put on something funky and you'll feel better."

"I don't think so."

"Oh, for chrissake, Abena, you have to get out of here. You're gonna wither up and turn into a ghost if you don't get outside. Tell you what. I'll take you out for dinner after, just you and me, and you can tell me again all about your travels to Africa and about just how luscious that man of yours is."

Abena smiled and swung her legs slowly out of the hammock. She sat there, letting them sway side to side for another minute or so before she finally jumped out and yelped, "Okay, okay, okay. I'm coming."

As usual, the café was full of friends and acquaintances, and they spent that day and others chatting, drinking tea and soaking up the jubilant atmosphere all around them. But soon Abena's health failed again. When Ruby visited her, Abena would frequently stay in bed and would have little to say. Ruby noticed certain things: the weakness of her hands; the overall slowness of her once lithe movements; the fact that her eyes had lost their lustre and were now simply uninviting.

Her friend was less and less inclined to go out or to reach out to folks. She stayed locked in her flat while Kwame, Mahmoud and Ruby tried to revive her and get her outside. Often she wouldn't pick up the phone, and she answered the door only begrudgingly. Though she was never rude, she remained sad and aloof. She abjectly refused her friends' entreaties to seek help, returning as always to the hammock to curl up into a ball and shut out the world. At these times the air hung thick as a sulky nightfall that seemed to be always upon her no matter what time of day.

One day Issam cooked up a big pot of stew and said, "Take this to Abena. Try to get her to eat."

Ruby went by with stew in hand and sat down to talk to her friend.

"Abena, you know you're depressed. Tell me what you're

thinking about. Try to get some of it off your chest—otherwise it will drag you down."

"Ruby, I don't want to burden anyone with my worries. How can you possibly understand or help?"

"Abena, you are on a long road now, and maybe we don't know where or how things will end up. But I can tell you that I fully understand the feeling of utter paralysis that comes with depression. Everyone keeps telling you to get up and get at it, but you feel like a piece of cement. The loneliness, the quiet, the dark become perfect companions. Sleep is the best escape of all. I've been there before."

Abena sat up a little. "What caused your depression?"

"Well, I got sick. I was hospitalized for mania and psychosis, which had been caused by stress and loss. Then I was depressed for a long time when I got out. Abena, listen to me. I'm sorry, I know your journey is much harder than mine was . . ." She faltered, not knowing what to say next. "But just let us try to help you."

Abena was still. She blew Ruby a kiss and then came over to hug her. "Time to go," she said, gesturing with her hand. Once out the door, Ruby leaned against the wall and wept.

Worrying about Abena's situation, Ruby became more wakeful at night, tossing and turning and having bad dreams. She was still dreaming about the man with no face. About rape. During the days Ruby hunched her shoulders in close and had started wringing her hands. Whenever he was around, Issam would try to soothe her by getting her to sit or lie down and staying with her. But he was at a loss as to what to do with her. She became more and more nervous and was often distracted from the tasks of daily living. She put the dish towel on the back of the chair next to the table and then spent ages looking along the countertops for it. She forgot to feed the cat and then ignored its insistent mews for hours. One night she stayed up late writing in her journal. Issam begged her to come to bed. Ruby ignored him. She jotted down thoughts, wrote bits of poems and paced the floors mumbling words out loud. When she finally came to sleep she was still agitated. She woke Issam and talked to him non-stop about Abena till he finally just covered up his ears and rolled over.

The next morning when she went to do some shopping, she was constantly looking around and over her shoulder, hyperconscious of any passersby. She took in bits of their conversations, expecting that they would hold meaning for her personally. Someone would say "The sky is so blue today," and Ruby would think she was responsible for making the sky sad, that it was her fault.

She knew these were bad signs, but she could still catch herself in the act and try to stop herself. The mania might be returning, but it hadn't taken over completely. She didn't want to call her doctor, afraid that it would mean hospitalization once again. So she took up walking more than usual, knowing that she might be able to keep the mania at bay with more exercise. But soon she was becoming too paranoid to be able to relax outside. It was like a concrete jungle with noises all around that she had to heed, that spoke out to her, with people signalling things to her all the time. She was constantly aware of the colours people were wearing, always trying to make sense of their meaning. She tried to drink calming teas and take valerian root before going to bed at night. She was scared; she knew that without sleep she was doomed. She knew that the paranoia was stronger than her: it would keep hammering away at her until she succumbed and lost touch. Finally, she called her sister and told her what was happening.

"Ruby, now listen to me good. You have to go to the doctor. He can help and you won't necessarily end up in hospital."

"Jess, understand this, I am terrified of going back to the hospital, of being totally out of control and drugged up once again. I'm terrified of losing my sanity. It's slipping away every day and I have no one to hang on to. Even as I speak, Abena sits spiralling into her own personal crisis. Issam has his own health issues to deal with. And Emma—she's wonderful, but there's only so much she could do. People don't understand. But you, Jessie, maybe you . . ."

"Ruby, I don't know if I can get any time off to come over. You know I would if I could. Let me see what I can do."

Ruby told Jessie she would try to hang on and would go to the doctor.

By the next day, though, Ruby had walled herself up in her flat. Kwame and Mahmoud had called to tell her that Abena was getting worse. Ruby kept saying that maybe the angels and spirits would come save Abena. Emma called her too, offering to take her to the doctor the next morning. Ruby acquiesced. But destiny was hers and she was starting to feel she could shape it. She felt she could save herself. Issam was going out for the evening, but before leaving he had called Emma and asked if she would come over.

"She's going crazy. I have to get out of here. Please come over, Em."

Ruby heard Issam call as he walked out the door that Emma was going to drop by for a visit. She went into the kitchen and took out all the spices, herbs, teas, nuts and grains that she had on her shelves. She got some paper and began scribbling the names and properties of all these things. She shoved a handful of walnuts into her mouth, thinking they would help purge her and clean her out. Ditto with the turmeric. She mixed it with some lemon juice and water and drank it all down. She put on the kettle and got out peppermint and chamomile teas. She had some fennel honey in the cupboard and that would help calm her, too. On and on she went, mixing up spices, drinking teas, all the while scribbling notes on the paper. She knew she was spiralling and headed for trouble, but she couldn't stop herself. She was caught up with the flow of her mania, entranced by the energy. She fiercely resisted the idea of returning to a hospital. This was her way of trying to make do on her own.

The phone rang. Ruby let it ring as she carried on but it kept going on and on. She went to the bedroom to pick up the receiver and it was her father on the phone.

"Hi, Ruby, how's my Dolly doing? I was just thinking about how you used to prance around the living room floor for all the guests. Ruby, Jessie told us that you called and that you're not feeling too well."

"Emma is taking me to the doctor tomorrow," Ruby said defensively, her mouth all prickly from a cayenne powder drink. "I'm trying to get better, I'm looking after myself, I am, Dad. You should see what . . ." Ruby decided not to elaborate and began thinking of the image of being all dressed up and bellowing out "Hello, Dolly" in a growly voice. She started singing the song over the phone.

Her father laughed, but his voice had an eerie timbre to it. "Jessie's coming over to see you again, Ruby. She'll be there in three or four days. She'll call to let you know when. I hope you do go to your doctor tomorrow. Tell Emma we said thanks for looking out for you."

"Dad, I gotta go, I'm cooking in the kitchen. Bye." She hung up. She was feeling flustered and overwhelmed but went back to the kitchen. She decided to make a pot of soup. She pulled everything she could find in the refrigerator—carrots, leeks, celery, a sausage, tomatoes and corn. Out of a basket on the counter she plucked two potatoes and some onions and some garlic. She looked to a shelf on the kitchen wall and pulled down her herbal remedies book. Marjoram, thyme, oregano and rosemary—she would use them all. She began chopping the carrots. The kitchen looked like a bomb had exploded, but Ruby worked around it all. The words *Hello, Dolly, Hello, Dolly* flung themselves at her as she wielded the knife. Chop, chop, chop, chop. *Hello, Dolly, Hello, Dolly.* She picked up the onions and went faster, trying to outdo the voice in her head. She could see herself as a little girl, bouncing up and down on the floor as the words spilled out of her mouth. She could see her mom and dad, proud smiles beaming across their faces as she sang. She started on the celery and was chopping fast, fast, fast. Ouch! She had sliced the tip of her finger, and popped it in her mouth. She could taste the warmth of the blood as it trickled down her throat. She stood there lost, the words still pounding ferociously in her brain. *Hello, Dolly, Hello, Dolly.*

"You're such a pretty girl. Come here."

The words spilled out at her as she heard the voice, warm and familiar, from her past. "Come, I want to show you something."

Then she envisioned trying to twist away as the fingers that belonged to the voice pushed in and around her where they shouldn't be; she felt him grab her and hold her up against him tightly as he breathed rapidly. She felt the life drain out of her as he put his mouth on her. She felt abandoned. Where was her mother? Where was her father?

Ruby started screaming. She sat down in the middle of the kitchen floor and sobbed away. What happened, what happened? How could this be? Finally she lay down on the bed as still as she could, like a zombie. Her head was throbbing with thoughts, but she kept repeating to herself, "If I wind myself up tight, nothing can get to me here." And there she lay, her body inwardly scrunched up, impermeable.

She tried to go back in time, tried to put pieces together. The man's voice sliced into her like the knife into her finger; it ripped her wide open. And she knew the voice! She felt herself spilling out onto the floor. This was the first time this memory had come to her, and nothing made sense. So many thoughts were hurtling through her mind. She wondered if somebody had planted them in her mind, if someone, or maybe the whole world, was out to get her. She felt violated and dirty, even though she didn't know if it could be true. After all, she knew that her mind invented all kinds of situations when it went off track. Still, they were always connected to some kind of truth, weren't they?

"Ruby, where are you?" Emma's voice rang out from the hallway. "I brought us some ginger ale. Wish we could spike it with some rum." She came into Ruby's bedroom and stood at the doorway gaping. "My god, look at you—you're a mess." It's true that she hadn't changed her clothes in two days and her hair was all mussed.

Emma put down her bag. "Ruby, what's going on? Oh my, what happened to your finger?" she said. Ruby looked down at the hand. She had wrapped a thick wad of toilet paper over her cut, but it was now soaked in blood. "I cut my finger with a knife, but it's okay now."

"Let's change that and see if we can find something bet-ter," said Emma. She rummaged in one of the cupboards at the far end of the kitchen, not saying a word about the mess there. "Don't you have any bandages?"

Ruby shook her head. "I don't think so."

"Let's get some tissue and some tape, then. Here we go, let's put this on," she said as she taped several tissues over the cut. "Ruby, tell me, what's going on?"

"Oh my god, I don't know. I'm feeling so anxious, I'm overhearing conversations outside, and I'm not sleeping well. Then tonight . . ."

"What happened?" asked Emma.

"Ummm . . ." Ruby was struggling to stay present.

"Ruby, snap out of it. Talk to me."

"Well, I spoke to my dad today . . ."

"Take a deep breath and try to focus your thoughts," said Emma.

"I started getting all revved up . . . I remembered this scene out of my childhood . . . I would sing and dance in front of my parents and their friends. But it didn't stop there." Ruby paused again, not sure of how to express her thoughts. "My head was flooded with the image of being sexually abused by a man who was a friend of the family. I could hear his voice, Emma." She stopped to clear her throat and shake her head. "I was floored. It just seemed so real." She jumped up and began pulling at her hair and pacing. "I feel . . . I feel so filthy all of a sudden, but I just don't know what to do with this information or whatever it is."

"Maybe it's just a delusion."

"Yes, no, I don't know. I've been getting shakier the past few days. Maybe I *am* semi-delusional, going in and out of it. But as outrageous as the thoughts can get, they're always connected to something fundamental at the core of my being." Ruby couldn't talk anymore, imprisoned with overwhelming thoughts. She could hear voices trying to distract her from her conversation.

"Ruby! Listen to me. Get out of your head. Stay with me here. You should talk to your parents about this guy. When do you think it happened?"

"I don't know. I'm not sure."

"Have you ever had this memory before?"

"No, never." She sat there thinking for a moment. "But I have had this recurring dream about being raped . . . I always thought it was just a dream. A very creepy dream."

The women stayed up talking for a bit, with Emma trying valiantly to keep Ruby from straying into the jigsaw puzzle that was her brain. Finally she suggested that Ruby contact one of numerous women's organizations in the city to see if she could get some counselling or just a sympathetic ear. After Ruby had pulled on a T-shirt and got ready for bed, Emma went home to sleep. A few minutes later, Ruby went down the hall to lock the door, opening it first, as she had a habit of checking the hallway at night. Luna came scrambling between her legs and bolted out the door and down the steps. "Luna, no!" Ruby shrieked. The cat had never been outside before, but if someone closed the front doors of the building she could be shut out for a long, long time.

Ruby took one look down the hall and then ran out the door in her bare feet. She had to find Luna. She hoped that the front door would be locked already but there was no guarantee. She crossed the courtyard in the dark; the front doors were wide open. She ran around the courtyard calling, "Luna, Luna," but didn't see her anywhere. She took off through the front doors with no idea which way to turn. She jogged south, calling out the cat's name. Someone had undoubtedly tried to kidnap her kitty. That's it, they were going to send her up in space—Luna, the moon cat. To her she represented the night, the moon, the galaxy. Others must see it, too. Ruby stepped through the open doors of a bar and asked if anyone had seen a white and grey cat.

"Sind Sie wohl verrückt?" Are you crazy? They looked with disdain at the wild-eyed, barefoot creature standing before them. Ruby moved on. She continued huffing and puffing along another street, carried away by her thoughts, wondering what would be done to her cat. They might shoot her up in a shuttle all by herself. She stooped to look under a car or two.

Ruby saw red lights flashing. A police car was coming slowly down the road. Ruby slammed herself up against a building. The cruiser stopped in front of her and the officer rolled down the window and offered to help her. *"Können wir Ihnen helfen, meine Dame?"*

"No, I'm sorry, I'm just looking for my cat."

"Ma'am, it's barely ten degrees outside and you're running around in your bare feet. Get in the car and we'll drive you home."

Ruby didn't like the looks on their faces. They must be part of the conspiracy. They were probably going to take her away and she would never see Luna again.

"No, no, it's okay."

"Ma'am, we've had complaints about you yelling your head off throughout the neighbourhood."

It was a one-way street. The cops were facing south. Ruby took off and ran north as fast as she could. She ducked into another street and ran hard until she had made her way home. What about Luna? Once in the courtyard Ruby was out of breath and stopped to stretch. She got down on her knees in a child's pose and prayed to the gods of the earth to set her Luna free. She turned to the north, the south, then to the east, stopping to pray each time. When she came to the west she found herself facing the garbage cans. She slipped into a cat's pose and began meowing. Sure enough before long a fluffy little head poked its pink nose around the corner. "Luna," Ruby whispered, not wanting to scare her. She crawled over to the cat, who rubbed up against her as if nothing had gone wrong. Ruby picked her up and said, "Luna, you can moon-watch from the window. No more going outside for you."

Issam arrived home in the middle of the night and found Ruby sitting up in bed staring at the ceiling, which was stuccoed. The cat was resting in her lap. "The flourishes are like a circus," she told him, "the trapeze, the trampoline, and the animals all swirling around."

"Ruby, please, you need to get some sleep. Come lie down with me." He reached over to rub her head.

She pulled back. "Issam, have you been meeting with people about me? I know you have. There's a conspiracy. People want to take my cat. And they want to study my brain."

"Ruby, I wish I could say that I had met with people about you—with a bunch of psychiatrists, that is. I never much believed in them before, but you need help."

"Aha! You see, psychiatrists. They want to use my brain—study it, dissect it."

"Why, Ruby? Why would they?" Issam almost yelled at

her. "Tomorrow's another day. You'll see the doctor. I'll give your shoulders a massage. Maybe that will help you relax."

Ruby gave in and tried to enjoy the massage while she looked at the ceiling, swirling just like her mind.

Emma took her to her doctor the next morning. Ruby was tired and in no state to cope with all the people on the subway, so they took a cab. Her doctor took one look at her and said he was giving her an injection of Haldol. If she wasn't better in one week, he said, he would try to get her into hospital again. In the meantime he was going to refer her to a psychiatrist, who might have a better handle on how to manage these bouts over the long term. He suggested she stay quiet, and not go out alone anywhere until he saw her the following week. Ruby tried to bring up the issue of what she had seen and felt the day before, but the doctor gently dismissed it, saying it was likely just another one of her delusions and that there was no point in trying to analyze it further because she needed to focus on the present.

When Ruby got home, Issam saw to it that she had something to eat and then she propped herself up in bed. She was thinking about Abena when she heard a sharp rap at the door. Issam opened up and Werner pushed his way in.

"I want to see Ruby," he said.

"Ruby's not feeling too well. This is not a good time to come by."

"Don't try to stop me, you monkey," he said as he shoved past Issam and strode down the hall.

Ruby was stunned to see Werner. She rolled on her side and turned her back to him.

Werner came around to face her. "Ruby, what are you doing? What's wrong? Are you sick again?"

"Werner, not now. Go away."

"Ruby, I know how to look after you. Are you sick? Maybe you need to go to the hospital again."

Issam stepped up to Werner and said, "Listen, she's been to the doctor, she's being treated. She doesn't want you here."

Werner looked at Issam and said, "Shh. Speak when you're spoken to."

Ruby wrestled herself out of bed and stood up in front of Werner. She drew her hand back and smacked him as hard as she could across the face. "Don't you ever, *ever* talk to him like that again. Get out of here and don't come back, you little pseudo-anarchist."

Werner's eyes were doing a crazy dance of anger. He leaned in to Ruby and said, "You'll learn to regret your words."

Issam grabbed Werner's arm. "Do you want me to call the police?"

"Ha! Sure. That would be really good for you, now, wouldn't it? How about a free ticket back home? Okay, I'm going. But I'm not finished here."

Ruby yelled out to him, "I've got Issam and Emma, and my sister's coming, too. I don't need a dickwad like you."

Issam looked at her and asked, "What on earth did you see in a guy like that?"

Ruby shook her head. "I don't even know how to answer that anymore."

An hour later Ruby tried calling Abena but got no answer. She was worried about her friend. She was hoping that she had found some determination and that it would carry her through this blackness and erase the storm clouds that brewed perpetually in her eyes. But Abena had told them, "I will not waste my time mincing words with someone who doesn't even know me and who would only put me on drugs. If I can't get better with the help of my friends then I won't carry on at all."

The next morning the phone rang early. It was Kwame.

"Oh my god, oh my god, it's Abena."

"Slow down, Kwame," Ruby said. "What on earth is wrong?"

"Abena just tried to commit suicide. She sat in a bathtub full of water and slashed her wrists. We're all at the hospital now, but we don't know yet if she's going to make it."

Ruby screamed, dropping the phone, and then she fell on the floor as hot tears streamed out of her. She called out Abena's name over and over. She grabbed on to Issam's feet as he entered the room and dragged him down, and he lay there with her while she rolled back and forth, gasping for breath, wailing and moaning. They stayed that way for a long while. Even Luna came out of hiding and came by to rub up against Ruby and sniff at her face. The cat crouched on the floor next to them.

Ruby knew that she was once again wrestling with the depths of her own madness and prayed that she would not be led down the same path as Abena. She had visited similar shores in her own life and knew how hard it was to dust off the soot of darkness and come out unscathed. She did not want to judge, but only to hang on to the love that she felt for her friend.

The next day she decided to go to the hospital. She was too afraid to go alone, so Issam accompanied her. Their friend was in no mood for communication; in a drugged haze, she drifted in and out of consciousness. Ruby sat there for a while, simply holding Abena's hand and then putting a palm on her forehead. They didn't linger for too long, and Ruby planned to return in a few days when Abena would hopefully be better.

CHAPTER TEN

Riot

JESSIE ARRIVED THE NEXT DAY. IT WAS SPRING, AND she wore a lemon-yellow jacket over tight black jeans.

"Jessie? Is that you?" Ruby yelled from down the hallway, her voice fully animated. The two sisters ran into each other's arms, hugging so hard that they had to stop to catch their breath.

"Jessie, you look wonderful," Ruby said, admiring her sister's long, frizzy tresses. "You stopped cutting your hair."

"Yes, now we really are opposites. I see you're keeping yours very short."

"It's easier to manage," said Ruby.

Issam gestured to both of them to come into the kitchen. "Coffee, tea?"

"Black tea would be great," said Jessie as she looked with concern at her sister's worn features, especially the large, dark circles around her eyes. Her short hair was tangled and her clothes were wrinkled.

"Sis, have you been to a doctor yet?"

Ruby moaned quietly. "Yes, yes I have. I got an injection of Haldol. I hope it helps soon. I'm starting to feel numb. That's a sure sign that things are beginning to work." She sighed. "I almost lost one of my closest friends the other day. She tried to commit suicide, but she wasn't successful. She's going to be okay. I went to see her yesterday, but she's not really present yet. It's been very stressful."

"I'm so sorry. That's awful."

"I'm tired. It's such a fight to maintain some kind of balance. I hope the meds will stop the thoughts from wrapping themselves around my brain and squeezing out all reality."

"I never understood how you could be undergoing all this and still be able to talk to me. I mean, I'm not doubting you, and I've seen it before, but phew!"

"It's only because I'm not totally gone yet. I guess I managed to get help before the delusions completely took over my mind. But even now, Jessie, as I am talking to you I'm wondering where you fit in the conspiracy of meddlers who seem out to get me."

"Who's in the conspiracy, Ruby?"

Issam was standing, tending to the tea and the soup. He listened attentively as the two sisters talked.

"Well, Mom and Dad—Mom's some kind of goddess who sits at a council where they make decisions about the world, including me. All the doctors I've ever been to are there—scientists want to use my brain for research. And the TV is part of it, too—on every show I watch, I think people are observing me and talking about me."

Ruby wanted to be honest with her sister now, when she was still in what she called the "middle phase" of her illness. She could still sort out her thoughts if she tried hard enough, and even if she sounded a little slow and stunned, she could hold down a conversation for a while as long as the other person kept actively engaging her. But she was sure no one could really understand what she was going through, not even Jessie.

"When it gets really bad, I think the whole place is bugged and they're all trying to get at me."

"Why? Why do they want to get at you, Ruby?" asked Jessie.

"They want a piece of my brain. It's somehow special. Remember that ear operation I had as a baby? Well, that's when they first got in. Hell, they even want my *cat*! Anyway, talk about being a megalomaniac. It's beyond my control . . ."

"Oh Ruby, none of this makes any sense. Why on earth would they want your cat? I didn't even know that you had one."

"Because she's a moon cat, she understands the moon. They want to send her up in space."

"I'd like to see this cat," said Jessie dryly, "the cat that's going to commandeer a spaceship. Do you think they have a spacesuit for her? Oh well, a dog's been up, why not a cat?" Jessie sighed. "Ruby, I think you need a rest and I know I do. I didn't sleep a wink on the flight. Why don't we both lie down for a little while?"

Ruby showed Jessie to her room and then went down the hall to her own bedroom. She tried to lie still and see if she could go to another place of consciousness. Could she get below the voices, beyond their reach? She thought about the times when she was in hospital and would search for a quiet place in her head away from all the hustle and bustle. It was very hard to find, but she had managed it once or twice. She lay still, breathing deeply, and shut her eyes, trying to fall into nothingness. After a time of struggling and refocusing she heard a deep voice, male and pleasantly hushed, saying, *Let me take you there*. She thought she recognized the voice and searched in her mind for who it could be. But nothing came. She gave in to its whisper. Darkness came upon her and she felt like she was swaying. Chirrups and the sound of crickets filled her ears and she felt as if she were surrounded by loam, soft and spongy. All around her were the sounds of the inner earth. Ants scurried, worms dragged themselves quietly through the mud. A bee buzzed right before her nose and it twitched. Her head was filled only with the undulating music of this murky bog. A dragonfly fluttered to the right of her head. It was bright green and gold. Everything else was suffused with grey-brown tones. It smelled damp and fetid, and she was not uncomfortable, but rather tingly all over, sucking life in. The voice was present again. *Make your peace with the world*, it said. *You can stay here forever if you like*.

Ruby rested like this for about fifteen minutes and then the cat landed on her belly, jolting her out of her dream world. The cat nestled up against her chest. Ruby closed her eyes again and began drifting off when she heard a voice again.

Have you left me so suddenly? Come back in. At first Ruby

thought it was the same voice, but as it continued it grew deeper and darker. *I've got you now, Ruby. I will tell your father what you did if you don't keep silent.* It was him again, her abuser. Ruby thrashed around in the bed, trying to escape. The cat went flying off her and scuttled off into a corner. Issam banged on the door and then opened it. "Ruby, are you okay?"

Ruby was crying. Jessie came in and wrapped her sister in her arms. "What's wrong, baby girl?"

Ruby shivered. She tried to explain what happened, but she felt as though she was talking nonsense. "I heard his voice again. I didn't tell you yet, Jessie, but a few days ago I had a delusion about being sexually abused. His voice sounded familiar to me, a lot like Daddy's friend Melvin Burns. Do you remember him?"

"Melvin Burns—get outta here! His wife and kids left him in the middle of the night many, many years ago. He was definitely a ladies' man. I always found him arrogant and more than a little unpleasant. But this—I don't know. You need to look into it. Maybe we can find out why his family left him."

"Well, I don't know whether there's anything to it—I just had the vision a couple of days ago. Maybe I should talk about it with Mom."

"Not just Mom. You should talk to Dad, too. And maybe you should get some professional help with this."

"How can I get help for something when I don't even know if it really happened?" said Ruby.

"That's why—to figure out if it really happened! If you were abused as a child, it might just put some perspective on all the bad choices you've made in men. Why you're such a floozy."

"Is that what you think of me? That I'm a floozy? Really, Jessie, have some respect for me. Just because I've had a few more sexual partners than you doesn't make me a loose woman. A floozy! Who created that expression? Men. In the name of oppression. Hmmph!"

"Oh, here we go, out comes the feminist." Jessie moved to her sister's bedside. "Ruby, why be so uptight? Everybody's bound to have some kind of illness at some time in their life."

"Jess, it's not the same. There's not the same kind of stigma attached to having cancer or diabetes. The mentally ill are still treated as pariahs and outcasts, or at the very least as suspicious. Jessie, I'm so surprised at you—with our mother and all. Where's your compassion, your understanding of the issue?"

"But our mother *is* crazy. On that point I will agree."

"You sound so callous when you say that."

"Ruby, she damaged us with her behaviour, with her bouts of mania. She wasn't always there for us when we needed her."

Ruby moved over on the mattress and gestured to her sister to sit down. "I don't feel damaged by her at all. She did the best she could. She worked when she could, she looked after us and Dad. In turn, can't she ask that we look after her when she needs it? She wasn't sick that often anyway."

"I'm older and I can remember how strange her behaviour could be, even in between hospital admissions," said Jessie. "It's hard to understand and therefore hard to forgive."

"But it was never her fault. How can you not forgive her?"

CAFÉ BABANUSSA

"Maybe she should never have had children."

"I can't believe what I'm hearing. Mom didn't even know she was manic-depressive when she had us."

"I know, I know. I just wish she hadn't been so sick. You don't remember everything. I wish she had been there for us more."

"Okay, I can accept that you might somehow feel shafted . . . but she did everything she was supposed to do. What's to blame?"

"Don't you feel any anger towards her for passing this on to you?"

"It's my lot in life. Sure, I'm frustrated. But I'm not angry at Mom. You gonna cry out again about not having children? That could be the beginning of eugenics. Do you really want that? Think about the history here. Think about the Nazis. I can't believe that you would echo that as we sit here in the capital of the former Reich."

"Oh, Ruby, you're overdoing it. I just think it makes sense to plan before you have kids, and if you have some disease, then maybe you shouldn't have them. It's just like the prenatal screening they do to make sure your child won't have Down's syndrome or be autistic."

"Yeah, and those things obviously don't always work. What do you do then?"

"I would probably give it up. And don't tell me you would keep it and things would be all rosy."

"Rosy, who said rosy? I cannot even begin to fathom what it would be like to raise a child with a disability. But why would I dismiss it outright? I know it sounds so hokey, but we really do need to share our love with all kinds. Everybody deserves a chance in this world."

"You're such an idealist. I could never be like you, but I love you just the same, Sis."

"Thanks, hon. I appreciate your support."

"Ruby, don't take this the wrong way, but have you asked yourself lately what more can Berlin give you? What with your illness and all. You have to get on with fixing you so you don't keep breaking. And you can do that better at home, in my humble opinion."

Ruby didn't want to start another argument, and it was true that she was overdue for a visit home, so she simply nodded her head.

"You need more rest. Tomorrow we're going to the Tiergarten with Emma, right?"

Ruby lay there thinking about the day and wondering about the murky bog. She decided not to try that pose again right now. There was another one she had practised in the hospital: the goddess pose. Both of these poses rendered her into a dreamlike state where she felt protected from the nurses and doctors and felt that her mind was temporarily safe from intruders. For the goddess pose she bent her arms and clasped her hands above her head. Her knees faced outward and the soles of her feet pushed together. But try as she might she could not find the release she was looking for. After ten minutes she gave up and curled herself into a ball much like the cat beside her. She slept fitfully and woke up when Issam came to bed. He shushed her and rubbed her back for a minute before turning over and falling asleep.

The next morning, as Ruby dressed, she worried about how she'd manage the subway. There would be a lot of people and that was still scary for her. But she had gone with Issam when they went to see Abena. She had been nervous but okay, perhaps driven by adrenaline to see her friend and be sure that she was really alive. She had kept her head down the whole way there and back and was nervous, but she had managed. Still, she worried about today. Every day was different.

Being in close quarters with other people, especially strangers, made Ruby paranoid. She knew she would feel as if everyone was prying into her mind, as if everyone were giving her signals. It had taken her over a month to ride the subway again last time. She just hoped that being with Jessie and Emma would keep her calm.

Ruby had been kicking around in T-shirts and old jeans for several weeks now. In honour of their spring walk, she chose to wear her good black jeans with a bright yellow wool pullover. She put on a pair of gold earrings and a floppy yellow crocheted hat and felt better immediately. It reminded her of how awful it was to be without one's own clothes in the hospital.

Jessie knocked at her door. "Why, aren't you just the Easter bunny. Love that hat!"

Issam had already left the house to spend the day with Magdi. They locked up and skipped down the stairs. The subway was only a ten-minute walk away. Ruby put her arm through Jessie's and kept her head down, to avoid making eye contact with people. She laughed bitterly to herself. *This is it*, she thought. *This is one of the pieces of how people become truly crazy—by always looking at the ground and avoiding the gaze of others.* She decided to be brave and try holding her head up instead and just making sure to look away when someone passed.

They rode the subway to Turmstrasse and waited on the platform for Emma, who appeared dressed in a black skirt and a black wool jacket that hung open. Underneath was an emerald-green mohair sweater that matched the beret that sat jauntily on her red curls.

Ruby dove into Emma's arms for a big hug. The three of them got back on the subway for the two stops it took to get to Zoologischer Garten. Emma asked after Abena. Ruby said that she was okay, but still in hospital on the psych ward. She was going to see her the next day. Ruby kept her eyes trained on the floor, except when speaking with Jessie or Emma. She looked carefully at everyone's feet, examining their shoes as she tried to squelch the paranoia that was rising. She could feel it snaking up around her throat. She could hear voices taunting her. "What's she doing out again?" "Hush, she's crazy." "Eyes down, don't make contact with us. We don't want you here."

Ruby couldn't resist tilting her head up and glancing briefly around to see who was talking. She held on to Jessie's arm again, for reassurance. She felt like a little child who didn't know how to be alone in this big world, and went back to looking at her feet, watching them as they got off the subway and ascended the steps, walked along Budapester Strasse and into the park. It was mid-morning and the sun was bursting through a few wayward clouds, filling the skies with light. Ruby stayed close to her companions. Though she could lift her head up a little more here, as there weren't too many people on the street yet, she instinctively ducked down whenever anyone came in sight. As they walked through the park, they began to hear the blare of loudspeakers.

"I heard there was a demo planned for today," said Emma, "but I didn't think they'd be this close to the park. The city government has just signed on to build a massive corporate complex. Most of us are appalled and think it's a huge waste, especially since they've begun slashing social programs."

"Let's go take a peek," said Jessie. "I've never been to a demonstration before."

Ruby sucked in her breath.

Jessie, sensing her discomfort, said, "You'll be fine. We'll be right next to you all the way."

Ruby didn't want to spoil the party and seem like a wimp, so they followed the sounds and the growing stream of passersby heading the same way. When they reached the street, Jessie stopped abruptly, her eyes now huge globes. "Oh my god," she said. People were milling about everywhere and marching down the street, bouncing signs up and down in their hands, chanting and singing.

Ruby recalled Werner's warnings about wearing balaclavas and running shoes to head out to a demo. The street was packed full of people, the sidewalks awash with protesters and onlookers alike. Parading by at that moment was a block-long group of women dressed in various shades of purple. They carried drums and tambourines and were singing songs as they pounded through the street. Following on their heels came the radical group, measuring at least three blocks long. Anarchists dressed head to toe in black, with balaclavas or scarves around their faces, Doc Martens on their feet. There was no singing here, but some carried signs and effigies. Ruby was surprised at the power of their presence. She could feel the tension in the air; her head seemed to pound in sync with the protesters' feet. The police gathered on foot, in full riot gear, at the intersections. They looked ferocious with their helmets, suits and masks, ready to do battle at the drop of a hat. As Ruby knew from past experience, it was not uncommon for peaceful demonstrations to end up as riots—often finishing up in Kreuzberg, with store windows smashed to pieces and many burning cars serving as barricades while the policed fired water cannons and tear gas into the festering crowds.

Emma interrupted Ruby's thoughts, saying, "Why don't we walk along for a bit to show our support. Ruby, will you be okay?"

"To be honest, I'm not sure. It's crazy down here."

"Come on," said Emma. "Give it a try. It'll be good practice for you to be among lots of people. We'll be here."

Ruby could feel the tension of the crowd mounting as they neared the next intersection. A sudden ripple ran through it, then she heard someone yell that they were being blocked off about ten minutes down the road. People started yelling and waving fists, and there was a surge of movement behind them. A swell of people pushed forward, taking Ruby along with them. She tried to see where Jessie and Emma were. She tried to push her way against the crowd to get back to them, but masses of bodies propelled her along. Ruby had to keep her head up and she felt a strange sickness mount in her as she twisted and turned and waved, hoping the two others could keep her in sight. It was wall-to-wall people, and Ruby couldn't breathe. In her head she kept hearing Melvin Burns's voice saying, *I gotcha now, girl.* She kept lunging forward and then trying to turn to look over people's heads for any sign of her lost companions. Someone yelled at her, "Quit stumbling around there, you're holding us up." The slight burn of tear gas and the cacophony around her matched the noise in her brain. Tears streaked down her face. There was now a choir in her head, filling in the breaks between Melvin Burns's cries. The voices ranted at her: *Don't be a fool, don't get lost, stand up, be strong.* As if to spite the voices, Ruby sank down to the pavement and sat crumpled in the middle of the crowds.

Someone hissed, "You stupid asshole, what are you doing? You can't do that. Get out of here."

Ruby started screaming, "I can't move, I'm stuck!"

Two men and a woman stopped to help her. They lifted her up and dragged her off to the sidewalk, bumping into people, cursing all the way as they inched their way through the throng. One of the men said, "You better get outta here and go home. It's only going to get worse." The woman told her, "You should cut back through the park up to Hansaplatz or over to the zoo." Then, "Be safe." With that she was gone.

Ruby stood on her tiptoes for a few minutes, scanning the crowd for her sister and Emma. It was impossible. So she ran into the park and ran and ran and ran. Burns's fiendish voice exploded into her head: *I'm gonna tear you apart, piece by piece. Ha ha ha. I've got you good.* Ruby writhed and twisted and shook her head violently, trying to remove him from her being. She collapsed on the ground and rolled back and forth, back and forth, but her voice seemed to be stuck in her throat. She kicked her legs and flailed her arms, struggling to be free of him.

"What's wrong, ma'am? Should I call an ambulance?"

Ruby jumped up and pushed the person away, yelling, "He's possessed me! He's coming to get me. I gotta keep going." Sheer adrenaline pushed her forward.

The skies were darkening, the clouds inky and bloated. Ruby kept running hard. She was too afraid to take the subway and decided she would run and walk all the way home, rain be damned. The choir was still singing in her head: *Gotta get home, gotta get home.* She was awed by the idea of a choir singing to her, but hated that it filled so much space inside her head with its repetitions. She shook her head again to see if she could get rid of it. It would be nice to turn it on when you wanted it. But she couldn't control it, and that made her angry. She continued quickly along the paths, trying to remember the way to Hansaplatz. A light spattering of rain began to fall on her head and she cursed the skies. Melvin

Burns seemed to have left the party, but she knew he would be back. His voice still echoed throughout her and she constantly looked this way and that as she slowed to a jog. She wondered where Jessie and Emma were, if they were okay. She knew they would be worried about her. Ruby picked up her pace as water dripped lightly from the sky. She eventually wound her way through the enclave of factories on the streets where Moabit met Wedding. The buildings looked lonely and ramshackle and she wondered if they were in use at all. It was quiet all around and the skies were still sombre. A fine drizzle trickled through her hair and onto her face. She looked up and heard a loud clap of thunder. The choir had stopped chanting and a voice erupted in her head. *I will suck your cunt dry, Ruby Edwards. Your flesh isn't as sweet and pure as when I last tasted it, and neither are you. Don't you dare talk about me—I will do you in, you hear! I will do you in.* Ruby sprinted down the street. She kept shaking her head furiously every few steps as if she really thought it would rid her of that slimy voice. She could still hear him shouting at her. A rush of adrenaline walloped her and she ran and ran and ran. She was screaming inside her head, "I want to go home, I want to go home, far away from here, home!"

As she neared her neighbourhood, the skies opened up and the rain flushed down over her. She was drenched but felt as if she were being cleansed of all impurities: the abuse at the hands of Melvin Burns, the thousands of questions about all her delusions, the confusion brought on by her illness. Let them all wash off her and disappear! She had slowed her pace to a jog, as she was now only about ten minutes from home. She felt comforted by the familiar landmarks and thought of how much she loved this city. But Jessie was right. It was time to leave.

She practically crawled up the stairs to the apartment and banged on the door while fumbling for her keys. Issam opened the door, with Magdi peeking around his legs. She fell into Issam's arms and he lifted her up and carried her down the hall to the bedroom. He lay her on the bed, removed her shoes and wet coat and then sat down beside her. She looked at him and said, "I just had the worst nightmare. Could you hold me, please?"

Issam lay down beside her and put his arms around her.

She said, "Tell me, are you thinking of leaving Berlin?"

Issam did not answer at first.

"Baby, you have to tell me what's on your mind," she said. "What your plans are. I'm thinking of leaving, too."

Issam sighed. "Yes, I want to go back to Africa. This is not the life for me here. Sudan is calling me to come home. I'd like to take Magdi with me, but we'll have to see. Ruby, I love you. But I am no good to you if I am unhappy. I can do more things, I can do *better* things, in Africa. It's where I'm meant to be. You could come with me."

Ruby tried to hold back her tears. "Somehow I knew this might happen. Just not so soon. Life is too cruel for you here. It's time for me to go home, too."

Just then there was a knock at the door. Issam got up to go answer it.

"Is Ruby here?" she heard Jessie say. "Oh my god, we lost her. We wandered all through the streets downtown looking for her. Please tell me she's here."

"Yes, she is. She's okay. She's soaking wet and tired, but okay."

"Oh, thank god," said Emma. "We were so worried."

The two women joined Ruby in her bedroom.

"I have never been so scared in my life," said Jessie. "But then Emma kept saying, 'Ruby will probably just go home.' And it's true, I guess. Where else could you go? Thank god."

"Speaking of home . . ." Ruby said, and she told them how after the demonstration she had been overcome by the feeling of wanting to go home to Toronto.

"I'll say," said Jessie, clapping her hands. "It's about time you came round to that."

"You were right," Ruby said. "Issam told me that he's making plans to leave. It may not be for a little while, but his mind is set on going." Ruby was tired; her brain felt like a tangled cluster of live wires. But she tried to stay up a little longer. Besides, who knew what sleep, or lack of it, would bring. She felt safer here with her sister.

Emma laughed. "It's going to be like a mass exodus. Everybody's going. Berlin has been good to us, but she's had her time. We need to move on."

CHAPTER ELEVEN

Leaving

ONE AFTERNOON RUBY WENT TO THE POOL AT HER local community centre. She loved the sense of solitude and peace that gliding through the water brought. She slipped into the water, submerging herself in its coolness. She pushed off, doing a breast stroke to warm up. As the pool was almost empty, she flipped onto her back and counted one, two, three, one, two, three as she propelled herself forward with the back crawl. This was her favourite stroke. She closed her eyes and it felt so rhythmic as she slid through the liquid that enveloped her. Her mind fell into nothingness for a few moments. Then his voice broke through the peacefulness with a stark and painful message: *I licked your cunt and I made you suck my dick. Ha ha. I'd do it all over again.*

Ruby careened frantically through the water, arms splashing wildly at her side. She swallowed gulps of water that rushed out backwards, burning through her nose. Her legs felt like they were struggling against dead weights. She couldn't catch her breath and couldn't calm herself. Her mind went black just as quickly as she heard cries around her.

It felt like an hour before she felt her body being yanked through the water to the deck. Someone was compressing her chest. She gasped and sputtered as water gushed from her mouth and her nose. "You're okay. You're gonna be okay," whispered the lifeguard. They brought her towel to her to cover her up. "What happened, ma'am, what happened?"

"Some kind of panic attack," replied Ruby, coughing between words and still shaking. And lying there shivering, recognized that to get better she would have to face her tormentor. What would she say? That he should rot in hell. But then, she didn't believe in hell, so what good was that? Still, she did believe in some kind of karma and felt sure that he would be made to suffer for his evildoings in some kind of afterlife.

When she got home, Issam could see immediately that something was amiss. She told him all that happened and of her new determination to resolve this in the only way she knew possible. He wasn't at all thrilled with the idea of her meeting up with Melvin Burns.

"Just go to the police when you get home. Let them handle it. Why trouble yourself?"

"The police wouldn't touch my story with a ten-foot pole. Remember, I'm a crackpot, a nutcase, wacko. Who's going to believe me? They'll just say it's the delusions. Besides, it happened when I was just a kid. It's too long ago."

Issam hugged her and then took her hand and led her down the hall to the bedroom. As he touched her breasts, her neck, and kissed her eyes he said, "I'm going to miss you so much, Ruby. Why don't you come to Sudan with me?"

Ruby cried. "I have to go home if I ever want to get better, Issam."

Issam made love to her at first with only his hands, roaming gently across her body. Ruby struggled to relax and put Melvin Burns out of her mind, and eventually she succumbed to her lover's touch. That night she felt something change in her body, a feeling of something taking hold of her and settling. Not long after, she knew for sure. She was pregnant!

She couldn't believe her good luck. She had begun longing for a child ever since Issam moved in with her, but knew she might not have much of a window of opportunity, given her illness. As of yet, nobody had diagnosed her as bipolar like her mother; at the hospital they had treated her psychotic episode as a one-time thing, despite her mother's history. Lately, she had been able to resist her tendency to paranoia, and the only persistent delusion was the one regarding Melvin Burns. If she went home and discovered it wasn't a delusion, maybe she could stay well. That evening at dinner she told Issam her news.

Issam dropped the bread out of his hand. "What do you mean? You can't be. Ruby, no!"

Ruby sighed. "Listen, Issam. That's not exactly the reaction I was looking for." Her voice took on a tone of harshness as she continued. "Don't you worry. I'll be raising this child on my own in Toronto. You won't have to do a thing. Okay?"

"That's *not* okay. It's not good for a child to be raised without a father."

"I will work hard at being the best mother I can be," said

Ruby. "I love you, Issam, and I want your child. And this may be my only chance."

"You know I love you, too. But what if you get sick again? You're not thinking this through."

"I'll have my family around me. They'll stand by me."

Ruby realized how lucky she was to be able to say that, and she hoped for her family's understanding.

Issam remained frosty for the next few days, and Ruby began to feel depressed. Her family in Toronto was beckoning to her and she wanted to follow their call. She had been away for almost five years.

She struggled to defend her decision and had to face the sorrow mounting within her. She loved Issam: the touch of his hand, his momentous smile, mischievous eyes and carefree spirit. So far she had felt sure of herself. Now every time she looked into Issam's eyes she experienced a sense of incalculable loss. Would he ever know his baby? Would she be able to travel to Sudan or could he come see them? How would she raise their child without him? Would her family's support be enough?

Emma was leaving in two weeks. They went out for drinks on a patio in Kreuzberg. Ruby drank iced tea and Emma settled for her usual Weizenbier. Ruby's friend practically jumped out of her seat when she heard the news. "That's so exciting! Oh my god, do you know if it's a boy or a girl?"

Ruby smiled. "I don't want to know. I'll find out in the end. That's good enough for me."

"You'll have to be careful with your health. You haven't been stable for long."

"But what about all those women with other illnesses—epilepsy, diabetes—what about them?" said Ruby. "Does someone tell them they can't have children and be good mothers?"

"I think you'll be a great mom. But to be on the safe side, maybe you should take up meditation."

"Mmm-hmm. And yoga, too, I guess."

"How does Issam feel about the situation?"

"He's not happy. In fact, he's not talking to me much."

"Do you want me to talk to him? Why don't I come home with you now and you can fix us something to eat while he and I chat?"

"You can give it a shot, but I don't know what kind of reception you'll get."

Back at home, Emma and Issam sat down together in the living room while Ruby put on a kettle for tea and got busy making dinner. Pasta with arrabbiata sauce was one of Issam's favourite dishes: a simple melding of wonderful flavours. It would be a peace offering to him. First she minced some shallots and garlic and then chopped up fresh and sun-dried tomatoes. She put two handfuls of olives on the cutting board, admiring their wrinkled yet silky skins. She smashed each one till the pits popped out. Then she put a handful of pine nuts in a small pan, leaving them to toast while she slivered the olives.

On the windowsill was a planter with lemon thyme, oregano, rosemary and basil. Ruby pulled off several stems of oregano plus a few sprigs of thyme and dropped them in the pan with the shallots and garlic. A few minutes later she added the diced tomatoes, slivered olives and a small red cherry pepper. The fragrance of the herb and tomato mixture permeated the kitchen and wafted through the apartment. Issam called out, "When are we eating?" Ruby laughed and called back, "When it's done."

I will definitely teach my child to cook and enjoy a meal with company, she thought as she splashed a glass of red wine into the mix.

As the linguine cooked, she rubbed some cut garlic into the halves of demi-baguette she had bought at the store that day, brushed the bread with olive oil and placed it in the hot oven. She tore up some basil leaves and tossed them into the sauce, along with several pinches of red chili flakes. Then she added several large handfuls of fresh tiger shrimp, making sure to not overcook them. She drained the linguine, saving some pasta water for the sauce, and then tossed everything together in the pan. She poured the whole into a ceramic bowl, sprinkled on the pine nuts and more basil, and then grated some parmesan on top. She called Issam to come bring the pasta, while she carried in the bread and the wine.

"If I could afford it, I'd hire you both to cook for me," said Emma as she smiled into her plate. "This is great."

"Thanks, hon. Let's toast to new beginnings for us all."

Issam solemnly raised his glass to the others and clinked dutifully. Ruby wondered how his conversation with Emma had gone.

That night Issam came to her. He looked at her and shook his head slowly. "I don't want to leave you and I don't want you to leave me. But what can we do? I don't think this is any way to bring a child into the world, and you'll never get me to agree with you."

Ruby sat cross-legged on the floor, alone in her apartment, the music of Sade wafting over her. She was packing a trunk— pictures and paintings, mounds of records—all the items that she had collected over the years. She wrapped up the hand-painted Italian dishes, the assortment of teacups and teapots, all plucked from flea markets across the city. She came across a beautifully beaded earthen coffeepot alongside bags of sandalwood, ridged and dark with fragrance. She envisioned the tales of Sudanese women seated naked in firepits hot and steamy as saunas, absorbing the scent into their skin, cleansing and renewing themselves as they rubbed their bodies till they shone like midnight pearls. She took out a piece and lit it, placed it in the ashtray on the coffee table behind her and watched the smoke rise towards the ceiling.

Ruby got up to change the music to something bluesier. Her fingers strayed over a cork box with a glass lid that encased an exquisite egg, hand-painted in shades of blue for her by Werner's mother. She lifted it out of its nest and cradled it in the palm of her hand. She recalled how his family had embraced her and smoothed her transition to a foreign culture. Even as she sought to whittle away at the obstacles Werner had placed around her and break free from his control, even as she prepared to leave behind the city she had called home for many years, she had never forgotten his parents' love.

She smiled as she placed the egg against her cheek, taking in the cool ripple of shell. She carefully placed it back in its box, and chose to wrap it up in the old red-and-white kaffiyeh that Issam had so often worn at Café Babanussa. Adrift in the old, she dreamed of something new.

One day she was resting at home when there was a loud knock on the door. When Ruby pulled open the door, there stood Abena. She was dressed in black pants, and her top was a mix of vibrant greens and black, the patterns of a kente cloth. Ruby saw that stretching out from the greyish circles beneath Abena's eyes were a few fine, feathery lines. She was still struggling. But she hugged Ruby as hard as ever and her voice was bright when she said, "Get your stuff, we're going out." Ruby grabbed a shoulder bag and put on some flats and they went down the stairs. Abena moved slowly, taking the steps one at a time. Ruby offered her hand, but Abena brushed her off and said, "I don't need that kind of help. So, just to let you know, we're going to Kreuzberg. Near Gleisdreieck. I want you to see this place and maybe you'll go back." Ruby asked for more details, but Abena just waved her hands. "Shh." Then, "Tell me about your plans." They sat down in the subway.

"Well, before I do that I have some other news. I'm pregnant."

Abena almost fell off her seat. "Oh, I'm going to be an auntie. Does this mean you'll stay?"

"Not at all. In fact, it underlines even more the need to go home. Issam is leaving, Emma is leaving. I can't raise a child by myself here. I'm worried about my health, but also about the racism. I don't think I could manage it. I'd like to be near my family."

"I can't believe you're leaving. I'm still here, I could help out."

"I know you could and you would. You'd be wonderful. But I need more than a couple of friends. It's been five fantastic years, but I think the spirits are telling me it's time to go. You'll just have to fly over sometime, and of course I'll come back to visit with baby in tow."

The women stepped out of the subway and locked arms as they walked slowly down the street. Abena soon stopped in front of a store named Zeitgeist. "We're here," she said.

The front room was like a hive, with young people rushing back and forth. They were mainly Turkish and German and they were busy printing out and organizing flyers about an upcoming demo and stacking posters that listed their services. A few people were on the phone. There was a meeting going on in one of the back rooms. Zeitgest also offered counselling for foreigners, and there was someone who was assigned to deal with racist incidents, to help people decide whether to go to the police or not. Ruby was surprised to see Isaac, the Black drummer from Dom's old band, talking strategy with a young German fellow. They hugged and high-fived each other, and she asked what he was doing there.

"Aw, I'm just here to help out in whatever way I can. Postering, leafleting in the cafés, you know. You should come to the demo next week. And the day after tomorrow there's a meeting about ways to influence public policy."

Abena turned to Ruby and said, "I just wanted you to know that there are people who care and want to make a difference."

They didn't stay for much longer and went to sit on the patio of one of the neighbourhood's many cafés. It was getting warmer now, and a light breeze rustled through the nearby trees. Ruby looked at Abena and felt sad to be losing another friend.

Despite everything, Ruby had loved living in Europe. She loved having history envelop her as she strolled the streets; she loved the French word *flâner*—to amble along, or to hang around. It applied here, too—you could stroll until you came across the perfect café or *Biergarten* and then just sit and absorb the sights, sounds and smells. Even more, though, Ruby thought about the tight circle of friends that had helped protect her from the dark elements of Berlin. She would especially miss Emma and Abena's steady presence. She wondered if she would find such incredible people to surround herself with back home in Toronto. Indeed, could she ever call Toronto home again? Ruby loved her family deeply, but she had spent years running away from them and she no longer knew if they would understand her. Still, she felt she could count on them to be there for her even if they didn't recognize her anymore. She could just hear her father muttering, "I knew it. I knew she'd have to come home and straighten herself out."

Ruby called home the next day. "Mom, it's me. Listen, sit down—I'm gonna tell you straight out. I'm pregnant. And I'm coming home."

"Oh, Ruby, that's wonderful! How far along are you?"

"Four months."

"I'm sure you've thought this out carefully."

"Mom! Of course I have."

"We'll be glad to finally welcome you home. Here's your father."

"Is that my youngest daughter? What's this I hear? You're pregnant? You better be packing your bags to come home."

"What about Issam?" Ruby's mom interjected. "What does he say about all this?"

"He's been planning to leave Berlin for a while."

"Is he coming with you?" asked her dad.

"No, he's going home to Sudan."

"Oh my, that's going to be hard on you," said her mom.

"Yes, it is. But I'm just trying to hang in there and stay calm. I'll be home by September."

Two days later she got a call from Jessie.

"I'm not going to hide my feelings. I think you're making a huge mistake. Knowingly having a child when you've not been well."

Ruby had expected as much from her sister after their conversations in Berlin. "Sick? You don't think it's possible that I might have long phases of well-being? Look at Mom—she hasn't had an episode in years. I'm fine now, Jessie, and you better damn well get used to the idea of becoming an aunt."

"Your life will change forever. Are you up for that? What the hell does Issam say? I bet he's not happy."

"You're right, he's not. But it's not up to him anymore. I will love this baby more than anything in the world. I will find a way to make it work. Hell, I'll even find a therapist when I'm home again. I owe my baby that much."

Jessie held off on commenting any further and their conversation wound down quickly.

Ruby planned to spend the night before Emma's flight to London at Emma's place so they could break bread together in the morning. When the time came, she was feeling the worse for wear, physically and psychically, and she constantly drank ginger tea and carried candied ginger with her wherever she went to ward off nausea. She didn't know how they would say goodbye, but she needed to confide in her friend one more time.

"I hope to go see Melvin Burns and confront him. I will ask him why he did what he did. I have to. I don't see any way around it."

"What if he tries to hurt you?"

"He's already hurt me. I can't get him out of my head. He takes over wherever he wants. I almost died the last time it happened." She told Emma about the incident at the pool.

"Oh my god, Ruby. Why didn't you tell me before? That's awful!"

"I'm tired of trying to explain the vagaries of my mind."

"Still, you should think long and hard before making yourself vulnerable to him. You just don't know what will happen. Anyhow, how do you think it will help you?"

"I don't know—maybe I'll just be able to stare him down and sense whether he did it or not. I know that sounds crazy, but maybe I won't feel so crazy myself if I see him."

"Take someone with you if you have to go, Ruby. Don't go alone."

The women ate dinner together on a patio and then went for a long walk through Charlottenburg, arm in arm, pointing out various restaurants and bars that they had once frequented.

"Aha! Do you remember this place?" Emma asked, pointing at the Schlosspark hospital.

"Oh my god, of course, how could I possibly forget? And not far from here lives Abena's friend Mouna. She used to braid my hair."

They kept walking, determined that nothing would break their conversation. But then they arrived in Moabit after an hour of meandering and decided to look in at Café Babanussa, for what would be Emma's last time.

Ali and Issam were working the bar, and there were a few other regulars hanging around. Joe, the resident musician, was playing a jazzy version of "Moon River" on the piano, and Ruby slipped into a momentary reverie as she listened to the tinkling of the keys and thought of her father. It was short-lived, however, because as soon as Joe had finished, Issam turned the stereo on, and the thumping bass beats that inevitably belonged to Bob Marley and his Wailers charged the air, filling every last space in the café. Walid, a fellow Sudanese, joined them at their table. He was young, tall and lithe, with the most beautiful smile that radiated out from his mouth and up to his big, round doe eyes. He put that smile to good use, as he loved to laugh. A little while later, "Is This Love" came on. Everybody hooted and cheered, and Walid pulled Emma onto the dance floor. Ruby grabbed Issam from behind the counter and they swayed in each other's arms like in their early days. Others joined in, and soon the café was glutted with bodies slipping and sliding across the floor. Joe danced by himself and then took turns with all the women. When the music ended, Joe went back to the piano and played a raucous rendition of Louis Jordan's "Yeah, Yeah, Baby" before easing into a quiet and reflective version of "Stardust." He kept accompanying their conversation through the night, and they were well into the wee hours of the morning before Ruby and Emma headed home, both a little teary-eyed.

The next day Ruby had to make the final decision on whether to bring Luna home with her or not. This little creature had brought her love and a stabilizing, almost spiritual element to her during her last psychotic phase. Many times Luna had nudged her or flicked her tail to suggest she move or look in another direction, which would somehow help clear her head. She had sat faithfully at Ruby's feet when she was scribbling in her notebooks and had curled up with her at night. Ruby felt as if the cat was working on her behalf, helping to guide her through her turmoil.

Ruby had called the airline but she hadn't told her parents.

She was worried about their reaction. Her mother preferred dogs, and her father did not share Ruby's love for animals at all. He disliked cats almost as much as he disliked birds. She paced her bedroom floor. She could not leave Luna behind. Issam wouldn't look after her. Emma was gone. Luna had to come with her. She would be living in her parents' basement, where the cat would be out of the way. Half out of fear, half out of stubbornness, she chose not to tell them. It would be a surprise.

Issam refused to accompany Ruby to the airport. He said he wasn't good at long goodbyes. He gave her some karkar, a Sudanese scented oil, and a leather amulet and held her for a few minutes before brushing her away. He stepped out the door, turning only to say, "Take care of the baby. Call me when it's born. Call me before then, too, if you feel like it."

He walked out the door and out of Ruby's life. Ruby felt sick to her stomach. Her indigestion and nausea had lessened in the past month, but here she was again, rushing to the bathroom to throw up. After cleaning herself up, she popped some ginger in her mouth and called a taxi to take her to the airport. She opened the door to the flat and there stood Abena.

"You didn't actually think I'd let you leave by yourself, did you?"

Ruby was thrilled, but it didn't stop her emotions from spilling over. Huddled in the back seat up against her friend, tears flowing down her cheeks, she suddenly realized the strangest thing about the city she was leaving. Berlin had introduced her to Africa and its music, literature and cinema.

Café Babanussa, Issam, Abena and the others had taught her to reach back into her own blackness and find comfort and a place of identity far more than that which she had derived from her own family. Having a child by a Black father was a way of growing even further. It seemed the natural thing to do.

The Edwards family sat gathered at the dinner table at the house in Don Mills, downing the last remnants of a roast lamb and scalloped potatoes that Ruby had prepared for the occasion. Ruby stepped into the kitchen to make tea and put the last touches on the linzertorte she'd made from raspberries, picked earlier from her mother's garden. Ruby had laboured over the lattice topping, as she knew this was her mother's favourite dessert.

Her family had been careful not to pepper her with too many questions in the past weeks. Ruby had made it clear that she was tired and disoriented from the move. Yet her parents had held out their arms to her and offered all the support they could to help her prepare for the home birth she wanted to have come autumn. Jessie was the exception. Ruby began collecting the dinner dishes from the table. If she looked closely at Jessie's hazel eyes, she could see laugh lines etched like feathers. Jessie and Ruby had scrapped a lot as children, but strangely all the fighting had just made them closer as adults. But now it was as if a wall had grown between them.

Ruby and Jessie descended upon the kitchen. The kettle whistled merrily, and Jessie grabbed it from the stovetop and handed it to her sister. She watched Ruby as she prepared the tea and finally blurted out, "You don't know what you're getting into."

"I know as much as I possibly can and that's good enough for me. Anyway, I don't want to talk about it if you're going to be rude, belligerent and inconsiderate."

"I'm just talking straight. No one else seems willing to."

"Jessie, what's the point? I can't turn back the clock now. I'm six months pregnant, so there's nothing to be done except to recognize that fact and get on with it. I love you. If you can't love me back and support me because of this, then I feel sorry for you."

Jessie backed away and slammed her fist on the counter. "Don't you see, you're ruining everything—for yourself and for the family."

"If I didn't know better, I'd think I detected just a hint of jealousy there."

Her father's voice boomed out from the dining room, "That's enough, you two. Jessie, quit worrying your sister. There's enough love here for everyone, including the baby."

Then, as if to deflect her sister, Ruby said, "Look, I've brought something to show you." She stepped into the dining room, reached into a bag that lay on the floor and pulled out piece after piece of colourful concrete. "Here it is, graffiti and all. Little pieces of history tumbling from my hands. I went and chiselled off a few pieces before leaving. Everyone is always trying to grab a bit of that wall. I hope it comes down someday soon." She gathered the rugged fragments of the

Berlin Wall into a large circle and then tried to arrange them as if they belonged in a certain pattern.

"Well, history and all, we're glad to have you both back," her father rumbled with a strange mixture of grumpiness and tenderness. He got up and motioned to Ruby to follow him.

They went into the family room at the back of the house. He put his hand on his daughter's shoulder.

"I am so glad you have come home. It's been a long time since we've heard the friendly tinkling of your voice around here. I'm so happy that I haven't even said a word about that damn cat of yours. Keep it downstairs and out of my sight." Ruby nodded in earnest agreement. Her father paused.

"I can't say that I'm not dismayed at your circumstances, but the main thing I want to tell you is that you are loved and you and the baby may stay here with us for as long as you see fit. I do think, and I want to stress this, that you should find a job by the time the baby is about six months old, so that you're not just sitting around. You have a child to look after now and you'll need a regular salary."

She hugged her father long and hard and then dried her tears. "Thanks, Dad. You don't know how much your support means to me."

Ruby felt an aching twinge every time she thought of Berlin. She missed Issam, she missed Emma, Abena, and Ali and his Café Babanussa. Would she ever find such a group of friends again? Such a wonderful place to gather? She felt lonely and somehow small again back in Don Mills. It was hard to get up in the morning and not see any beauty around her. The architecture in Toronto seemed so bland—new and ugly high-rises stretched out everywhere. Almost every night she went to sleep crying for what she no longer had. She thought of Issam and his gentle caresses and cried some more. Ali had called to enquire about her, but the father of her child had not. Ruby cried herself to sleep and then wept again in the morning. For weeks she wrestled with the dark clouds that seemed to follow her wherever she went. She was tired and listless. Her family was gentle with her, yet they tried not to let her lie around too much. Her mother would always come down to the basement and say, "Ruby, it's time to get up. You need some fresh air." Ruby felt she had made a mistake, that she shouldn't have left Berlin after all. It was so hard, leaving all those good people behind, leaving her beloved Europe behind.

In time she came to accept that there was no going back. She had made her bed and now she would have to lie in it. Her father would offer to go for walks with her to get her out of the house. Her sister would do the same. Often she would sit outside on the back patio with her mom, who would regale her with tales of Ruby and Jessie's childhood. Everyone put in an effort to keep her going and not let her sink. Eventually, with her family's quiet insistence and her own need to move on, she pushed through the sorrow. She was determined to find her place in her family, to rediscover Toronto, to find joy wherever she could.

Toronto had changed while she was away, and was

changing still. She loved catching the College streetcar from Main Station out to High Park and then ambling through the grounds before heading up to Bloor Street to window shop. She carried her camera with her wherever she went, snapping photos of the pastel-coloured houses that greeted her eyes in Kensington Market. Here was the Chinese pastry shop where her father had so often taken her and her sister when they were young. Nothing about the eatery seemed to have changed, especially the old bench where she could sit and gorge on the barbecue pork buns and almond cookies. She strolled along the boardwalk by the lake and sat on the rocks, gazing out to the skyline. Staring into the distance where clouds and turquoise sky met the deeper blue of the water, feeling the spray of mist murmur against her face, she felt renewed.

The months inched by. Although she had more or less settled in, the back of her mind was suffused with questions: Should she have left? Should she go back? She still hadn't heard from Issam. Ruby became restless as the bustling breath of autumn filled the air. The baby was late, and Ruby's laboured breathing slowed her down at every step. Finally she decided to take in an afternoon of comedy, mainly old flicks, including her father's favourite, Buster Keaton, in the hopes that a belly laugh would deliver relief.

It worked. Early the next morning her baby was kicking and pushing, head bobbing and feet dancing, as it prepared to burst into the world. Ruby was set up for a home birth and duly called Jessie to join their parents and the midwife to celebrate the coming birth. The contractions were occurring steadily but she moved about freely. For a while she kept her father company in the kitchen while he prepared soup and cornbread. But she returned to the basement, too distracted for conversation. By the time the midwife arrived, and Jessie shortly after, her water had broken. The pain of the contractions had increased tenfold. For the next eight hours, Ruby heaved and sighed and cried and grunted and howled, at times wildly cursing her choice of a natural birth. Her mother and her sister helped her as she moved from bathtub to bed and back again. The warm water lifted her spirits and calmed her. In between she paced and squatted, with the midwife holding her up by her arms. In the meantime Ruby's mother recounted the stories of her own pregnancies. When she had been expecting Jessie, their father had been late coming home from work. Her water had broken and she was down on her knees from the pain. He came in to find her on the floor and rushed her into the car. Traffic was heavy; when they finally got to the hospital, Jessie popped out while her mother was still lying on the stretcher, waiting to be transferred to a room. Ruby had been much easier.

Jessie laughed. "See, I had to fight harder to get into this world. That's why I'm made of steel."

"No comment," Ruby replied.

Sweating and exhausted, Ruby finally asked to lie down. The midwife stood at the foot of the bed, Jessie rubbed her shoulders and her mom held her hand. She pushed and strained, gasping for breath. This scene repeated itself for ten minutes before a little head covered in flowing ebony curls and milky white drizzle was rounding out of her. The baby was the colour of café au lait, with almond-shaped eyes, high cheekbones and a little pug nose. She was the picture of her father; Ruby wondered where he was right at that moment.

Gently hugging and rocking her baby girl, Ruby held her to her swollen breast and touched the baby's barely open eyes. "You, my child, you will be my star and my moonbeam, guiding me through any darkness that may come, filling the night air with joy and light." She kissed her baby's forehead, whispered "Nyota," then closed her eyes.

Jessie came into the bedroom with a towel for the baby. "You're something awesome, Sis," she said softly.

Ruby called Issam to let him know he'd had a baby girl. She didn't comment on how hurt she was that he hadn't called. He was ecstatic and offered a name for the baby, Soraya. Ruby explained that she had already named the little one but would gladly use Soraya for her middle name. Then she said, "I miss you."

"I miss you, too. I think about you all the time. Take care of yourself and Nyota Soraya Edwards. I will write you with my address in Sudan. Maybe one day you will come visit me."

Ruby knew it was time to put her plan into action. Now that the baby was a few months old, she could leave her with her mother for a few hours without worry. Nobody was home, so she sat down to write up a few questions to ask Melvin Burns about Black history in Toronto and then picked up the phone to dial his number.

What would he say? She hung up the phone. Would he know why she was calling? If he were guilty, then yes. She tried again, but this time her hand was shaking so badly that she couldn't dial the numbers. She paced around the kitchen, making up possible conversations in her head. *You'll just have to do it*, she thought. She took a number of deep breaths and tried again.

The voice at the other end of the line sounded soft but firm. When he realized who he was talking to, he sounded momentarily happy and asked her how she and the family were doing. But when she asked if she could meet up with him, he left the question hanging in the air. Then he began blustering in a pitiful voice, "I don't usually have visitors over."

"I won't bother you long. Just a few questions to help me with a paper I'm doing."

"I don't think I can do that."

"Sure you can. You're a fountain of knowledge, Mr. Burns. That's why I chose you to interview."

"How much time do you need?"

"Not much."

"Well, maybe I could spare half an hour next Tuesday afternoon. You can come by then. But only for half an hour, you hear?"

"Great, Mr. Burns. Is one o'clock good?"

"Yup, that's fine."

"Okay, see you then."

Ruby hung up the phone and realized that she was shaking all over. She picked up Nyota and went to the living room to sit down and put her feet up. She snuggled and then fed the baby, loving the feel of her mouth gurgling at her breast. She had done it. Now she was halfway there.

The following Tuesday Ruby left Nyota with her mother. She took the bus and then the subway downtown and hopped a streetcar on St. Clair and rode it west. She only had a few blocks to walk. As she made her way towards Melvyn Burns's house, she felt the slow burn of panic arise within her. Her body started to quiver. She still hadn't figured out what she was going to say. She continued forward but felt blackness and confusion coming on. The urge to vomit overtook her, and she leaned over the curb and retched into the gutter. She stumbled a few feet farther along and then sank down onto the curb. His house was only a block away. After five minutes Ruby steeled herself to carry on. She came upon the house, a little stone bungalow with a blue porch. There was a lovely garden full of irises and peonies to her left. The door was wooden, with a large brass knocker. She rapped three times. After some time had passed she lifted the knocker again and the door creaked open. A pretty young woman, about her own age, opened the door.

"You must be Ruby. Come in. I'm Susanna, Melvin's daughter." She ushered Ruby towards the living room. Ruby had blanched and was uncertain of her steps. Then she stuck her shaking hands in her pockets and summoned the courage to speak.

"I vaguely remember playing with you and your sisters a few times way back when."

"Yes, I do too," said Susanna, smiling wanly. "My father isn't well. He has liver cancer and hasn't much longer to live. You won't be able to spend too much time with him."

"I see," said Ruby.

"You should know, I've only been here a few weeks. I hadn't seen him for twenty-five years until this week. We left him when I was five," she said, her voice now hushed. Ruby stood rooted to the floor, straining to understand what she was hearing. "I've been in therapy for ten years because of him. My sisters, my mother . . . " She was practically stammering. "They couldn't do it, they wouldn't come. They can't stand the thought of being near him. But I wanted to look him in the eye after all these years . . . and then say goodbye. I don't know why, I feel compelled." She paused, her hands trembling ever so slightly. "Go on in. But don't expect much in the way of niceties. It's the door on the right," she said, pointing down the hallway.

Ruby's mouth went dry and she broke into a sweat. She wanted to march right back out the front door and keep going straight without ever looking back. But she was here now, she had come this far. She would have to go through with it. Her body felt limp, but she turned down the hallway and pushed open the door.

A slight, balding man, with ashen skin and sunken eyes, was propped up on a large, bright white pillow. He looked a decade older than he actually was. Fumbling, Ruby forgot everything she had planned to say and stood in the doorway, wringing her hands. She was struck by the pathetic sight of this enemy she felt she had come to know so well in her delusions.

"Hello, Ruby. I'm surprised to see you here. You look lovely, my dear."

Ruby could feel his eyes coursing over her body, as if trying to recognize something he once knew. She felt violated and shuddered, still at a loss for words. Slowly, as if drawn by a magnet, she brought her gaze to meet his. She saw flinty bits of haughtiness and fire in his eyes.

"You are an awful man," she finally sputtered. "How many children did you hurt?"

"I knew you were going to say that. Your father was so successful. I had to bring him down a notch by taking something that was his. And you were so precious. But then, he never knew, did he? You were a good girl, you stayed quiet like I told you to. You must have buried it deep inside."

"You should be ashamed. You had no right."

Ruby watched astounded as she saw him wrestle with a kind of sadness. His face metamorphosed as the sorrow trickled through and dampened the light in his eyes.

"How true. That I am, that I am. Nobody said that being nice would get you anywhere. In the end I am paying for my sins."

"Not soon enough. How unfair that you should go unpunished while others suffer because of you."

Burns's face collapsed now, any arrogance gone. His voice broke as he tried to spit out the words. "I'm so sorry. Please tell me you forgive me. Look, you have your whole life ahead of you still. I am dying now."

Ruby looked down at the floor, chewing her lip, and then back into his face. "That would be very hard. You have crawled into my head, taken up space with your nasty words that I remember so well. You caused so much fear and pain. I can't think of forgiveness right now. I just needed to finally know."

She took one last look at the pathetic sight of this dying man crumpled on the bed. "I feel sorry for you and especially for your family, too." She left the room and closed the door behind her.

Susanna was standing right outside the room. "Did you get what you were looking for?"

Ruby looked at her morosely and nodded. "More or less."

"Listen, Ruby. I have a card here for you. It might be of use someday when you're ready." She turned into the living room, rummaged through a desk drawer and then handed the card to Ruby. It read "Abuse Counselling for Women" and listed the names of several psychotherapists.

"It helped me a lot, and it would probably help you, too. Give them a call sometime."

Ruby smiled her thanks and felt her eyes begin to well up. She struggled with her words. "I have to go, but thank you so much."

Walking down the driveway, Ruby felt relieved and agitated at the same time. It took her a few moments to regain her composure. When she did, she continued down to the street and walked towards the streetcar stop. She found a seat at the back. She watched the vistas passing by her as she gazed out the window, heart still throbbing. Tears rolled down her cheeks as she sat thinking, turning the card Susanna had given her over and over in her shaky hand. So it was true. She felt ill and her mouth was still dry as a bone. There was nothing left to do but grieve and get help. She wondered if she would be free of the delusions and dreams that had stalked her so. She hadn't told her parents about Melvin Burns and tried to imagine their surprise, their hurt for her. She would have to tell them soon now. She sat shaken and dishevelled, leaning against the window.

An hour later, Ruby walked up the driveway to her parents' home. The front door was open and the September sun was streaming into the hallway. Her mother stepped out of the kitchen with Nyota in her arms and came to greet her at the door. Ruby scooped her daughter out of her mother's embrace. She squeezed her tight and sat down in the living room. She lifted her top and prepared to let her baby suckle at her swollen breasts. She rippled her fingers through Nyota's hair and gently rubbed her skull, then she tweaked her little nose. She thought of all the stories she would tell her when she was older. She smiled. She was home. She was safe.

On Being Crazy

By Karen Hill

I TOLD MY EIGHTEEN-YEAR-OLD DAUGHTER THAT I was sure they were going to kill me. She insisted that I call her hourly that night from the psych ward, to reassure her that I was all right. It was December 2008, and she was away at her first year of university. She cajoled me through my fears and supported me with her love. Only that was supposed to be my job. How did the tables get turned like this?

They're pretending to be busy but they're watching me. I know that they even have cameras in the washrooms and the showers out on the floor, perverts!! Uh-huh! Today they're all wearing colours for the different guys I'm enamoured with, to show their support for one or the other. Purple, red, black, white. The guys, they're always yacking at me and arguing but I can barely hear them. What do

317

*they expect; they're all talking at once. Then they get mad 'cause I
can't seem to respond to each one individually. I want us all to live
together under one roof. Crazy me. The head doctors are constantly
trying to hypnotize me with their eyes again. Drain the information out of me. Can't fight against it; they always win.*

In my family, the incidence of mental health problems runs
high. My mother and her twin sister are both bipolar. On
my father's side, one of my aunts was bipolar and two of my
cousins are schizophrenic. While some people dispute the idea
that mental illness can be hereditary—and I, too, believe in
the importance of social and environmental causes—you can
nonetheless see that the odds were pretty high that someone
else in my immediate family might get hit over the head with
it, too. The only mitigating factor was that, having witnessed
my mom in periods of illness, we already knew something
about it and were well aware of the signs.

In 1979 I graduated from university and took off to
Europe. Six months later I was twenty-one and living in
Berlin. I was too busy living my adventure to worry about
mental illness. I worked under the table cleaning houses, travelling whenever I could. After two years I married the young
German man I was living with and got my work permit. I
landed an excellent job at the Max Planck Institute for Human
Development. In the summer of 1984 the institute asked me to
attend a conference in West Germany on my own as a member
of the *Betriebsrat*, a kind of internal watchdog for the institute,

with something like a union role. This conference brought together *Betriebsraten* members from across Germany, and it was an honour to be asked to represent my workplace.

My German was very good by then. But when I was wrangled into presenting complicated findings from the week's working meetings, I felt like the lamb led to slaughter. The pressure was intense, and I found myself not sleeping, walking the halls, then tossing and turning in bed and then up pacing again. Underlying all this was an increasingly unhappy relationship with my husband. I was a wreck by the end of the week, not able to think straight, totally at a loss. I made a mishmash of presenting the group's findings in front of a crowd of two hundred and then collapsed in a sobbing, ranting mess. Someone drove me the three-hour drive back to Berlin because I wasn't fit to get on a plane. From there on in I just got worse. A week later I was going to the doctor's office to get injections of an antipsychotic drug, Haldol, and about three weeks later I was an inmate at the Schlosspark hospital.

This first experience of psychosis with delusions and hallucinations was a surreal nightmare. Emotionally I was petrified—and soon physically petrified as well, as the side effects of the medications slowed my reflexes and made me feel as if my body was slowly turning to stone. I met with the staff psychiatrist regularly. He was never arrogant or condescending, nor was he intrusive or threatening. Our meetings were always one-on-one, and we usually met in his office, unlike at the hospitals in Toronto, where there is almost always a small group of doctors peering at you while you're sitting uncomfortably on your bed. Other meetings at hospitals here in Toronto sometimes took place in small conference rooms, and again there was always more than one doctor present and I always felt intimidated. When I told my psychiatrist in Berlin that I didn't want to go to group therapy, instead of badgering me, he immediately suggested I join a music program instead, and that worked wonders for me.

My brother Larry came to stay in Berlin for a few weeks as soon as he could get there. He saw me at my worst, before I was hospitalized. In November 1984 my parents came over, and I remember our many walks on grey autumn afternoons through the palace grounds behind the hospital. In December, after two months and countless visits from friends, I was released. By February 1985 I was in a deep depression, and my brother Dan came to visit and took me swimming almost every day. By the end of his stay several weeks later, I was finally coming to, shaking off the vise of blackness that had me in its grip.

One of the most important pieces about this story is that the German doctors deliberately chose not to diagnose me with anything, despite knowing of my family history of mental illness. Instead, immediately upon my release they embarked upon a plan to have me weaned off the antipsychotics over the course of a year and a half. When I was completely off those drugs I wasn't on any other mood stabilizers or other medication. For the following thirteen years I was drug-free and incident-free.

I know they're following my every move, my every thought. I can tell. I know better. I have to get out of here. Don't want to sleep. The staff will get me in my sleep. That's why they always push the extra Ativan—to knock me out. To study me and then do away with me. The windows in my room look out onto tall buildings full of people studying me and controlling me. I'll give those nurses a little wave. To let them know that I know . . .

The choir is singing in my head—constantly singing at the back of my head, bluesy gospel-like singing, call and response. I know it's been put there by friends to help me, to soothe me. Also to guide me to action. I hate that it's there all the time. When it's not the choir, it's an Aboriginal drum circle sent to comfort me and let me know that people are thinking of me. But I can't stand the constancy. It doesn't let up. I don't want anyone to guide me. The worst thing is that sometimes the bad guys—doctors, scientists—try to imitate the sound of the choir or the drums. But I can usually tell the difference in a few minutes. Everybody's inside my head pulling me every which way all the time.

In 1985 I left my German husband and within a year was involved with a young visual artist from Sudan. In 1988 I became pregnant and decided to move back to Canada the following year. My partner stayed behind in Berlin until 1996, when he was able to follow me to Toronto. (He returned to Sudan in 2002 and remained there.)

In 1997, I was rehired as an ESL lead instructor with the Toronto District School Board after a temporary layoff of nine months. During the layoff I had found a less interesting but still demanding job, and I was trying to ghostwrite a biography of someone at the same time. With the switch back to my regular work it was all too much. I soon became manic and then delusional.

This time I went to Women's College Hospital. There they diagnosed me as being bipolar and as having seasonal affective disorder, and I was put on lithium. I remember my brother Dan bringing me music and a Walkman, and I would constantly walk the halls listening to *The Best Hits of Van Morrison*, and later in my room to Babyface. Nobody seemed bothered by my constant rounds of the halls, and I remember that the nurses seemed friendly.

The following year stress led me into sickness once again. The Mike Harris government had decided to close or amalgamate many hospitals or hospital departments, and the psych ward at Women's College Hospital was closed. Instead I had a horrible seven-week stay at the Clarke Institute, precursor to today's CAMH, or Centre for Addiction and Mental Health. The doctors at the Clarke couldn't figure me out. Despite the lithium, I continued to struggle with psychosis. I felt like I was left pretty much on my own. Soon, I started acting up on the ward, pacing constantly in front of the nursing station, yelling that my brother Dan had told the CBC about me and they were following my plight and the doctors had better take care of me. At the same time, I believed that O. J. Simpson was coming to Toronto to see me for a match of the wits where I was going to tell him off. It was just after his trial, and while I believed that he had rightly been acquitted given the missteps of the LAPD, I inwardly felt he was nonetheless guilty. I was a mess and not getting much attention from any doctors.

My family complained formally, with a written letter, about inappropriate care. The doctors finally put me on a different mood stabilizer, Epival, plus the antipsychotic olanzapine. Still I believed that the outside world was paying attention to my situation, and I continued to march back and forth every day in front of the nursing station. Finally I tried to bust out past a security guard posted at the door to the ward, and because of this, staff insisted I be put on a Form 1, committing me to the institution for seventy-two hours. I refused to sign the papers and was locked in a small room for three days. My parents came down every day begging me to sign. I finally capitulated. Being on a Form 1 meant I could no longer leave the ward at all, not even in the company of family or friends. I was very upset about the whole situation. Three weeks later, though, my mental state had improved and I was deemed well enough to leave the Clarke under directions to continue with my medications. Six months on olanzapine saw me gain thirty pounds. A common side effect, the doctors told me. I recently read that there is now a class-action suit regarding this drug, as many people became diabetic and suffered strokes due to the massive weight gain. I couldn't stand it, so I took myself off the drug.

From 1997 to 2001 I continued working at the Toronto District School Board. However, my job—and those of many other colleagues—was about to be cut. I struggled with this, as I had been at the school board for almost ten years, but I eventually found work at the Canadian Race Relations Foundation. The atmosphere there was politically charged and stressful, and I became unwell and eventually had to leave the position. The following year my father died, and then I found a temporary job marking Grade 10 literacy tests for the Education Quality and Accountability Office. With the extreme stress of this job and the loss of my father, I found myself once again on unstable ground.

Between 2004 and 2010 I was hospitalized five more times, each time at Toronto General Hospital. I switched from Epival back to lithium, and the antipsychotic of choice had become risperidone. Although perhaps not as nefarious as olanzapine, it still caused weight gain along with the usual numbness and slowing of the mind.

In the summer of 2004 I was an outpatient in a group therapy program at Mount Sinai Hospital that caused me a lot of grief and anxiety, and at the same time I was not yet on disability so did not have the money to pay for my next set of prescriptions. I would take what medication I had left only every second or third day. Of course, chaos ensued within a week or two and I was hospitalized again. A few other times, I reduced my antipsychotic medication on purpose in the hopes of going off it completely, wanting to be rid of all the nasty side effects and extra weight. I never tried to go off lithium, as I felt it was my baseline and didn't mess with my mind or my weight. But the overall common denominators were always extreme stress leading to lack of sleep, followed by increasingly erratic behaviour.

Sick again in 2010, I paid another visit to the hospital. I no longer remember what propelled me there, except that I was once again delusional, and as my family insisted, I didn't really have a choice. I couldn't look after myself at home, and it would be too difficult for my mother or anyone else in the family to look after me, either. Even though I was deeply resentful and scared, I never truly resisted going back to the hospital, perhaps because deep down I knew I couldn't function on my own and needed help. My family was always there for me, visiting me regularly during my stays, meeting with doctors and frequently checking in on me when I came out. I cannot stress the importance of family involvement in the healing process and of making them aware of the resources that are available (to name a few, CAMH and in particular its Workman Arts project and its Empowerment Council, the Mood Disorders Association of Ontario, Across Boundaries, the Gerstein Centre, the Canadian Mental Health Association, Sistering and the Creative Works Studio).

As usual, as soon as I got into hospital I felt like I was stuck in a prison and wanted desperately to get out. Programming cuts meant there wasn't much to do during the day. Watching television only fanned the flames of my various conspiracy theories (I believed the newscasters could all see me and read my thoughts; that the other programs were all about me, but were also often mocking me). I did a fair amount of lying around. I felt very strongly that if I lay on my right side, I was offering resistance to the system. Along with refusing to eat most of the time, it was for me a way to give a finger to psychiatry. When I lay there, I could feel the eighth floor and all the people on it tense up and prepare for battle. It never took very long before a group of nurses would come down to check on me, eyeing me. They didn't say so, but their fake smiles and cold, hard eyes yelled at me that I was acting out and was to stop. When I wasn't lying around in protest, I made use of supplies from the art program that had fallen victim to Harris's mania for cost-cutting.

Art lends itself easily to my maddened mind. In the early stages, my mind is too erratic to focus on reading, writing or puzzles. During my 2010 stay at the Toronto General Hospital, I made one painting for each of my family members, flinging and dribbling paint about in my best Jackson Pollock mode. I was sure staff was hostile to my whipping brushes in the air, but my mind was jumpy and well suited to the frenetic activity. While I created, I thought about how I hated the condescending head doctors. Most of the nurses weren't much better. It seemed to be all about robotically lining up to take my meds and eat meals in silence with others. I often felt locked in a power struggle with them. I wanted out.

On a grey late-December day, as I splashed more paint on more paper, I figured out that the easiest and most sensible thing to do would be to watch for a group of people leaving the ward and hide among them as they filed through the ward doors and onto the elevator. I got ready, and an hour later that's exactly what I did.

Time to run. Mom's coat is too small but there's nothing else. Go. Go down the hall. Try to be normal. Grab my paintings. Go through the door, quick, with the others. Out! Fast! Before they see. People I don't know in the elevator. They're all watching me. I can't remember if I'm supposed to look up or down when the elevator is going down. So many rules. I can't remember them. Who made them up? The people who made them up, how do I know if they're on my side?

So now I was making my getaway. I had escaped from Women's College Hospital years before. Here I was again, zigzagging in my mind, trying to discern the best way to get out and stay out. On the ground floor I strode towards the main doors, not wasting a step. Big, wet snowflakes greeted me, floating down from a darkening late-afternoon sky. I stepped outside with an armful of newly minted paintings slapped carelessly at my side. College and Spadina were crowded in the afternoon rush hour. I stuck out my tongue to taste the snow, and it felt fuzzy and soft as it melted in my mouth. The coat my mother had left me was thin and too small for me to do up over my risperidone-bloated body. It was no match for the frigid January air.

I stumbled east along College Street. My paintings kept slipping out from under my arm and I watched them transform themselves yet again as they met with snow and slush. I kept looking over my shoulder for the hospital workers I was sure would be coming after me.

It's cold out here. Where am I going? Head east on College. The paintings are floating away from me. Somebody must be calling for them. Where am I going? Dan's. Dan won't want me. Mom's? She's old. She's my only ally. Walk in the middle of the sidewalk? Walk left or right? I don't remember. They've told me over and over again. But I always forget in between. Left foot first, going uphill, keep your head down. Right foot first, going downhill, keep your head up. What to do on a flat stretch?

There is a sea of people floating around me, all talking to me. A hundred voices. Think this, think that. "Oh, there's that woman everyone's talking about. She's certified . . . Who do you think you are, wasting our time? You're not working hard enough to change. Walk left, no, now right. Walk. Just go." Where am I going?

I trudged along, my feet thoroughly soaked in cheap runners. I wanted to go home, but I didn't have a key. The nurses had taken my personal belongings. I wondered if I could walk to Don Mills, where my mom lived. I was agitated. Always, in my delusional states, I know that everyone is talking to me, signalling things to me with what they're wearing, what they're saying, how they're gesturing. It's as if the whole world is in my head telling me what to do. My solitary walk east-ward through the late-winter evening was filled with pressing people, pressing messages.

I found myself at Sherbourne and Wellesley. I went inside a dingy coffee shop, but didn't order anything. I sat at the back, my brain chattering as much as my teeth. I was still worrying about how to get home, wondering if people were following me. The woman at the counter made me nervous, and I tried to figure out if she was with me or against me. I had decided that the City of Toronto was tired of me, tired of me not learning my lessons, tired of the entire ruckus that happened when I was in hospital, tired of me not being able to see the truth. And it was true, I couldn't see the truth. My mind was a constant to-and-fro, not knowing who to believe, not knowing who had my best interests at heart. The conspiracy theories continued to mount, and before long I had decided that the counter help was an enemy. I crawled under the table, huddled up against the wall. The woman at the counter was clearly avoiding me, and it wasn't long before a small group of paramedics and police officers entered the premises. I was terrified at the sight of them and stayed put.

"What are you doing down there?"

"Hiding."

"Who are you hiding from?"

"You."

"But we haven't done anything to you."

"No, but you're going to."

"No, we're not. You can't stay there. You have to come out. Nobody will hurt you."

They asked me other questions. Speaking in firm, insistent tones, they moved the table away from me and coaxed me out. They told me they were taking me to St. Mike's Hospital. I was confused and jittery, but still I managed not to tell them that I had just run away from the psych ward at Toronto General.

They dropped me off in the hive that was the ER. I sat unattended for a very long while, fidgeting away, swinging my legs recklessly like a child and wondering what my next step should be. Someone came along. She told me to lie down and asked me what medication I was on. I told her. She left. I lay there, becoming more and more absorbed by the frightening sounds of the hospital. She came back about half an hour later. I felt the steel of a needle tear into my arm. I wondered what they were giving me. She said the doctors would be here soon and then left me alone again. I was convinced that the whole hospital was planning to lock me up and put me in some kind of coma so they could examine and play with my brain. What was in that needle? I sat up, waited for the hallway to empty out a little and took off into the winter night again.

Those who are supposedly helping me on the outside say that I talk out the back of my head, swearing, screaming vicious vitriol. That's why they hate me even if they say they want to help. I can't control it. They keep trying to tell me how, but I'm always mixing things up. There's too much in my head. It happens mainly at night, my yelling. That's why everyone hates me. That's why they're trying to lock me up, drug me up and hide me.

I briefly toyed with walking down Queen Street to the Beaches, where my brother Dan lived, but I didn't think he and my sister-in-law would let me stay. I really just wanted to go home to my co-op in Riverdale. Near Queen and Parliament, I ducked into a grubby little bar and sat down at a table near the door and by the window. Once again I was left alone. I was grateful. I stayed put at the table, but didn't outstay my welcome. I was just trying to warm up, as I was improperly dressed for the weather.

Outside, the streets were now dark and relatively quiet. Snow was falling on top of snow, swirling in great big whorls like white lace—the winds had picked up. Taxis flashed by and I wanted to flag one down but I had no money. Besides, I was sure a bulletin had been put out to the taxi network not to stop for me. I waved, but every driver looked the other way. It was cold and I was moving slowly. Although my mind was like quicksilver, my movements were unsure. I was afraid of everything around me. Two guys grazed me as they passed. I was sure I heard them whisper, "Home base, ya gotta make it to home base. That's where it is." I wondered what "it" was and what I'd find at home. I turned homeward with renewed energy. I started noticing sirens. The cops were out to find me. Better stay off the major streets.

I'm trying to use the security button at the top of my head so that no one can hear or read my thoughts, but I can never tell if it works. If it does, I'll be more protected and they won't hear me and find me. I hear sirens, the cars, the blasts of horns, terrifying. Run, get off this path. They never told me anything about running. My paintings are all gone now, lost to the world. No choir, no art, no drums to help me. I wasn't supposed to leave.

To get home I had to cross the bridge just beyond Queen and River. There was a couple standing at a streetcar stop. They looked at me intently as I passed and I heard them mutter, "It's your goddamn mother."

My mother is a goddess and right now she is convening a panel of gods and goddesses from many religions to deal with the question of me. Me, the mortal, but insane. She knew that I had been operated on at three months and that they had seen remarkable things in my brain. They inserted a chip to monitor my every movement and thought. Mom, the all-knowing. I loved to watch her sing to the birds all day in the backyard, to see her communicate with the animal world. The last time I was sick in summer the birds sang to me, the flowers, gay pansies and all whispered sweetly and the insects ground their way through my brain in a slow-motion screech about the impending apocalypse.

In actual fact I did have an operation at three months. I was having constant and serious ear troubles, and doctors recommended performing a double mastoidectomy in which they cut open both my ears and scraped them out. When I am mad, I always maintain that this was the first interference of scientists with my brain. When I am sane, I find it interesting to note the interconnectedness between delusion and reality. In fact, most of my paranoid delusions stem from something concrete that has happened in my life. It's like someone has taken a jigsaw puzzle and tossed it in the air, letting the pieces fall where they may. That is my psychotic brain. Actual facts and events all cast about, tumbling about in my head, their now jagged and unfitting edges no longer in synchronicity.

I eventually found myself about twelve blocks from home, at the corner of Dundas and Broadview, taking refuge in the Coffee Time. It was late at night by now. I sat down at the back in the corner. This time folks weren't so friendly. An old man came over waving his hands fiercely at me. He stuttered that I should get out if I wasn't buying anything. He came closer. "Get out, lady. Get out or I call the cops."

Keeping to the side streets, I made my way home, shivering, and unsure of what I would do when I got there. It was now about one in the morning. When I reached the co-op I went to a friend's unit and banged on the door. She was looking after my cats and would have a key. She didn't open and I could hardly blame her. But now I was stuck.

A dog barked as I passed through the laneways back to my unit on Logan. I thought about all the dogs in the park across from my unit and how they always seemed to be telling me to stop what I was doing and shut my mind up. This was unlike my cats, who gravitated to me when I was sick. They would nudge me, directing me to sit in a certain place or to look at certain things that they sensed had meaning and would be helpful with my healing. They would knead me endlessly and then curl up and help keep me warm. I had one cat that lived upstairs and communed with the moon while keeping me company at night, and two cats that lived downstairs and watched over me there, while focusing on more earthly things. Between them, they tried to keep me on track, with their affection and guidance.

I want to go home and see the cats. They help me, the way they turn their heads. If they rest their paw on me, they tell me through their motions which way is safe to lie on the couch so that my thoughts can't be heard or stolen or manipulated as easily. Which way to lie in bed to try to talk with different people in my head. Luna is left— my brother Larry, my mom and a few others. Magic is right for Dad, Dan, Malaika . . . Luna will be talking to all the other cats throughout the night in the co-op, updating them on our situation. Oscar is centre, the protector of the middle ground. They are love.

When I got to my front door, I pulled on the knob but it didn't yield. There was a picnic table in the small front yard and I sat down on the bench and cried. I wondered what my father would tell me to do were he alive, but the vision of his warm, brown face faded quickly. I went to the door and called out to the cats, but I knew they couldn't save me. I decided to brace myself up against the wall and do some yoga poses. I felt the hardness of the brick seep into me and give me strength. I stood there with my knee bent and my arms splayed, pressing into the wall for a long, long time. I was so frustrated that I had made it home but couldn't get in. Inside was my sanctuary. I could crawl into bed and sleep. Except that within me there was still that knowingness, the deeper level of thought that reminded me that I probably wouldn't sleep at all. I would be up all night cavorting around the place.

I began singing songs to myself. I loved Joni Mitchell's "The Circle Game" and I had taught it to my daughter many years before. We would curl up in her bed and sing it to each other till we fell asleep. Later I would crawl back into my own bed, the song still like a lullaby in my head. On this late-December night, "The Circle Game" comforted me for quite a while.

I went and lay down on the bench and tried to rest. It was too cold and snow was blowing in my face and felt like little icicles pricking against my skin. I was so cold and weary. I went back to the wall and stood there again, stoically flattening my back into the bricks as hard as I could. I continued this back-and-forth until finally I could see that the eastern skies were starting to lighten. I decided to walk up to the Danforth to see if the Tim Hortons would be open. I walked up the hill dreaming of coffee. But I didn't know how to get a hold of any money. I swung open the side door at Tim's and sat down at the nearest table. It wasn't long before a big, burly woman in uniform started snaking her way over to me. I didn't even try to argue, I just got up and left. I cursed the fact that I had no money and I cursed myself that I didn't have the gumption to find any. I cruised on foot along the Danforth, peering into windows along the way, till I reached Broadview. I had no place to go. I had to go home.

Back at the picnic table in front of my door, one of my neighbours stepped out. We didn't really know each other. He looked at me for a bit and asked if I was okay. I shook my head no. His eyebrows were raised and he stood there for a moment silently. Then he said, "Come on in." I followed him up the stairs. His girlfriend was sitting on a chair at a desk, typing on a laptop. They invited me to sit down. But the woman kept looking at me like I was some kind of animal and I was sure she was typing nasty things about me. I was very uncomfortable and after five minutes, I jumped up and went back outside. Fifteen minutes later my downstairs neighbour opened her door and yelled out my name. "Karen, here you are. Come on in. Have some tea." She pulled up a chair for me. The apartment buzzed with the sound of kids getting ready for school, a dog waiting to be walked, people getting ready for work. It was just after seven. I sipped on my tea and sat quietly. My neighbour also sat at her computer, and it looked like page after page of names of companies, associations and people were flying by on the screen. I thought these must be some of my supporters and she's showing me that they're here to help. But instead, half an hour later the doorbell rang and a dear friend of mine stood there with her arms wide open. "We've been looking all over for you, Karen. Dan is on his way." We hugged for a few minutes in silence but my mind was hissing. *Christ*, I thought. *It figures.* I knew that Dan would take me back to the hospital, and at that moment I hated him for it.

If I could go home, I could at least be myself again. I think. On the TV they watch me, too. The newscasters see my face, my actions, read my thoughts. They've hacked my email. There is nowhere safe.

Ten minutes later, my brother Dan showed up. "Hi, Karen. Are you okay? We've been looking all over for you." I nodded my head. "Come on, Bev and David are waiting for you in the car." I had survived the hospital many times before and I would survive it again.

Again, a profound inner consciousness tugged at me, and it registered somehow that I indeed couldn't make it on my own and needed help. I just wished it didn't have to be the hospital.

On a number of occasions my elderly mother had taken me into her home when I was at my worst, or she had come to stay with me. But my behaviour wore her down in no time. There weren't many options, so I didn't struggle. I was very lucky to have family and friends who cared.

She's been punching all kinds of names and numbers into the computer while I wait here drinking tea. Whose names? Maybe she's watching me, too. They all hate me; just want to get rid of me. If

I were in my place I'd just curl up into a little ball and try to block out the voices . . . What does Malaika know? Is she in on all this? One of the scariest things is everyone reading my mind so that there's absolutely nowhere to hide.

When I arrived back on the eighth floor, doctors and nurses crowded around me and berated me. Because of my behaviour I was going into the intensive care unit—no street clothes, no phone, security guards pacing the hall, only occasional visitors. In short, lockdown. I felt like a child being punished. I fought and pushed and yelled, but to no avail. I was a voluntary admission, but sometimes you are not treated as voluntary at all.

There was nothing at all to do in lock-up. I couldn't think straight yet, so I was lost in the nebulous world of my mind. Trying to sort out the voices in my head: who was a friend, who was a foe. How could their words help me to get out of here? Other people's thoughts and directions intermingling with my paranoia. Family came to visit, and I would walk up and down the little hall with them, trying to stay with the conversation. I had pastels, so I drew a lot. Eventually the medication started to clear the fog, but I was more subdued than ever. After four or five days I was released back onto the general ward. I was happy, mainly because I knew I'd be able to go outside and smoke. My cigarette addiction was always worse when I was ill, and I don't know how I made it through those days without smoking.

They're lending me cigarettes and I know it's crack. The Belmonts I buy at my corner store are laced with cocaine. But near the hospital they're crack. I wonder how they do it. Why are they trying out all these drugs on me? Some of the patients are in on it and they give me their cigarettes, probably dope, too. They want to try mine because they know it's coke. But I'm so out of it I can't even tell the difference anymore. They can do anything they want. Nobody can protect me.

Being back on the ward meant I could wear real clothes again. Clothes are a marker of identity and security. There's nothing worse than roaming the halls day in and day out with only a gown that you have to fumble with. But back on the ward there was also one nurse who I was certain didn't like me. I was intimidated by her steeliness and her bossiness. When there's not much to do, you walk the halls round and round again. One night I couldn't sleep, so I decided to go up and down the corridors to wear myself out. While I strode purposefully back and forth I felt like raising my fist in defiance, but I didn't. Years before I had paced the floors with a raised fist at the Clarke Institute and had gotten staff in a dither. In the confrontation that followed, I had tried to force my way past a guard and was slapped with a Form 1. Now I didn't feel like pushing my luck again. I just wanted to walk. Nonetheless, this one nurse was not happy with me going round and round the corridors. Finally, she stormed over to me and said, "You have to go back to your room. I will not have you pacing the floors on my watch." I was upset. My paranoia had kept me from sleeping, but I didn't want to take even more Ativan. Sometimes I was afraid that someone would do something to me. I felt unsafe and didn't want to be totally knocked out. The next day you would feel so hungover. I wanted to walk off my vexatious mood. But I was stymied and was too afraid to make a scene.

I found another way to resist: by fasting. My mind had told me that my ex-husband was fasting in Sudan so he could be released from prison. The people cluttering my mind suggested that I support him by joining him in this fast. None of this was true, but I decided to try it out.

White stands for my husband, Seif, in prison in Sudan. That's why he hasn't come back. I want to understand what happened to him . . . My brothers just shake their heads—they don't understand. White is solidarity for Seif, who's in trouble. That's why the others want me to fast. To help him. They tell me to kneel down and pray to Allah for him at least twice a day. I try, on the bed and on the hospital floor, but it feels wrong. Once I hear his beautiful voice calling out to me, so fleeting, then gone. Canada won't let him back in. They think he's a terrorist. I have to fast with him.

I only fasted for two or three days at a time—drinking coffee, tea, juice and water. Then one of my visitors would bring in some snacks and I would start eating again.

Three weeks after my escape I went home, armed with new prescriptions for lithium and risperidone. I was subdued, tired and anxious to settle in and find my old self again. Going home after any kind of stay was always a blessing. However, it could take months before I would feel truly well again, free of paranoia and delusions. It was an arduous climb back to sanity.

I will always have concerns about my medications and will continue to wish I could just ditch them altogether. You might think that I would be happy to have medication that calmed my mind. You might think that I would see I'm not alone: my brothers remind me that they have to take medication, too, for their diabetes. But my medications cause serious weight gain and wind my brain function down into a slow-motion fogginess. And yet, each and every time I try to cut my doses, I run into trouble with paranoia and psychosis. For many years I was compliant. I took my meds because, as a single mother, I felt I owed it to my daughter to be as stable as I could be. Now that she has grown, I still toy with the idea of setting my sights on freedom from medication.

I often wonder what the ongoing treatment would have been like in Germany.

If I could set my own treatment plan, it would definitely involve weekly visits to my psychiatrist and with my fabulous visiting mental health nurse and maybe a round of psychotherapy with someone else. I feel that I would need the help of not only my GP but also support from a naturopath or homeopath. It would mean living with as little stress as possible and the unconditional support of my family as well as friends. That's asking a lot in these busy times.

But I do have some good news. I have started on a newer medication that doesn't cause weight gain. I've lost twenty pounds in a few months. And I've found a useful and pleasurable outlet. An occupational therapist I saw for a while helped me find my way to the Creative Works Studio. Here my passion to create outranks my fears and anxieties, albeit not without a struggle. Creative Works has provided me with a place to create, a place to go when I'm lonely and need to get out, as well as a place to go when my mind is full of ideas bursting to express themselves on canvas or otherwise. I am not trying to become an artist per se. I am simply trying to unlock doors to help the beauty of creating flow through my life more evenly, to let my inner voice soar in as many ways as possible. This distracts and soothes me from the regular paranoias of my mind. I recently took a hiatus from the Studio to finish writing a book. I missed it sorely while I was gone and am now making my way back in, slowly putting together paint and pieces of cloth and objects for a wall hanging, much like I am always trying to reimagine my life.

Is it surprising that I occasionally miss the bouts of hypomania? People who have never experienced them don't always recognize that they bring with them such creativity and confidence and outright joy. However, I never miss the aftermath: the months of depression or the struggles with acute psychosis.

And I never want to see the inside of a psych ward again. It has now been more than three years since I was last hospitalized, which is something of a milestone for me. I am blessed with family and friends who care, with a visiting nurse and a good psychiatrist and the occasional help of an occupational therapist. I feel I have finally reached a place of some stability. From here I can reach out and become a healthier and more active participant in the mental health and wider communities. Sadly, this is still not true for many others who struggle with mental illness.